When at last

they lay side by side, spent,

she turned to him and asked,

"DO YOU LOVE HER?"

"WHO?"

"YOUR WIFE."

If you're married to the world's most beautiful and desirable woman, you aren't likely
to forget it—unless you're Brian O'Neal,
formerly the world's greatest actor, present-
ly a Hollywood superstar with spectacular
appetites—and a strange shocking idea of
just what a marriage should be . . .
**If you thought VALLEY OF THE DOLLS
was something, wait until you get a load
of this . . ."** Publishers Weekly

THE
BEAUTIFUL
COUPLE

A NOVEL
by William Woolfolk

A SIGNET BOOK

Published by
THE NEW AMERICAN LIBRARY

Library of Congress Catalog Card Number: 68-31467

This is a reprint of a hardcover edition published by The New American Library, Inc., in association with The World Publishing Company, 2231 West 110th Street, Cleveland, Ohio.

SIGNET TRADEMARK REG. U.S. PAT. OFF. AND FOREIGN COUNTRIES
REGISTERED TRADEMARK—MARCA REGISTRADA
HECHO EN CHICAGO, U.S.A.

SIGNET BOOKS are published by The New American Library, Inc., 1301 Avenue of the Americas, New York, New York 10019

FIRST PRINTING, MARCH, 1969

PRINTED IN THE UNITED STATES OF AMERICA

... tell me if the lovers are losers
... tell me if any get more
than the lovers
... in the dust ... in the cool tombs.

from *Cool Tombs*

BY CARL SANDBURG

THE
BEAUTIFUL
COUPLE

CHAPTER ONE

This was the morning on which she had decided to die. The plump, satin-covered pillow yielded beneath Jacquelyn Stuart's head as she looked up. She was in the bedroom of the Royal Suite at the Plaza. At each corner of the panel moldings, just under the ceiling, in the sumptuous Louis Fifteenth room, there were small golden cherubs, angelic creatures, chubby and smiling, with masses of ringlets. They're not dancing, the wicked little creatures, she thought. They're fornicating somewhere in the blue empyrean, somewhere beyond care.

"Wherever you are, my darling, angels will watch over you," Mother had said.

Mother's face, saying this to her, did not quite come into focus; it kept trying to become Mother and changing into someone else entirely. Then she realized that Mother never said that to her. It was a scene from *The Lord Is my Shepherd,* the movie in which she played when she was nine years old; the mother was fine, old sympathetic-looking actress Bessie Crawford. Drunken, vindictive old bitch. Jacquelyn could remember Bessie tucking her in bed, the reek of whiskey fumes so strong it made her nauseous.

Jacquelyn sat up suddenly in bed. The whole scene in which she believed her real mother spoke to her had never happened. It was so easy to slip away and lose herself entirely in that grossly magnified portrait up there on the screen. Bigger than life and twice as wonderful. Jacquelyn Stuart, queen of the cinema, the common people's royalty.

What an unholy stink there will be in the newspapers tomorrow. The last time I'll make the headlines.

The telephone rang.

"Good morning, Miss Stuart. It's eight o'clock." The operator hesitated. "You asked to be wakened at eight."

"Thank you. What sort of a day is it?"

"Lovely—sunny and cool. You'll enjoy it, I'm sure."

She closed her eyes.

"Shall I have room service send up your breakfast?" the girl asked.

"Yes, please. Thank you."

The washbasin and bathtub in the bathroom had carved golden dolphins for faucets. She shrugged off the slender straps of her nightgown and looked at her naked body in the gold-rimmed full-length bathroom mirror.

Well, Jacquelyn, darling, she thought, millions of men would like nothing better than to see you the way you are right this moment. Take a last look, boys. Good-bye, dark-haired fairy princess. Every time you saw that face in a mirror, even as a little girl, it seemed to be more something you owned than something you were. No one knows the thoughts hidden behind that portrait of innocence. Her hair was pinned up in loose curls, dark as midnight. Brian would remove the pins until the long strands fell limply down to her shoulders and he would put the seal of his kiss on her breast.

My God!

She looked into the mirror and could almost see the shadowy outline of Brian behind her. She even heard his voice. But when she turned, there was no one. Their marriage had lasted three years and seven months and fifteen days, and every moment, all the passion and all the fierceness, was wasted. It was going to end like this. She wished it were possible to go on living in the past, or carry it into the present like some great jewel on a velvet cushion.

When she returned to Jacquelyn Stuart's face, it was crying. Stupid. The tears wouldn't stop, they seemed to have a will of their own, welling up and following each other down the streaky path that other tears had taken.

When the telephone rang again, she debated whether to answer. Everything was flooding in, wave after painful wave, and this was the time to cut off pain forever. There would always be telephones ringing. In a short while she wouldn't hear them.

She flung herself on the bed to reach the canary-yellow telephone on the bedside table.

"Jacquelyn?"

"Oh, it's you, Morey. I don't want to talk to anyone."

"Is something the matter, pumpkin?"

"I just want to be left alone."

"I've fabulous news for you, pumpkin. Can I come by to talk to you a minute?"

Morey Bloom, her agent, drew excitement from some inexhaustible well in his body.

"I'm tired, Morey. You woke me up. I'm going back to sleep."

"This can't wait, pumpkin. It's the dream deal we've been waiting for. We have to move while the frost is on the pipe."

She could imagine him on the phone, tight-faced, biting his fingernails.

"I don't have to do anything, Morey. Not one god-damned thing!"

In sleep you were wrapped warm, swaddled about, insulated from the terrors of the world. Her sleep would be deep; safe, she would sink into the crib of unconsciousness.

"I'll sum up the message in four words," Morey said. "*Death of a Peacock*."

Despite herself, she felt a tiny dart of quickening interest. *Death of a Peacock* was the smash dramatic hit by the nation's most important young playwright, Armstrong Johnson. A beautiful fag, Mr. Johnson, but one hell of a writer. Every major Hollywood studio was falling over itself in an attempt to buy the screen rights.

"This is from the inside, pumpkin—latrine number four. Mammoth Studios came up with a bid to top all competition. They even topped Liz Taylor and Richard Burton who were trying to buy the property to star in themselves. I can't reveal the terms, pumpkin, and you wouldn't believe me if I told you. I don't believe them myself. But they need you, gorgeous, because with the investment they got in this property they need every known form of box office insurance."

"Tell them to go stick it," she said wearily.

"The whole thing will be shot on location in Brazil." Morey began to hum a samba. "You got the rhythm, pumpkin? Those caballeros in Buenos Aires are gonna go nuts over you."

"Buenos Aires is in Argentina, Morey."

"What's the difference? It's all south of the border.

Pack your bags, honey. You're taking off in the next day or so."

"No, I'm not, Morey."

A spluttering over the phone: "Are you serious? I thought it was some kind of a gag. Are you knocked up? Even if you *are* knocked up, find yourself a doctor. Have an abortion. You can't pass up this one, pumpkin. It's the one they'll remember you by when you've got gray hair and started to play character roles."

"I've got personal reasons, Morey. I can't explain now."

"This picture'll do for you what *Gone with the Wind* did for Vivien Leigh. You'll be immortal. They'll pay your price, sugar—a cool million. *And* they'll give you the negative after seven years, provided they recoup their costs. That means *you* own the picture. And *Death of a Peacock* is bound to be one of the screen's all-time grossers."

"I won't discuss it."

"There isn't a top star in Hollywood who wouldn't trade her tits for this role. Off the record, pumpkin, I've got an important client so hungry for it she's been throwing temper tantrums in my office."

"Gerda Andersen?" Interest flickered again.

"Mentioning no names, pumpkin."

She had forgotten how her dislike for Gerda started, one of those intertwined relationships that cannot be unraveled because they are entangled in coils of mutual revulsion.

"Morey, I have other things on my mind."

Morey fought to control his exasperation. "Is it Brian? I know you two go together like bagels and lox. But he's busy on that Greek turkey he's shooting over in London and you couldn't be with him anyhow unless you went over there. Right? Right! And you never liked London in the fall." He began to hum a samba again, with marked vocal emphases. "Brazil is the climate for you, pumpkin. You'll love it there—and they'll love you."

In the bathroom medicine cabinet the way out was waiting. There was no turning back. London Bridge is falling down. . . .

"I'm sorry. The answer is no, Morey."

"Do you know what you're doing? Whoever gets this role is going to be the hottest female star in Hollywood for a helluva long time to come."

"It doesn't matter, Morey. It simply doesn't matter."

"What do you mean? What kind of an answer is that?"

She imagined Brian walking with funereal tread in the cortege behind her coffin. The picture blurred. Not Brian. He'd perch atop the hearse, legs straddling it, a bottle of liquor aloft in one hand to toast the dear departed, and he would be laughing, with his head back and his tousled thick hair across his forehead. How he would laugh! Solemnity always amused Brian. *We all stand teeter totter on the edge of the world, love, and it can go either way with us at any moment. The thing to do is have a cosmic sense of our own insignificance.*

Toss him onto the blazing funeral pyre! She would die happy, if Brian were turning charcoal beside her. He deserved to suffer, the rotten adulterous pig!

"Morey, do you really think it's an offer I can't refuse?"

Morey chortled with relief. "I'll get a memo of agreement drawn up. We'll finish the contracts later."

She put two fingers against the phone as though to restrain his enthusiasm. "I need time to say good-bye to Gene. He's at that private school in New Hampshire."

"Okay, okay. You can leave any time after that. You're not making a mistake, pumpkin. This is the biggest break of your whole beautiful life."

In the bathroom she took out the vial of blue pills and shook her head with impatience. In her depressed mood she had lost the real Brian in a succession of tender images. The real Brian was arrogant, self-centered, a boisterous drunkard and a compulsive philanderer.

She emptied the vial of pills into the toilet bowl. That son of a bitch. I wouldn't give him the satisfaction!

For the meeting with her lawyer, Arthur Eakam, she chose a simple black wool dress and a rose turban. She picked up the telephone in the foyer. "Will you ask my chauffeur to have the car in front of the door in five minutes?"

"Yes, Miss Stuart."

She found her long kid gloves, put on the sealskin-lined cloth coat. She hesitated for a moment, knowing that she had forgotten something and unable to recall what.

Then she opened the drawer of the table in the foyer and took out her sunglasses. She never went anywhere without her sunglasses. The huge dark rims covered the upper portion of her face. When she glanced a final time in the foyer mirror, her image was dim through tinted lenses. You really think you're an ostrich, darling, and if you put your head into the sand no one will ever see you.

In the lobby of the Plaza, the murmuring began. A bellboy intercepted a couple who tried to approach her. She had left strict orders that she did not wish to be disturbed by autograph collectors, and she stayed at the Plaza because their staff was alerted to make sure her orders were obeyed.

Outside the hotel her metal-gray Silver Cloud Rolls waited, with smiling discreet Edward beside it in his vi-sored cap and uniform. A crowd had gathered on the sidewalk opposite the park, having learned in the mysteri-ous way that crowds do that she was about to leave the hotel. Was there some sort of tom-tom telegraph? How did they find out so quickly?

Voices crashed around her like a booming surf.

"Jackie!"

"JACKIE STUART!"

The two doormen of the hotel were struggling to hold people back. Edward shielded her with his arm as she got into the limousine. The windows were already rolled up, but outside them she saw reaching hands, flat palms against the panes, agitated white faces, open mouths shouting unintelligible messages.

"JACKIE . . . JACKIE STUART!"

Edward got into the driver's seat, closing the door against the surging press of the crowd.

"Edward, get us the hell out of here!"

The Rolls began to glide forward. Moist hands made sticky imprints on the windows. A plump teen-age girl shouted so loudly that the words rose above the hub-bub:

"Oh, Jackie, you're so *beautiful!*"

Jacquelyn twisted her face like a gargoyle and *blatted* her tongue. Everyone smiled happily. They thought she was charming. Those people didn't have any minds of their own anymore—they were part of the crowd and only thought crowd-thoughts. This year she was charming. She could remember times when the crowds had been shouting for her blood like the mobs at the guillotine during the French Revolution. There had always been crowds, as far back as she could remember, even when she was a little girl. Prisoners waiting in the damp chill for brief rays of sunlight to invade their celled darkness; curious, forsaken people gathered at the gates of the huge studio for a glimpse of a star, the stock characters of a human repertory company playing their assigned roles as idolaters.

She had been seven years old on the morning Mother first took her to the studio. Mother drove there in the family car, an old Plymouth sedan, and parked in the studio lot that was reserved for ordinary visitors and not for Very Important Persons. It was a warm sunny day and Jacquelyn could feel the sun on her face and on the beribboned straw hat she wore. Her hand was held tightly in Mother's hand as they crossed the parking lot and went up to the guard at the gate.

"Who would you like to see, ma'am?"

"We have an appointment with Mr. Orrin."

"What's your name, please?"

"Mrs. Eve Stuart."

The guard consulted some sort of register.

"Oh, yes, ten o'clock." He leaned out of the window to point down the sunlit main street of the studio. "Mr. Orrin's office is the second one on the right as you go down the street."

"Thank you."

The guard smiled. "Don't mention it. A mighty pretty girl you've got there. Cute as a button."

Jacquelyn smiled her prettiest smile.

Inside the building, in the waiting room, they sat for a long time before a secretary came out to see them. She said that Mr. Orrin was busy, in conference, and it might be quite a while before they could go in.

"We could go for a walk," Mother suggested. "I'd like to show my daughter what it's like in a big movie studio."

The secretary was shocked. "I don't think that's a very good idea. When Mr. Orrin *is* ready to see you, he mustn't be kept waiting."

Jacquelyn sat on the maroon sofa, her legs dangling, being careful to keep her white pinafore spread out the way Mother had told her. Her knees were bare. She wore short white stockings and white patent-leather shoes with a strap. Mary Janes, the shoes were called.

From the moment she had opened her eyes that morning she had been aware that this was an important day. Her sense of excitement had quickened through breakfast.

Mother was outwardly calm and controlled, but she had never spent more time over Jacquelyn's curls, or deliberated longer in choosing the proper bows for her hair, or worried so about how her dress fit and whether the dimples in her knees showed. When Mother was finished with all the preparations, she took a deep, deep breath before saying in an odd voice, "Let's go, darling." Somehow, to a child's eye, all this nervous preparation was translated into expectancy.

After an hour she became impatient, but only showed it by swinging her legs. Mother was pretending to read but kept her gaze on the open doorway of the secretary's office. The secretary hardly glanced in their direction as she occasionally went through the reception lounge to the small adjoining alcove where there were steel filing cabinets and two people typing at desks. Once or twice messengers came, but they left whatever they were delivering with the people working in the alcove. One of the messengers was a nice, white-haired old man who smiled at Jacquelyn and seemed about to speak, but then glanced at Mother and decided not to.

Lunchtime came, and Mother took her several blocks from the studio to a lunchroom where workmen ate, staring at them all the while. She hardly touched her chicken sandwich and milk, and when they returned she was close to tears.

At a quarter to four, when they had been waiting almost six hours, the secretary came out to tell Mother Mr. Orrin could see them now. Mother took her hand tightly as they went into the secretary's office and beyond that through a door into a leather-furnished room with a cigar humidor and window blinds drawn against streaming sunlight. A huge vase of flowers stood in a corner of the room, and a dictating machine was on the immaculate, wide, glass-topped desk.

Seated behind his desk, Mr. Orrin seemed to be rather a large man. He was fat and chalk-colored and bald, and chewed on a cigar that wasn't lit. In profile his face was birdlike, protruding at the nose and mouth, going in at the forehead and the chin.

"Well, well, this is the little girl you were telling me about," Mr. Orrin said, never taking his pale eyes from Jacquelyn.

"Jacquelyn, this is Mr. Orrin," Mother said.

Jacquelyn curtsied and Mr. Orrin chuckled around his

cigar. He had a queer mouth. It looked all right from the front with the cigar in it, but from the side his lips protruded like a flounder.

"Very pretty," he said. "Very cute. Prettier than she looked in those pictures you sent me."

Mr. Orrin stood up and came around his desk. He was shorter than he had appeared when sitting.

"So you want to be in picures, Jacquelyn?"

"Yes, sir."

"A lot of little girls would like to be in pictures. Hundreds of them ask for the chance every week. But I don't see too many of them. Do you know why I wanted to see you, Jacquelyn?"

"No, sir."

"Because you were so very, very pretty in the photographs your mother sent me. And because your mother wrote such an interesting letter about you. Can you sing?"

"Yes, sir."

"Dance?"

"Yes, sir."

"Of course, we don't want any more Shirley Temples. There's only one Shirley Temple and she gets all the singing and dancing roles. We need a different image for you. It won't be so easy to find. We've got quite a problem cut out for us."

Jacquelyn sat in a deep leather chair with her legs close together, her bare thighs flattening and merging above the hemline of her pinafore.

Mr. Orrin appeared to notice Jacquelyn's pretty legs. When his pale eyes looked at her she had an impulse to pull down the hem of her pinafore. Then she decided not to.

She hardly dared to breathe as Mr. Orrin and Mother began to talk about business matters. There was some mention of a screen test, a contract with options, approvals by a new talent committee at the studio, "all preliminary, of course, nothing definite," and problems that were a matter of routine and problems that (Mr. Orrin said gravely) were serious considerations and would require the earnest cooperation of everyone concerned.

Finally, Mr. Orrin said, "We seem to understand each other, Mrs. Stuart. I don't want to promise too much. I don't want you to be disappointed, or to accuse me of bad faith . . . No, don't shake your head. You'd be *surprised* how many people say that I promised something definite when I did nothing of the kind, when I only said that there was a chance. Yes, definitely, I think there *is* a chance I can do something for Jacquelyn. But there are so many factors to consider. One, of course, is the child herself. I know so little about her. It might help if we had an hour or so to talk. I think I'll learn a good deal more in that way than by a whole month of interviews."

Mother thought that was a very good idea. She was sure that Jacquelyn would be delighted to talk with Mr. Orrin. As she was leaving, Mother managed to give Jacquelyn a glance that said, Do your best, darling, charm the man; it's up to you now; Mother has done everything she can and don't let me down, we've come too far to have anything go wrong now. Jacquelyn got those messages without needing the words; they were transmitted along the direct line that connected her emotionally with Mother.

The door closed.

There was something peculiar about Mr. Orrin, she decided. He was rather too short and fat and rather too white and soft. He had a fringe of white hair around his startlingly light-colored eyes.

"Well, Jacquelyn, I think it's time we get better acquainted, don't you? I'll call you Jackie, if you don't mind. That sounds more friendly than a long name like Jacquelyn, doesn't it?"

She preferred Jacquelyn, but only smiled and nodded in answer.

Mr. Orrin leaned back against a corner of the desk; he had short fat legs.

"Now, Jackie, wouldn't you like to tell me about yourself? Don't worry about how to start. Just tell me anything that comes into your mind."

Jacquelyn told him about her school, her teachers, her favorite subjects, what her home was like, and about a friend who had a dog called Leader. She knew exactly what not to tell him. She didn't mention the time she and her best friend Emily had gone to the five-and-ten-cent store together and she had secretly taken a pretty ring with a red stone from a counter and slipped it into the pocket of her dress, or about the day when, jealous of a new classmate—a plain, wispy little girl who had become the teacher's favorite—she had told the new girl that she was ugly and that nobody wanted her in the class.

Mr. Orrin listened, his eyes disturbingly fixed on her,

and while he *seemed* to be listening very hard, Jacquelyn had the feeling that he wasn't really hearing anything.

"That's very interesting," Mr. Orrin said. "Yes, Jackie, I can tell you're a most unusual girl. Have you ever played any make-believe games?"

Jacquelyn nodded.

"What are your favorite make-believe games, Jackie?"

"Oh, all sorts. Sometimes I play nurse with my friend, and sometimes we play with dolls and dress them up like real grown-ups who get married and—"

"Boy and girl dolls?" Mr. Orrin's pale eyes flickered.

"Oh, yes." Mr. Orrin was a silly. How could dolls get married if they weren't boy and girl dolls?

"How do you dress the boy dolls?"

"There are suits that came with the dolls. My favorite is one who wears a real dress-up suit like you wear to a wedding."

"He's probably very handsome," Mr. Orrin smiled. His smile was an imitation made with lips and teeth.

"He's just a doll," Jacquelyn said defensively.

"There's nothing wrong with it, Jackie. You mustn't be ashamed if you like to play with dolls, or dress and undress them. Everyone has make-believe games he plays. Even grown-ups like me. Would you like to see a game I play that is very much like your game?"

"Yes, sir," Jacquelyn said dutifully. She did not enjoy being alone with Mr. Orrin, and wondered how much longer the interview would last. She was afraid she might not be able to be charming for as long as Mother wanted. When she had to pretend too long for grown-ups, her real feelings started to show through.

Mr. Orrin took a small key on a chain from his vest pocket. He opened a drawer of his desk and took out a very large scrapbook with a black cover that had a soft velvety feel.

"I keep a scrapbook with pictures of my favorite people. Look at it and tell me if you recognize any of them, Jackie."

She turned the stiff pages with the full-sized photographs covered in protective sheets of cellophane. She did not recognize any of the first girls she saw. They were all about her age, some younger, and none were wearing any clothes. Then she turned another page and saw a girl who looked familiar.

"Isn't this Judy Lester?"

"That's right, Jackie. You're very clever. That's Judy Lester—a very big star today. Of course, she's grown up now. That picture of her was taken when she was only eight years old. How old are you, Jackie?"

"Seven."

He knew that.

"I think you're much prettier right now than Judy Lester. Prettier than almost any of the girls in my scrapbook."

"Thank you."

"I like you, Jackie. Wouldn't you like me to take your picture for my scrapbook?"

She thought Mr. Orrin meant sometime, and nodded. But she couldn't help being a little embarrassed. Mr. Orrin noted this.

"You don't think nice girls like Judy Lester would do anything wrong, do you, Jackie?"

She shook her head.

"Of course not. Neither would any of the other young ladies in my scrapbook. They knew how much I admired them and they wanted me to have a little memento to remember them by. I have hundreds and hundreds of pictures of my own family. I have two daughters. They're both older now; one of them is married. Would you like to see a picture of me with my family?"

She dutifully looked at the framed photograph that showed Mr. Orrin with a small, dark, plain-looking woman who was apparently his wife, and two young girls who were also small and dark and plain. They were all wearing clothes.

"I love my family," Mr. Orrin said. "I'm very proud of my two daughters. Aren't they lovely?"

"Yes."

"I'm glad you think so. That means a lot to me, Jackie." Mr. Orrin had tears in his eyes as he replaced the handsomely framed photograph on his desk. "Now I'd like to take a picture of you just the way you look right this minute. I want it to go right into my scrapbook."

Jacquelyn looked around the office, but there was no camera in evidence.

Mr. Orrin said, "I have everything set up in the next room. Would you come in there for just a minute, Jackie?"

The adjoining room was long and narrow, and there

was no furniture except for the large black camera on a tripod at one end of the room, and a red chair against the red draperies at a window. She recognized the chair and the draperies. Most of the photographs in the scrapbook had been taken in this room.

Jacquelyn began to feel uneasy. She wanted to leave, but she remembered how Mother had looked, and she knew how bad Mother would feel if she left now. Mother would tell her it was silly of her to be frightened, because Mr. Orrin certainly was not going to hurt her.

"You have such a pretty face," Mr. Orrin said. "It's quite remarkable. I can tell what a lovely woman you're going to be when you're older."

Mr. Orrin had come near, and his hand was beneath Jacquelyn's chin, lifting her face.

"Such a pretty face," he repeated. His pale eyes seemed moist, but not in the way they had been when he showed her the photograph of his family. His flounder lips worked forward as though forming imaginary kisses. She did not know what had happened to his cigar.

"I know you must be pretty all over." Mr. Orrin undid the top button of her pinafore.

Jacquelyn lifted her hand as though to stop him, but Mr. Orrin was already undoing the other buttons, working swiftly and expertly. As he slid the pinafore off her shoulders, he began to breathe heavily.

"What a lovely child you are," he murmured. His soft hands touched her bare shoulders and moved slowly down to her hips. He lifted up the white ruffled slip she was wearing, taking it over her head. She wore only brief white panties and white socks and the shoes with straps.

She crossed her hands on her shoulders. "I'm cold." She was not really cold, but she did not like to admit she was frightened.

"It's warm enough in here," Mr. Orrin said, and indeed he seemed to be. His forehead was dotted with perspiration.

"Just the same, I'm cold."

She drew back from him when he reached out to her, and his hands slid off her narrow hips.

"I want to put my clothes back on."

Mr. Orrin had been leaning toward her; suddenly he straightened up and looked at her almost blankly. His flounder mouth was working.

"Don't do that," he said. "I'll turn up the heat. It won't take long. It'll be all right in a minute, you'll see."

He turned up the radiator. The steam hissed.

"There, that's better. Now, will you finish undressing so I can take your picture?" He indicated the camera on the tripod at the other end of the room.

Jacquelyn studied Mr. Orrin's stomach, a folded-over protusion of abdomen. He was quite an ugly little man, but she was not afraid of him any longer. In a mysterious way she had gained power over him.

"You have to turn your back," she told him.

Mr. Orrin turned obediently while she kicked off her shoes and rolled down her socks. Mr. Orrin's bulky back was turned to her when she hooked her thumbs in her panties and stepped out of them. She stood naked for a moment, enjoying the fact that he was not yet aware of it.

"All right. You can take pictures now."

When Mr. Orrin turned, his plump, moist, pale face betrayed emotion only in the sudden upward quirk at one corner of his mouth.

Jacquelyn smiled at him. "Where do you want me to stand?" she asked.

Mr. Orrin gestured blindly with his arm. "Over there," he said in a voice so harsh it sounded like a frog croaking.

She was feeling quite composed and even beginning to enjoy it a little.

She posed by the drapes, one leg in front of the other, holding the edge of the draperies with one hand. She had seen a movie star pose that way in a photograph in a magazine, and thought she had looked very appealing.

Mr. Orrin cleared his throat huskily, bent to his camera, and then looked up. He pulled the skin of his neck at the juncture of his receding chin.

"Hold that pose. Fine. You're doing very well, Jackie."

He took a good many pictures while she was standing by the drapes and later when she sat in the big red chair. He lost his nervousness and became eager, almost gay, snuffling with enthusiasm. He told her a dozen times how extraordinarily lovely she was. While he was posing her at exactly the angle he wanted, he touched her upper arm, and his fingers squeezed affectionately. She did not protest. The next time he shifted her to a new pose he let his fingers trail over her bare legs. She liked the sensation.

At the end of half an hour, Mr. Orrin showed no signs of tiring. He still fussed with his camera equipment and returned again and again to Jacquelyn to adjust her pose. Finally Jacquelyn decided that if he was not going to put a stop to it, she had to.

"I think you have enough pictures," she announced in a firm voice.

Mr. Orrin was stricken. He looked as disconsolate as a small boy.

"I'm not sure I have just the right picture I want. It has to be right. Your picture is going to have a very special place in my scrapbook."

"Well, a few more then. But I'm getting tired."

Mr. Orrin speeded up his picture-taking, and when Jacquelyn finally stood up, he appeared to be both disappointed and resigned. He sighed deeply, and his lips quivered.

"You've been very sweet," he said. "May I help you to dress?"

He helped her with lingering care, taking much too long with every article. When he put the pinafore around her he seemed genuinely sad.

"Perhaps I'll come again sometime," Jacquelyn said, in an attempt to brighten his spirits, "and we'll take some more pictures."

Mr. Orrin beamed. He put his arm about her and hugged her.

"That would be wonderful," he said. "We'll have such fun. This was fun, wasn't it?"

"Oh, yes," Jacquelyn lied.

"It will be our secret. We won't tell anyone else about it"

"All right."

"Not even your Mother."

"No."

A few minutes later Jacquelyn was sitting in Mr. Orrin's office, in the chair facing his desk, chattering away. Mr. Orrin sat with his hands folded on the desktop, beaming at her.

When Mother was announced, Mr. Orrin gave Jacquelyn a slightly anxious glance and then, reassured, told his secretary to have Mrs. Stuart come in.

He greeted Mother with both hands extended. "Your

daughter is a marvelous young lady. Absolutely entrancing."

Mother was surprised and pleased, and she put her hands into his. "I'm so glad you two got along so well." She smiled over at Jacquelyn.

"I've never had a more interesting interview." Mr. Orrin's voice was light and sounded as though there were bubbles in it. "I'm sure Jackie is going to have a fine career. I've never met a more beautiful child. Can you bring her back Wednesday at ten o'clock for a screen test?"

On the way home in the Plymouth, Mother could hardly contain herself. She said in an excited low voice that she had known it was going to happen like this, had known exactly what it would be like; the very moment Mr. Orrin said he wanted to interview Jacquelyn alone, she was sure everything was going to be all right.

"You must tell me everything that happened," she told Jacquelyn. "Every single thing from the moment I left you two alone."

Jacquelyn felt queasy. "We just talked, Mother."

"What about? You know how interested I am, darling. Tell me *everything* Mr. Orrin said."

"I don't want to."

Mother was astounded. "You don't want to. Why not?" She stared out the window.

"I just don't, that's all."

Mother pulled the car to a stop in front of a theater, parking between two no-parking signs. She seized Jacquelyn's arm so tightly that Jacquelyn whimpered.

"Now, you just listen to me. After all I've done, I don't expect to be treated like an outsider. If it wasn't for me you'd never have set foot in Mr. Orrin's office. Don't get the idea that you can treat me like some nobody because you may get to be in the movies. You keep in mind it's your mother who got you there."

Jacquelyn's arm hurt where Mother gripped her.

"I don't want to be in the movies. I don't ever want to go back into Mr. Orrin's office again!"

She felt tears starting to come. She concentrated on the few people lined up at the theater box office to buy tickets. With one part of her mind, Jacquelyn noted that the movie was *The Conspirators,* starring Robert Taylor and Hedy Lamarr. She could not see the marquee, but the posters on the side display cases showed the two stars in passionate embrace.

The tears began rolling down her cheeks. To be a star was to have everything, to own the world. A star's every wish was fulfilled. A star lived in an enchanted world outside ordinary human experience. She did not think this in words but felt it in the yearning of her heart.

Mother shook her roughly.

"What are you saying? What are you talking about, Jacquelyn? Why *don't* you want to go back into Mr. Orrin's office?"

Sobs broke in her throat and she wept and wept.

Mother was taken aback. "What's the matter with you? You've never acted like this. Are you sick? Did Mr. Orrin make you nervous, is that it?"

Mother had become concerned and did not sound hostile any longer so Jacquelyn decided to tell her.

"Mr. Orrin . . . isn't a nice man."

"What do you mean? What did he say to you?"

"He didn't . . . say anything. But he made me . . ." her voice trailed away.

Distant, icy: "What did he make you do?"

"He made me take my clothes off . . . and . . . and took pictures of me. He said he would put them in his scrapbook."

Her first indication that anything was wrong was when she realized Mother had not moved at all. Jacquelyn turned, and at that moment Mother pushed her with such force that she fell back against the car door. She gave a startled gasp. She had never seen Mother like this, the lean white face frozen, fiery pinpoints in her deep-set hazel eyes.

"You little . . . liar!" Mother said.

"I'm not lying. I'm not," Jacquelyn cried. Her voice was high, desperate with the need to make herself believed.

Mother's mouth had become thin, and her face had a queer, frightening expression.

She said in a voice so tight with the effort at control that each word was like a separate blow: "You're letting your imagination run away with you, Jacquelyn. I won't stand for it."

"It did happen, Mother. It really did. Mr. Orrin made me take off everything and—"

Jacquelyn was talking to stave off some terrible thing from happening, but she had no inkling how terrible it would be. Mother brought the palm of her hand down across Jacquelyn's cheek with all her strength, leaving a stinging pain. The shock of the blow took Jacquelyn's breath away. She fought to regain it, as the pain began widening through the nerves of her face and her head.

"What's the matter, Mamma?" At the end of the question her voice rose to a shrill shriek.

"You ... dirty ... child. I'll teach you once and for all to make up stories like that. Once ... and ... for all!"

Mother's arm rose slowly.

"Mamma ... Mamma!"

She cringed back, but that punishing arm came down again. The blow turned Jacquelyn's face to one side. She howled in fear. It seemed to her that Mother had gone out of her mind. She fumbled at the catch of the car door to get out, to escape. She was locked in with a kind of madness she could not cope with, being dealt a punishment she had not earned, could not understand, and for which there was no conceivable limit. She was trembling, her hand on the door handle while she looked back at Mother, trying to speak but only moving her lips.

As quickly as rage had come upon Mother, it seemed to pass. With an effort that made her shudder all over, Mother brought herself back into control.

"I mustn't blame you ... not entirely ... no, no, that wouldn't be fair. It's my fault for letting your father put such ... filthy ... ideas in your head. I should have stopped him ... I should have known."

Jacquelyn sensed that the threat of further punishment was abating. She put her face in her hands. The sobs in her began to break through.

Finally Mother's arm came around her shoulders. Her voice was soothing, vainly trying to comfort for the injury that would never be forgotten.

"It's all right, dear. I'm sorry I lost my temper. You're a very special, very talented little girl. Just because you are talented you have a very vivid imagination. Much too vivid for a little girl your age."

Jacquelyn turned her face against her mother's chest. She wanted to protest that she had been telling the simple truth about what happened in Mr. Orrin's office, but she knew better than to do that. Besides, she was crying so hard no words would come.

"Try to remember," Mother said slowly and tenderly, patting her shoulder now, "that millions of girls all over the world would give anything to be in your shoes. You're going to be a movie star. You mustn't do anything to endanger that. If you go on telling lies, it will only harm you. It will ruin all the plans we've made. You don't want that to happen, do you?"

Jacquelyn was hollowing down in the warmth of an affection that, somehow, nearly had been lost. She managed to shake her head.

"You must not speak that way about Mr. Orrin again. Do you understand why, darling? He would be very very angry if he heard you were telling such lies. And it would be bad for you too. If you tell lies you get so that you can't tell any longer what is really true and what isn't."

That appeared to Jacquelyn to be happening already. What she had told Mother was the truth, but children were never never punished for telling the truth. So it couldn't have happened just the way she told it. But she was sure it had. Perhaps grown-ups did not always want to know the truth or perhaps they told lies and believed in them.

Close, comforted, secure and warm in Mother's embrace, Jacquelyn made an important decision. If grown-ups did not care for the truth, then she would only tell them what they wanted to hear. She would keep her private truths as a secret, forgive. It was better that way anyhow because she could do just what she wanted and nobody would have to know.

Jacquelyn touched the rim of the sunglasses with her fingers, adjusting them to shield her eyes. The Silver Cloud Rolls slowed down outside an office building on Madison Avenue and Fortieth Street. It was October, a brilliant, tingling day when the city almost sparkled in the fresh, clear air. It was the kind of fall day Brian loved. Something in his Irish constitution responded to brisk weather. She enjoyed sultry weather, the hot blow of a strong sun, the soft warm nights, but she had tried to love his kind of weather too. She had tried to change herself in so many ways for Brian, make herself become the kind of woman he wanted. What more could she have done?

She turned away from the limousine window. She hated October now, with its cool sun, the unbearably cool weather that disclosed the onset of winter.

She stubbed out her cigarette in the silver ashtray on the center bolster of the rear seat.

The names Eakam, Trencher and Dyne were lettered on the fine-grained wood door of the office. She opened the door on a reception room with subdued lighting, deep carpeting, and a reverential silence.

A girl working at the desk looked up, smiled mechanically, and suddenly looked again.

"Miss Stuart!"

"How do you do. I'd like to see Arthur Eakam, please."

"Mr. Eakam. Yes, yes, of course." She fumbled for the office intercom.

Arthur Eakam came out to meet her, took her hand and kissed her formally on the cheek. Arthur was a tall, impressive-looking man of fifty, with a small bay window beneath his vest; he wore milk-colored spectacles and maintained an air of shrewd but pompous gravity.

He led the way to his private office. "Good to see you again, Jacquelyn. You're looking beautiful, as usual."

"Thank you, Arthur."

She sat in a deep-cushioned chair that faced Arthur Eakam's desk. The large double windows showed a fine panorama of midtown New York skyscrapers parted by a canyon that led to Bryant Park and the New York Public Library.

Arthur spent the first few minutes in the minor pleasantries that he firmly believed put his clients at ease.

Finally he said, "Well, my dear, why did you want to see me?"

Even now, trying to be most sincere, she caught herself pausing for maximum dramatic effect: "I'm divorcing Brian. I want you to start proceedings, Arthur."

Arthur Eakam sat back very slowly. "I don't believe it!"

"Nevertheless, it's true."

"How did it happen? Good Lord, as I went past my newsstand today at least three cover stories of top magazines had to do with The Beautiful Couple—you and Brian."

A vapor of emotion rose in front of her eyes, but her voice was perfectly composed when she answered: "Brian and I just can't live together any longer."

"I know this must be a painful topic, Jacquelyn, but if you want me to institute divorce proceedings, I have to know more about the background. How long have you and Brian been married?"

Three years, seven months, fifteen days, and at this precise moment, twenty-two and one-half hours.

"Three and a half years," she said.

"When did the trouble start?"

"I've only been aware of it, of how serious it is, for the past few months."

"Serious? In what way?"

"Can't we get to the legalities, Arthur? I want your services as a lawyer, not a psychiatrist."

Arthur Eakam dangled his Phi Beta Kappa key on a chain from his vest pocket, twisting the thin golden strand in his fingers. He smiled in an avuncular manner. "The difference isn't as great as you seem to think."

"Arthur, you're a dear sweet man, but there are times when you give me a swift pain in the ass."

Arthur Eakam's smile became a nervous twitch. He squeezed the Phi Beta Kappa key tightly between forefinger and thumb.

"Jacquelyn, why do you stoop to these childish attempts to shock?"

Arthur's sententious manner went over well in courtrooms, but Jacquelyn found him a bit trying. Moreover, he was clearly having difficulty keeping his gaze from wandering. Her large breasts projected nicely, she had a small waist with real woman's hips, and her thighs were well shaped, but she did not enjoy the feeling of having them under such close scrutiny. Not now, particularly.

"Do you want to act as my lawyer, Arthur? Then get down off your high moral horse and start acting like my lawyer."

Arthur's head wobbled slightly as though he had been cuffed behind the ear. He got up and walked to the window; he seemed to be looking out of it in search of his dignity.

"I'm going to need grounds, so you'll have to tell me, no matter how disagreeable it may seem. Are you and Brian having career differences?"

"Oh, the usual. He thinks he's a great artist and looks down on the sort of movies we've been doing together. But that has nothing to do with the divorce."

Arthur returned to the security of his desk. In his chair, facing Jacquelyn, he seemed to find solid support again.

"Is it his drinking, then?"

"I knew all about that when I married him."

"I'm sorry to bring it up, Jacquelyn, because it's a

delicate topic. But you realize that anything you tell me will be kept in perfect confidence." Arthur hesitated. "Is it another man?"

"Oh, Christ, Arthur, getting a divorce isn't even my idea. Brian wants it."

Arthur gazed at her shrewdly. "It's another woman, then. Who is she?"

"Her name is Merrill Yeaton."

"I've heard of Thomas Yeaton, the head of International Business Data. Is she his daughter?"

"Yes. She's only twenty-five."

"And she and Brian . . .?"

"Yes. She and Brian."

Arthur Eakam shook his head. "I don't doubt that Brian may be having a fling. You know what he's like. He has to go after every woman he meets."

"Well?" Jacquelyn crossed her legs in the way directors always made her cross them. There really should be a special screen credit: Legs by Jacquelyn Stuart.

Arthur Eakam removed his eyeglasses, tore off a sheet from a pad of cleaning paper, and absentmindedly began to clean the lenses.

"Jacquelyn, you certainly should be able to overlook casual infidelities. After all, you're the most beautiful, most desirable woman in the world. I just can't conceive of anyone else interesting Brian as much as you do."

"I'm not here to get marriage counseling, Arthur. I'm here because Brian has asked me for a divorce and I intend to give it to him."

"Perhaps if you didn't act impulsively. If you gave it time, used a little patience . . ."

He seemed about to launch on the sort of pontifical lecture he liked to give.

Jacquelyn stood up abruptly. "If I don't get the divorce, Brian will. He's made that plain enough. It's over. There's no use pretending it isn't. Just get the preliminaries underway, will you?"

Arthur Eakam patted his vest. "Do you realize the furor this will create when the news breaks? It will knock everything else off the front pages. Are you sure there isn't *some* chance of a reconciliation. Why, you two are practically a symbol of marital happiness . . ."

"I'm going to be out of the country for a while. When I come back, Arthur, I expect everything to be ready for me to get the divorce."

His professional manner, vaguely challenged, asserted itself: "I don't suppose, in view of the circumstances, that Brian intends to contest the suit."

"He won't."

"Then it should be relatively easy. There is no question of alimony or support. Of course, we can't disclose the real reason for the suit, but I suppose mental cruelty is adequate."

"It was good enough for my previous divorce," Jacquelyn said.

Gene moved back, back, lifting his hand, and threw the football in a wobbly arc. A tall narrow-backed boy, running downfield at a slanting angle with two defenders in pursuit, reached up to gather the football in. Then he rocketed forward across the goal line.

Standing up in the first row of wooden benches that made up the spectators' seats, Jacquelyn cheered with the others. Gene looked in her direction, then went back into the huddle.

A few minutes later the game ended. Gene came off the field with his arm about the boy who had caught the pass. They had their helmets off, and Jacquelyn saw with surprise that the other boy was a Negro.

"How'd you like the game?" Gene asked.

"Great. You scored the winning touchdown."

Gene looked at her with annoyance. "I just threw the pass. Nellie caught it."

"Nellie?"

The annoyance became more distinct. "Nelson Redfield. My friend. Nelson, this is my mother."

"I'm pleased to meet you," Jacquelyn said.

"Wait until my folks hear about this," Nelson said.

"Mom, give him your autograph," Gene commanded.

Jacquelyn produced a ballpoint pen and, after some indecision, finally took Nellie's helmet and autographed the side: *Admiringly, Jacquelyn Stuart.*

Nelson Redfield held his helmet carefully in two hands. "Thanks, Miss Stuart. Well, I'll be seeing you," he said to Gene.

"Wait up. I'm going with you."

They started toward the door of the locker room.

"Where shall I meet you?" Jacquelyn asked.

"I'll find you when I get out," Gene said.

He disappeared in a crowd of boys making their way

into the locker room. In the corridor, amid a throng of youngsters pushing past, Jacquelyn felt abandoned. After eleven years, Gene was more a stranger to her than ever. He could hardly share in the worshipful regard of a Nelson Redfield, because she was not a glamorous movie star to him. *The trouble is, I'm not a mother either. I can't help it. I don't know how to be.* She had got to the end of maternal emotion without ever really beginning, without knowing why, or being able to figure how to make a fresh start. The first day she brought Gene to the school he had cried, out of fear more than at the thought of leaving her. Within a few minutes after his arrival he had made friends and was too busy playing to say a proper good-bye.

At least it was an improvement over the first time she had taken him to school. Then, she had watched from the window of the principal's office, at recess time, to make sure that he was not left out of the game-playing. The psychiatrist had told her that it would be better if Gene gave up private tutoring at home and went to school to meet other boys and make friends. But Gene did not join the group of boys lined up at the slide, or the group playing touch football, or the smaller group that began a game of immies in a corner of the yard. He hung around the edge of those taking their turn at the basketball hoop. He never stepped up to toss a basketball, but pretended to be a distant part of the activity. Finally he drifted off to watch the immies game. After a while he picked up gravel and rattled it in his hands as though he were going to shoot an immie too, then sprayed the gravel back where it came from. Then he began having trouble with his socks. He kept stooping over to pull them up, one at a time. At last he could think of nothing better to do than to stand with his back against the concrete wall, his thumbs hooked into his pockets, watching all the activity with a smirking superior smile. Watching from the window, Jacquelyn wondered if she should mention it, but decided not to. Gene had to learn by himself how to get along with other boys. She didn't know how to teach him. She couldn't even talk to him about it without shocking him into a silence that might go on for days.

She wished she knew how to act like a mother. It was a duty that consisted of strange intangible things that could not be measured. She tried to be affectionate; she brought presents and wrote and came to see him when she could.

But she didn't feel that she had much to do with Gene or with the course of his life. They had never really touched each other.

She strolled around the gymnasium until finally Gene came out in his jacket and trousers, freshly washed, his hair wet, and his bow tie in place. She liked him better when he was dressed like this; a boy who looked like that was easier to deal with.

"Where would you like to go now?"

"No place in particular, Mom."

"You don't want to just talk, do you?" She gave a forced little laugh.

"Did you bring anything for me?"

"Don't I always?"

"What is it this time?" Gene didn't seem interested, merely curious in a polite, greedy way.

"Wouldn't you rather wait to see it? I had them bring it up to your room."

"You can tell me."

"Well, all right." She waited to be sure she had his full attention; the timing which served so well in most situations never seemed right with her son. Then: "It's a model railroad. Everything. Tracks, locomotives, signals, everything. It's the very best model."

She added the last sentence lamely, aware of some resistance.

"Gee, Mom, that's great."

His tone was lifeless. She had done something wrong. What? she wondered, in panic.

"You don't sound as though you think it's so great. Aren't you interested in railroads?"

"I like sports cars."

"Oh." She knew he was interested in motors, but there didn't seem to be that much difference.

"It's all right, Mom. Thanks anyway."

"You might get to like it."

"Did you see it?"

"What?"

"The model railroad."

"That's a funny question. Of course I saw it." She had seen the pictures in the brochure and read the descriptions, even if she hadn't actually picked it out. Janet handled those details for her.

"I don't think my room's big enough," Gene said.

"Oh, I'm sure it is." A picture came into her head of

the small room he shared with another boy. There was floor space for a few feet of track but not all the rest of the equipment. *Damn.* She should have thought of that. "Isn't there someplace they'd let you put it? In the basement where you can play with it when you want to?"

"I don't think so."

"I'll speak to the headmaster."

"Please don't bother, Mom."

They strolled aimlessly about the campus. One day a few years ago, when they were living in that big house in the canyon, she took him for a walk. They had rarely been alone together. It was a dry, hot summer's day and everything seemed brown and scorched, dried out and cleaned by the heat. When they reached the lower slope of the hill, Gene asked, "Where are we going?" "Just taking a walk. I thought we'd climb to the top of the hill." "That's no fun," he told her. "What would *you* like to do?" she asked. "Walking is no fun," he repeated stubbornly. She became angry. "Well, that's what we're going to do, just the same. If you don't like it, you can go home." "I don't know the way," he said. "All right then, do as I say." "No, I won't!" he almost screamed. He dug a fist into his eye. "If I get lost, it's your fault." He turned and ran, while she chased him, stumbling, falling on the down slope. He ran out of sight, and she called and called but he didn't come. When she got home he wasn't there, and after an hour she called the police. Three hours later they found him wandering in that wilderness of mesquite and tangled chaparral. His legs were scratched and white lines in the dirt beneath his eyes revealed that he had been crying. But he did not shed a tear in her presence. He was such a difficult boy to understand. Like the time when Margaret, the best maid she ever had, accidentally knocked over one of his toys. It broke and he exploded in anger; she had to slap him for being so rude to Margaret. He didn't cry; he became curiously cold, as though his emotions had congealed. She couldn't get through to him at all.

They stopped in a soda shop near the school, a favorite during visiting hours when the children could leave the campus.

"Order anything you want, darling. How about a banana split? It looks scrumptious."

"I don't eat things like that."

"Why not? You don't have to watch your weight. You look positively skinny."

"I've got acne."

"An eleven-year-old boy shouldn't be too vain about his looks."

Gene slouched in the chair at the table, carefully balancing his tall glass of milk shake on the imitation marble top. It seemed to her that chocolate was as bad for acne as banana. She glanced covertly at her wristwatch. My god, only two thirty.

"Your grandmother sends love," she said.

"That's fine. Send her my love too, Mom."

"I will." She sipped her lemonade, and felt desperation gaining. There had to be something to talk about. She did her best to be a good mother. She kept him away from bad influences. When he was visiting just a few months ago, he had wanted to see one of her movies. She hadn't let him. Instead, the sliding wall with the paintings had gone up and she showed an Ingmar Bergman film. Part of it. When the movie, which she hadn't seen before, began to show a lesbian masturbating, she jumped up with a shout. "Stop the film! What the hell kind of a picture is this?" Brian was annoyed because he thought all Ingmar Bergman films were wonderful and didn't believe anything was capable of corrupting the young. "They do that well enough for themselves, love." They compromised by showing some awful Italian thing by Antonioni. "Whatever happened to those Gary Cooper westerns?" she asked Brian later. Brian said that in the new westerns, when the hero climbed on his horse he didn't want to go anywhere; it was for an entirely different reason.

At other tables parents and their children were talking and laughing.

"Tell me about Nellie. Are you and he good friends?"

That was a good choice. She could see interest begin slowly inside of him and come gradually to the top.

"I'll say."

"He seems like a very nice boy."

"Nellie's great. He's the best pass catcher I ever saw. I had to fight to get him on the team, though."

"Didn't they think he was good enough?"

"A couple of fellows didn't want to play with a colored guy. Jerks!"

"What did you tell them?"

"I had to fight with one. Cecil Ramsey."

"A real fight?"

"He got a black eye."

Jacquelyn regarded her eleven-year-old with surprise. "What made you such a roughneck?"

"Brian says if you believe in something enough you have to fight hard for it."

There had been a succession of "fathers" in his life, beginning with Charles, his real one, but never a man who fascinated him the way Brian did. Of course, there was a good deal of the child in Brian too—unpredictable, mercurial, mystifying.

"You're not mad, are you, Mom? You don't think Brian's wrong, do you?"

"No. I don't think he's wrong." She had intended to tell Gene about their separation, perhaps even their impending divorce, but she couldn't tell him now. She couldn't risk having him stiffen up. Mamma needs you, she pleaded silently, more now than ever.

"When is Brian coming up to see me?"

"I don't know exactly. He's very busy. He's in London."

"I wish I was in London. I got a letter from him last week. I'm going to write and tell him about my fight with Cecil Ramsey."

"He'll be glad to hear from you."

"I'll tell him about Nellie too. He might grow up to be another Homer Jones."

"Homer . . .?"

"Jones. The Giant end. The one who catches all the passes."

Jacquelyn rumpled his stick-up light brown hair.

"You know, this is the last time we'll see each other for a while. I'm going away. I have to make a movie in Rio de Janeiro."

"How long will you be gone?"

"Two or three months."

"When Brian comes back, do you think he'll take me to a football game in New York?"

"I'm sure he will."

They left the soda shop and walked back toward the school. They entered the gate and started along the winding concrete walk.

"Do you think Brian will come up to watch me play?"

"He'd like to, darling. He will if he can."

"I always have a good time with Brian."

"He loves you too."

He grinned and matched his steps to hers as they went along the walk.

They reached the stone wall of the main building. Jacquelyn pulled Gene to her, held him tightly, and kissed his head. My dear. If there was some way I could make up to you for everything.

"Good-bye, darling."

His reply was muffled inside her coat. She had to release him to hear.

"Mom, I don't mind about the trains. Honest, I don't."

CHAPTER TWO

In his office, slumped in his chair, Lester Mitchell chewed at the already chewed end of a yellow pencil and wondered where in samchrist a skirt-flicking, mother-pinching whoreson of an Irishman named Brian O'Neal had vanished. Meanwhile, he listened to two scriptwriters arguing about changes he had asked for in the script. Waiting for appointments were the technical advisers, the assistant production men, and the wardrobe designers. He had a request in writing on his desk from Dame Sara Thomas, who wanted a half hour of his time to discuss the interpretation of the role of Oedipus' mother, Jocasta. Later this afternoon he was scheduled to oversee costume fittings and hire extras needed for the mob scene.

Lester frowned. The reason they were shooting the mob scene today was also the reason his faith in this production was ebbing away. The scene originally scheduled needed Brian O'Neal, and no one had seen or heard of Brian O'Neal in three days.

As far as Lester Mitchell was concerned, *Oedipus Rex* was his biggest challenge as a director, and he had looked forward to working with Brian O'Neal, who, while a lush, was a fine, serious actor, one of the gifted few who could apparently detach a character from acetate and give it a shape in the real world, who could move on a stage and make you feel that his costume was moving with him. In Lester's more rash and optimistic moods he still felt that a sensitive, modern film could be made with Brian O'Neal, but the hope was rapidly fading.

A knock at the door of his trailer office.

"Come in," Lester said.

Pete Hendrickson, his assistant, appeared in the doorway. Lester stood up instantly.

"That's all for now, gentlemen," he told the two

scriptwriters. "I'll think about what you said, but I can tell you right now that I still want those changes made. It will speed matters up if you stop arguing and get back to your typewriters."

As soon as the two writers left, Lester turned to Pete.

"Well?"

"We found him, Lester."

"Where?"

"A hotel in Soho. He checked in three days ago and hasn't left since. The local liquor store has sent up half a dozen bottles to his room. Apparently he's been living on Irish whiskey and sandwiches. I left Joe Kelly on guard in case he tried to check out."

"Pete, you take over the rest of my schedule for the day. Do the best you can. Lock up when you leave, and don't take those flats down. I want to see them tomorrow first thing. And get that goddamn Number Two hookup fixed."

"Aren't you going to be back today?"

"How the hell do I know? I'm supposed to be directing a picture. But I'm really playing wet nurse to the star."

"Good luck, Lester."

"I ought to wring his goddamn neck. But am I going to do it? Not on your life. I'm going to be polite, because Brian O'Neal is a big star. And in this business nobody gets tough with a star." Lester Mitchell curled back his thin lips. "Sometimes this business makes me sick!"

He left the office and banged the door violently behind him.

Lucia rolled over, the sheet now covering only the lower part of her beautifully sculptured body.

"That's the way," Brian O'Neal said. He was ready again to exhaust himself in the ritual act until stupefied, drunk with abandon.

He slipped his hands under her shoulders. Sex is a thicket in which I can lose myself. Easier to be me than to understand me.

A shudder ran through Lucia's body.

She gasped. "I can feel you. I can feel you."

A plain bloody miracle if she couldn't. In his long experience no one ever had complained he was small.

A new voice cut in: "Don't use yourself up, darling. You won't have anything left for me."

Brian, holding on tightly, winked over his shoulder at

Caroline, seated in a chair near the bathroom door. Caroline had no clothes on, her legs were crossed, and she had a whiskey tumbler in her hand.

Lucia cried out sharply. She began to thrash about. In a few moments, frenzy waned and she lay quiescent, squirming.

Caroline came over to the bed on Lucia's side, put her hand in Lucia's tangled dark hair, and yanked. Lucia shrieked and quickly disengaged from Brian. She flung herself on Caroline. The two nude women tumbled to the floor and rolled over and over.

Brian put a pillow behind his head. A carnival, he was thinking. A joyless carnival. Nothing endures for a shorter time than sexual pleasures, or leaves a man with so sharp an emptiness. Why did he pursue it? Moth wings vanish in the flame that summons.

Without taking his gaze from the flailing scratching females, he took a cigarette from the pack on the night table, lit it, and sat smoking as the battle mounted to a crescendo. The floor thumped.

By rights, he should not be here. He had no business in this tawdry hotel room. His business was elsewhere, with the majesty of Sophocles, the inevitability of imagined tragedy, not the triviality of Soho drama. Nothing was more important to him than the movie he was making. Nothing. Acting was for him a substantial offering of himself.

But a woman's smile was an invitation he could not refuse. It held the suggestion of all the other things he craved—the impact of himself accepted and admired. He revealed only a little of himself to women, but what he did reveal was true. I am no better than what I do, although sometimes I wish I were. I would like to perform such deeds as would make the very air catch fire. All his passionate impatience to achieve something clothed itself from time to time in a ferocious need for women.

"What's going on in here?"

Nora came to the door of the bathroom. She wore a towel looped around her middle.

"What are those two fighting about?" Nora asked.

"Caroline got impatient. Next thing I know, this free-for-all started."

Nora sat down beside Brian on the bed. Her eyes were partly closed, her full mouth was open, and her blond hair trailed down over her exquisite bare shoulders.

"I could use a cigarette," she said.

Brian took the cigarette out of his mouth and turned it over. She took a deep drag.

Caroline was getting the worst of the battle. Lucia was on top, working her knee expertly.

"You must be all pooped out, Nora said, exhaling a blue haze of smoke.

"My strength," said Brian, "is as the strength of ten because my heart's impure." He laughed, and put his hand on the smooth inside of Nora's thigh.

Nora said tenderly, "You're trying to kill yourself, lover."

"I have an appetite for confronting problems—and my chief problem is sexual appetite."

Nora said, "I really thought you couldn't make it again today."

Brian said, "Beautiful, I'm Irish. The Irish know how to handle liquor and women."

Nora took another puff of the cigarette, nodded, and stubbed it out in the ashtray. She reached up to undo the looped knot of the towel. Slowly she lowered herself onto him, lifted slightly, and settled.

Brian closed his eyes and let himself go along, deliberately holding back power and coasting for a long ascent to another climax. He must have been averaging one every few hours ever since he checked in. There had to be a limit somewhere, and he was interested to know how long he could keep going. Nora, Caroline, Lucia. There were times in these past days when he hadn't been sure which was which. It wasn't surprising. The faces and bodies of all the women he had known sometimes blurred into one huge, soft, white female body that absorbed him, drew him into the belly, devoured him. Women were his passion and his cross, and he was forever crucified with need for them, forgetting them as soon as his need passed. He had often met women who acted as though they had some claim on him because he had been to bed with them. Most would have been terribly shocked to know that he did not remember them at all. Yet each must have been important to him at the time. It really wasn't hard to figure how Oedipus made his mistake and laid his mother. Mothers were only women, after all, and women are hard to remember.

Nora crossed one arm in front of her eyes and began thrusting her abdomen forward and back. She was getting to him even though he was sated, surfeited, with the act of love. His strength began flowing down to his loins.

He closed his eyes. He felt like a dog in the sun, looking for a way into the shade. Copulating dog! Everything below his waist was suspended from a string. Only two women he remembered, really. He married them both. Conferred on them the words of the tribe that were an aid to memory. Ah! Nora working on him, until he felt like a cork pulled out of a bottle . . .

He met Fabia at the poolside of that fancy hotel in Juan-les-Pins. The one where Scott Fitzgerald stayed . . . Ahh! He was aching, the room contracted and expanded with need to let go . . . Think of Fabia, large-breasted, self-contained, inaccessible—the most forbiddingest. When she swam in the pool she moved as gracefully as a dolphin, and what a huge, yielding, bountiful creature! When he finally approached her, she treated him coldly, and it was not until much later that he plunged down into the dark dark of her. His heart hurled itself against her unmercifulness. How could he believe she loved him? He wanted forgiveness for the sins of his childhood. He swam in her bovine content just as she did in her heated pool.

Months later, on a rainy night, they walked down Fifth Avenue in New York, followed by a photographer . . .

How long can a man lie here holding himself in? In my prayer I am inserted into the orifice and at the tip of me a bubble grows like a tiny infection. I fester. Where is the thump coming from? The thump of a bed—we are making love! Nora! . . .

"Now, Brian, don't start up. Let him take his pictures and go, or we'll have him trailing us back to the hotel."

"He will anyhow, if I don't put a stop to him."

Black roadway, light glittering in rain under street lamps.

He tossed the photographer by the seat of his pants, and threw the camera down a sewer grating.

"Brian, why did you have to spoil our whole day?"

Her eyes coal-black, accusing. Mother's eyes.

"If you give him leave he'd come to the room and snap us under the covers."

"We'd have nothing to be ashamed of if we were married, Brian."

In marriage she still tried to be Mother, shrewish, autocratic, replete with tiny tyrannies. Once she told him off in front of people, and gave him a kick under the table when she caught him stealing looks at a pretty girl. When he got her home they settled that between them. He pulled all the draperies down and hurled the lamps against the wall and kicked over the furniture. Fabia was afraid for her life when he brandished the butcher knife. She promised to be better. After that, she limited herself to nagging, but he could overwhelm her in words. She was a good cook and a fine mother, and fantastically neat. He was sure that she was good for him. Most of all, she was entirely honest; he always knew where he stood. She took him back after his indiscretions, and never used tears to implore him back to fidelity. She preferred the wearing-down process, capacious mother-forgiveness. It always worked until Jacquelyn . . .

Now his body below felt hollowed out; hot tropical winds were blowing. It will not be long, dear Nora! I will look into the undersides of my lids and see nothing for half a minute. I will pretend they are sewn together. Then you will know the power of the coming . . .

Jacquelyn was altogether, completely, and supernaturally different. She was not just a quick tumble beneath sheets. Fabia remained haughty, but fear winked. She guessed that he had something going with Jacquelyn that he never had with anyone else. Oh, a little, I suppose, but with Jacquelyn a lot. It was their religion, the top experience. Offensive, vulgar they were, and he made crazy demands, but she liked the game and wanted to play it. Learned all she could about him. Excitement, variety, adventure. A man really did not have to look elsewhere for what he needed. In that last violent scene, Fabia said, She's no better than a whore. She added, I will not soil myself by talking about her . . .

His whole body shimmered like a fountainhead. He was overflowing. Multicolored rockets exploded across barred eyelids . . .

When he closed the last door behind him, Fabia took a bottle from her dressing table and flung it. The crystal shattered, and he got the bare scent of the sticky sweet odor that was filling her room . . .

I am fucking my life away. The dog was panting in the shade. Lightheaded, he opened his eyes. Do you want me now? Here we go!

Nora was rolling and writhing, and beyond her he saw the bulb in the ceiling light which grew more and more swollen in appearance until it was ready to explode.

Go in for the kill. Break the glass. Shatter the bulb.
HERE I COME!

He felt as though the back of his skull were coming off. The effect on Nora was even more shattering. She began sobbing and crying.

"Oh, God, I love it. Oh, don't stop. *Please* don't stop. Don't stop. Oh, God, I could ride you forever. I love it so. Keep sticking me. Oh, God, God, God."

Her head fell forward and her whole naked body collapsed against him like a pricked balloon.

A loud knocking on the door roused Brian from sleep. He sat up. Nora was sprawled on her face beside him.

Lucia sat before the dressing table. She was wearing a black slip that set off the whiteness of her skin. Her full mouth was sullen.

"Somebody's at the door," he told her.

"I can't answer it," Lucia said. "I'm not decent."

"Where's Caroline?" Brian asked.

"In the bathroom, making repairs. The bitch!"

Brian nudged Nora with his elbow; she stirred soddenly, without a sign of returning consciousness. Brian grinned.

"The hell with it," he said.

The knocking on the door became much louder.

"Come on, Brian. I know you're in there. Open up!"

"Who is it?"

"Lester Mitchell. I have to talk to you."

"I'm busy. Go away!"

"It's important, Brian. Honestly. It's about Merrill."

Brian fingered three days' growth of beard.

"What about her? She's in Switzerland."

"She got back this morning. She telephoned and wanted to come down to see you."

This sounded authentic, so Brian got out of bed, fumbled into his shorts, and started for the door. Then he remembered something, glanced back at Nora lying on the bed, and returned to drape a sheet about her nakedness. As he passed Lucia at the dressing table he muttered, "Beat it." She gave him a disdainful glance in the mirror, but she got up and went into the bathroom to join Caroline.

Brian opened the door.

Lester Mitchell, blond, tall, loose, sauntered into the room. His gaze took in Nora, sheeted on the bed.

"I hate to break it up, Brian. But we do have a picture to make."

"What's this about a phone call from Merrill? Is that true?"

Lester made a mocking cross on his chest. "She called from the airport. Fortunately, she doesn't know you haven't been at your hotel for a couple of nights. So she called me on the set and asked for you."

"What did you tell her?"

"I made up something on the spur. Told her you'd gone into seclusion for the afternoon to study the script. She wants you to call as soon as you get back."

"That's clever. Suppose you hadn't found me."

Lester's mouth smiled. "She'd have known I was a liar. You do put your friends into some embarrassing predicaments."

Brian pulled on his shirt. "You're no friend, Lester. We just work with each other. How did you find me?"

"Hardly an accident," Lester said. "I've had everyone from Pete Hendrickson to the public relations men, even one of our cameramen, tracking you down."

"I led them a merry chase."

"They combed every hotel and pub in this area," Lester said, his voice taking on a more accusing tinge. "We checked out the whereabouts of every broad, from secretaries to slave girls, you might have scooted off with."

"Enterprising of you," Brian muttered.

"Lucia turned out to be our lead. When she wasn't around for her walk-on in the temple scene, Joe Kelly deduced she was with you. And this hotel room is registered in her name."

"You ought to be a private detective."

"I'd probably get into less sordid situations," Lester said coolly. "By the way, where is the lovely Lucia?"

"In the bathroom."

Lester regarded Nora's figure with interest.

"Then there are two."

"Three. The other one's name is Caroline."

Lester Mitchell pursed his lips. "Most men who talk of what they've done lying in bed are lying in their teeth. You're the exception. I hope you save some of your energy for acting."

Brian caught the unmistakable note that he had been hearing too often lately in people's voices. They would like to dismiss me as an alcoholic clown, but they can't because they know that something not pitiful but tragic is going on—a man is being destroyed offstage. My life is being played behind the scenes and I am being murdered. By me. So their voices take on a tone made equally of irony and rebuke.

"I've had my bit of relaxation," Brian said. "After a shave and a cold bath I'll go to work." He fingered his beard. "I'll give you the best damned film performance you ever saw."

"I'd like to believe that. *Oedipus* isn't exactly a walk-on— even for a graduate of the Royal Academy."

"I've been doing all right so far."

"You've done your best acting *off*stage."

Time to call a halt to this sort of thing.

Brian's heavy fist clenched. "I don't care if a man says I drink. That's true. I don't care if a man says I'm a whoremaster. That's true. But when you start casting aspersions on my *acting* ability . . ."

Lester's smile was a bit sickly. "All right, I apologize. I must try to remember that you're Irish and the Irish have nasty tempers. Now, do you think we can begin clearing the girls out of here, and get you shaved, showered, and presentable?"

At five o'clock, Lester Mitchell received another telephone call from Merrill Yeaton. Her cool tones chilled his ear.

"Lester, I would hate to believe you were hiding anything from me. Brian has not returned to the hotel yet. Is he there with you?"

"Well, Merrill . . ."

"If you don't tell me where he is, I shall come there and find out for myself."

"I saw him just a little while ago," Lester said. "He's going over script changes with a writer, and you know how he is when he's working. I didn't dare break in on him. I'm sure he'll call you the moment he's free."

"I'll talk to him now, if you don't mind."

"Merrill, he'll be in a foul mood if I interrupt . . ."

"That's my concern. I'm quite sure Brian will want to talk to me. Tell him I'm waiting on the telephone, will you please?"

Lester Mitchell had no difficulty distinguishing between a request and a command.

"All right, Merrill," he said wearily.

In the dressing room he found Brian lying on a rubbing table while a muscled masseur pounded his back.

"What is it now, Lester?"

"Merrill. She insists on talking to you."

"Insists?"

The masseur began to use the sides of his hands in a chopping motion up and down the muscles of Brian's back.

"She doesn't believe you're here."

Brian paused for a second or two, his head slightly cocked as though to keep his judgment dispassionately fair.

"You tell her to go straight to hell via the nearest down escalator."

"Brian, be reasonable . . ."

Brian lifted his head off his pillowed arms. The masseur stopped pummeling.

"No woman ever insists on anything with me—and that goes for Miss Merrill Yeaton as well as for anyone. Tell her that if she asks to speak to me in her nicest, most humble fashion I will take the matter under serious consideration."

"She'll flip her lid, Brian."

"Tell her!"

Lester Mitchell sighed and shrugged. "Okay, I'll do it. I'll tell her every word you said, and don't blame me if this blows the whole ballgame."

He returned to his office, picked up the telephone, and repeated the precise message Brian O'Neal had given him. He waited for the explosion.

There was none.

Instead, Merrill Yeaton's cool voice turned languid: "That does sound like Brian, so he must be there after all. Sorry to have bothered him. Will you simply convey this message—in my nicest, most humble fashion? I'll be waiting, impatiently, for him at the hotel, and I am looking forward to spending a delightful evening in his company."

"Do you want to talk to him?"

"No. I wouldn't dream of interfering with him when he's working. Thank you so much, Lester."

Lester Mitchell replaced the telephone receiver in its cradle with faint bewilderment. Trying to follow the roller-coaster course of Brian O'Neal's romantic life was like watching one of those stupid old cliff-hangers. Come back next week and see how the hero gets out of this impossible scrape. Somehow, the hero always managed, although Lester was double-damned if he knew how. Lester hoped he would not be in the audience when the next chapter of this serial was played out. His nerves were not what they used to be.

"Why didn't you talk to me when I called the first time?"

They were dining alone in her suite at the hotel. The table with its faultlessly white linen cloth gleamed with her personal silverware; the heavy, solid-silver coffeepot was also a Yeaton possession. Merrill never traveled anywhere without bringing her own linen and tableware.

Brian picked a green Tuscany grape from the bunch displayed in a bowl of crushed ice.

"Because you really are something of a snoop, my darling."

Merrill smiled. "Do you think so?"

"I know you are and, what's more, so do you. You've gotten to the point where you think your father's money can buy you anything you want. But you don't own me. I've made it my job to disabuse you of that vile notion, and thereby save the remnants of what is doubtless a very sterling little character."

Merrill stared at him. "You have a beautiful speaking voice," she said. "Strong and masculine—and sure."

Brian chose another grape. "You would not, by any chance, be trying to seduce me?"

"The thought crossed my mind."

"I'll have another cup of that delicious Irish coffee."

"Don't you want me?"

"I've wanted you ever since I first saw you. I always want you. I'm likely to keep on wanting you for reasons that are not even very clear to me. Would you like to know the image you bring into my head?"

Across the table, her hand, lean and manicured and subtle with uncolored polish on perfectly shaped fingernails, covered Brian's hard muscular hand with the tangle of dark hair growing on its back. "Your hand is like *him*," she told him once. "That's why I love to touch it."

Now she said, "Please tell me, Brian. Tell me how you feel about me."

"You remind me," Brian said, "of a particular pub in Dublin."

She started to withdraw her hand, then did not.

"A rather odd simile, isn't it?"

"I deal in oddities, darling. They're my whole stock in trade—or nearly. Now, about the Irish coffee? Keep a steady hand on the proportions."

Merrill shook her head in amused annoyance as she got up and poured a cup half full of Irish whiskey and added coffee and whipped cream. She brought it to him and he took a sip of the steaming sweet brew.

She sat on the arm of the chair beside him. He felt the yielding flank of her thigh against his elbow.

"Tell me more."

He nodded. "The pub? It was when I was a boy. Only six or seven I was, and looking for my father. The old rascal was hiding out on Mother and hadn't gone to any of the usual places. At last I found him in this one. There was such a fine sound of revelry from behind the swinging door. I opened it a little and peeked in, and there they were, all gloriously drunk, gathered at the bar and playing darts and singing the fine old songs. No nation in the world has ever written songs like the Irish. Do you know the one they call 'Eileen Aroon'?"

"Brian, really . . ."

Brian O'Neal sang:

> Beauty must fade away,
> Castles are sacked in war,
> Chieftains are scattered far,
> Truth is a fixed star, Eileen Aroon.

"You're a madman, that's what you are. I love you for it."

"Don't you want to know why you're like the pub I saw that night? There are such lights in your lovely face, Merrill darling, such a revelry in your voice. When I look at you I hear the old songs, the wild songs of my youth, but somehow, you're always a little out of my reach. I can still feel with you like that little boy, peeking in at the door to where all the joy of life is."

She caught her hand in the thick growth of his black hair and held his face against her breast.

"You make me ache, I want you so badly, Brian."

The soft breast against his cheek was alluring. He was tired, heartily sick and tired, of being on his worst behavior. He tried so hard to displease everyone, and why did he, if not to prove that he was still Brian O'Neal, rebel, outcast, little boy who stood in the dark street and watched the lights of the pub and picked a rock from the gutter and threw it through the window. What a shattering crash! His father whipped him that night. Old Billy was properly angry because he'd had to pay for the window, but he never understood why Brian did it. Not to summon Father out of the light and warmth, the singing, or the comradely drinking, not that at all. It had been to make those inside know that he was there, a presence that could not be ignored.

Merrill came out of the bedroom in a nightgown that must have cost her at least two hundred dollars at Gorringe. The light behind her revealed the slim willowy shape within the nightgown.

"Do you like it, Brian?"

"I like you," he said. He had stopped thinking. His brain had become a gland.

She looked at him. "You do respond to me, don't you? Look at you. You're ready now."

"I'm an animal. I tried to warn you the very first time."

"I'm so glad I didn't listen."

She came into his arms with swift urgency. Her lips demanded. He put one hand on the neckline of her gown and pulled the silk until it came apart with a tearing sound. Merrill stepped forth, Aphrodite from her bath—a creature of loveliness and elegance. He passed his hands over her finely sculptured breasts, down her curving waist to the flat, hard abdomen. Everything gracious and cool to the touch, he thought, and was driven with a great need to be with her, to be in her.

She expected him to sweep her into his arms, to be taken masterfully, to be conquered by a knight of old.

But he was no knight, and chivalry was another demand that he rejected.

Instead, he put his hands on her bare shoulders and bore down. She was forced to her knees beside him. She looked up, almost imploring, her lovely clear complexion flushed beside the rock-hard prominence.

"Kiss it," he said roughly.

Tenderly, she touched him. She said wonderingly, "You must have been a good boy, Brian. You couldn't have been with anyone else while I was away and still want me like this."

She buried her face against him. She was a lovely, very willing girl. A lady, even in the heat of her passions. It was not fair to hold against her the fact that her father had eighty million dollars.

It wasn't fair at all.

CHAPTER THREE

Jacquelyn Stuart entered the lemon-hued, thick-carpeted, mirrored, and chandeliered interior of the couturier's grand salon. A slim gentleman in a dove-gray suit fawned on her.

"Miss Stuart," he said, "we are honored."

He led her to a *fauteil d'honneur,* one of the seats reserved for the elite. Mother was waiting in her seat. She had the look of an aging bas-relief Madonna.

"I called you yesterday. You weren't home."

"I went up to see Gene at school."

She managed a smile. "Oh, yes. How is he? He's ten now, isn't he?"

"Eleven. He's fine."

"I have such a crowded schedule this week, but I must find a day soon to visit him. He writes me such lovely letters . . . Oh look, they're about to begin."

The slim man in the dove-gray suit peeked through the curtain shutting off the main salon from the *cabine des mannequins.*

A moment later, the first mannequin emerged, moving and turning with carefully executed precision to display a stick-thin figure in the swirling folds of a brilliant plum-colored gown. She paused, turned, twirled, and the folds of the gown rose and slowly settled again.

The dove-gray man looked hopefully toward Jacquelyn. Several other women in the main salon were also looking at her.

She barely shook her head. The dove-gray man looked disappointed and the other women promptly lost interest in the plum gown. The mannequin interrupted her mannered saunter about the room, turned, and ambled away.

"Mother," Jacquelyn said in a low voice. "I have something to tell you. I'm afraid it's bad news."

52

Mother's face tightened with anxiety. "What is it?"

She had to tell someone; it could no longer be her concern alone. The visit to Arthur Eakam had been too professional to offer any relief.

"Brian and I separated. We're going to get a divorce."

The creases in Mother's forehead vanished.

"Is it Meyer? I knew you'd been seeing him occasionally while Brian was in London. I never guessed it was anything serious."

"Actually, the divorce is Brian's idea."

"You mean *he* asked *you* for a divorce?" Mother's voice remained cautiously low but was traced with indignation.

"I'm afraid so."

"The ungrateful wretch," Mother said. "Well, I suppose it's all for the best. The sooner you're rid of him the sooner you can marry Meyer Whitney."

She should have known Mother would be no consolation. She had learned that, slowly, over the years, yet she continued to seek for it, like a small girl who had lost her pet dog and kept looking for it in the accustomed places.

"I don't feel quite that casual about it."

"I know Meyer will ask you to marry him as soon as he knows you're free."

"He's already asked me."

"Wonderful! That must mean the sordid romance he was having with Gerda Andersen is finally over. I'll bet she's furious. But you'll be so much better for him than Gerda."

"I'm not sure yet whether I will marry him, Mother."

Often Mother did not seem to hear what was being said—as if her real self were absent somehow, and it took her a moment to bear down on the reality. When she finally did hear, she turned to stare incredulously. "Do you have any idea how much money he has? I saw an article in *Fortune* the other day that lists him among the fifty wealthiest men in the world. And that doesn't include the rest of his family. You know how wealthy Jews are. They keep it all in the family."

"I didn't think you'd approve of my marrying a Jew."

"There are Jews and Jews, dear. Besides, everyone knows they make the most marvelous husbands. You can train them to do *anything*."

"I wouldn't like a man I could train to do *anything*."

Mother gave this the polite smile that was due an untrue, although socially necessary, statement.

"Where will you get the divorce, dear? Mexico?"

"No."

"Reno, then? Idaho? I understand Idaho has a six weeks' residence requirement."

The feeling she had wanted to share was reduced to a location in space, a matter of geography.

"Mother, I'm starting a new picture. I'm leaving on the one o'clock plane tomorrow for Rio de Janeiro."

"What sort of divorce laws do they have down there? I never heard of anyone going to Rio de Janeiro for a divorce."

"It has to wait until I finish the picture."

"Oh, dear. Once you make up your mind the best thing is to get it over with."

"I've signed for the lead in *Death of a Peacock*."

"*Death of a Peac*—my, that's wonderful!" Mother's expression lit, then darkened. "But you can't afford to wait too long, darling. Men like Meyer Whitney don't grow in every bank vault." She looked approvingly at a mannequin who had appeared in a glittering creation of white silk. "Isn't that gorgeous? It's more exciting than anything else I've seen. You'll look ravishing in it."

"I'm too heavy for it."

"Nonsense. You have a perfect figure."

"Well, a dress like that might encourage me to diet. I'll try it on."

She nodded to the dove-gray man who clasped his hands with delight. The other women in the salon began to buzz.

"Darling, will you listen to me?" Mother asked.

"What about?"

"It's always bad to leave things in a state of uncertainty. I know that *Death of a Peacock* is a wonderful opportunity. But you have to think in terms of your whole life. The sooner you're rid of Brian the better."

"I know how you feel, Mother, but it isn't necessarily the way I feel."

"I never did understand what Brian had to offer you. Certainly not financial security or social standing. Besides, that kind of man can't be faithful to any woman."

"We were happy together."

Mother dismissed this with a snort of impolite derision.

"Happy? I know what that kind of happiness is based on."

"What's wrong with it?"

One corner of her mouth twitched. "We're not going to discuss that."

They had never discussed it. Mother had never given her the sort of sex talk that most adolescent girls get. That topic was forbidden in the Stuart household, and even when Jacquelyn was grown up, it was referred to in contemptuous or disapproving terms.

"You can get that sort of thing from any man," Mother said.

On impulse, Jacquelyn said suddenly, "You never got it from Father."

Mother's mouth formed a round O of shock. "What a perfectly terrible thing to say."

"Sex is a very good reason for people to stay married. You and Father never had that going for you. I don't blame you, but it's a fact."

Mother flushed deeply. "I've never told you anything like that."

"You didn't have to. By the time I was old enough to know my father, he wasn't even a man."

"Jacquelyn! How can you talk like that?"

"I felt sorry for him. I feel sorry for you. Do you know something? When I first learned what men and women were supposed to do, I tried to picture you doing it with Father. And I couldn't."

"I don't have the faintest idea what you're talking about." The crimson slowly receded from her face. "Are you going to see Meyer before you leave for Rio?"

"I'm meeting him for dinner tonight."

Mother nodded. "Wonderful. I hope you have a good time, darling."

Jacquelyn had often watched Mother make these small social recoveries. This time she determined not to let her.

"I'm not going to bed with him, Mother, if that's what you mean. Not tonight, anyway."

"Jacquelyn!"

Mother looked around nervously to see if anyone had overheard.

The bottle of Dom Perignon was chilled and waiting in the ice bucket in the secluded alcove. Meyer Whitney rose as the headwaiter, radiating joy, brought her to the table. He was a distinguished-looking man, slim and faultlessly tailored, with just the proper tint of gray in his smoothly combed hair, and a well-shaped, taut, bony face.

He took her hand and brushed her cheek with his lips.

"As beautiful as ever," he whispered. "I've been so impatient to see you again."

She could not imagine Meyer Whitney being impatient for anything. He had his emotions under too strict a control.

Meyer held out the chair and she sat down. The headwaiter poured a few drops of champagne into Meyer's glass and won his approval.

"There's only one toast I can make tonight," Meyer said, raising his glass to hers. "To us. To our marriage."

Jacquelyn sipped her champagne. "Something happened today you're not going to like, Meyer."

His gray eyes shielded slightly. "Is there some hitch in the divorce?"

"Not exactly. It's just that I have an offer of a movie. *Death of a Peacock*—to be filmed on location in Brazil. Every star in Hollywood has been after the part."

"That can wait. When you get the divorce, we'll honeymoon in Brazil—and you can do your movie."

Jacquelyn shook her head. "They need me down there right away. They're starting on background shots, and I have to be in some of them."

"That would delay all our plans for months."

He put his fingers on her bare shoulder, pinching her skin a bit tightly with possessive pressure. It was his way of demonstrating, in a physical way, his domination of her. She resented it, and for a moment considered the possibility of telling him that a delay might not be the worst thing that could happen. In several months, she could hear herself saying, anything might happen. We may decide we aren't really suited to each other, or—and this she could not tell him, for the hope was light as a breath, hardly perceptible—Brian's romance with Merrill Yeaton might burn out. Then there could be a chance to try to salvage some part of what she and Brian had had. London Bridge is falling down ... falling down ... but it hasn't fallen yet.

"I don't know what can be done about it," she said. "I'm planning to leave tomorrow."

"Tomorrow!" A startled exclamation.

"I have a one o'clock reservation."

"I'll deal with one problem at a time. The first thing is to cancel your plane reservation."

"I can't."

"I'm going to be in town for only two days. Then I'm flying to Casablanca on a business deal."

"I'd like to stay with you, Meyer. But I can't do anything that will make me lose this part. It's terribly important to me."

"My private plane will fly you down there in two days. I intend to spend these two days with you."

"Do you always get what you want?" she asked with a slight laugh. She nervously twisted the thirty-carat diamond ring on her left little finger.

"Not always. I let you get away from me once. It won't happen again."

Her hostility ebbed a little. "I wish it didn't matter so much, but this isn't just an ordinary movie. It has everything going for it. The right script, the right director—and the best woman's role written in the past twenty years."

"If it's that important to you, I'll underwrite any sum the studio loses by delaying production two days."

"I don't think they'll agree. They can get anyone else they want. Everyone's after it—including your old friend Gerda."

If she meant the remark to provoke a reaction from Meyer, it failed. She was never able to really shake his composure. There were times when he appeared to be some graven idol, a lean Buddha without the benevolence, obsessed with concerns that rendered him impervious to earthly clamor.

She shook her head. *How unfair I am. Perhaps because he is so utterly different from Brian.*

"Leave the details to me, dear. The part's yours. And you're *not* leaving on the one o'clock plane tomorrow."

"You're surer of that than I am."

"I'm accustomed to having my way."

"So am I," she reminded him.

"Only because people spoil you and want you to have your way. No one ever wanted the Wilenskis to have it."

Wilenski was his family name—it had been changed by grandfather Abraham shortly after his arrival in the United States. Abraham was an admirer of Eli Whitney, and he mistakenly thought that the given name Eli meant that Whitney was Jewish. Because he changed his name, the Jewish community in his new homeland always looked on him as something of a religious turncoat, but Abraham never attempted to explain. When a powerful railroad tycoon once remarked that the Whitneys were not to be trusted because they "were neither true Americans nor true Jews," Abraham acted in a characteristic way. He quietly bought up control of the man's railroad and informed him that he would be dismissed at the next meeting of the board. The man begged for an interview and was told that Abraham would meet him at the Temple Emanu-El. When he arrived and found Abraham among the worshipers, he made his way to a seat beside him. "There's only one thing I want to say to you," he whispered. "You have won and I apologize." Without looking up from his prayer book, Abraham replied, "I accept your apology and you're still out of a job. As a Jew I forgive you, but no one can say I'm not a true American."

It was typical of the Whitneys that no concessions had since been made in naming their children. Meyer's father had been named Elijah, and his four sons were named Lazarus, Ezekiel, Samuel, and Meyer. A powerful close-knit group, the four Whitney brothers were multimillionaires in enterprises as diversified as merchant ships and steel fabricating, business machines, contracting and building, photographic equipment, theaters and entertainment and a host of interlocking corporations. Jacquelyn had met brother Samuel, a leaner, grayer, sharp-nosed version of Meyer; he had looked her over, she thought, with an approving eye as though she were a valuable new acquisition.

"You don't realize how important a production this is, Meyer. They can't afford postponements."

"Will you excuse me a few minutes? You can order dinner while I make a phone call. I recommend the duckling."

He returned a few minutes later and took his seat. She wondered who the telephone call had been made to. Meyer operated within the inner circles of power, turning that giant wheel by which all the other little wheels are moved.

While Meyer was ordering a venison cutlet, very rare, the maitre d' brought a white telephone to their table and plugged it in. She heard Meyer exchange only a few words with the party on the other end before he hung up and turned to her.

"It's all set, dear. The studio has agreed to a forty-eight-hour delay in your Rio schedule."

"Who was that?"

"Jim Reynhout. The head of Mammoth Studios."

She said weakly, "I don't understand how you do it. It seems so effortless. There should have been all kinds of maneuvering. Phone calls between the studio, and my agent, and lawyers."

"Secondary people. The trick is to deal only with the principals."

She could not help admiring the clean edge of power that, when necessary, cut through his perfect decorum, his surface willingness to oblige. He was like a soft-spoken interrogator, observing the civilities, but knowing all the while that he carried the signed death warrant in his pocket. What sort of warrant had he carried in his pocket this time to compel an unexpected concession from Mammoth Studios? She decided not to wonder.

"What are your plans for the next two days?" she asked, content to let things go the way Meyer wanted them to.

"I thought we might go to my lodge. It's in upstate New York. I only use the place a few weeks during the hunting season, but I steal up for an occasional weekend when I can."

He took the bottle of Dom Perignon from the ice bucket and poured. Frothy amber glittered with light.

The headlights of the long sleek Jaguar XKE racing up the Taconic Parkway revealed startled pale clumps of trees along the roadside. He drove at seventy miles an hour, hardly varying the speed. It was typical that he drove so swiftly, moving purposefully at a rate exceeding the legal limit. He acted within rules that he set himself and he inhabited a world whose boundaries were his own.

They drove up in front of the lodge, a long, low-lying redwood house on the slope of a hill above a valley with the river far below. It was too dark for her to see the view, but Meyer had shown her three-dimensional color slides. There were two bright lanterns on either side of the door they entered, and a woody aroma inside the lodge prepared her for the immense living room with its timbered walls, huge fireplace with piles of kindling, and the

bearskin throws on the oaken floor. On the far wall a
stuffed deer's head projected with sad stricken eyes.

"Do you like it?"

"Very much." She wondered how many other women
had been brought here for those occasional weekends.
Gerda must have been here many times.

"It's pretty masculine, I know. But there are all the
conveniences. Have you ever been hunting?"

"Never. I don't think I'd like it."

"I suppose not. You're much too feminine."

Brian did not like hunting either; in fact, he despised
hunters. Brian never liked to kill any living creature.

"Can I take your things?" Meyer asked.

She slipped out of her coat and as she turned, Meyer
crushed her in his arms. His kiss was so beseeching that
she responded at once. A few minutes later they were in
the bedroom, and she was lying back on the quilt.

"Darling," he stammered. "I hope you don't mind . . . I
didn't mean to have it happen so quickly—but I can't help
myself . . . I've thought of nothing else since we were in
the car. I couldn't wait to get here . . . to have you alone
with me."

His voice had grown lighter, less sure. He seemed a
young bridegroom approaching his bride on their wedding
night. His assured mastery, which she so much admired,
did not reach into the bedroom.

He held her hand and rubbed her fingers as though to
warm them. Finally she reached out to him. For a moment
he held back, oddly tentative. Then he groaned, "I love
you so much. I want you more than anything in the
world."

It began happening. It was pleasant. There was pleasure
to be derived from the physical sensations, and she wanted
to abandon herself to them. Meyer's ardor augmented her
feeling. She was satisfied, appeased, by the obvious
strength of his need for her. Her hands were holding his
shoulders, and she felt him tremble.

He moved up until his cheek brushed her bare breast.
He did nothing disturbing, nothing to make her body
flinch. She slid her hands about his shoulders and for a
moment she felt something.

Then the moment passed; his urgency became simple
animal need. Even as she writhed beneath him, heard his
grunting labor, she realized that she had crossed over the
threshold of disappointment again.

They lay side by side while the heat that had mounted to her brains slowly subsided and flowed out through her limbs.

"Was it all right, darling?" he asked.

"Of course."

She shivered slightly. A thought slipped beneath her guard, a saddening thought. He could not give himself wholly to anything.

"I'm sorry. I didn't mean it . . . to happen so fast."

"It was wonderful."

"Really?"

"Yes."

"I mean, did you really come? I thought you did."

"Ummm."

"My dearest."

He covered her face with kisses. Men were so strange. Nothing they accomplished in the world, nothing they built or bargained for, could rid them of one besetting doubt. How did they measure up as lovers? Poor Meyer. He had reason to fear that other men's steel was truer than his own in that ridiculous testing place of a man: the bedroom.

Luxuriating beneath silken sheets, she looked up when Meyer Whitney opened the door and came in. He was wearing casual outdoor clothes, a red checked shirt and muffler tied like an ascot, corduroy trousers and boots. He looked perfectly at home against the timbered walls of the bedroom of his hunting lodge.

"Good morning, darling. How did you sleep?"

"Very well. It's so quiet here in the mountains. I didn't hear a sound all night."

Meyer chuckled. "Don't give too much credit to the mountains. The windows are double-paned and the timbered walls are sound-proofed. I believe that when you live the rugged life you ought to have every modern convenience."

"I wondered why I didn't even hear birds singing."

"You can hear them if you really want to. I'll have bird singing piped in through the hi-fi system. Do you have any particular bird songs in mind?"

"Oh. You're impossible! You think you can arrange everything."

"But I can."

She pretended to throw a pillow at him, then did. He caught it in one hand.

"If you'd like proof of how I can arrange things, I'll tell you what happened this morning."

"What?"

"I've been on the telephone with lawyers in New York and Rio de Janeiro and Mexico."

She sat up suddenly. "What about?"

"Working on a way for you to star in your movie and get your divorce at the same time. I think I've found it."

He tossed the pillow back to her. She was glad to have something to hold.

"It's a matter of knowing how to organize," Meyer said, sitting beside her on the bed. "You have to know the right buttons to push."

"I'm impressed. But I still don't know what you did."

"What would you say if I told you you'll get your divorce in Rio within the next few days?"

"I wouldn't want to do anything wrong, Meyer. After all, what's the harm in waiting?" She felt a lightheadedness. "It isn't as though we were missing anything while we waited to get married."

Meyer looked at her approvingly. "I'm not just a young stag in rut, my darling. I want much more of you than the pleasure of you in bed. I want you as my own. No other man in the world can have any claim on you. I want you as my wife."

"That's very romantic, but I don't see why you go to so much trouble. I've already said that I'll marry you."

"That's why I've been at such pains to be sure you get your divorce quickly. Don't worry, pet. Your little hegira to Rio won't cause any delay. We can't fulfill residential requirements in Brazil, but you can in Mexico."

"I won't be in Mexico."

"Technically, you will. The Mexican consulate in Rio is literally and legally Mexican territory. I've made arrangements for you to spend a day in residence at the consulate and for the divorce to be granted there."

"It doesn't sound legal."

"It is. We'll get Brian's consent and he'll be represented by counsel, so there won't be any hitches. Before the ink is dry on your divorce decree, we'll be married. I may even pull a few strings and have Brazil declare a national holiday!"

Meyer put his arm about her. He seemed to exude excitement like an actual physical odor.

"Darling, you'll never have to worry about anything again. Depend on me. I'm going to give you a personal written guarantee of happiness—the sort you've always deserved and that no other man has ever been able to give you."

She wanted to be caught up in his confidence, to share some of his happiness, but her spirit stayed numb, heavy, and inert.

Above her seat, in the front of the jet, the microphone crackled.

The captain's voice: "Miss Stuart, we will be landing in a few minutes. Would you mind securing your belt and not smoking?"

She was alone in the eight-passenger private jet Meyer Whitney owned. She sat back on the comfortable love seat and buckled her safety belt, then put out her cigarette and stared out the window. Traveling for a length of time, even in such luxurious quarters, made her feel stiff and grubby. She was glad to be alone, away from the retinue of social secretary, personal maid, public relations man, and business manager who usually accompanied her. They would all be following on a commercial airline jet tomorrow. Within the hour she would be at a villa that the studio had rented for her on a hillside beyond Rio. She looked forward to the luxury of bathing, reading a book, being out of touch with everyone for an evening.

The clouds above the horizon were like mountains, dark and absolutely motionless; they seemed projections of her mind. When she had parted from Meyer, a few hours before, they exchanged the usual "I love you's" and "I'll miss you's." Words always sounded the same, even though in one place or another they never were quite the same. But the words of parting had brought back memories, some tender, some full of guilt. She had always thought love was going to last. It never did, of course. Promises were vain, even when the promises seemed an echo of truth in the heart. She had always desperately wanted love to last, from the very first, with Jeffery . . .

She had first met Jeffery Robertson on an afternoon she would not forget—it was as sharply clear to her now as on that day, when she was two weeks short of seventeen, that he walked onto the set of *Tomorrow Is a Moment*. She was playing a romantic scene with Mark Vaughn, whose profile was almost as beautiful as Jacquelyn's and who was so aware of it that he kept his chin-line firm and his head slightly lifted, even during the most impassioned speeches. He had the slightly ridiculous appearance of a man protesting fervent love sideways to a mirror. This was their fourth try at wrenching Mark Vaughn away from total self-admiration, and at the end of the scene the director announced tiredly, "Okay, cut and print it."

Jacquelyn, feeling uncomfortably warm from working so long under the lights, wandered off the set. An assistant director came over to mop her neck with his handkerchief.

At that moment, Henry Orrin appeared with a squad of six young men in uniform.

"Jackie, I'd like you to meet some young gentlemen who have been defending our country in Korea. I know you've heard about them. Each was a famous athlete before he decided to sign up and defend democracy."

Orrin twittered on, introducing each stalwart young man in turn. Jeffery was a decathlon champion who had seemed assured of winning that event for the United States in the Olympics before the Korean War interfered. He had served for almost two years, won a Silver Star for gallantry, and had been wounded in action.

Jacquelyn kept a mechanically bright smile on her face as she shook hands and murmured what a great honor it was to meet them. She was flattered at the impact she made on them—at sixteen she looked fully developed as a woman, and was playing her second co-starring role opposite a much older leading man. These young men, ranging from twenty to twenty-three years old, obviously did not consider her juvenile. Their handclasps were moist and, in two cases, slightly trembling.

Except for Jeffery. His handclasp was firm and dry. His voice was deep and well controlled with only a slight trace of southern accent.

"Miss Stuart, I've been looking forward to meeting you ever since you were a youngster of fourteen. That must have been at least two years ago."

Everyone laughed, including Jacquelyn, and she quickly appraised him anew. Six foot four. His shoulders kept going out and out to there, and his neck was sturdy and muscled. She saw the biceps move under his coat sleeves. Oh my, she thought.

She did not remember what she spoke about with the young men for the next half hour while they were busy on the set positioning lights for the next scene. In the light quick babble of conversation, she was aware that Jeffery's voice seemed to sound a definite baritone note.

"What is this movie about, Miss Stuart?"

She tried to tell him, slightly disconcerted by the direct blue gaze intent on her.

He said gravely. "Seems to me they've stolen that plot out of Shakespeare. *Measure for Measure*."

She was impressed. How did this superbly physical young man know about Shakespeare?

"I wouldn't be surprised," she answered lightly. "I guess a lot of movie plots can be traced back to Shakespeare."

Jeffery smiled. "No harm done. Shakespeare stole most of his plots from the *Holinshed's Chronicles* and *Plutarch's Lives*. I guess he wouldn't have a right to complain."

Henry Orrin bustled back onto the scene, fluttering over his charges. It was time for them to go.

The assistant director came over to Jacquelyn.

"We're ready to shoot the next scene, Miss Stuart."

She quickly shook hands with each of the young men, in turn, reserving Jeffery for the last. She held his hand a moment, while the others moved out of earshot.

"I'm having a birthday party tomorrow. Would you like to come?"

"I'd love to come, Miss Stuart."

An hour later she called Mother to tell her she wanted a birthday party to be given in her honor tomorrow.

"But Jacquelyn, you're not going to be seventeen for two weeks."

"I have to speed things up a bit in order to invite a certain young man."

Dancing with Jeffery on the evening of the party that prematurely celebrated her birthday, she was suddenly very conscious of his arm encircling her waist.

"When you went off to war and became a hero," she said lightly, "did you leave anyone pining for you at home?"

"I had a girl."

"Oh. Are you engaged?"

"I gave her my class ring. I got it back a few weeks ago."

"Oh. I'm sorry."

"It's just one of those things you have to expect when there's a war going on."

"That depends on the girl."

He said slowly. "Don't get me wrong. Nancy isn't that kind. There's nothing wrong with her."

He likes her, Jacquelyn thought hollowly. Nancy's face appeared before her—a little dim and unreal. But they're not engaged any longer. She doesn't have any claim on Jeffery anymore!

"As long as you're not officially engaged or anything, you don't have to clear it with anyone. Why not let me show you around Hollywood?"

He smiled in an odd, rueful way. "Any and all favors are greatly appreciated, Miss Stuart."

She saw Jeffery every night during the next week. By then the story got into the newspaper columns, and she and Jeffery hardly had a minute alone. Reporters and photographers followed them everywhere and there were invitations to parties, to fund-raising affairs, to patriotic rallies. Television shows offered fabulous sums for a live appearance, even a walk-on by the storybook lovers, the wounded war hero and Hollywood's most glamorous young star.

She finished the last retakes on *Tomorrow Is a Moment* and the studio rushed it into release to capitalize on the publicity of her new romance. After the premiere, Jeffery drove her in a studio-supplied convertible to the moonlit Palisades. There she asked him to park for a little on a cliff high above the beach where waves beat silvery against black rocks.

She leaned against him, her head on his shoulder.

"Wasn't the premiere exciting, darling?"

"I enjoyed being with you, and you looked beautiful."

"You were so handsome in your uniform. I'm so proud of you."

The distant roar of waves sounded like the roar of blood in her veins.

"Jeffery . . ."

She pulled him down toward her, and when he kissed her she opened her lips. There would never be any other man for her, no matter what happened. His grasp tightened. She thought: There is no way of saving up love, we have to spend it when we can. Tomorrow she would be going through an ordinary day and no one, not even Mother, would know that she was no longer a virgin.

He broke away. His breath came hard, and with arms stiffly before him, he gripped the wheel of the car.

"What's wrong?" she asked.

"I'm even more of a damn fool than I thought."

Everything around them was silent; even the noise of the waves seemed to be stilled. This moment which was going to be transformed into its own kind of immortality for her, the time that she would never forget, was ruined.

She turned away. "You'd better take me home, Jeffery."

She expected him to call to apologize the next day, but he didn't, and when she called him the day after that, she learned that he had left Hollywood with the others to continue their nationwide tour in behalf of Army recruitment. She went into her room and wept and wouldn't come out even to eat. Mother came to comfort her, but when she said it was just as well Jacquelyn hadn't become too serious about a man at her age, Jacquelyn began sobbing so uncontrollably and at such length that Mother was forced to relent and say she was sorry and that Jeffery was a wonderful young man with whom Jacquelyn had every right to fall in love.

She wrote to Jeffery, a passionate declaration, and she was disappointed that his reply did not say more than it did. He merely informed her when he would arrive in Los Angeles and signed the letter, Love, Jeffery. She clung to those last two words as though they were proof that everything was going to be exactly the way she wanted it.

Mother informed the studio publicity department, and when at the appointed day and the appointed hour Jacquelyn was at the airport, most of Los Angeles was also on hand. Roads on the way to the airport were choked with cars, and police were everywhere to keep enthusiastic crowds from spilling onto the airfield itself. Out of the multitude sprang a forest of tiny, waving American flags. The flags were on sale at the newsstand in the airport and vendors sold them everywhere. When the jet appeared and began to let down for the landing, the crowd's cheers mounted and mounted until they were heard above the tremendous roar of the plane's engines. A phalanx of police ushered Jacquelyn onto the strip and toward the plane as it rolled to a stop.

Several spectators vaulted the wire fence and ran toward Jacquelyn, but police intercepted them. Then the gate was pushed open by the press of the crowd. The police line strained to hold, then broke. Across the strip raced the enthusiastic welcomers.

Waiting at the bottom of the landing platform, Jacquelyn was terrified that she was going to be mobbed. The police hastily reformed their lines around her in a tight double circle and were assisted by reporters and photographers who wanted to keep their own vantage point.

When Jeffery appeared at the top of the landing platform, flashbulbs popped and the crowd cheered. He came down the steps to Jacquelyn, and she rushed into his arms. A forest of microphones quickly surrounded them, and Jacquelyn, through tears, kept murmuring, "I'm so happy, I'm so happy," and Jeffery managed to avoid answering the question that everyone was asking: "When are you two going to be married?" He looked rather peaked, and there were grim lines at the corners of his mouth.

They drove through cheering, shouting, gesticulating crowds to the Beverly Hills hotel, where they held their first joint press conference in the crowded Polo Lounge. Two women reporters actually cried. Jacquelyn held Jeffery's arm tightly, smiled, and answered questions readily. Jeffery was withdrawn, silent and strange. He never smiled at all.

That evening he took her dancing at the Coconut Grove. She wore a long pink velvet evening dress and a crown shaped diamond tiara atop her dark hair. The dress had been made for her by Chanel in Paris. Everyone stared at them. Bernie Trell, the orchestra leader, came over to get Jeffrey's autograph. Bernie stared approvingly at the Purple Heart on Jeffery's tan tunic.

It was not a successful evening. They only danced twice, and Jeffery did not hold her close and did not talk to her at all. He had too much to drink and became a bit surly when she suggested that he shouldn't order another.

"What do you know about it?" he asked. Then, apologetically, he added: "It's all such a lot of crap!"

"What is?"

He waved his arm at the other tables, at the crowded dance floor. "All of this!"

She understood then, and his words transformed all the false glamour. Jeffery was right. This tinsel and frivolity when he had been in the midst of a living horror. Probably, he had seen men killed. He must have. And killed men himself. She blanched. It was hard to believe this quiet, broad-shouldered young man seated at the table with her had taken another human being's life. He had no choice. Over there it had been kill or be killed.

Her hand touched his across the table.

"You're right, darling. I didn't realize how silly all this must seem to you, now."

She had made up her mind to begin an affair with him as promptly as possible, and she had chosen the occasion on which it would happen. A picnic, alone together, at a secluded spot she knew a few miles from La Jolla. Jeffery did not seem especially interested when she mentioned it to him—in fact he turned sullen and hardly spoke to her.

On the way home from the Coconut Grove, with Jeffery driving, they did not exchange a word. When they stopped in front of her house, she turned to him and held out her arms. He smiled slightly—the disconcertingly ironic, off-center grin.

"I think we'd better stop this before it goes any further," he said. "It can get pretty ridiculous if we let it."

"What do you mean?"

"I'm not going with you on that picnic, and I'm not going to see you again. This is it, Jacquelyn."

She felt a pounding at her temples. All the shattering tensions of youth and need burst into anger.

"What's the matter with you? Don't you want to make love to me?"

His voice came quietly to her: "I can't."

"What?"

"You heard what I said. I can't." He gave a hoarse chuckle as though some pain inside him were dissolving into sound. "Our whole romance has been a triumph of propaganda. Both the Army and your Hollywood studio can make a lot of bricks without straw—but there's one thing they can't do."

"I don't know what you're talking about. I really don't!"

He said gently, "I don't think you'd be very happy with me as a lover, Jacquelyn. I don't think any woman would. Not after what happened in Korea."

She stared at him incredulously. "After what happened?"

"Do I have to spell it out? I can't make love to you or

any other woman. Ever." As he reached across to open the car door for her, he seemed a very tall, bitter, and powerful figure. "That's why Nancy broke our engagement. It wouldn't have been much use marrying a man like me. I would have been luckier to have been killed outright."

Humiliation and shame made her cry out, "Damn it, you might have told me. You didn't have to let me make such a fool of myself!"

She flung out of the car, and as she hurried up the walk, in tears, she was terribly sorry she had said it. She had been cruel.

But life could be cruel, sometimes . . .

Bump and jar of the plane wheels.

Good-bye Jeffery. Only the present matters.

She looked out at the runway running swiftly past the plane window. The terminal building swung into view, and she saw the crowds. They had swarmed out to the gates, were black against the roof gallery, and beyond in the huge field people were stetched out as far as the eye could see. Streamers were flapping in the wind. There was a band playing.

Over the years she had come to fear crowds. Packs of animals snapping at her heels.

The plane's motion stopped. The captain opened the door into the cabin.

"Looks like they're expecting you, Miss Stuart. Most of the town has turned out."

"Can you talk to the control tower?"

The captain's voice was slightly surprised. "Of course, Miss Stuart."

"Have my car meet me here at the plane. Tell them I'm not having any press conference and I'm certainly not going on display for the mob. They'd better find some other way to get me out of here."

"Yes, Miss Stuart."

She looked moodily out the plane window at the airfield.

CHAPTER FOUR

The telephone rang.

Distinguishing himself from the rich men, and their beautiful kept women, married or not, and the assorted hangers-on, company presidents, idlers, Blue Book regulars, and titled heads, Brian O'Neal called out:

"Oh, let the fucking phone ring. I'm in the middle of a story."

The ringing echoed through the ballroom of the Crittenden mansion while everyone studiously ignored it because Brian O'Neal said to. Such bloody fools. The guest list at Crittenden's fancy ball included the ripest rotten fruit falling from the branches of England's noblest family trees, yet no one dared to speak against Brian's vulgar assumption of command. There's the proof, if any more was needed, that their blood has thinned. I'd have been drawn and quartered and my tongue sliced off if I'd presumed as much a couple of centuries ago.

A servant answered the phone, which was ringing and ringing from the gatehouse where outside calls were being intercepted. The relay meant it was important, but Lord Crittenden didn't move when the servant indicated it was for him. The servant finally hung up the phone.

Brian went on with his story. It had to do with the time he'd been an altar boy. "The finest sort of training for being a pubkeeper, which was my secret ambition. All that muckin' about with wafers and wine, you know, and changing over of one thing into another—like pouring cheap whiskey into fine labeled bottles."

A nervous whinnying came from a paunchy, pale, snub-nosed man standing on the fringes of the crowd. Stephen Innis, the irreverent dog. Not likely anyone would challenge Stephen either: this party was in his honor. Ireland's poet laureate, they called him, and who had a better right to the title? Stephen was drunk, mad with the power of his new-found, new-minted speech—but they would ruin him. There was already talk of adapting one of his long Irish narrative poems into a movie and having Stephen himself do the screenplay. It would be a commercial disaster, and it could also be his unmaking. He would be hired for more screenplays on the strength of it, and what would happen to the glorious mystic roar of his Irish verse? Perhaps no matter. All would be lost one way or the other, bartered for Hollywood gold or drowned on the long binges or frittered away in salons where silly people punctured him with tiny pinpricks of admiration until all the fluid of poetry seeped out of him.

He winked at Stephen and went on: "I rather enjoyed being an altar boy. It was like being the assistant in a magician's act. You give the head man the props and watch him befuddle the multitude. If he's a little leaning in the wind, you remind him whether he's conducting Low Mass or High Mass. I can't say it was dull. That was really my first introduction into show business—to performing before an audience. I missed the applause, but I had all the rest of it."

There was embarrassed laughter. Merrill's tinkling chime joined in with it. Merrill looked especially beautiful this evening in her white gown, diamonds sparkling like a million icicles. Beautiful, impeccable, far-from-untouchable Merrill—how far a distance he had traveled from the boyhood years. Merrill was a strange conquest for a boy who worked after school in dark rocky fields to help poor farmers and served drinks in his father's pub at night.

"I even got laid in a church," Brian said.

A young girl near him put her hands to her face. "You didn't!" She was charmed. She'd have gone behind the altar with him on Ash Wednesday. What a resurrection there would be with the two of them rising a hundred feet into the air before the eyes of the startled worshipers.

He said, "Not in the church proper but in the graveyard. We had a wonderful good time. She wasn't exactly a pro, but she had certainly long ago abandoned her amateur standing."

This time the laughter was led by Lord and Lady Crittenden themselves. Brian turned for a new drink and found that Merrill had materialized near him.

"It's midnight," she said, "and you've gone past the

manic into your outrageous phase. Would you like to take me home?"

Brian said loudly, "Are you making indecent proposals to me, my turtledove?"

"Brian . . ."

"I'm in a receptive mood. Meet me in the hothouse in half an hour and we'll see what we can do about raising the temperature."

Merrill flashed him a look that said he was drinking too much. She was quite right. He had begun the evening on champagne, a mistake for him because it took a magnum to have any effect, and by then he had switched onto the hard stuff and was beyond his true capacity. Just as well, considering what the evening would have been like if he remained in the slightest degree sober. Poor Stephen Innis was working on his second bottle of Irish whiskey and smiling at everyone in gap-toothed fashion while feeling as many ladies' bottoms as he could reach. In the society columns tomorrow the party would be written up as a magnificent success. It was a dismal bore that only liquor made endurable. He was tired of contributing his shocking all to the merriment. He shook off Merrill's arm and crossed the room to where Stephen had a blonde in a low-cut green dress cornered against a wall. Stephen's hand was on her bottom as he spoke with her, and the girl kept sliding along the wall in a vain attempt to disengage his hand while keeping him in conversation.

As Brian came up, the blonde was saying, "What Kierkegaard means when he says that Don Juans are irresistibly demonic is that Don Juans *expect* to be victorious simply because they are erotic . . ."

"You have a beautiful behind, my dear," Stephen said.

"Don't you agree with me?" the blonde asked Brian.

"I agree with him," Brian said, indicating Stephen. "You do have a beautiful behind."

The blonde blinked. "Is sex all you men ever think about? There are more serious things in life."

Stephen made an attempt to reach her lips, but she evaded him. "My dear," he said, "I am perfectly serious about sex. I'm even willing to talk about it provided the talk leads to something more practical. Now you take the typical Don Juan. Think of the mad cunning with which he insinuates himself into the affections of his desired object. He is a master of the seductive arts. What should interest you is the high degree of art, the magnificent control and direction, of Don Juan as a seducer. A boff isn't just a boff to him. When the fucking is over, Don Juan can get as much pleasure, maybe more, in thinking back over his own cleverness in leading up to fucking."

"I wish you wouldn't use that kind of language," the blonde said.

"What kind of language?"

"I'm really very disappointed in you."

"Do you or don't you?" Stephen asked.

"What?"

"Fuck."

"I certainly do not!"

"Then I," Stephen said, drawing himself up to his entire five foot five inches, "am very disappointed in *you*."

The blonde finally departed in a state of indignation, and Stephen looked after her reflectively.

"I still say she has a beautiful behind."

"I've seen better," Brian said.

"Why don't we forsake this old ladies home and go on an ass hunt?" Stephen asked.

Brian said, "I'll pretend to go to the men's room and get the car. Then I'll be ready for a getaway in front when you show up."

Stephen flung an arm about him. "Fellow conspirator. Great-hearted seeker." Stephen put a finger beside his nose. "Outside the house, in five minutes. Then forward to Meehawl's."

Meehawl's was the best pub this side of St. George's Channel. It was dark and smoky and leathery looking, and no one paid any more attention to Ireland's poet laureate and Ireland's most famous actor than if they had been two dockworkers stopping by for a draft of the warm, brandy-colored beer.

"Do you think they've missed us by now?" Stephen asked.

"It would have to have been a mighty long pee," Brian told him.

Stephen's whinny was cut short. He jabbed his plump elbow into Brian's side.

"Look there," he said. "The young thing with the mane of honey hair. Like a palomino mare."

"She can't be more than eighteen."

"Ah, but she's well broken in. You can see the look in her eyes."

"You can't see her eyes from here, you liar."

"I can see what I need to. If I can't have her, Brian, I am going to stand here and drink myself insensible."

"What d'you want me to do?"

"Is she alone?"

"No. That's her boyfriend over there, playing darts."

"Will you give me half an hour with her, Brian? Would you do that for an old friend? I'll leave a sonnet to you in my will, I swear it."

"I'll do what I can."

Brian sauntered over to watch the dart game in progress. The boyfriend had a steady hand and a good eye, and seemed sure to win in jig time. Brian glanced at the booth where Stephen was in earnest converse with his palomino mare, who seemed both bewildered and flattered by all the attention. Brian noted that from time to time she cast anxious glances in the direction of the dart game. That indicated to him that Stephen was being treated merely as an interesting diversion, a possible provoker of jealousy, rather than as a serious contender.

The dart game ended. The boyfriend collected his shillings, and was about to start off when Brian intercepted him.

"I'll have a game with you. And I'll wager half a crown to a shilling I can beat you."

The boyfriend, a cocky little squirt, winked at his friends.

"You're on."

The contest was no contest at all. It was a rout. The cocky little boyfriend won hands down going away. Brian, chuckling, shook hands and congratulated him, and offered to stand him and his friends a round at the bar.

When they finished their drinks, Brian glanced over at the booth and noticed it was empty. He called the pubkeeper and paid the tab. As he was pocketing his change the boyfriend noticed his girl was missing. There was a hubbub for a few minutes, interspersed with comments of an unfavorable nature on the girl's ancestry, and fumbling attempts at sympathy from his friends.

Finally the boyfriend said, "She can go straight to hell for all of me," and joined in a new dart game with his friends.

Brian left Meehawl's. As he was crossing the street he heard a whispered halloo.

"Brian, it's me, Stephen. I've someone who wants to meet you."

Stephen emerged from a dark hallway, with his palomino in tow.

"See, do you recognize him now? Isn't he Brian O'Neal, the actor?"

The girl's eyes widened. "Mr. O'Neal, I never expected to see you in a place like this."

"It's the only sort of place you can expect to see me, my dear. But we shouldn't stay around too long. It's nearly closing time. That boyfriend of yours will be leaving soon and if he finds you here . . ."

The thought bestirred her. Moments later they were in a high-riding black taxi, heading toward Stephen's sublet in Chelsea.

In the taxi Stephen treated the girl alternately with respect and mockery, with a real attempt to be charming and with humorously grandiose fantasies. She reacted with a placid smugness that seemed to say, I know what you're after, and which finally baffled, fascinated, outraged, and defeated Stephen.

As they were getting out of the taxi, the girl took Brian's arm instead of Stephen's proffered one.

Stephen gave him a reproachful look. "If there's one thing my dear father, who owned a bit of land, taught me, it was to hate poachers."

Brian shrugged and they went upstairs in a groaning, old elevator. In Stephen's two-room flat the palomino became animated. She put on a rock 'n' roll record, and while Stephen mixed drinks she kicked off her shoes and did a fairly abandoned dance. Watching the slim lithe figure wriggling inside her clothes, Brian deduced that she was only wearing a bra and panties underneath her white wool sweater and miniskirt.

She held out her arms to Brian.

"Come on, let's dance."

She was disappointed when Brian shook his head and let Stephen take over instead. Watching them together, Brian wondered why this porcine unattractive man was in a constant state of heat for pretty young girls who would never understand the hundredth part of his riotous eloquence. The needs of mind and body are so wonderfully different.

Stephen joined in the spirit of the girl's dancing, ripping off his shirt and twirling it about his head, while he matched her step for step. He began to use the shirt as a cape, inviting the palomino to charge at him. When she did, she went lurching drunkenly past and down to the floor where she lay on her stomach convulsed with laughter.

Stephen promptly tried to mount her from behind. For a minute or so she did not protest; then she uttered an impatient exclamation and rolled over, sliding Stephen off to the floor.

Brian mixed more drinks all around. Stephen put on another record.

At shortly before two A.M., Brian decided to get out of his warm sticky clothing. He stripped down to shorts and stretched out on the bed with his drink. Stephen and his young palomino were dancing to a very slow rhythm now, standing face to face and hardly moving, with only their hips revolving against each other.

Stephen gradually worked his hands up under her sweater, lifting it so that her waist was bare. She dropped her honey-colored head wearily on his shoulder.

Stephen glanced over at Brian and with a jerk of his head indicated that he should retreat into another room.

Brian was starting to obey when the girl suddenly came to life. She lifted her head and looked around suspiciously.

"Say, what time's it?"

"It's still early, honey," Stephen reassured her.

"I've got to be getting home. My mother'll kill me."

"Don't be in a hurry. We're just starting to have fun. Aren't we just starting to have fun, Brian?"

"Sure," Brian said. He lay back on the bed and finished his drink. There was nothing he could do to help in the seduction except put forth the kind of effort that would undoubtedly win the girl away from Stephen. He had learned when he was a very young man that he had an animal appeal for women—he had noticed how some women looked at his strong stocky body, the head with its heavy shock of black hair, the regularly chiseled but masculine features. It wasn't just his looks, however; he knew many men better looking than he was. He had seen it happen to women while he was talking to them, when he was far more interested in what he was saying than in them. Their gaze would become a little bit fixed, their smile a trifle unsteady, and he would think here was another one ripe for the plucking.

There had been hundreds, literally hundreds without meaning, a brief quiver in the loins. None of them meant as much as Jacquelyn.

Jacquelyn.

A man's real mistress is sometimes his wife.

He drained the last of his drink hurriedly. If Stephen didn't hurry to bed down his palomino, he was likely to stage one hell of a bawling scene. It wasn't manly, but he was Irish and beginning to be drunk, and everything he was doing seemed strange. I want to live warmhearted and bravely go forth to die. Instead I live a clown's life and will perish of a liver turned to sawdust. What am I doing here? I ought to be with Jacquelyn right this minute. She ought to be beside me in bed. How could he be horny for a woman he had bedded down a thousand times?

"I'll bet you don't think I can," the palomino said. She was standing, legs astraddle and challenging, at the foot of the bed. She must have been talking to him, but he hadn't heard a word she said.

"If anybody can, honey, you can," Brian said.

"Would you like to see me do it?"

"I'd love nothing better. First I want to get myself another drink."

At the bar he poured a glassful and took a deep swallow from it. Jacquelyn is gone, he thought quietly. She's gone for good with all her beautiful, enticing, insidious blandishments.

"Hey!" Stephen called. "How d'you like that?"

Brian turned to see the palomino standing on her head at the foot of the bed. Her miniskirt had slid up around her hips. He had been right. She wore nothing but panties.

"That girl's got talent, Brian." Stephen went over to where she was standing on her head and held her legs together in one arm. He ran his other hand down the smooth length of her thigh. "A shame to have a girl keep so much talent hidden."

"I can do it like this for minutes," the girl said in a muffled voice.

"That's all I need, honey," Stephen said soothingly. He got hold of the top of her panties and pulled them up over her legs.

Brian smiled. He had come with Stephen and the girl, as inevitably as if no other place of refuge were offered.

Now he had had too much to drink, and still the edge of self-disgust was not dulled. Is the throne of my reason ever occupied or do I only cast an occasional shadow across it? He looked on without interest as Stephen worked the palomino's panties up over her ankles.

Brian went into the bathroom, sat on the toilet, and finished his drink. No doubt I overdo it. They are not long, the days of wine and roses. Or the weeping and the laughter. A man seizes what he can. Does no good to swear to be better. When you make a vow to the Lord your God, do not put off fulfilling it, for the Lord your God will require it of you, and you will have incurred guilt, whereas you incur no guilt if you refrain from vowing. Old Testament boys knew how to get along with the Deity. Don't make promises you can't keep.

When he came out ten minutes later, Stephen was sitting on the floor, with his back propped against the bed. The girl was on her stomach, her bare behind showing. Stephen looked exhausted.

"Maybe we ought to take her home now," Brian said to Stephen.

Stephen's glassy gaze rolled over to him. "What for?"

"It's getting late."

"Don't be silly. Rosetta has all kinds of tricks she hasn't shown us yet. Haven't you, Rosetta?"

The palomino put her head on her crossed arms. "I'm not a bad girl. I don't want you to think I'm a bad girl."

"Nobody thinks that, honey," Brian said. He bent over her and patted her bare behind. "You get up now and I'll take you home."

Instead she turned, half lifting herself. She flung her arms about Brian.

"You're the one I want," she cried. "Why did you let me do it with him?"

She began to cry against his shoulder. "You don't respect me anymore. You think I'm cheap!"

"No, I don't. That isn't so."

Her teeth bit his bare shoulder.

Stephen waved a magnanimous hand. "It's all right with me, Brian. Have fun."

"Thanks a lot." He had no intention of making love to her.

She began to squirm and move until the silken soft touch of her skin began to rouse him.

"Come on," she said. "Come on. Please."

Her hand fumbled with the front of his shorts. She looked down, and a flush spread over her face. Her lips parted. She flung a strand of loose hair back over her shoulder.

"He's right, you know. I have a lot of tricks I can show you."

He lifted her with him and drew her toward the bed.

She brought to their wild antics a strange and disturbing purity. While he was waiting for her to join him and ride on to climax he saw in her white, strained, harassed face a silent indication that the lights were red. He stopped his motion, held himself with an imperious gesture. He wanted to break through the little seductive ways that still defended her innocence.

Then he let himself go, and over the noise of traffic from the streets, above the hoarse hooting of Stephen's breath from the foot of the bed, he heard her rising cry.

The way to learn about satisfying women is to be brought up doing it. He had learned imperceptibly, a session here and there, and grew up acquiring further knowledge of the small signs by which a woman would tell what she wanted. There was almost a blueprint, and he grew adept at reading the female sexual diagram, starting with Molly on the upper floor of Kinsella's barn, and continuing through the others in his nearby villages. Alice Quigley had taught him more than anyone since. After Alice he never had any doubt about his proficiency in the art.

Alice Quigley lived in what had formerly been the old Loughran house. She had once been an actress. There were framed photographs of her onstage and in costume; a handsome woman then, tall and lean, with long black hair at shoulder length and a well-ordered face. In those old photographs she wore black, with white pearls, often with long, black leather gloves. She apparently had a following in her heyday, but her charms had faded now. Her tall figure (she was at least five foot eight) had become long and stringy, and her erect posture made her appear a haughty heron moving about on long long legs.

When she announced an evening of dramatic recitals, everyone in the village and the surrounding area received invitations. Kathleen and Bridget intended to go, and Old Billy gave Brian permission to accompany his older sisters.

In all, perhaps a hundred people gathered at the local

theater which had been closed down two years before but was reopened for this occasion. When Alice Quigley appeared in her black dress with the black gloves and white pearls everyone agreed that she was a striking-looking woman.

The program consisted of scenes and readings from some of the worst plays ever written. Afterward, Brian and his sisters went backstage where four or five other people had gathered. Brian knew that at a moment like this it was proper to say only kind things and voice no criticism. But nothing that he felt was hidden, for his face was like a transparent pane of glass as far as registering emotion was concerned.

Alice Quigley turned warm attention on him, appreciatively taking in his black hair, blue eyes, and rosy complexion. "How did you like the plays tonight? You're Billy O'Neal's boy, aren't you? My, you've grown into quite a handsome young man."

"Thank you, Miss Quigley. I had a very nice time."

She laughed and clasped her hands together in a girlish gesture. "How sweet of you to say that." She held out her hand to Brian. He took it with some awkwardness. "You must come tomorrow night and see our little theatrical again. I've been thinking of adding a short piece by Pinero. Will you come?"

"If I've nothing else . . ." Brian was stopped by the glares from his sisters. "I'd be glad to," he finished lamely.

"Wonderful," Alice Quigley said. "You must all come," she said to the room in general with the sort of inclusiveness that, because it was not directed to anyone, could not be construed as a real invitation.

On the next evening, there were fewer people present. It was even a bit embarrassing, all the empty, staring rows. The handful of spectators distributed themselves carefully throughout the small auditorium.

Brian sat in the second row of the orchestra, and Alice Quigley saw him there just before she began reading the new piece from Pinero.

"*Cead mile failte,*" she cried. A thousand welcomes.

He did not think the Pinero piece any better than the others. When the evening ended, he hesitated about whether to go backstage. It was late, and he had three miles to walk home. On the other hand, Alice Quigley had recognized him and called out a greeting, so she would probably expect him to call backstage. Kathleen and

Bridget, who had decided not to come, would ask him what had happened and would think him foolish and rude if he did not go backstage.

Alice Quigley greeted him with outstretched hands. There was no one else in her improvised dressing room, and she seemed sadder and paler than before, her mouth redder. He felt a little sorry for her.

"What a sweet boy you are, Brian O'Neal," she said. "You shall have your reward for coming to see me again tonight. You shall take me home."

It did not seem a very great reward to Brian. Alice, after changing to street dress from her stage costume, led the way to the lot at the rear of the theater. She owned a rather battered little blue car. Brian had only been twice behind the wheel of a real automobile, and then never for more than a few minutes at a time.

"Do you know how to drive?" Alice asked.

"Oh, sure."

He drove back along dark unlighted narrow roads, and once or twice Alice cautioned him about going too fast and once she grabbed at his elbow and her face turned as green as a husk of corn.

"Are you sure you've driven before?" she asked.

"Am I going too fast for you? I'll slow down."

"And would you try to keep more toward the center of the road?" She smiled, a little apologetically. "I know I'm a nervous passenger. But I'm used to driving myself, you see."

Brian drove with a flourish into the back yard of Alice Quigley's house. The car's wheels jolted a bit going over something in the dark.

"Was that an obstruction?" he asked.

She replied faintly, "It was the hollyhocks. But no matter. We're home safe."

Brian got out to open the door for her. She sat still for a moment, as though regaining composure, and then put her hand lightly in his hand and got out.

"A gallant gentleman," she said. "Would you care for some tea before I send you on home?"

"Oh, I wouldn't trouble you, Miss Quigley."

"You may call me Alice. And it's no trouble at all."

The high-ceilinged living room was a bit chilly, and she asked him to build a fire in the grate. There were chintz covers, freshly cleaned, on the furniture, and the wood seemed to Brian oiled and polished. There was a fine-looking painted clock on the mantel above the fireplace.

"It's past ten," Brian said. "I can't stay long."

"I'll have tea on in a minute." She took off her coat, a bit damp with misty weather, and handed it to Brian. "Just hang this up somewhere, will you?"

The coat's fur collar was sleek and wet to his touch. He put it among feminine things in a closet with a feminine aroma.

When he returned to the living room, Miss Quigley was gone. He took a seat on the chintz sofa, stretching his legs toward the growing fire.

In a few minutes she returned, wheeling a tea wagon that had pot and cups on the top shelf, and cakes and biscuits and cheese and jam on the bottom. She had changed again, this time into a long, close-fitting dark robe that reached to her ankles. She took a bottle that had been on the bottom shelf, and held it up to the light.

"I thought you might like to taste a bit of port," she said. "It's very good."

The port was dark, the color of blood. He took a big swallow and felt the warm shock go all the way down to his stomach.

Miss Quigley poured herself a glass of port too, but she sipped hers, watching him all the while. He finished the port in another big swallow.

"Would you care for another?"

"That might do. It's very good."

"I'm not allowed to drink myself," Miss Quigley said, pouring for him. "I take a little sip, but I really shouldn't do that either."

He took a piece of cake. "Why not?"

"I've been ill. I was nearly four months in bed before I moved here. It was a terrible weakening illness. I haven't got over it yet. I'm not allowed to drink, or eat eggs or anything that's cooked in butter."

"That's too bad," Brian said.

"When you come close to meeting your Maker," Alice Quigley said, "you begin to realize what things in life are important."

He bit into the cake. I hope this isn't going to turn into a religious lecture. She went to the eleven o'clock Mass on Sunday, and his family went to the ten o'clock so he never saw her in church. Not that he would be able to tell from that whether she was religious or not.

He finished the glass of port and the last of the cake.

"Love is important," Miss Quigley said. "Don't you agree, Brian? But then, how could you know? You're such a young man. You've never been in love, have you?"

Brian thought of Molly Kinsella and rolling with her in the hay in the barn.

"I guess not," he said.

"Have you ever really ... *liked* a girl, Brian?"

"Oh, I suppose so. I've gone out with a few girls I thought were pretty nice."

Her laugh tinkled merrily. "Pretty nice. Hardly an enthusiastic reaction. Your glass is empty. I think you'd like another glass of port."

"I have to be going. They expect me at home."

"Oh, the evening is young yet. Do have a glass. There. Now, you were telling me about the girls you've known."

Brian did not clearly recall telling her about the girls, but he could not be sure. He was warm and comfortably fuddled. The effort of concentration was not worth it. Miss Quigley's eyes were gray. They seemed very large at such close range. She listened with enormous concentration while he told her something about Molly Kinsella. Mentioning no names.

"She doesn't sound like the right sort for you, Brian."

"I didn't intend for it to be serious. Neither did she."

Molly, naked, lying on the straw. The fear began in his stomach and came up into his empty, sick head. He was standing on the rim of a chasm and had to jump, fearing he would never make it to the other side. But he had.

"I was married, you know," Alice Quigley said. "It was when I was seventeen—a mere child. I was divorced two years later. The real marriage only lasted a few months. He was wealthy, and my family thought I should marry him, but I did it against my better judgment. He was so much older and wanted to possess me. He was always wanting to make love. A woman doesn't like to be possessed, Brian, unless she really wants to be."

"I understand that." He drew his head back to keep Miss Quigley in focus; she was that close. Her lips seemed even redder than they had in the theater. Redder than port wine. She was smiling. She had rather good teeth, a bit prominent and large, but very white.

"Would you like to kiss me, Brian?"

"Miss Quigley ..."

"Alice ..."

Her lips were strong, and not afraid of work.

"I like you, Brian."

"I like you too, Alice."

Her eyes had turned smoky. She sat beside him and kissed his ear, then her teeth pinched the lobe. She was almost athwart him, and his arm touched the softness of her breasts. Big ones, he would imagine. Then he did not have to imagine. The dark robe was open to the waist. Two, soft, flat mountains spread over the front of her, with large, round, purple nipples. He had never seen nipples like those. Molly's were tiny red points, her breasts were firm and small. He felt Alice Quigley's weight, and tried to roll her off him; she went easily over and down on her back. He slipped the robe off her shoulders.

"You're not ready," she said then.

Truth was, he was frightened. Here he was on the edge of the chasm with a woman so much older and more experienced than any he had had before.

"It's all right. Just sit back and relax. Leave everything to me."

She gave him a fond kiss and disappeared. Down lower, he felt her bare breasts against his bare skin. She was drawing him up out of himself. Her mouth felt soft and purple inside. He began to want her. He wanted her to do everything to him that she could think of.

Artful woman.

"For Jesus' sake, let me do it to you now."

"Yes. I think you're ready."

Almost past ready. As she ground her hips down, it was over.

"The first is always a bit hasty." She smiled with her red lips.

They went into the bedroom and took off their clothes. A second time was beyond his powers, he was sure. But she knew how to call out the reserves ...

"When will I see you again, Brian?"

"I don't know when I can manage to get away from the pub."

"You want to see me, don't you?"

"You know I do."

"... Alice."

"Alice."

"Say it. 'I want to see you again, Alice.'"

"I want to see you again, Alice. I just don't know how I'll do it, but I'll manage somehow."

"I have an idea."

He was pulling on his trousers.

"Wouldn't you like to be an actor, Brian?"

"I never thought of it." He buttoned his shirt.

"I could arrange to give you lessons. Then you could come to see me twice every week."

"My father wouldn't pay for lessons."

"He wouldn't have to. I'd say I was giving you free lessons because I believe in your ability, and you'd promise to pay when you got a job in a theater."

He strung a tie about his neck and underneath the shirt collar. "You really think I could?"

"What?"

"Act."

"You might. You have the looks for it. And your voice is well placed."

He approved himself in a mirror. "I might have a go at it."

"It could be fun, Brian. And we would have whole afternoons to ourselves. Twice a week."

"I'll talk to my father," Brian promised. "When he's in a good mood."

They wantoned away many delightful afternoons over the next six months. He would have been willing to take on more lessons a week, but Alice had other commitments. There was Clifford the carpenter and Walsh the shoemaker, and the gentleman from the north village whose name he discovered was Fitzgibbon. Alice always told Brian that he was her favorite and made mocking comments about the others' ability to perform in the league with Brian.

"You're so young, that's the difference," she said.

Going about the village, in pride of loins, he regarded with amused superiority the middle-aged physiques of Clifford and Walsh. Crumpled horns.

He was learning both in the bedroom and in the parlor. Alice Quigley taught him something about the art of acting. She taught him to have faith in his imagination, to develop the power to project himself into a character through intense concentration, to remember emotional states from his own experience and use them in expressing an emotion felt by a stage character. They would each take roles in a play and act them out. Brian liked *Antony and Cleopatra* or *Dr. Faustus,* where he could make mighty mouth-filling sounds roll out of him, although it was a bit awkward pretending that Alice Quigley was Cleopatra or Helen of Troy. Her face would not have launched a small-sized canoe.

Still, custom had not staled her infinite variety between bedsheets. She always had some new little goodie for him, and drew him on and on to ever more masterful conquests. He could hold back for as long as half an hour, in full erection, with such subtle modulation of stroke that he drove her half out of her wits.

There came a time when he began to suspect that while he had not learned all the secrets of her boudoir he had exhausted her repertoire in the parlor. For Brian, this new game of acting was uncovering more facets every day. He was consumed with curiosity about it, and anxious to try new roles. He wanted to do things with gusto and insight—to make people feel the heart beating in him. He had found his true vocation, but did not know what to do about it. Alice told him that acting was a terribly hard profession and that all too few who aspired to become actors ever really did. Since she was his only authority in the matter, her verdict was discouraging.

Clearly there was no future for an Irishman who stayed in Ireland. Brian's older brother Timothy had joined up with the British during the war and escaped poverty and marriage by getting himself killed at Dunkirk. That was six years ago. Brian was now Timothy's age, eighteen, and if there had been a war going on, he might have joined himself. Instead he was doing what Timothy would have done, working as assistant to his father at the pub. It was either that or farming, and he had had his fill of working in the fields during his summers out of school. He was no man to spread manure to raise berries that would go to feed the birds. His younger brother Patrick, who was sixteen, was frantically taking home courses at night in accountancy—that was his plan of escape. Brian did not have the ambition for it, or the head for mathematics.

So he worked for his father at the pub, drawing suds for hard-handed farmers, and dreaming that Alice Quigley's lessons would open another prospect to him.

One evening, while he was serving drinks at the pub, two men and a woman stopped by. It was raining bats outside, the woman said, and all three looked drenched. They said they had been driving for hours and were on their way to Galway to appear that evening in Synge's *Riders to the Sea*.

Brian had read the play with Alice two weeks before.

"You're actors, then?" he asked, serving up two Guinnesses and an Irish coffee.

"In the repertory," said a man, blowing off the top of his Guinness.

"I've done a bit of acting, myself," Brian said.

"Have you, now?" the woman asked, with a sly look at her male companions.

That led to a conversation at a table, in which Brian stood the next round, and the next, and the woman, whose name was Judith, told him that he should look them up if and when he ever came to Galway. She was full-blown and red-haired, with plump rosy arms and a chest that was a treasure.

"Perhaps we'll find a place for you in the company," she said. "A fine lookin' lad like you, there are plenty of parts."

"Oh, yes," said one of the men with her, giggling as he said it.

"There are indeed," said the other man, and solemnly they all drank. Brian ordered another round on the house.

When they left, Judith gave him a copy of the program at Galway, and pointed out their names in the credits in the small print near the bottom.

"Now, you be sure to come see us," she called back as they rode away in a gale of laughter.

It was only a matter of time until he went, and the prompting for his decision came less than two weeks later when Alice Quigley came down with a slight recurrence of her illness. She was in bed when he called to see her, and she said she was feeling too poorly to have a go at the parlor lesson. He had been counting on rehearsing *Shadow of a Gunman*. Sean O'Casey had almost as wild a way with words as William Shakespeare himself.

"Perhaps I'd better go," he said, disappointed.

"No. There's no need to run away so quickly." She held out bare arms to him. She never shaved beneath the armpits. He sat down on the edge of the bed, but she would not be content until she drew him into her embrace. She pushed a breast against his face and he kissed it and took the solid tip between his teeth. Her gray eyes were wide.

"I don't want to hurt you if you're feeling poorly," Brian said.

She raised her hands above her head and slowly swung her body back and forth. Wobbly soft mounds, cool white and powdery with the large circles. Bull's-eyes.

He told her he was leaving for Galway. He had meant to tell her anyhow, but the timing was punishment. If there was to be no Sean O'Casey, there would be no sliding of his body into her.

They had a royal battle. Her large gray eyes were wild and bloodshot.

"You vulgar boy!" she cried. "Do you think I've given you the dearest gift a woman can give only to have you toss me aside like an old rag when you're done with me? You've ruined me, and now you want to abandon me. Oh, you heartless thug. You Celtic cocksman, you."

The same trouble as with her interpretation of a stage role. Too emotional.

"Alice, I've got to try to better myself. We've had some good times but let me be."

"I won't. You hear me, you lout? I've made you into six pennies' worth of man. You owe me something! You can't sneak off when you want to. Is there decency in that? Is there justice? Don't you love me at all, you rattlesnake bastard?"

"What did I do to you? Am I the only lover you've got? What about Clifford and Walsh and Fitzgibbon? You'll have no trouble replacing me in your bed."

"Are you trying to give me a bad name, you festering chancre? I'm a decent woman, and you've ruined me. God will never forgive you. I'll call your father. Billy O'Neal is an honorable man. He'll throttle you for what you've done to me."

That's all she knows about Billy O'Neal, but the thought did nothing to check his rage.

"God damn it, one more threat from you and I'll ram this bedpost up your hole. You hear me?"

He worked himself up into such a fury (call my father, will she?) that he swung his fist, and the breakfast tray she had put on the table went flying into the air, scattering crockery and noise about the room.

Her cries dwindled down to a whimper, and a vague crafty smile came to her mouth while her bloodshot eyes streamed gray tears.

"Brian, dear, don't go in a fury and leave me. Show me some love before you go."

"You're a terrible woman."

A glimmer was in her eyes. She lifted her nightgown. "Would you come in for a drink?"

"No, I will not."

She reached and touched him. "Let me have a feel of him then. Let me have him in my mouth."

"You're an awful woman."

"Ah, but you like it, Brian. You like what I do."

After a time, moving slowly, she had him in her power. He was absolutely forced to submit.

"Lie down beside me. Tippytoe."

Ah, a pleasant way for saying farewell. It would be a long joyous hour that would see him through the tiresome long journey to another woman's arms. She had such gentle fingers. He began moving over her body, burrowing, while her artful hands moved on his legs and a soft purple mouth urged him. He felt a hammering inside his skull and at the same time wanted to roar with explosive releasing laughter. Oh, she was a black beast of a lover. They could set her free among a flock of sheep and she would turn them all into goats. Circe! Ulysses would have torn down his mast and shoved it into her for safekeeping. All his blood was descending out of him into his groin. What a blast there is going to be, my lady. Through the back of the throat and onto the pillow if I know my projectile force.

"EEEOWWW!"

He should have known when he stopped hearing the slurp of her purple mouth. She shifted gears. Teeth came down deep onto the root, biting him off like a link of sausage. Chords of pain swept up like a blazing fire into his brain as he pulled free. Decapitated, by God. Do not nod your head, said the headsman, or it will fall off. YIIIEEE!

She was laughing, with the red color of him on her lips, when he picked up the tray and swatted her. It made a cymballing sound and her mouth opened. O, and she fell back on the bed. Serve her right if I fractured her cannibal skull. Ohh, Jesus Mary and Joseph, I am coming undone!

When he got back to the house and took a look at it under the faucet it was not all that bad. She had made a grievous tooth furrow, but the bleeding had stopped and he was intact.

He poured iodine until the pain made him jump about the bathroom, and when he had to urinate his aim was unbelievable. There was no doubt she'd tried to leave her mark on him.

He was well rid of her.

Two days later he arrived in Galway, and went to the local theater. *Riders to the Sea* had departed more than two weeks earlier, and the company had ridden out with it. The watchman did not know for sure where they had gone; he thought Manchester, perhaps. The theater was dark and would be until a revue came in three weeks. Singers and dancers only.

He had a ten shilling note and a few pence in his pocket. There was no turning back. Alice Quigley would have the horse laugh on him.

He got a job drawing drinks in the local pub, and three weeks later returned to the theater. They gave him a job as an usher. He wrote his father on the letterhead of the theater, saying he was going to keep on with his stage career now he had made a start.

He was young and sure of himself. No wounds festered.

Morning now.

Through a dim haze he saw the chapel where he had been baptized, along the green flowing river that ran a half mile or so from the village. There were willow trees bending down to the surface of the water to wash their leaves, and frogs gaped at the human invaders. The water was chill, he was chilled through by it.

Ahhh, the water was cold.

He opened his eyes.

He was in his own bed in his own room. Merrill removed the icy washcloth from his temples.

"Are you feeling better?"

"My head is going to blow apart any minute."

"You've had a good deal too much to drink."

Hangover.

"How did you get here?"

She began to soak a new washcloth in a bowl filled with ice and water.

"I've been calling your room at hourly intervals since approximately half past midnight last night. That was shortly after I decided you and Stephen Innis were not coming back to the party. Then I left word with the desk clerk to call me as soon as you returned. He did and I came over. As simple as that."

"What time was it?"

Her smile was quizzical. "You really don't remember?"

"No."

"Six o'clock this morning."

He groaned. "What time is it now?"

"Shortly past noon."

She made him feel guilty and worthless, and he hated her.

"You're an exceptional woman, Merrill. I don't deserve you."

"Of course you don't. Lie back and let me put this cold washcloth on your head."

"I love your cool hands and your quiet eyes," Brian said, lying back. "I love everything about you, Merrill."

"You just feel guilty and worthless," she said. "You mustn't, or you won't really love me at all. You'll start to hate me."

Good God. She could read his mind.

"I don't feel well."

"You shouldn't, after the amount you probably drank. I don't understand why you keep doing it, Brian. You know what the doctor said."

"I'll outlive him. No teetotaler lives long. Medically proven fact."

"It's nothing of the kind. I wish you'd take his warning seriously. You can't keep on like this forever."

He did not wish to hear any more about it. Any sensible man has to be terrified of the grip death holds him in.

"Ah now, Merrill, don't try to change my ways. You knew what I was like when you picked me. Don't be one of those reforming women. I never could stand them."

"All right. Lie back and let me put this cold washcloth on."

The fierce cold of the cloth on his head made him start and quiver. Icicles were stealing down the veins of his arms, and at the same time those parts of his body that were not touched by the cold were burning up with a kind of fever. He lay there, freezing and burning. It reminded him of a poem. *Some say the world will end in fire. Some say in ice.*

Jacquelyn. The last time he had come home to her drunk there had been a whing-do of a battle. One to remember. Jacquelyn was sharp. There was no fooling her as to where he'd been or what he'd been up to. Maybe Merrill wasn't fooled either, but she reacted differently. Jacquelyn treated him like the bloody bastard that he was. *Bloody joker.* They were well matched. She flung things with a good right and an accurate left. He gave as good as he got, though, first with bruising talk she could not parry, then with pulling hair, and arm-twisting when needed, to keep her from killing him.

What a fury she had, a lifting thing to a man's spirit. She was especially beautiful when she was angry, a demon out of the fires of hell, a shrieking witch on the eve of All Soul's Night. All brimstone she was and sulfur. At the height of blaspheming they sometimes tumbled into bed, and he took her, with her fighting and struggling against him as rich a taste as blood in the mouth. *From what I've tasted of desire* . . . Merrill would never never fight him, no matter how he hurt her. She would always be cool and self-possessed and full of concern for him even when he stuck the invisible dagger into her heart to give a mortal wound. Cool as ice. *I hold with those who favor fire* . . .

Ah, Jacquelyn . . .

What memories we make.

CHAPTER FIVE

Her villa was out toward the end of Copacabana on a folded, crumpled hillside surrounded by crags and peaks that protruded at impossible angles. Out of its surrounding jungle the villa appeared like a coral reef emerging from the sea.

It was a delicious morning; the air was warm and the sun brilliant. In the dense foliage surrounding the house, bright-colored birds hopped and chattered.

Breakfast was served on the terrace by the maid, a tall woman with high cheekbones, black wiry hair tied in a bun at her neck, and a skirt that fell almost to her ankles. Jacquelyn, looking exotic in a flame orange and gold caftan, had a soft-boiled egg and black coffee. A breeze fluttered the tablecloth while she lingered over coffee, blinking even behind dark glasses in the strong sunlight and looking over the *Death of a Peacock* script.

A stoop-shouldered, gray-haired man appeared.

"*Senhora*, this arrived by messenger a few minutes ago."

"Thank you, Gilberto."

She opened the small box. Inside, on a cushion of black velvet, lay a necklace of rubies and diamonds. The red and white brilliance against black was dazzling. There was a note on a small white card. *For my beautiful Princess from her adoring Meyer*.

How perfectly sweet, she thought. The words came to her mind because they were the words that were supposed to come to her mind.

From her terrace she had a clear view of the curving three-mile crescent of Copacabana beach where each patch of sand had its striped umbrella and straw matting.

"Jacquelyn!"

Janet, her secretary, was on duty in one of the second-floor bedrooms, which had been transformed into an office. Jacquelyn looked up, sliding her sunglasses down on her nose to see more clearly.

Janet was at the window, holding a telephone. "There's a call for you."

"I told you I'm not accepting calls this morning."

"I thought this one might be different. It's Bobby Randall."

"Bobby!" Jacquelyn put down her script. "What's he doing in Rio?"

Janet was smiling. "He sounds anxious to talk to you. Would you like me to have the call put on the extension down there?"

"Yes, do."

While Gilberto was setting up the phone on the terrace, she thought it would be nice to see Bobby Randall again. How many years? It must be five or six, and ages before that when they made their first big movie hit together. She had been twelve years old, Bobby fourteen—she played the little daughter of a rich landowner and Bobby the hired man's rambunctious young son, and in the movie they won the blue ribbon for their favorite sow and by the end managed to save her father's property from destruction by tornado and a hard-fisted local banker. An unlikely enough plot, one that she would never have approved for herself once she won script approval. But in those days the decisions at the studio were made not by stars or their agents but by Henry Orrin, who ran the studio like an Oriental despot and whose imperial commands made amazing commercial sense for a long time. Only now, when she herself was confronted with the problem of deciding which script, which package of director, leading man, producer, pre-sold property of best-seller or hit play or even original screen play would lead to the unpredictable smash at the box office, did she fully appreciate the intuitive wizardry of Henry Orrin in selecting attractions that would keep the studio's star names on the lips of an adoring public and theater box offices across the nation jingling with profits.

Gilberto handed her the telephone.

"Bobby?"

A gruff, grown-up voice answered, a voice with only tiny echoes of boy in it: "Jackie, isn't this a gas? You and me doing the Rio bit together. I couldn't wait to get in touch with you."

"Where are you calling from?"

"The airport. I haven't even unpacked my bags."

"You poor thing. Why don't you call me when you get settled? I'm absolutely dying to see you."

The gruff voice sounded pleased. "Yeah, we can really cut a slice off old times, eh Jackie? I got a million stories to tell you. You know old Bobby—always good for the laughs."

He's trying so hard, why is he trying so hard? But she knew.

"Don't bother to call," she told him. "Come over as quickly as you can."

Bobby arrived at a few minutes past one o'clock. She was signing letters that Janet had written for her that morning when the front doorbell chimed. There was noisy hubbub in the entrance hall, and then Bobby Randall erupted into the cathedral-like living room that was paneled in expensive Brazilian wood, with stained-glass windows and a huge wall mural of a tortured figure of Christ crucified.

Bobby reminded her of a slightly oversized Mickey Rooney, a compact, fleshy man only five foot six inches in height, with quick movements, a staccato manner of speaking, an enforced gaiety, and an apparently inexhaustible well of energy.

He spread his arms. "Jackie!" but didn't wait for her to come to him. He surged over and clasped her before she had gotten to her feet, and whirled her somewhat off-balance across the room.

Janet watched with modified amusement. She stooped to pick up a letter that Bobby's abrupt entrance had sent to the floor.

Still holding Jacquelyn in a bear hug, Bobby chortled in Janet's direction: "I love this gal. Always have! I'da married her if I had any sense."

"Bobby, I can't breathe," Jacquelyn said.

He released her at once, too quickly, with a note of apology that bordered on fear.

"I didn't hurt you, did I, honey? Sometimes I don't know my own strength. Bobby Randall, the circus strongman, that's me. The mighty midget. How's that? Well, it's one act I never tried. And I bet it's the only one. You're sure I didn't hurt you?"

"I'm sure." Jacquelyn straightened her dress and touched her hairdo to make sure it was still in place. Then she flashed her radiant smile. "It would be worth spraining a few ribs to see you again, Bobby. But I don't dare. I'm supposed to be on the set tomorrow to start work."

"Yeah, yeah. I heard about it. That *Peacock* script, right? It'll be a real gasser. You'll be terrific in it, honey. Really terrif. But it won't be another *Too Long at the Fair*. They don't make 'em like they did in the old days, do they?"

Too Long at the Fair had survived barbed reviews and had gone on to make a fortune and find a niche in the motion picture hall of fame. It was still shown occasionally in theaters, and was a staple of the early evening television shows at an hour when children were around to watch. She had seen the movie on television not long ago, and closed her eyes during it, not to shut out the incredible mawking sentimentality but only to black out the images of herself and Bobby, so young, with so much of their lives ahead. If either of them had foreseen then what was ahead for them . . . But what could they have done? Nothing. The downhill torturous road would still have to be traveled. Still, if anyone offered her a chance to change places with the sweet-faced dark-haired twelve-year-old girl whose face was alight with the beauty of innocence and to live those years over again, she would not have accepted. That part of her life was over, and she had survived it. That was what was important. She had survived.

Janet gathered up the rest of the unsigned letters. "I don't suppose you'll want to finish these now, will you, Miss Stuart?"

"No. I'll get to them after lunch. Have you had lunch, Bobby?"

"Sure." He winked. "A seven-course special. Six martinis and a peanut." He bellowed laughter.

"We'll have it served on the terrace," Jacquelyn told Janet, who nodded and left the room.

Bobby looked after Janet and he was still smiling, but his mouth twitched slightly. "I don't think she likes me."

"Don't be silly. Of course she likes you, Bobby." She picked up a cigarette out of the box, and Bobby was quickly there with his lighter. He managed these little gestures with a flair.

"You're looking as beautiful as ever, Jackie," he said. "The years haven't done anything to you."

"You're looking fine too, Bobby."

"You don't have to lie, Jackie. I know what I look like. Fat, foolish, and forty. Of course I'm not forty yet, but I look every minute of it." He shrugged. "But what the hell? It's no wonder with the kind of life I've led."

Bobby was becoming sadder, sinking into self-pity. She tried to change the subject.

"What's been happening to you lately, Bobby?"

"Oh, I haven't been in the headlines exactly. I'll get back again shortly, though, when the papers pick up my divorce. She's in Reno now."

"Katherine?"

Bobby grinned. "Katherine was my fourth. This is Sheila. She's my fifth. We *have* been out of touch, haven't we?"

Jacquelyn sat down on the sofa. "You always were hell on women."

"Yeah." Bobby turned a chair around and sat as he usually did, with his legs straddling the back of the chair. It was a pose that made him seem taller than he was. "If I had back a penny for every dollar I spent on women I'd be a rich man today. Right now I owe more in back alimony and support than I'll earn in the next five years."

"They can't put you in jail if you haven't got it."

"They can try—and they keep on trying. That's one reason I came flying down to Rio. I had a deal on the front burner. A movie here, y'know carnival time and the nightclubs and all that razzmatazz gay stuff. I'm good at cooking up action in a small pot. That was the idea, me to emcee a kind of tour of the Rio hotspots. The money was being put up by some Brazilian promoters with a kick-in from the government."

"It sounds interesting."

"It fell through. It was dead before my plane landed in the airport. I knew it, but what the hell. I had a free ticket to Rio and I figured I might as well use it and get away from some of my ex-wives." His face contorted, and there was a twitching beneath his left eye. "I needed a rest anyhow. I've been three months on the cure. That's a new record. But it kind of gets on my nerves, y'know."

"I know. But you mustn't give in to it again, Bobby."

"Oh, I'm all right this time. I got stamina. I learned my lesson when they sent me up for that term as a user. I swore off then. Slipped back a coupla times, but I'm in control of it now." He shook his head. "Thank God you'll never know what it's like, Jackie. It's rough."

"Kicking the habit is something you can always be proud of, Bobby."

"Yeah. That's about all too. I've been riding the rims on luck lately. You won't believe it, but I landed in Rio with seven dollars in my pocket. And I used two bucks to get out here to see you. I haven't got enough to pay my room rent."

"How much do you need?"

Bobby squinted with embarrassment. "I hate this, but you know you'll move right to the top of my list. The first money I lay hands on goes to you and screw my other creditors."

"How much?"

"Can you spare a thousand?"

"I haven't got that much cash. It's all complicated now, Bobby. There's some sort of corporation that pays all my bills and gives me a spending allowance. And that's only three hundred a week."

Bobby's voice grew a bit harsh. "No kidding? I heard you're getting a million for doing *Death of a Peacock*."

"It's all paid to my corporation. You know how I am. All those coins and bills don't mean anything to me; and I never could keep a checkbook balanced. I need some protection against myself."

Bobby rubbed fingers over his face, and the flesh seemed rubbery as he molded it. "I don't want to press you, but I don't know what to do about the hotel or even getting out of Rio if I can't find any work to do here. I might have to do something I'm fighting against."

"What's that?"

"I got an offer for my story. You know, the real inside stuff of the past few years. No punches pulled."

"Everybody's doing it these days."

"I hate to, because I'd have to hurt a lot of people I don't want to hurt. It doesn't matter what I say about me. How can anything hurt me? But other people—they've got a lot to lose."

His shape before her began to seem less appealing. He was still attempting to look forlorn, but there was no mistaking the malice.

"By other people, I suppose you mean me."

"You're one of the real people, Jackie. I love ya. You're

a real broad in this phony racket. I'll never forget the Academy Awards when you . . ."

"How much are they offering, Bobby?"

"Five grand. That wouldn't have been spitting money a couple of years ago. But it's big now. It could solve a lot of problems." He was beginning to sound confident.

"And for five thousand dollars, you'd turn yourself inside out," Jacquelyn said coolly, "and show what sort of a skunk you really are."

"Now, wait a minute . . ."

"Don't pretend, Bobby."

"For a guy on his uppers five grand is worth thinking about."

"You've gone a long way down. I suppose you might as well finish the job and slide all the way. Tell these people—whoever they are—you'll take their offer."

Bobby Randall blinked nervously. "They want everything. Nothing held back. That includes a couple of items you wouldn't want to see in print."

"I'm used to reading lies about myself."

"These aren't lies."

"My lawyers will say they are. They'll sue your publisher—and get an injunction that'll hold up publication indefinitely. Where do you think you'll be the meanwhile? When I pass the word, nobody will hire you—even to clean toilets. You'll be a leper, Bobby, a real leper. The only thing you've got left is a few friends like me. Go ahead and write your filth—and you won't have one friend in the world. It'll be Bobby Randall winging it alone—and you haven't got the stuff anymore."

It was like kicking a dog. He looked so crushed that she was instantly touched with pity. In the jowly defeated man she willed herself to see a young boy with curling golden hair who had played with her in so many hit movies. When she did see that boy, the vision made her throat contract suddenly.

"I don't know where to turn," Bobby Randall mumbled. "I got my back against a wall." His throat filled. "I wouldn't do anything to hurt you. We're buddies. But a guy gets desperate." He made an effort and stood up. "Okay, I'm ashamed. I won't take the five grand. I'll kill myself first."

"That might be a better idea than trying to make a living as a blackmailer."

"Jackie, don't say that word. I only wanted to scare you

into a handout." He lowered his head and stared at the floor. "It sounded like you were giving me the brush. You'd be surprised how many people do that. People I did a lot for once. Now they act like I don't have a right to live."

"I told you the truth, Bobby. I've only got about a hundred in my purse."

He didn't raise his head. "Whatever you can spare. I'll pay it back when I get straightened out again."

The back of his head was almost completely bald and there were deep crease lines in his neck. She had to fight down an impulse to touch him and tell him everything would be all right.

"Wait a minute! I think I may have the answer."

She hurried upstairs to the bedroom and came back holding a box. She pressed it into his hands. When he opened it and saw the red and white brilliance of the gems against the black cushion, he shook his head in disbelief.

"Jackie, honey, this is worth a fortune!"

"I imagine it is. The man who gave it to me can afford it."

"I can't take this." The gesture offering it back was a mere polite reflex.

"Consider it a loan, a stake. You can pawn it and send me the tickets."

Tears flowed from Bobby Randall's eyes. He put his arms awkwardly about her.

"Jackie, you're the queen."

"Sure," she said. "And you're the king."

Then he was gone, and she was watching the empty place where he had been. There was nothing you could rely on in this business. It was all quicksilver, less than quicksilver. She had never known a time when she felt really rich. The joke was that the biggest stars were always simultaneously rich and broke, making staggering sums of money but living on allowances, or indulging themselves recklessly and then coming up against the hard reality that they couldn't pay their income tax.

In the end, the bill always came in.

Her mother had been her first manager. The money paid to her had gone into a trust, and Mother was the guardian. That was true all through her teen years, while she was becoming a big star and newspaper columns were full of stories about the glamorous life she led. Actually, she spent most evenings at home watching television because she had to get up at five thirty to get ready for the drive to the studio. She never had enough spending money. She never dated seriously, and she had no close girl friends to confide in. Off screen, she led a curious life, as unreal, as lacking in content as the roles she played on screen. When she was eighteen she was in many areas of experience as naive as a ten-year-old.

Then, just when she arrived at an age and an income bracket where she could enjoy all the perquisites of a movie star, the bottom fell out of the bucket. The TV panic began.

There had never been anything quite like it since the advent of sound dismantled the silent film industry, overturning accepted story formulas, ruining established stars, catapulting unknowns into fame.

In the immediate postwar era before TV gained acceptance, the movies had enjoyed their most prosperous years. But the interlude was brief. As more and more millions of TV sets were sold, as the challenging new medium created its own stars, deepened its own pool of talent, the motion picture industry began to feel it was waging hopeless war against an electronic monster.

TV spilled gallons of red ink onto movie company ledgers, forced overhauls of top echelon executives, turned flourishing movie theaters into wastelands of empty seats. A hush fell over the Hollywood film colony, the traffic seemed to move in studio streets as though cushioned on wheels of fear. Behind the shuttered windows of executive offices there were conferences in which one could almost smell despair. There was a demand for new and tantalizing movies that would discover a new audience. There was a demand for boldness and maturity. New voices were needed, everyone agreed, to echo new problems that were occupying the attention of a new America.

Meanwhile, box office grosses dipped steadily. Nothing was a good risk. The average film, a B budget, became a prescription for disaster. The top-budgeted films, with topline stars, failed to earn back the negative costs. Thousands of motion picture theaters closed and became parking lots or supermarkets.

Even Jacquelyn Stuart's film, *The Betrayers,* failed to attract customers away from the insidious television screen. It was a typical script; she played a young Hungarian girl, stranded without a passport, who unknowingly falls in with a ring of international smugglers. Apparently her pub-lic was tired of watching her as a young innocent in peril, an unanimated Snow White.

At a meeting with Henry Orrin and his production chief Paul Greenfeld, Jacquelyn and her agent Morey Bloom were told it was time to change Jacquelyn's public image.

"How long can she go on playing naive young girls?" Paul Greenfeld asked. "She's a grown woman. She's built like a sex siren."

"It's dangerous to monkey around," Morey argued. "Jacquelyn's movies all made money—up to this last one. And that was a clinker of a story, right? Right. So why blame her?"

Henry Orrin said, "No one's blaming anyone." He held a crumpled handkerchief to absorb the perspiration in his hands. "But Mammoth Studios can't keep taking losses like it's been taking. We've got to grow up. We've got to move with the times."

"How do we know anyone's going to accept Jacquelyn in a new image? Try to change her over into a sophisti-cated glamour babe and you'll make millions of people sore. They like her just the way she is."

"Have you read *The New Yorker?*" Paul Greenfeld asked. "Their critic wrote a review of *The Betrayers* that says exactly what we mean."

"Who reads *The New Yorker?* Smart-alecky jerks who don't go to anything but foreign films. You want to put Jacquelyn into some arty-farty movie? Make it about Welsh fishermen, shoot it off-focus, and give it a tragic ending. *The New Yorker*'ll love it. But who'll go to a theater to see it?"

Jacquelyn asked quietly, "What does *The New Yorker* say about me, Paul?"

Paul opened to the review with satisfaction. "The movie we don't have to discuss, except to say they hated it. About you, here's what it says. 'She parades across the screen in the sad guise of a senescent and overblown twelve-year-old. There are no virgins like Miss Jacquelyn Stuart, but if they exist they should be treated as the singular creatures they are—in a class with the unicorn.' "

Henry Orrin's protruding lips worked into a nervous circle. Morey Bloom sneered.

Jacquelyn smiled faintly as she thought that, while *The New Yorker* critic might be astonished to hear it, most of her lovemaking actually had been done in front of a camera. She still belonged with the unicorns.

"Maybe it is time I started acting my age, Morey," she said.

Paul Greenfeld beamed. Henry Orrin simply clutched the handkerchief tighter in his fist. Obviously the decision to change Jacquelyn's screen image was not entirely his. In the face of the onslaught from television, with the standards by which he had lived and risen to power crumbling around him, Henry Orrin was shaken.

"Pumpkin, don't let them sell you a bill of goods," Morey said. "You're still rated in the top four on all the popularity charts."

"I'd like to stay there. If there's one thing I hate, it's becoming a has-been at eighteen."

"Nobody's going to believe you as a wicked woman."

"Then I've got to make them believe me. It's time to start appealing to the grown-ups, so I might as well learn how to do it. I've got the natural equipment."

She sat back and let the men in the room look her over. There was no sign of dissent.

Morey said weakly, "It's a dangerous move, pumpkin."

"Have you read the script for the movie I'm supposed to do next? *The Crystal Palace?* It's down my usual alley—but it's a blind alley. No more sweet little girl-women for me. I'm going to stay on top—even if in my next movie I have to strip down to the buff and climb into bed with a gorilla. If it's what the public wants, I intend to give it to them."

"You'll like the new property we've got in mind for you," Paul Greenfeld said. "It's based on a best-selling book, *The Gorgon,* a real steamy novel with a strong feminine lead. And we've got Seth Rosen to direct it."

"Seth who?" Jacquelyn asked.

"A very promising young talent," Henry Orrin intoned.

"One of the imports from television, pumpkin. Began as a scenic designer, graduated to doing a Western series on TV, got his chance with *The Maloneys,* a realistic, low-buget movie drama. It made money. Now they want to move him up in class."

"How do you feel about it, Morey?" Jacquelyn asked.

"I like big names. Why take a chance with a newcomer? You don't have to."

Paul Greenfeld said, "We're signing Jon Edgar to co-star with you."

"I'm entitled to a top director too," Jacquelyn said.

"Seth Rosen *is* a top director. He's going to be one of the best. And he's perfect for your new image because he doesn't start off with preconceived ideas about what you can do. He'll treat you like an actress."

"I'll see what he's done," Jacquelyn said. "Then I'll make up my mind."

The next afternoon she went with Henry Orrin and Paul Greenfeld and Morey Bloom to a screening of *The Maloneys*, and then watched two episodes of the TV Western series Seth Rosen had directed. She was impressed. Seth Rosen appeared to have a modern touch, quick, nervous, daring, in contrast with the more florid, slower styles of the other directors with whom she'd worked.

"All right," she said, when the screening was over. "He's good."

The production of *The Gorgon*, co-starring Jacquelyn Stuart and Jon Edgar, began on the Mammoth Studio lot four weeks later.

Most directors were a little afraid of Jacquelyn, and they suggested changes in her acting with the greatest reluctance. But on the first day of shooting, Seth Rosen took charge.

When the first hour's shooting was over, his narrow dark face had an intense, troubled look.

"I don't like the way you're approaching Gloria. You don't have an idea of what she's all about."

"I think I do."

"You're wrong. This girl is wise in the ways of love. She's learned that by using sex appeal she can get almost anything she wants out of a man. By setting her web in the right place she can get all the flies for dinner. You need a better overall view of the character and how she acts at different stages of the story."

"I read the script. I know what Gloria's like."

"You're not giving me what's in the script. You're giving me warmed-over Jacquelyn Stuart. A sugar girl."

"I don't happen to agree."

Seth had been about to give instructions to the head cameraman. He stopped, and turned back to Jacquelyn.

"One thing we've got to get straight—right now. This is my picture, not yours. Motion pictures are a director's medium, and I'm a good director. You do what you're told and you may end up with a real performance."

"I've done all right so far without you."

"How many times have you read the script?"

"Isn't once enough?"

"I've read it fourteen times by actual count. I read it as a book, and I worked on the screenplay. I've been over it with the writer a dozen times to make new changes. There are going to be more changes—every day. Your job is done in bits and pieces, a thirty-second take here, a minute-and-a-half take there, and all shot out of sequence. I'm the one who keeps the whole story in mind and charts your way through it."

"I don't work that way!"

"You'll get used to it. Now, in this scene, try to remember it's your first meeting with George, the character that Jon Edgar's playing. He's a married man. His wife's your co-worker on the fashion magazine. But even in this first meeting you're sizing him up as a possible conquest."

She played the scene simmering with resentment at how rudely he had spoken to her in front of the other actors. When she was halfway through she heard the dreaded "Cut!" She looked at Seth, who was pushing back a thick mane of wavy black hair.

"Oh, Christ, what's wrong now?"

"You're not in shouting distance of what I'm talking about."

"You could be wrong. I know you think you're a genius, but you're not!"

"We're still going to do it my way."

"Not unless I agree, I won't!"

Seth ignored her. "Now, this scene takes place in a café. It's the same set for the next two scenes. All three will have the same setting but different moods."

"Moods?" she asked sarcastically. She was determined to make him pay attention to her.

"The first meeting shows you gay, fresh, everything just starting out for you. Spring—that's a clue. In the next scene, your romance with George is in high gear. I want a summer mood. Rich, luxuriant."

"Do you *believe* him?" Jacquelyn asked of a bit player standing near.

Seth gave no indication of having heard. "The last mood will be autumn. It occurs near the end of the story, Gloria returns disillusioned to the café where her romance began. It's the last splurge of loveliness before the winter; everything dying."

"You really know how to pile it up," Jacquelyn said.

"Let's go," Seth said, as though she had not spoken. "Remember—spring, summer, fall, that's your clue."

She was tired and irritable. During the take she barely dragged herself through the motions. Again Seth called, "Cut!"

"It's still more like a romantic scene played by Jacquelyn Stuart than by the girl in our story."

She burst out, "I don't understand what you want! Nobody understands all that crap about spring, summer, and fall. Who talks like that?"

"I do."

"You sound like some damn fruit if you want to know the truth!"

He drew his head back so that he could observe her at a slight distance. "We'll do it again. This time you follow instructions. Pretend I'm an usher in a movie theater and you want to know the way to the can."

"I can't go through it again."

"Even if you can't act, you *can* find your way to the bathroom. If necessary, I'll draw you a map!"

No one had ever dared speak to her like that before. She felt absolute, hopeless, dumb anger. She turned and rushed from the set to her dressing room.

A few minutes later Seth arrived. He walked up to where she was lying in tears on the couch, turned her around, and sat her up. Then he cupped his hand under her chin, forcing her to look up at him.

"How about a truce? I'm willing to forgive and forget if you are."

She sobbed, "I don't know how to give you the kind of acting you want. I don't have it in me!"

"Oh, it's in there all right," he said. "But you have to feel it. A real actress can't keep cool in her heart—can't be outside the character smiling at it, mocking it a little. You have to turn yourself inside out to become the character you're playing. That isn't something you can do simply because you're getting paid to do it. You can't fake it."

Jacquelyn snapped, "I'm not faking!"

"Maybe the real trouble is that you've never been laid."

Jacquelyn fought back tears. "That's all you know!"

Seth patted her cheek. "Well, if I'm wrong, he couldn't

have been very good. You don't have the right experience to draw on. But you are an actress—and all that emotion I need is there, in embryo. Use it. That's all I ask."

"What if I don't have any?"

"I've seen enough to know that you do, and my job is to dig it out of you and put it in front of a camera. If I don't get it from now on, it's my fault, not yours."

After an hour she returned to the set. On the eighth take, Seth said he was satisfied, but she knew he still hadn't got the effect he wanted. He put his arm about her shoulder as they walked off the set. She felt empty, exhausted, but oddly relieved to know that she had been bested in fair combat and didn't have to struggle against him anymore . . .

After the first week she began doing better. Seth didn't go so far as to compliment her, but his stream of complaints dwindled.

After the second week they were on friendlier terms. Seth got into the habit of dropping by her dressing room for short visits. He had a treasury of funny stories and could always start her laughing, no matter how troubled she felt. One Friday afternoon, when they were finished shooting, he suggested that he stop by her place the next day and take her for a drive in the country.

They sped south on the highway past Laguna in his red Lancia. It was a sunny beautiful day, and she was far away from the problem of herself. Seth was an amusing companion, bright, observant, gay, yet beneath his brittle sophistication he was a genuinely involved artist who wanted very much to do meaningful work. She felt strongly drawn to him.

"Where are we heading?" she asked.

"I know a beach not far from here. Believe it or not, it's very private, very secluded. A cove surrounded by rocks."

"You didn't tell me we were going swimming," Jacquelyn said. "I haven't brought anything."

"Neither have I. Does it matter?"

She felt excited, reckless; she was having such a good time. Everything ahead seemed so easy.

"No, I guess not."

Seth parked the car on a rocky shoulder of the road almost directly above the beach. Twenty feet below, fronting the ocean, was a small oval of sand and pebbles, flanked by huge projecting rocks. Waves came in with long, low growls.

"Are you sure it's all right?" she asked.

"It's a private beach. I know the owner." He noted her continuing hesitation. "You can undress behind the rock down there. I'll undress in the car."

She nodded and, carrying her shoes, descended the narrow gravel path to the beach. When she looked back to where the Lancia was parked, she did not see Seth. He must be inside the car, undressing. My goodness, she thought with a nervously irrepressible giggle, I never thought it would happen like this. Or today.

The rock was about twelve feet high, black with tiny green patches of lichen growing in the crevices. As she was undressing, a seagull fluttered down to rest momentarily at the top. The gull stared everywhere except at her. A perfect gentleman. The gull flew off while she deliberated about removing her bra and panties. She had just about decided to do it when she saw Seth come out onto the beach, wearing his shorts. She was relieved and disappointed. It would have been easier in a way to get everything over with at once—there would be no further embarrassment.

Seth was splashing to his knees in the white, broken swirl of waves when she appeared from behind the shelter of the rock.

He looked over at her and waved, smiling. "You'll like it. The water's fine."

He accepted her near nudity so completely that she immediately ceased to feel awkward. She ran toward him, slightly aware of her full breasts swinging.

They ran in and out of the threatening waves, escaping in front of the careening crash. Soon they were laughing, half soaked. His shorts were clinging to his body, and she could not keep her eyes away. Once as they turned their backs to the crashing surf, he put his arm about her and his hand touched the side slope of her breast.

A few minutes later a giant wave broke earlier than anticipated and, struggling to keep her footing in the rapidly surging cross-currents, she went down. He held her hand, keeping her from going under while the wave ebbed with powerful suction. Laughing and sputtering, she tried vainly to scramble to her feet. She was so thoroughly soaked that there was hardly any use pretending even to herself that she was concealing any part of her body. He held her by the elbows until she was standing up, then his arms slipped about her waist and drew her against him. His face was warm and kindling. She could feel him pressing between her legs when the next receding wave pulled at their footing, scooping the sand from under their feet. His body was so tight against her that she almost imagined he was inside her. She shook wet spray off her face, and saw him look at her with naked hunger.

He led her out of the water, and a few yards up the beach to the shelter of the same gaunt rock behind which she had undressed. There he lowered her gently to the sand.

They kissed, with her head pillowed against his forearm and his body obliquely atop her. His body was lean and perfectly firm; she felt a hardness against the inside of her thigh. His hand, at her waist, gradually moved her into position, and his fingers pulled at the soaking wet panties she wore. She closed her eyes, ready to feel the slow molten thrill of him moving through her veins.

She opened her eyes abruptly. Seth was starting to his feet.

She saw a man in a blue uniform, boots, and visored cap and sungoggles standing on the beach.

"You two better get dressed," the state trooper said.

"What's the matter, officer?" Seth asked. "We haven't done anything."

"We'll find out what the judge thinks about that."

"You can't arrest us for swimming."

"How about illegal trespassing?"

"This is a private beach and I know the owner. We have every right to be here."

"There's also a question of indecent exposure."

The state trooper, taking out his book, eyed Jacquelyn with appreciation as she picked up her clothes from the rock and hurriedly began dressing.

She could tell that the state trooper really wasn't too upset. No doubt Seth would be able to handle the situation easily. Perhaps a little money would change hands and everything would be forgotten.

Instead, Seth's voice rose angrily, "If you make a charge like that, you'll regret it all your life. I'll break you! I've got friends who'll see that you never wear a badge again."

The trooper's bronzed face set. "I've heard that kind of talk before." He flipped open his book. "While you're getting decent, mister, I'll take down a few facts. What's your name?"

"I'm not going to tell you anything!"

The trooper's voice turned harsh, "You're in trouble, mister. I wouldn't make it worse."

"The smartest thing you can do is walk away and not bother us anymore. We have every right to be on this beach. We stopped to go for a swim."

The trooper sneered. "Dressed like that?"

"We didn't have bathing suits. Since this is a private beach we had no reason to think that anyone would inter—"

"Say." The trooper pushed back his visored cap and stared at Jacquelyn. She had gotten into her dress and was trying to zip it up. "Haven't I seen you before, miss? Aren't you Jacquelyn Stuart, the movie actress?"

"Never mind who she is. If you try to arrest us you're going to look like a damned fool. In the first place, we weren't doing anything wrong. In the second place, no one could see anything from the road. Only if some idiot came down here would he see us at all."

"You say you know the man who owns this beach?"

"That's right. His name is Henri Breton and he lives less than half a mile from here."

The trooper was feeling for his back pocket with his charge book. He found it, slipped in the book, and buttoned the pocket.

"Okay, get your clothes on. We'll go see this fellow and find out whether you're telling the truth. If not, you may be in a hell of a lot more trouble than you think."

Seth turned to Jacquelyn and said in a low tone, "It's going to be all right. Trust me and don't say a word. I'll get us out of this."

She was numb with fear, shivering with cold, yet her skin was burning with shame. She would have given anything, absolutely anything, to be out of here and away from this situation. But she obeyed Seth's injunction and said nothing when they returned to the car. Seth dressed quickly, and they followed the state trooper's car. They pulled up in front of a huge rambling structure of white stucco, with grilled windows and a wide lawn with statuary and a fountain. The trooper got out and came back to Seth and Jacquelyn, who were still seated in their car.

"This the place?"

Seth nodded.

"Okay, you and Miss Stuart get out. We'll find out soon enough whether you've been telling the truth."

"There's no need for both of us to go in. I'm the one he knows," Seth said. "The lady can wait here." To Jacquelyn he added, "This won't take more than a few minutes."

It was the longest few minutes Jacquelyn ever spent. She sat, slouched in the front seat, wearing concealing sunglasses. Warmth and sunlight mocked her. All she could think was: If I ever get out of this, I will never never get into trouble again. If I ever get out of this I will never never. If I ever get out of this.

The next morning, while Jacquelyn was having breakfast in bed, the door opened and Mother stood in the doorway. She had a newspaper in her hand and seemed to be in paralytic shock.

The moment Jacquelyn saw her, she knew what had happened.

"Jacquelyn," Mother said. "How *could* you?"

She dropped the newspaper with a nerveless hand on the coverlet. Jacquelyn saw the headline through blurred eyes: JACKIE STUART AND MOVIE DIRECTOR PICKED UP IN BEACH FROLIC.

Seth had succeeded in getting the owner of the beach to identify him and had won their release, but when the state trooper told a reporter at headquarters about the episode, the story got on every news wire.

"How could you?" Mother asked.

Upsetting the breakfast tray, Jacquelyn flung herself face down on the pillow and held the edges up around her head to muffle her hearing. If she could have muffled all her other senses, she would have.

It was just too awful.

The rest of the day was a waking nightmare. The telephone rang constantly. Mother finally had a mechanic install a toggle switch to stop the ringing.

Jacquelyn did not touch a morsel of food, and found that she could stop crying only at intervals. What had happened seemed irrecoverably tragic. She was exposed for the miserable sex-ridden creature that she really was, and her feelings of guilt and shame clustered into a single intense emotion of bitter remorse. If someone would only give her another chance, she would never look at a man again—at least not until after marriage. She would be more respectable than the most provincial small-town matron. One chance was all she asked, one more opportunity to arrest the downward curve of her life.

"Your brother is here. Do you want to see him?"

"Yes. Oh, yes."

Richard was twenty-three, finished with college, actively engaged in a small business selling boats. The lean boy in sweater and jeans had become a tall, slender, balding man with pock-marked face and down-turning sardonic mouth.

"Richard, it's the end of everything, isn't it?"

"What is, Jax?"

Jax was his particular pet name for her, and he only used it when he was feeling especially affectionate.

"I'll never get a role in a picture again. How can they risk it, after the scandal?"

"Scandal? Jax, you were just caught skinny-dipping with a man on a beach! As far as your career goes it's probably the best thing that could have happened. It'll help you break out of the little-girl stereotype. You're old enough." He brought both hands down on his knees. "By Jesus, I'd have loved to have been there when that trooper stumbled onto you. It must have been something to see."

"It was awful." She raised her eyes when she heard an odd rumbling sound. "Richard! You're laughing!"

"I'm sorry, Jax. I can't help it. The thought of you and that director in the altogether with a puritanical cop breathing fire and brimstone at you ..." The rumbling in his chest erupted into open laughter. She stared at him, amazed, and then began to giggle. Soon she was laughing too.

"Richard, you don't take *anything* seriously! You don't seem to realize what an awful ..." She couldn't go on. Laughter quite overcame her.

A full minute passed before she regained control.

"Mother says I'm cheap because of what I did with Seth Rosen. Do you think I am?"

"If Mother said that, my advice is for you to move out of here. Find an apartment of your own."

"Mother would never stand for it."

"She can't stop you once you make up your mind."

"What would be the point? Oh, I know what you'll say. To have a place to bring men. If you're interested, I didn't go that far. I'm still a virgin."

"I'm extremely sorry to hear it. At your age, it's perfectly natural to go to bed with a man. Probably you haven't found one that interests you enough—but you will. Sex is fun. Girls as well as men should enjoy it."

She considered him a grown man, full of maturity and wisdom. She had always wanted to know.

"Have you had . . . intercourse . . . with a lot of women?"

"Just like that, eh? I'm not going to tell you, Jax."

"Have you ever been in love?"

"I am right now. I was going to tell you. Her name is Mady—and we're going to be married in a month."

"I don't believe it!"

She had spent some of her happiest hours on his sloop, with his bare feet going padding past on the deck to change the rigging. She had gone there to have hurts soothed, to confide secrets. Richard was her only confidant. Even when he had personal problems, they didn't carry over into his relationship with her. He was so direct, and he really concentrated on anything she revealed to him. A solid T-bone steak of a man, who had never been impressed by her value as a public commodity; through the years he had managed to stand apart from her fame, from the money and the people who worshiped money. She could not imagine Richard loving any other woman; it was somehow an intrusion on the special character of their feeling for each other.

"I'll see to it that you and Mady get together as soon as possible. You'll like her, Jax. And I know she'll like you."

She could not quite meet his eyes. "We've always been so close. Why didn't you *tell* me?"

"I wasn't sure how serious it was until a little while ago. Now I know. This is what I've been looking for. I'm going to give up my boat business and move to Carmel. I'm buying a pharmacy."

"It sounds awfully . . . sudden . . . to me."

"It's time I started to find out what it's all about. I've been knocking around, wasting myself. I want a home and a family like everyone else."

"You're only twenty-three."

"I feel a hell of a lot older. I was practically a bum in college. I need a stabilizer, Jax, and Mady can be it. This business I'm in is a farce. Just gives me another excuse to hang around boats. From now on things will be different.

I'm really going to settle down and amount to something."

"You're too good to work in a drugstore."

"Thanks for the vote of confidence. But you'd better let me be the judge."

She was no longer preoccupied with her problem. This woman, Mady, might love Richard, probably did, but Richard was not in love with her. She wished she could be firm with him, as firm as he had been with her. He didn't understand the sort of trap he was getting into. He was so wise about other people—how could he be so stupid about himself?

The next day she made a telephone call to Henry Orrin. She told him she wanted a favor, and what it was; a week later, she and Richard and Henry Orrin had lunch together at Mike Romanoff's.

"Your sister thinks pretty highly of your talents," Henry Orrin told Richard. "We have an opening in our international distribution for a bright young man like you. Someone with a forceful personality who's willing to learn the business from the ground up."

"I don't know anything about the movie business, Mr. Orrin."

"The job pays twelve thousand a year," Henry Orrin said.

Richard's expression became solemn. "Well, that's a good deal of money."

"Try it for a couple of years. If you don't like it, you'll have enough money put by to give you a headstart in some other line. You might be surprised. Once movies get in your blood, it's hard to get them out."

"I don't know. I'm planning to go into a different business. And I'm getting married soon . . ."

"For an opportunity like this," Henry Orrin said, "she'll wait."

"I don't want her to wait."

"It wouldn't be right to take a bride along. This is an overseas job, you understand. Your home base will be in Tokyo. You'll be traveling a lot. You wouldn't want to leave a new bride at home alone in a strange country."

"No, I certainly wouldn't." Richard's voice slowed with suspicion.

"There. You see?" Henry Orrin beamed as though he had scored a personal triumph.

"Yes, I think I see." Richard's forehead furrowed with a question. "You set it up, didn't you, Jacquelyn?"

"I don't know what you mean."

"You thought I'd take this job and put off the wedding."

Henry Orrin cleared his throat. "Well, how about my offer? Are you going to take it? It's the opportunity of a lifetime for a young man like you."

Richard said, "I'm afraid Jacquelyn is the only member of this family who's ever going to be in the motion picture business."

Henry Orrin's silly face opened like a hooked flounder. Jacquelyn stared down at her plate.

"I'm sorry, Jacquelyn," Richard said. "But I've made up my mind and there's nothing you can do."

"I only want you to be happy."

"I'll make a deal with you," Richard said. "I'll keep butting into your private affairs if you promise to keep your nose out of mine. How's that?"

She did not raise her eyes from her plate. "Okay."

When she did look up, Henry Orrin managed to give her a weak smile. She returned a venomous glare. The fat old fool had ruined everything.

After Richard's wedding, three weeks later, Jacquelyn returned home and spoke to Mother. Mother said it was ridiculous—of course she could not have an apartment of her own, she was much too young. Jacquelyn was no longer frail enough to be crushed. There was a terrible scene. Mother entreated heaven, draped self-sacrifice as a banner across her chest, and accused Jacquelyn of every crime short of treason. Her whole body went limp and she simulated a fainting spell. Jacquelyn was a little awed by such histrionic determination, but she held fast. Finally, the argument turned to the matter of funds. Mother would not allow Jacquelyn a penny. Jacquelyn threatened to go to court, swore she would never sign another contract in which her mother acted as her guardian, reminded her that in a very few years she would be old enough to keep all her money, and cut her mother out entirely. Mother's voice broke—she stared at the approach of the awful, black hour. She reached for a pastel-colored Kleenex and wiped her nose. "Very well, then, if you're determined. Remember I warned you. I've tried to protect you and this is the thanks I get. I suppose it had to happen." Her face was like a puffed-up, wrinkled, white pillow. Her eyes were like enormous buttons. "Go. Move into your own apartment. You'll get an allowance, and I'll continue to look after your money. After all, you are my daughter."

And so the deed was done. Jacquelyn was on her own at last.

Jacquelyn looked down the table at Hernan Ramirez's dark face, illuminated by the tiny, yellow, flickering lights of the three-branched candelabra. Hernan was a handsome man, no more than forty, but his hair was thickly blue-gray and his long, handsome face was marked with grave lines.

She had invited him to dinner alone with her at the villa, and she wore the ermine-trimmed white dress with the low neckline. He was the Mexican consul in Brazil, and it was through him that Meyer Whitney had made the arrangements for the divorce proceedings to take place in the Mexican consulate on what was legally Mexican territory.

Hernan explained the technical regulations that would govern the divorce proceedings; she pretended to listen with interest.

Hernan's gaze smoldered from the opposite end of the table. He had been oozing charm and compliments from the moment of his arrival. He made discreet references to his wealth, to his promising future, even to the rumors he might be a candidate for high office in the next elections. It was somewhat unusual behavior for a man supposed to be carrying out a mission in behalf of Meyer Whitney. The only explanation was that Hernan liked her. Her thoughts turned delicately to a problem that would have surprised him. Did he like her enough to take the risk of venturing beyond the boundaries of his assignment?

"One day you must come to Mexico," he was saying now. "Our country would be most honored to have you stay there. I have a home a few miles outside of Mexico City. Perhaps you would graciously consent to spend some time there with your husband."

"With Brian?"

Hernan laughed—white teeth flashed in the swarthy face. "I was referring, of course, to your fiancé, Meyer Whitney. No doubt by the time you visit Mexico, you will be husband and wife."

"I'm not entirely sure, Hernan. There are so many difficulties, so many obstacles."

"From what I have heard of Meyer Whitney he is not one to allow difficulties to stand in his way. Especially when the prize to be won is as lovely as yourself."

"*Gracias, señor,*" Jacquelyn said. "Nevertheless, sometimes I wonder if everything is worth the trouble."

"I am very sorry that trouble should ever intrude on the life of such a beautiful woman. You can rely upon me to do all I can to make your difficulties smaller."

His hand passed hers with a whispering touch to light her cigarette. He moistened his lips as her lips closed over the filter end. Yes, there was no doubt of his interest. If she could exploit that interest, she might find a way to postpone the divorce.

"But it's asking so much of you and your government . . ."

Hernan nodded. "It is an extraordinary procedure. But then, of course, Señor Whitney is an extraordinary man."

Jacquelyn sighed. "Sometimes, I can't help wishing . . ."

He hung breathless over the incompleted thought.

"Wishing what, Señorita Stuart?"

"We have known each other only a few hours, yet I feel that I can trust you."

"I hope you will allow me the honor to be your friend."

Her timing was exquisite. "The truth is, I'm not entirely sure in my own mind. Meyer is a wonderful man, strong— as you say, extraordinary—but that sort does not always touch the emotions as deeply as others."

She turned her emerald gaze upon him, and one would almost have thought that the glance penetrated, for he turned a faintly greenish tint.

"I understand, señorita. In affairs of the heart one must care deeply. It is not enough merely to admire." He met her gaze with tentative boldness, then became transfixed again in concentration on her mouth. He grimaced slightly and pursed his lips. Close-pored skin glinted in the lamplight with tiny bubbles of perspiration. "I speak to you as a man who has lived the sorrow of a life without love."

"I knew it. I sensed it, somehow."

"I married as a very young man. A most admirable woman, the daughter of the mayor in our village. She was considered pretty, but there was not . . . what you would call . . ."

"Passion?"

". . . there was not passion between us. And very soon I

was unable to feel what a husband must feel for a wife. *Que lástima!* Who can deny the truth of what he is? I became . . . enamored . . . of others. For a time my wife did not know, and all went well. Then she discovered."

"What happened?"

He tapped the left side of his chest significantly. "An attack of the heart. She suffered it, and I was given to know that I must cease at once what I was doing. There was no choice. I agreed, and became again a good husband. Despite her illness, she was very demanding. I did not complain. I conquered aversion. Her doctor said she had not a long time to live and the next attack would finish her. I believed it. *Ya lo creo!* I waited upon her as a servant. I spent night after night in the house. We had few friends and went nowhere. She preferred to spend her last months alone with me."

"Did she die?"

"*Madre de Dios!* She is healthier than I! I discovered after years that the doctor was her friend and made up a lie. I was so furious I could have killed. But by then my father-in-law was prominent in the government. I became consul, and my name was mentioned, as I say, among possible candidates for high office. You see how I am completely without luck."

Jacquelyn managed to look sympathetic. "Not completely. Perhaps that is why you have so much understanding."

Hernan bowed slightly "I am honored, Señorita Stuart."

"Please call me Jacquelyn."

"In my country that is not a privilege one assumes lightly."

"I did not mean it lightly."

He swallowed. "You fail to understand. It is sometimes taken as a token of intimacy."

"You may take it in whatever light you care to, Hernan."

His eyes widened a trifle. "You are very kind."

"I have an intuition that we have much to offer each other, Hernan."

"You will find me very devoted." He touched his napkin to his temples.

She touched his arm and felt a muscle jump beneath the jacket. He turned to her with an expression that was almost agonized, and his gaze seemed to founder on her face.

"Jacquelyn." His full lips moved without volition. "*Cara mia* . . ."

"Hernan," she put a finger to her lips, "we have said too much, far too much, already. I wouldn't have, except that I sensed how *simpatico* you are." She shook her head, as though regretfully. "In a few days, I will be married to Meyer Whitney."

"Señorita . . . Jacquelyn! . . . you must not allow it to happen!"

"I may have given you the wrong impression, Hernan. You see, I do care for Meyer. Very much."

"If it is without passion, you cannot be happy."

"I need time to learn my true feelings. And there is so little time."

His swarthy face was a mask of anguish. "You must not throw a chance for happiness away, Jacquelyn. Do not permit this!"

"How can I prevent it? You know what sort of man Meyer is. He won't allow *anything* to stand in his way."

"There must be something we can do."

Their relationship had swiftly progressed from friendship to intimations of something more, to calculation, desire, and now with the possibility of a liaison dangling before him, to his becoming a willing accomplice.

She pushed back her chair and rose. "One should not take advantage of friends."

"I assure you, Jacquelyn, that nothing is too much for you to ask."

"I am grateful that you are here and willing to help."

"I am your obedient servant."

"Well, a few moments ago, you said that what you are doing to make the divorce possible is an extraordinary procedure. I'm sure your government would not like its honor or integrity to become questioned."

"That is a risk we have considered carefully."

"Do you realize how much publicity there will be, Hernan? Nothing about my private life can be accomplished in secrecy. My divorce will be front-page news in every newspaper in the United States."

"*Claro*. That is clear."

"That means that afterward there will be hundreds, maybe thousands, of requests for similar divorces. Some will be by prominent people. If they are refused, they will accuse your government of discrimination. There may even be accusations of—bribery."

Hernan touched the napkin to his temples again. His skin had gone chalky beneath the eyes. "There are highly placed people in my government who have opposed this granting of a divorce. They do not believe that certain legalities should be . . . er . . . skimmed past."

"It is very dangerous. I am thinking of you now, Hernan, and your future. If you should commit a blunder . . . why, you might even be accused of assisting foreigners to get around the laws of your country."

"That would be most unfortunate." Hernan's brown gaze was turning liquid with self-pity.

"I might also be making too much of it."

"No, no, these are matters which must be weighed."

"I suppose nothing is lost if we put off the divorce for a little while. Perhaps, during the time of waiting, we shall even have a chance to become better acquainted."

She offered her hand. He kissed it, lingering a moment longer than courtesy demanded.

"Good night, Hernan."

"Will you have dinner with me soon? I must see you again, talk to you. And perhaps deepen our friendship."

"I'd like that, of course. I'll be too busy for the next week or so with my new picture. But call me after that, and if I have an evening free . . ."

"I can hardly wait. I can hardly breathe."

He bent to kiss her hand again, and still perspiring slightly, turned, and left. From the window she saw him enter his limousine.

When he called in a week she would be very sorry that she was still too busy to see him. She might keep him dangling with regrets for quite a while before shock and disillusionment finally set in. He would not become too annoying because the pride of these Latins was great, and there was also his diplomatic position to consider. That was important to him. In a way, she would benefit from a form of diplomatic immunity.

The thought amused her.

CHAPTER SIX

Shortly after midnight, Brian O'Neal opened the second bottle of Irish whiskey and filled Lester Mitchell's glass and his own.

"I'm out of ice," he said.

"At this point I couldn't tell the difference," Lester said, "unless you put it in a bag on my head."

"You discourage too easily," Brian told him. "You ought to have been born Irish. We always go forth to battle ..."

"... and never win," Lester finished for him. "But I'm not satisfied with a losing struggle, Brian. I gave up some promising offers to make *Oedipus* with you, and I hate to be stopped for lack of money."

"You won't be."

Lester indicated the papers scattered on the table, filled with penciled scrawls. They had spent most of the evening grappling with the unavoidable harsh reality of figures.

"You saw for yourself. We're scraping the absolute bottom of the barrel. Unless we get new financing, there won't be enough to buy film to shoot with next week. Not to mention paying the actors, and the rent on the studio, and the staff, and—"

Brian filled his own glass to the brim. "I was never meant to be involved as a producer. I should have stuck to my trade, acting, and left money problems to people who like to deal with money problems."

"Have you talked to Merrill about this?"

Brian finished half his glass in a single swallow. "She volunteered last night to go to her father."

"Well?"

"I wouldn't let her."

Merrill, sitting up in bed last night, the upper part of

her long lovely torso bare, while she watched him going over the preliminary report from the accountants.

"Darling, I can't see you worry like this," she had said. "It's my fault. I wanted you to do something important, make a movie that would say important things. I still think that's where your energies should be spent. If you'd been willing to keep on playing Hollywood lover-boys you wouldn't have had trouble with money. Why don't you let me see what I can do about solving your problem?"

"You've done enough already," he told her. "A lot of your father's cash is going down the drain with this production. I never realized costs could go up so quickly. Why, the costumes alone—"

"You shouldn't have to concern yourself with things like that, darling. You're not a wheeler-dealer. You're an artist, a fine artist, and I simply won't allow you to be frustrated for lack of a few dollars."

"Money is a damn straitjacket, that's what. I've never had to bother my head about it."

"You don't have to, darling," Merrill reminded him. "Thomas Yeaton isn't exactly on poverty row."

"And I'm not exactly in the business of accepting handouts."

"My Irish rebel," Merrill said as she lay back and slowly moved the sheet away from her. . . .

Lester Mitchell said morosely, "If we could only get some other producer interested."

"I've tried everyone," Brian said, "and I know a lot of producers. All of them turned me down. They can't see *Oedipus Rex* as a commercial property, and they're probably right. It's the sort of film that puts theater cashiers out of work. You know what one man suggested? He said that he'd take over and guarantee financing if I would get Jacquelyn to play Queen Jocasta."

"I don't blame him. None of your co-starring pictures with Jacquelyn ever lost money."

"I'm going to make it on my own," Brian said. Then he laughed. "Besides, can you imagine what Jacquelyn would say if I asked her to play my *mother?*"

"An absolutely delicious idea," Lester said. "It makes me positively shiver with delight."

It was comments like this, Brian decided, that made some people think Lester Mitchell was a homosexual. It wasn't true, however. Lester was merely a member of the new intellectual elite in the arts who tried to make a virtue of unmanliness.

"Well, we can't have Jacquelyn and we've got to have the money," Brian said. "Would it do any good to have another go at Runnymede?"

Runnymede Studios Ltd. was Britain's largest film production company and had recently formed a partnership with Celestial Films in Hollywood in a worldwide film production network.

"I've been to them twice," Lester said glumly.

"What did they say?"

"They were too involved in the details of the merger to discuss financing any new movie."

"It might be different now that the merger's gone through. And I know the president, Lyle Wesley."

"How well?"

"Dates back to my time with the Royal Academy. I was pretty active and Lyle was just getting his feet wet as a producer. We had this wild idea of making a film of *Macbeth*, with me as the star. It never happened because the money men wouldn't consent. Wise old birds. It would have laid a giant-sized square-shaped commercial egg."

"You'd need a new approach," Lester said, musing.

"How about turning over the production to them and just keeping a percentage of the profits, if any."

"That's what I offered before."

"I could promise to appear in another picture for them."

Lester looked hopeful. "Would you be willing?"

"I'll do anything to get this production over the hump. I can't have it suspend, Les. There's not only Merrill and her father to consider. There's Jacquelyn, too."

"Jacquelyn?"

"I wouldn't, for half the world, give Jacquelyn any reason to feel sorry for me."

When he called Lyle Wesley at Runnymede Studios, Brian was told that Mr. Wesley was "not available," then another higher placed flunkie informed him that "Mr. Wesley is out of town and, I'm afraid, incommunicado," and when Brian's Irish temper got the better of him, he was put through with alacrity to the Great Man's private office. There, his personal secretary informed him that Mr. Wesley was not in the office but that Mrs. Wesley had stopped by for a visit. Would he care to speak to her?

"Margot? I'd be delighted. Put her on."

Margot was equally delighted; her voice trilled. Margot Wesley had the sort of voice that could trill on command.

"Brian, dear, we haven't heard from you in ages. Lyle is going to be so disappointed. But he really is off and away. It's supposed to be a secret, but he's in Greece trying to set up some sort of a production deal with that terribly talented Michael Cacoyannis."

"Can I reach him? I have a business proposition for him I think he'll be interested in."

"Why don't you come to the house tonight? I expect Lyle to call at about seven. We can have drinks before he calls and afterward you can take me to dinner."

"Sounds wonderful, Margot. I'll be there."

He was rather pleased that Margot was so friendly because he had always considered her more Fabia's friend than his own. After the divorce, he had written off any possibility of further intimacy with the Wesleys. No matter what past he and Lyle had shared, women determined the future of a friendship.

Lyle and Margot Wesley lived in a grand Georgian house in Mayfair. As his chauffeur-driven Bentley crossed Trafalgar Square in a gray drizzle, Brian looked up to Lord Nelson towering high on his pinnacle above the live pigeons and the stone lions. The pavements were blue with the rain and Lord Nelson was looking a bit under the weather, not to say weatherbeaten.

In Dublin, stalwart Horatio Nelson had suffered a worse indignity than any conferred by weather or winged creatures. He had been artfully blasted from his foundation by a pair of Irish revolutionaries who were not of a mind to have English heroes celebrated on the soil of the Free Republic.

That episode had been the inspiration for the raid on the Cuchulain burying grounds. A raw, wild, and boisterous night it had been—and the escapade was planned for neither pleasure nor profit—for no good reason, which is the best reason of all, as Stephen Innis pointed out. Stephen had always been overfond of Gaelic and the later warriors of the Ulster saga and the singing bards who helped to make Gaelic a deathless melody in the hearts of certain men. He could recite whole passages of fine jawbreaking sounds, and rise to impassioned lyrical heights in *The Pursuit of Diarmaid and Gráinne*. When they were students, their teacher had once taken them to the Cuchulain burying ground, to point out the reputed resting place of mighty Cuchulain himself. Stephen had wept.

Therefore, it should not have been surprising when he showed up, more than a little drunk, and raging, at half past midnight of a stormy night in the lobby of the hotel in Dublin where Brian was staying with Jacquelyn before they were married.

"I am sorry to be calling you at this hour, Mr. O'Neal," the desk clerk said, "but a man here claims to be a friend of yours. He's creating a disturbance about seeing you."

"Who is he?"

"He claims to be the poet laureate of Ireland."

"Stephen? Stephen Innis?"

With accents of faint distaste, the clerk replied. "That appears to be the gentleman's name, sir. He is a bit under the influence."

"I know him," Brian said sourly. "What does he want?"

"I can't make out too clearly."

"Put him on."

Stephen's bawling baritone took over: "Brian, are we going to let them do it? Not while there's a man's drop of blood left in our veins. Are you with me?"

"I'll be with you tomorrow, Stephen. It's too late now. I want a good night's sleep." He listened for a knock on the door of the room connecting to his.

"Are you going to let the sacred bones of Terg Dall O'Higgins be scattered to the five winds?"

"Four winds. I'll see you at Old Billy's place in the morning. Good night, Stephen. Go home and sleep it off."

"Don't evade me, Brian. Are you an Irishman?"

"As good a one as you."

"Then prove it. Come with me. There's glory enough for both of us this night. Link hands with our noble brethren who blew the top off Lord Nelson. Strike a blow for the deathless soul of Ireland."

"Stephen, I'm not going anywhere on a night like this. I've got other plans."

Just then he heard the tapping on the door of the connecting suite.

"Hold a minute," he told Stephen on the phone.

He crossed the room in his pajamas to open the door to a lovely vision in her nightgown with her sly, shy grin.

"I'll be with you in a minute, love," he said. "As soon as I get rid of a mad poet."

Jacquelyn sat nearby and listened while he protested with Stephen who invoked the ghosts of the powerful Irish dead to curse the poor bloodless descendant of the warlike family of O'Neal. He called Brian a black-hearted Protestant and the bastard son of a Black and Tan.

At one point Brian simply held the phone away from his ear as the chanting went on in a wonderful hurry of eloquence.

"What's it all about?" Jacquelyn asked.

"I'm not sure I get the whole drift of it," Brian said. "But I gather there's a housing development going up on part of the Cuchulain burying grounds. It involves displacing the bones of one of Stephen's favorite poets—Terg Dall O'Higgins."

"What does he want you to do?"

"Dig up the bones and find some fitting sacramental ground to rebury them. Or else shoot the chief officers of the housing development. I'm not quite sure which at this point."

"Let me listen," Jacquelyn said.

He held the earphone toward her. They were inundated in the hot molten lava of Stephen Innis's anger.

"If we don't preserve the sacred bones of our immortals," Stephen said, "we are not fit to be called a reasonable folk. Ireland will sink into its bogs, forgotten and unsung, a dirty, shamed, and ignorant people whose silver lakes are only to catch fish and not for men to swim in. Fish are fitter to live in Ireland than we Irish. Oh, for shame, Brian O'Neal, that you would dishonor the brave soul of Terg Dall O'Higgins and send his ghost wailing over the hills."

"Stephen, I'll talk about it with you in the morning."

Jacquelyn caught the phone and put her hand over the mouthpiece.

"Let's do it," she said.

"What?"

"Whatever he wants. Anyone who can talk like he can is the rightest man in the world."

"You mean it?"

She nodded, almost laughing. "Yes!"

He took her hand from the mouthpiece.

"Give us ten minutes," he told Stephen. "We'll meet you in the lobby."

"We?"

"Jacquelyn is coming."

They met Stephen downstairs. After one look at Jacquelyn in her green slicker and hood, Stephen shook
Brian's hand with vigorous apology.

"You're a better man than I thought, Brian. If it's the
likes of her you're giving up for the evening, it's a dear
price to pay." Stephen took off his shapeless rain-soaked
hat and bowed. "I salute you, O Queen of Beauty. Knights
of old never jousted for so fair a lady."

"You're soaked through," Jacquelyn said.

"I have enough slosh in me to keep me warm for a
fortnight. The red wine is bubbling in my heart. No
man is damp who can do great deeds—as we shall do this
night."

"Let's get on with it," Brian said.

He ordered his car brought around to the door of the
hotel and got into the driver's seat. Jacquelyn got in beside
him and restrained Stephen from getting into the rear.

"I can't sit up front. I'm in too wretched a condition."

"Sit here beside me," Jacquelyn said, "and tell me all
about Terg Dall O'Higgins."

That invitation Stephen could not resist. He sat beside
her and as the car sped through the pouring night, he
quoted great gobs of unintelligible Gaelic.

"O'Higgins wrote in the times of England's cruel victory
—when they were robbing our land and dishonoring our
altars. A bardic poet who had a fine fury in him for all
things English."

"But it's the Irish who are digging him up."

"All landowners are English in their hearts."

Brian parked the car at the edge of the burying ground,
a long expanse of rolling plain and marsh grass. Mud
came up to the top of their boots and made sucking
noises. Stephen led the way with a flashlight probing the
dark. Brian followed carrying two long-handled spades.

"Hold on, Terg. We're coming," Stephen muttered.

"Not likely he's going anywhere," Brian pointed out.

Jacquelyn asked, "Does anyone know where the grave
is?"

"I make a pilgrimage once a year," Stephen answered.
"A bit to the left. A hundred yards or so beyond the
monument to Cuchulain."

On the far edge of the burying ground the first signs of
invasion were in evidence. The ground had been cleared

of shrubbery and grass, and earth was rolled up into mounds now spotted with glimmering pools of water.

Stephen flashed the white beam on a moldering slope-shouldered slab of granite. "The poor musical man. The noise of hammers and drilling in his stuffed ears all the day long."

"Here's your shovel," Brian said. "Get to work before we all drown out here."

Jacquelyn held the flashlight as they set to work. Their spades made clinching noises in the rain-soaked ground.

"It just occurred to me," Jacquelyn observed, "that we could all probably get a year in jail for this."

"Throw all lawbooks into the fire," Stephen said, in short bursts of labored breath. "When there's no more law, they'll still be reading poets."

Rain pelted down. The ground turned squishy underfoot. Brian found it slippery footing as he struck in, dug up, lifted, heaved, and struck in again.

He stopped to rub his hands together. "Are you cold, darling?"

"I'm fine."

"Well, I'm cold. Terg Dall O'Higgins isn't feeling anything. He's better off."

"There's an odor here, though."

"Sheep's dung. They use it for a pasturing ground. The cemetery's been long abandoned."

"The more shame to Ireland," Stephen cried as he flung another spadeful over his shoulder.

They got down a few feet, with water running into the hole, and the soft sides crumbling. Then they struck wood.

"Well, that's a blessing," Brian said. "They buried him shallow."

"Ah, Terg, it is friends who come so rudely at this hour of the night," Stephen said. "We will not let you be built into the foundation of some damnable solicitor."

He tossed his spade aside and lowered himself into the pit.

"Brother," he cried. "Great-hearted poet. Stephen Innis comes to welcome you back to the light."

He struck the wooden coffin lid, and gave a cry. His feet went through the rotten wood.

"Help me out, Brian. He's grabbing me. I feel him holding on to my ankles!"

"It's all right. We'll have you out in a minute!"

Jacquelyn put down her flashlight, keeping it steady on the pit. She joined Brian at the grave's edge and they extended hands to Stephen who reached for them like a drowning man at a spar.

"He's trying to pull me down into the grave with him. It isn't my time! Jesus, Mary, and all the Saints, save me!"

They hauled Stephen, belly flat up, through the muck.

"Wow!"

"I guess he mistook you for an English landlord," Brian said, laughing.

As Jacquelyn was going back to retrieve the flashlight, Brian heard above Stephen's frightened blubbering the unmistakable whine of an approaching car. Spinning wheels trying to find a surface in the mud.

"Someone's coming. It might be the caretaker—or even the police," Brian said. "Switch off the light."

Jacquelyn picked up the flashlight, found the switch. They were plunged back into the night.

"Don't leave me alone in the dark," Stephen whimpered.

"Quiet. Do you want them to find us?"

"I'd rather be found by the living than the dead," Stephen said.

"Courage," Brian said. "Remember Clontarf and the Boyne. Think of Daniel O'Connell and Charles Stewart Parnell."

"Safe in their tombs," Stephen reminded him.

The approaching car came into view through the rain, its orange headlights flattening out to irregular shapes in the wet air.

"It's the police," Brian whispered. "We're for it, now."

Stephen answered with a burst of Gaelic.

"What's that? More O'Higgins?"

"That damnable ghoul! This is no time for blasphemy. I said a short prayer looking to the salvation of us all."

"I have a more practical idea," Jacquelyn said. "You two get down out of sight."

"What for?"

"Don't argue. Just do as I say."

The police car vanished around a bend in the road, and before it reappeared Jacquelyn flashed on her light and ran toward Brian's parked car. She was almost beside it when the police car pulled to a halt behind.

The policeman emerged, a huge man in a black rain-coat, with a head that did not seem large enough to suit his body or fill his helmet. From his hiding place nearby Brian overheard their conversation.

"What's wrong, miss?"

"I'm afraid my car won't start. I don't know what's wrong with it."

The policeman grunted and went around to the front to lift the hood.

"Looks all right to me. It may be the battery. Try your lights."

Jacquelyn got into the front seat and turned on the lights.

"It isn't the battery, then."

The policeman reached beneath the hood and did something.

"Now try to start it."

Jacquelyn turned on the ignition, and the engine gave a satisfactory answering roar.

"That was it," said the policeman with satisfaction. He seemed very pleased with himself as a mechanic. "You'll be all right now, miss."

"I don't know how to thank you."

The policeman moved to the side window. "You must be daft, miss, to be out in this forsaken place on such a night. Where were you heading?"

"I went for a drive to see the countryside. I got hopelessly lost."

"Would you like me to show you the road back to Dublin?"

"If you would just tell me, I'm sure I can find it."

"You'd only get lost again. I'll show you the way. Follow me."

As she pulled out to follow the police car up the road, Jacquelyn shrugged in the general direction of the shrubbery that bordered Cuchulain's burying ground.

"She's gone," Brian said.

"She'll never find us again. We'll die out here and leave our bones to fertilize a lawn."

"Stop your lamenting. We'd better start walking."

Brian and Stephen trudged along the road in the downpour. In twenty minutes they heard the thrumming of a car's engine.

"I never thought you'd find us again," Brian said as he climbed shivering into the front seat beside Jacquelyn.

"I memorized the route when he was taking me out of here."

"Jesus Christ, it's good to roost again," Stephen said. "A black plague on all poets. May their bones be lost in sewers."

Jacquelyn began to laugh. "I thought, all things considered, it was a jolly good show."

Then, on the dark road between Culligmane and Dublin, Brian put his arm about her and held her, green-slickered and trembling, in his arms.

"You're a proper madwoman," he told her. "I'll not rest until we're married. What do you say to that?"

"Answer quickly," Stephen pleaded. "Or I'll die a death of cold and wet."

"I think it's a perfectly lovely idea," Jacquelyn said.

The chauffeur pulled the car up before the Wesleys' home in a heavy drizzle. Brian leaned forward.

"Don't wait for me. I don't know when we'll be going to dinner."

"Very good, sir."

Margot Wesley was an attractive older woman. She was quite small, but her figure was trim, and her long auburn hair was held by a barette at the back. She wore a simple black shift.

"Brian, darling," she said as she hugged him. "You're right on time. I can't tell you how nice it is to see you again. How long has it been? Three years?"

"You look at least three years younger than the last time I saw you—and you looked twenty-one then."

"I love Irishmen. They're lovely liars."

At the bar in the library Brian became aware of the silence in the large house.

"Are we alone?"

"I'm afraid so. I give the servants one day a week rather than stagger their time off. Then I make arrangements not to dine at home that day. That's why you weren't invited to dinner. I'm a terrible cook. Completely lost in a kitchen." She smiled. "I suppose you still drink Irish whiskey. Straight up, and with nothing in it?"

"I'm surprised you remember."

"Is it for patriotic reasons—or because you like the taste?"

"Because I like the taste."

She poured a tumbler of whiskey for him, and mixed a

whiskey sour on the rocks for herself. As she sank into the deep-piled sofa, Brian finished his drink.

"I'll make another, if you don't mind."

"I don't suppose I'm the first one to tell you that you shouldn't drink so much, Brian."

"You're not the first," he agreed.

She laughed. "You remind me of my father. He never liked anyone to comment on how much he drank."

"Did you?"

"I couldn't help myself. After all, he was my father. I couldn't help caring about him."

"I suppose not." At the bar he refilled his glass.

"I can't help caring about you either, Brian."

He glanced at her. He was probably mistaken, but there seemed more than mere politeness in the remark. He met her eyes steadily and suddenly he saw that she was flushing. By God. He had certainly never thought of Margot Wesley in that way.

"What is this business proposition you wanted to talk to Lyle about?" she asked.

"It has to do with this movie I'm making. We've got into a bit of a bind. I want Lyle to bail me out of it."

"*Oedipus?* Lyle told me that Runnymede had been approached about investing in it. I was disappointed when I heard the studio decided against it. I think it's a fine idea and you'll be wonderful in it."

He knew Margot to be an intelligent woman who often acted as Lyle's unofficial adviser in business matters. She had worked with Lyle as his assistant in the early days, and still maintained an active interest in the business side of film-making.

"The question is, can we make a bloody nickel? Would you care to hear the proposition I'm going to make to Lyle when he calls? You might have a suggestion or two to make it sound more appealing."

"I might. Go ahead."

He outlined the new proposal. If Runnymede would take on the production, leaving a percentage of the profits for the original investors, in return Brian would agree to star in another picture under contract for Runnymede. Margot listened intently, sipping her drink while he talked, and when he finished she sat for a moment saying nothing.

"Does it make sense to you?" Brian asked.

Margot nodded absently. "I suppose so. How much money do you think you'll need?"

"Half a million ought to swing it."

"This is important to you, isn't it, Brian? I mean it isn't just another movie."

He would have preferred to answer such a question lightly, but he found he could not.

"*Oedipus* has been a classic for a good number of centuries. Sophocles had this marvelous idea, you see, and a Johnny-come-lately like myself shouldn't unload pigeon-droppings on his memory."

"You're not likely to do that. You're a fine actor. You've been wasting your talents on the kind of garbage you've done lately."

"An actor can't always pick and choose."

"No, he can't. The movies with Jacquelyn were pot-boilers. Profitable potboilers, but no more. They didn't scratch the artistic surface of Brian O'Neal. You feel that too, don't you, Brian?"

"Yes." He finished his glass morosely. "There's a poem by Edgar Lee Masters that describes me:

> The earth keeps some vibration going
> There in your heart, and that is you.
> And if the people find you can fiddle,
> Why, fiddle you must, for all your life.

"It's time you stopped fiddling. I agree that you should do *Oedipus*—do it the way you want to." She put her glass down on the table and looked at it as though to find an answer reflected there. "You might be able to persuade Lyle to give you the money, but I honestly doubt it."

"You don't think it's a good deal?"

"*Oedipus* is going to lose money, and we both know it. The only thing you have to offer is an agreement to star in another production. But I happen to know that Runnymede has no big budget movie in the works that would particularly suit your talents. So that isn't much of a selling point."

"I see."

"No, you don't." There was a curious inflection in her voice. "Because I intend to persuade Lyle to back your movie—on the terms you've outlined."

He looked at her with surprise. "Do you think you can?"

"Lyle always takes my advice. I've been making most of his business decisions for some time. You might be shocked to know that it was I who originally vetoed his plan to star you in a film of *Macbeth*."

"You were probably right about that."

"I don't believe *Oedipus* has any better chance of making money than *Macbeth*. But things have changed. Lyle was barely starting out then and a mistake could have ruined him. Now he's the head of a big studio, with money to burn, and if they put some of that money into *Oedipus* it won't hurt them much. It might add a little to their prestige. Runnymede has very little to lose, the way I see it. Any big studio always can use properties for release to help justify all the extravagant overhead charges. They can't sit still and do nothing."

Brian did not answer at once. "You'll be doing me a big favor. I'm not a man who'll forget it."

"It's almost seven o'clock and Lyle is due to call. I'll talk to him, then you can take me to dinner."

Across the table in the restaurant, Margot appeared a different woman. She wore a white silk dress with a jade pendant, and her auburn hair was done up in a French twist and fastened with a jade comb. Artful use of makeup highlighted her high cheekbones and gave her face a masklike Oriental beauty.

She seemed to feel his approval.

Brian said, "Yes, I *was* thinking that you're quite lovely, Margot."

A hint of color appeared in her cheeks. "You're sure you're not trying to pay me back with compliments because I set up the deal for you with Lyle?"

"Quite sure. You're like a Dresden Doll—with a hint of Javanese somewhere."

Color heightened. "I thought you preferred lush, shapely types like Jacquelyn. I've always thought I was too small for your taste, Brian."

"I like small women. There is really no such thing as a taste for certain kinds of women—except for undiscriminating men. A man likes a particular woman, then she helps to form his taste."

"It's the same with women. When I married Lyle I thought he was my ideal type. Lean, distinguished, with that sort of haunted, ravaged look around the eyes. I still think Lyle is attractive, but my preference in men has taken quite a different turn. I can pinpoint the time it happened. It was ... four years ago."

Brian watched her carefully. Margot must be in her late forties, he thought, but her age didn't show tonight. She might have been a dozen years younger.

"What kind of man do you prefer now?"

"Stronger looking, not necessarily tall, but broad and powerful. Handsome in a rugged undisciplined way. A man with a sort of mantle of protective warmth and concern for a woman. That concern shows out of his eyes whenever he looks at you, for he has a very direct way of looking at a woman."

"It sounds a though you have someone particular in mind, Margot."

"Does it?"

"How long have we known each other, Margot?"

"Four years this month."

"And has it been like this with you ever since?"

Margot closed her eyes. She seemed to have expected the question but, surprisingly, did not reply to it. Instead she asked, "Do you love her?"

For a moment Brian did not know what to say. Then he countered, "Who?"

Margot's eyes flew open. "Your wife."

"That's an impertinent question."

"You haven't answered it."

"Probably because I have no intention of doing so."

Margot smiled. "That's a good enough answer. I'd like you to take me home now, Brian."

That evening, standing by the window on the upper floor bedroom of the large house in Mayfair, Brian saw the pale globe of a street lamp reflected palely in the dark window. The only other light came from the small space beneath the bathroom door.

When the door opened, the light expanded to the size and shape of the open doorway. He turned and saw Margot for an instant before the light went out. She had an exquisite little body, everything in proportion, from delicate shoulders to small white breasts, to the narrow waist and the subtly flaring hips and slender, rounded legs.

She came into his arms. Her lips were warm and eager.

"You're still wearing too much," she whispered.

He pulled open the clasp buttons on his shorts an
them   fall.

"Is that better?"

Margot looked down at him. "Oh, yes," she breathed.
She held him. "I'm a little afraid of you. You're so much
bigger than Lyle."

He put his hand on her breast. "I won't hurt you."

She looked curiously at his hand cupping her breast.
"You have strong hands. You'd have made a wonderful
sculptor or stonemason or woodcarver. You could do anything with those hands."

"I'd rather do what I am doing," Brian told her.

As a boy, in the pub, his fingers held the handle of the
tankard while ale frothed into it from the spigot. His
fingers were cooled and cleaned by the spillover. All the
workingmen's hands were broken and blackened with
grime. He had been lucky. So few escaped the grinding
monotony, the soul-destroying toil. A hard thing to stay
alive, or prosper, in that green country.

Later, her head was turning on the pillow to and fro,
and he put his hand under her chin and commanded her,
"Look at me."

"I can't."

"You're ready now. You're not afraid, are you?"

"Please don't hurt me."

"I won't. Trust me."

"I know you won't. I do trust you."

He came to her, not thrusting or pushing, lowering
himself with gentle strength. He waited until she brought
her legs together. Then he moved his legs outside of hers
lying straight beneath him. She began writhing and he held
her head steady. She had to stay still and feel his warmth
inside her and experience all of the mounting tension.
There would be no cheap way out for her. The richness of
it became overpowering. He could see her drowning in it.
The poor lass, face tight-clenched, mouth open to show
small white teeth. How she struggled to evade, to push
away or control everything she desired. She would not
evade him.

He held in her until her mouth contorted and her
tongue licked wildly against her teeth. When her first cry
broke, he drove against her and brought the breath wrenching out in a strangling scream of delight.

Later, they lay side by side in bed with only their hands
touching.

"I always thought it was my fault, that there was something wrong with me."

"There's nothing wrong with you."

"How long could I have let it go like that?" she asked. "Without knowing?"

"Until it was too late. I've known women like that. Is Lyle the only one?"

"Yes."

"That's the trouble, you see, with the whole crooked notion of fidelity. Where is someone to get experience?"

She began to cry, and the tears rolled gently down her cheeks.

"It'll be all right now," he said. "That's how it works. If one knows, that's enough for two."

"I hope you're right, Brian. It would be such a relief not to . . . want any more. To know that I'm woman enough for my husband."

She turned away and Brian turned her face back to him. He looked at her steadily as though to see into her heart and read its secrets.

"You're woman enough for any man," Brian said almost harshly.

She drew a deep breath. "I believe that because I want to. I have to know one thing more, Brian. Will you answer me honestly?"

"Yes."

"I wasn't . . . a disappointment to you?"

He didn't speak.

"I'm not asking for reassurance, not really. I want to know. And it won't help if you try to lie to me. I've always been able to see through polite answers."

"There's only one possible answer a man can give to a woman who asks a question like that."

He drew her toward him, and felt the soft yielding. There was a troubled, anxious look in her eyes.

"You're not doing this for me, are you? It's for you, too?"

"It's for me too, Margot," he said.

When he took her again, she knew the answer. It had to be for him too. There was no lying, no hypocrisy in such moments. It was impossible to deceive in an experience so completely shared.

Just before the climax, when thunder was breaking in his ears, Brian had this swiftly vanishing thought: I am paying her in full for anything she's doing for me.

CHAPTER SEVEN

In the hot twilight when Jacquelyn returned from a preliminary conference with her director, H. T. Wallace, on the set of *Death of a Peacock,* Gilberto brought a list of telephone calls that had come in during the day. Her eyes scanned the list. Calls from Hollywood, from the Ministry of Culture welcoming her to Brazil, from Senhor Candido Vargas, one of South America's wealthiest and most notorious girl-hunters, from people who wanted to give a ball in her honor, from Piñata, a prominent young artist who wanted to present her with a painting—the list went on and on. Meaningless, all of it meaningless. There was only one telephone call in the world she wanted.

One name on the list suddenly leapt out at her. Marta Moran. Marta was the leading gossip columnist in Hollywood, syndicated in more than two hundred newspapers in the United States, with a sizable following in Europe and in Latin America also. Marta had recently married the aging Latin Casanova whom she had shamelessly pursued for years. Captured and caged, her Latin husband wrung from Marta a final concession: a villa in his home town of Caracas where they spent a couple of months each year.

Unfortunately, Caracas was not far from Rio. While on her holiday, Marta Moran had flown over to cover the shooting of *Death of a Peacock.* She would expect to get exclusive interviews. Jacquelyn, of course, was first on her list.

Opposite Marta's name was the penciled notation: *Please call at once.*

"Marta, darling, how are you? ... Jacquelyn. I just got in a little while ago and saw your note. How thrilling. You're in Rio. I can't wait to see you."

"You won't have to, darling. I thought I'd come over, if it won't bollix up your schedule too dreadfully."

"You mean—tonight?"

"No time like the present."

"I've hardly settled down, darling. I've been running around so much I'm afraid I may be a little tired."

"It's bound to get worse from now on, darling. You'll be starting on the movie."

"How about sometime over the weekend?"

"Can't make it. I'm leaving Rio tomorrow."

Aggressive pushy bitch. Jacquelyn had crossed rapiers with Marta on several occasions, and the bitterness in their relationship came from Marta's discovery that her enmity did not affect Jacquelyn's popularity in the slightest.

"I won't be my sparkling self, Marta darling. What do you want to interview me about?"

"Oh, the usual. How you like Rio, what kind of interpretation you're giving to the role of Diana in *Death of a Peacock*." There was a slight pause. "How much you miss Brian, being away from him."

"Are you sure there won't be more interesting things to talk about when the movie is underway?"

"Anything about you is interesting, Jacquelyn dear. Your public eats it up."

"You don't want to give your public the same old stuff. I don't have anything new to tell you."

"I'm an expert at making bricks without straw, darling. Just give me a little newsy item to start me off and I can turn it into a masterpiece of suspense with a little tug at the heartstrings thrown in for good measure."

Poor woman, she was only semiliterate. If anyone took away her three dots she would not know how to write a simple sentence with subject, verb, and object.

"Then of course come," Jacquelyn said. "I'm simply dying to see you."

Marta Moran appeared an hour later in an electric blue envelope of soft crepe with floating front and back panels. She was a shapeless stick woman of fifty-plus years who wired herself into the shapeliest haute-couture Parisian designs. A rope of heavy Oriental pearls at a simple neckline concealed the arid flatland of her bosom, and the dress camouflaged the perfect pencil shape of her figure. She always wore a white turban as some kind of personal signature.

They embraced each other.

"Are you still drinking Chateau Yquem?" Jacquelyn asked.

"How dear of you to remember."

They sat side by side on the living room sofa. Marta sipped her Chateau Yquem and Jacquelyn drank a glass of tonic water.

They covered mundane matters, impressions of Rio, of the movie, of the co-stars and director and producer, and at the end of an hour the interview shifted to personal matters.

"How about Brian? Do you miss him?"

"Of course."

"How often does he write?"

"Every day. Sometimes twice a day."

She had not heard from Brian in weeks.

"Telephones constantly, I suppose?"

Jacquelyn smiled. "I keep telling him that all our money is going on those transatlantic phone calls."

Marta would discover the truth in a few days, when Jacquelyn filed suit for divorce. Marta would be furious at having been deceived, and it rather pleased Jacquelyn to think of that.

"What does Brian talk to you about when he calls?"

"Oh, the same things any husband tells his wife. We enjoy sharing even the little events of our day together."

"Then of course Brian has told you he's been seeing quite a lot of Merrill Yeaton."

Oh! Cards on the table. It is not going to be so easy to deceive Marta.

Jacquelyn smiled blandly. "They're good friends. I like Merrill."

Marta touched the spongy fullness over what should have been her left breast. "You aren't jealous of Brian? Not even when you're apart?"

"I have no reason to be."

"I suppose that's because you find consolations of your own."

"What is that crack supposed to mean?" Jacquelyn asked.

They exchanged glances as sharp as swords in the air. Then Marta altered her face into a sweet expression.

"Meyer Whitney is such a fabulous man."

Her big suction machine is pumping and hoping to draw up dirt. This is why she was so insistent on having an interview tonight.

"Meyer is a good friend. Period."

"I understand he's quite dazzled by you."

"I don't know who told you that. If this is a fishing expedition, Marta, you might as well cut bait and clear out."

"Oh, I trust my sources." Shark smile. "There isn't much that goes on that escapes Marta Moran. Do your plans with Meyer include marriage?"

"That's a stupid question. I *am* married."

Marta's thin lips formed an insinuating sneer. "I have it on good authority that you're planning to ask Brian for a divorce."

The dark-faced, sunken-eyed, nervous, intense, prying egomaniac.

Jacquelyn finished her glass of tonic water. "You mustn't believe everything you hear, Marta. That could get you into a lot of trouble."

Marta blinked. "I happen to know Meyer Whitney is thinking of marriage. I have that information from a most reliable source."

Gerda Andersen.

"I certainly hope you don't intend to print that."

"I've been checking the rumors. I believe they're true. You and Brian have reached a parting of the ways."

"Remember the libel laws, won't you? I have a *very* good lawyer."

"I know all about the law. Truth is an absolute defense against libel."

"I wouldn't mind hauling you into court, Marta. It would enable me to say some of the things I truly think about you."

"Jacquelyn darling, I don't blame you for not wanting to lose Brian. He did add a certain touch of class to you. Goodness knows, you need it."

"You wouldn't know what class was if it grew teeth and bit off your nipples."

Marta's hand strayed nervously over the front panel of her dress. "You don't want to fight me, Jacquelyn."

"Of course not. It'd be like stepping on a toad. You'd go all squishy—and I'd get sick to my stomach." Jacquelyn glanced at her opal-faced, diamond-encircled wristwatch. "Isn't it time for you to go, darling?"

A look of pure black venom. "Read my column tomorrow. You might find it very interesting. It's going to have an exclusive on your divorce from Brian—and your plans for a remarriage."

"Who could possibly read your slush, darling? You don't write. You just dribble in print. Anyone can taste the drool and saliva in every paragraph."

Marta stood up. She was trembling with outrage.

"I understand why Brian picked Merrill Yeaton over you," she said. "After all, Merrill *is* a lady!"

"Why don't you fuck off?" Jacquelyn asked sweetly.

She picked up the telephone.

"I'd like to make a person-to-person call, please. To Mr. Richard Stuart, in Carmel, California ... Yes, that is in the United States."

Waiting impatiently, she tried to remember just when the ritual of calling her brother the day before she started in a new picture had begun. It must have been when she was a child.

"Your call to California is being put through. Please stand by."

"Thank you."

In a moment she heard the low, distant sound of ringing, then Madeline's voice answering. "Mr. Richard Stuart, please," the operator said. "Long distance calling."

"Mr. Stuart is not at home."

"Is there anyplace we can reach him by telephone?"

"I'm afraid not. He's gone off sailing and won't be back for several days. Who is this calling?"

"Never mind, operator." Jacquelyn hung up.

Madeline would have recognized her voice, no doubt, but she had no desire to talk to her. They didn't like each other. She suspected Madeline was jealous of her closeness to Richard. Or, perhaps, to be absolutely fair, she was jealous of Madeline having Richard entirely to herself.

The phone sat on the table, crouching, waiting. She was disappointed because she wanted badly to talk to Richard. Not being able to struck her as a bad omen.

The silence in the room beat at her in waves, pulsing and sending shuddering rhythms through the whole length of her body in synchronized time.

Suddenly, to the beating of her heart, the room began closing in, a matrix in which unwelcome images were born. Brian sitting beside her at their favorite bar at Governor's House; Brian laughing, his fist clenched on a whiskey tumbler, unruly hair flying; Brian reading passages aloud from Shakespeare to wide-eyed Gene, a performance complete with flourishes, swordplay, even the sound of trumpets. The boy had been no more entranced than she. Brian, oh, Brian.

She grabbed the phone as for a spar to keep her afloat in a drowning sea.

"Yes, please?"

"Long distance."

In a moment the long distance operator came on. She had to say twice that this was long distance before Jacquelyn raised her courage to speak.

"I'd like to make a person-to-person call to Brian O'Neal, please, in London, at the Fotheringay Hotel."

"Certainly. What is your name and telephone number, please?"

Her thoughts shot ahead to her name being repeated at the far end, to Brian. He might not be alone. Merrill might be with him. Even if he were alone, what would she tell him? Brian despised weakness. She had nothing to say, really, nothing to make except a crack of noise, a cry of loneliness. She would end up telling him that nothing mattered but him, that without him her whole world was collapsing. She would hate herself thoroughly while she was saying it, knowing she was not winning him back with this ultimate sacrifice of self-respect but only inviting his contempt.

"I've changed my mind, operator."

"I beg your pardon."

"I'll place the call some other time. I don't want to make it now."

She put the phone down gently. What a damn fool. Women in love are not to be trusted.

At five o'clock the following afternoon Jacquelyn lay back in a contoured chair, relaxed and drowsy, while the masseuse gave her a cream facial. Her day had begun at seven o'clock in the morning, and it was not over yet. Jacques, her hairdresser, was due shortly, and Toby Dolan was coming to the villa to do publicity stills that evening.

She looked forward to the evening with Toby, though. He was one of her favorite people. He had started out as an actor in movies, a child star, and when his career was over he took up his real love: photography. He was very good, and what was more important, she could trust him.

Toby never tried to sneak in candid, unflattering shots of her, the kind of photographs that would sell for a high price to *Life* or *Look* but wouldn't do her any good. And he never argued. When she marked his proof sheet with the heavy grease pencil X that meant she rejected a particular shot, he promptly destroyed the negative.

Yes, she liked Toby, and it would be pleasant to see him again. She leaned back in the contour chair, her legs crossed at the ankles, while Estelle worked cream deep, deep into her face.

Suddenly the kneading fingers stopped.

Jacquelyn opened her eyes. "What is it?"

Estelle was looking toward the door of the dressing room where Janet had appeared, carrying the telephone.

"Telephone call for you, Miss Stuart. It's from Mr. Whitney."

The chair came upright with her sitting-up motion. "All right, I'll take it. You can have a ten-minute break," she told Estelle.

Janet plugged in the telephone and left.

Meyer Whitney sounded upset. "Have you talked with Hernan Ramirez?"

"I had dinner with him the night before last."

"How did he act? Friendly?"

"Yes. Very."

Meyer said, "I don't know what's wrong. Everything seemed set for a quick divorce. Now Hernan says there are complications. He's a little vague about what the complications are, except that they involve the honor of his damned country. Sounds to me like he's stalling.

"I can't imagine why he would do that."

"Neither can I. God knows I'm paying him enough. I tried to make plain to him that I won't stand for any delays."

"I'm sure he's doing his best, darling."

"I'm not so sure. I'll be coming down to Rio to handle the details myself. I promise you it won't be long, love."

"I can wait, if I have to."

"I can't wait. We'll be together very soon. And the moment you get that divorce decree we'll be married."

She wondered whether Hernan could delay Meyer Whitney very long. It would be like trying to turn back Niagara.

They talked a few minutes longer and Meyer finally

said, "I'll call you in the morning. You know how much I love you, don't you?"

"Yes, I know, darling," she answered quietly.

Her face in the mirror was streaked with cream. She felt trapped in glassy mirror walls.

A flashcube glowed brightly, then faded. Toby replaced it and moved to a position on the sofa, resting on it with one knee and angling his camera at her as she chose a book from the bookshelves.

A flashcube glowed again.

"Okay," Toby said. "That's all. We'll take some out by the swimming pool later."

"In a bathing suit?"

"A bikini. You want this layout in a national magazine, right? That means we need at least one smashing example of respectable sex. Or at least semirespectable sex." Toby's lean face, until now so intent and serious, brightened with a smile. "That ripe, Rubens figure of yours in a bikini, darling, might even persuade me to convert."

"I hope not, Toby."

"What a nice thing to say, darling. Do you mean it?"

"Of course. I like you because you don't make demands on me, not even the hidden kind that the quiet letches make. Some of the worst are photographers. They use their cameras to satisfy all their instincts as peeping Toms."

"I could tell you some stories about Rolleiflex brethren as voyeurs. There's this fellow who's supposed to do fashion photography, and he simply insists that he must photograph the girls in the altogether first so he'll know how the clothes ought to hang. Can you *imagine?* He'd never get away with it except that he has such a reputation that the poor dumb mannequins now do absolutely *anything* he says. They're all crazy to get into the movies . . ."

Toby was always able to draw her into his gay chatter about one thing or another, to share his wide-eyed innocent delight at the outrageous way people behaved. Later, at the swimming pool, she posed in a bikini on the stepladder to the diving board, standing and lying flat on the diving board, and coming up the handrail out of the pool. The skimpy bikini clung to her wet body, and Toby had to rush a robe to her because the night air had a chill. Laughing together over drinks at the poolside table, she asked, "How was I? Did you get any good shots?"

"Beautiful. You're unself-conscious in front of a camera

these days, darling. Not like the first time. Do you remember Princess Annette?"

"The Wooden Princess? How can I forget her? That was the day we first met."

"And I was a courtier in the French court who was absolutely smitten with you. What was the name of that turkey?"

"*Pont Royal.*"

"You looked gorgeous in a white wig. Positively breathtaking. But you couldn't act your way out of a pocket handkerchief. That's why everyone tabbed you the Wooden Princess. But you've certainly come a long way."

"Funny. My career doesn't seem that important to me anymore." She looked around the square, white, ultramodern terrace, shaded by palm trees and dotted with curly, fluted, white-painted iron chairs and tables. Dangling from a roof overhang, in a cage shaped like a Chinese lantern, was a vivid-colored cuckatoo.

Toby's voice was suddenly serious. "It isn't true, is it, darling? The story about you and Brian. It's in Marta Moran's column today."

The air hung heavily, and seemed to have absorbed a musty odor like air locked too long in a vial. "Take me away from here, Toby, will you?"

Toby had a quizzical smile. "Would you care for a taste of the low life?"

"Anything you say. I want to get my mind off me for a little while."

"I know just the place. Get dressed, darling. I'll show you the rawest nightspot in Rio."

The place to which Toby drove her was reached along a network of narrow muddy roads. At the entrance to the club, several Brazilian men were standing, in wide-brimmed hats and boots red with mud.

Inside, the noise was deafening, and the large low-roofed room was crowded with tables and dense with smoke. In the center was a cleared, square area where some couples were dancing, and on a stand the four-piece orchestra blared away in screeching harmony. The place was full of furious gaiety.

Neither the cloakroom attendant nor the waiters paid any attention to Jacquelyn. In that dim interior it was hard to make out anyone clearly, and there were far too many pretty girls for one more to attract any notice. The girls were young, expensively dressed, extravagantly made-up. A blonde of no more than seventeen wore a Greek robe of startling white that opened all the way up both sides and showed the entire length of her naked body beneath the crisscross of white ties that held the dress together on either side. Another girl, tall and willowy, sat at a nearby table with a gigantic Negro who was dressed in a spotless tuxedo, his frizzled hair tied in a matador's ringlet in the back. His face had a gentle, smooth look, and he paid scarcely any attention to the ivory-colored beauty with the high-piled sloping hairdo that made her look like Queen Nefertiti.

"Where do they come from?" Jacquelyn whispered to Toby. "I've never seen so many lovely women."

"They come from all over Brazil, looking for a husband or a lover among the coffee barons. This is a wide-open country since the military dictatorship."

Everyone was drinking Scotch, which was contraband and very expensive in Rio, and men were flashing thousand cruzeiro notes from bulging wallets.

Jacquelyn ordered a Scotch on the rocks, and Toby a *cachao* with lemon. In the thick heat, Jacquelyn sat, disconsolate, stirring the melting ice in her untouched drink.

She looked up, and realized that Toby had been speaking. She must have given the impression that she had been listening, for he did not appear to notice her abstractedness. What was he talking about? Oh, yes, the spur-of-the-moment party he had given to celebrate the successful completion of *Pont Royal*. Toby seemed to remember it as a hilarious evening.

Toby was such an angel, so good-looking too. There were still traces of the darkly handsome young boy who once had been a screen favorite. As a young man he could have had his pick of almost any starlet in Hollywood. He must have tried with some; perhaps then he discovered that he really wasn't interested in girls. The roots of homosexuality began in childhood. He needed feminine understanding, not dominance. It was all so clear to her. She might start him on the road back, and that would be more than the simple act; that would be an event that would change his whole life. She was so very fond of Toby.

She leaned toward him, really listening now, as Toby recalled the merriment, the abandoned drunken gaiety of a long-vanished evening.

"That was when that pretty girl—what's her name— damn, I've forgotten—got up and started to imitate a burlesque dancer. She had such long black hair, remember?"

"Sylvia Brooks."

"That's right." Toby was delighted, then sobered. "She died a couple of years ago. They found her in her car in a locked garage. Poor crazy kid. But she had a lot of fun while it lasted. That night everyone began yelling for her to take it off, and she did, the whole way, and somebody tore down the curtains for her to do the dance of the seven veils."

"That was Larry Whiting."

"Oh yes, Larry. A lovely chap. Such fun. He joined in the striptease with that awful Claudine woman. We got a regular conga line of strippers going after a while."

In the nightclub now, the blare of the orchestra suddenly ceased and the couples stopped dancing and began slowly to find their way back to their tables. The lights dimmed, plunging the huge room into semidarkness. Even the light on the bandstand softened to a shadowy orange-gray against which the musicians stood out sharply like black silhouettes.

A spotlight struck down with hard conelike brilliance onto the empty dance floor.

A voice boomed over the loudspeaker: "Introducing Madame Sosostris!"

A long-legged blonde appeared, wearing fishnet black tights that clung to a provocatively bosomy figure. She was toying with a long, black fox fur. She wrapped the fur around her arms, sliding it slowly, then undulated it over her hips in time to strongly rhythmic music and a nifty brush underlay from the drums. She pulled the fur between her legs, inching it higher, moving and rocking her torso back and forth on the length of the fur until finally her knees bent and she fell to the floor. She began writhing; holding the fur between her legs she reached up and pulled away the fishnet bodice to reveal huge bare breasts with glittering sequin points at the nipples. She bent her torso backward from the knees, writhing the fur to and fro between her legs.

Jacquelyn glanced at Toby. He was watching the performance with merely polite interest, sipping his *cachao*. Jacquelyn felt suddenly warm and protective toward him. She would let him take her home and she would manage, without frightening him, to make known to him that he could have her. Everything would be very gentle, very slow, and Toby would be so grateful, afterward, and the whole episode would mean so much more than a mere seduction. She would give him a new orientation.

She heard a gasp from spectators around her, then laughter and applause. On the stage, the long, leggy blonde dancer had whipped off a blonde wig. She had also pulled off the fishnet binding her too tightly between the legs. She wore a short jockey strap beneath the binding, and the "she" was unmistakably a "he."

Toby broke into high peals of laughter and applauded enthusiastically. "Wasn't he wonderful? I never would have guessed. Would you, darling?"

"He has a bosom. I don't understand . . ."

"It's that plastic stuff that doctors insert under the skin. Women use it to develop bigger bosoms, but I never saw a man do it. What an original fellow. I'd love to meet him, Jacquelyn. Would you like to come with me?"

"No, thanks. I'll wait here."

She couldn't bear to see the grotesque fellow at close range. Toby had no qualms about it, though; he was chuckling with anticipation as he got up and hurried off through the tables toward the rear of the club.

He really is hopeless, she decided. I don't know what made me think anything could be done. He's content to be exactly what he is.

The next act was announced: The Newly Married Mrs. Sabine. Mrs. Sabine was a beautiful girl, slim, redheaded, and curvaceous, and she appeared in a wedding gown which she gradually took off, an item at a time, until she was wearing only the bridal veil and a pair of diaphanous panties. Mrs. Sabine admired herself in an imaginary mirror as she readied herself for the wedding night with her new husband. At last she removed her veil and her panties, and stepped nude into a tub that had been wheeled onstage. As she was playing with soap bubbles a man appeared, a Negro, wearing only a pair of ragged trousers and rope sandals. Apparently in the next room, he went through imaginary drawers seeking valuables, then noted the open door of the bathroom where the bride was bathing. He entered and saw her, and as she tried to scream he was upon her in a bound. They struggled, the redheaded Mrs. Sabine being pulled halfway out of her bath to display her spectacular torso, before with a backhand blow the Negro apparently knocked her out. She lay draped enticingly across the side of the tub while the Negro slowly undid his trousers, and removed his rope sandals. As the lights dimmed he got into the tub with Mrs. Sabine. She raised her head, felt him with her, and started to scream again. His hand came across her mouth to stifle the sound as the lights went out.

The lights came up, the stage was empty, and the crowd began to cheer the rape of Mrs. Sabine.

A fanfare from the orchestra announced a new act about to begin. Jacquelyn had seen enough. Toby had been gone almost fifteen minutes and she would not wait any longer. She got up and started the way Toby had gone. The path through the tables had become crowded, as more tables had somehow been squeezed onto the floor. Someone patted her on the rump—then she felt the quick cold shock of a hand venturing quickly up beneath her dress. She did not glance back to see who it was but began to hurry, almost running. She had lost all semblance of equanimity, and was behaving badly, indefensibly; people at a table were laughing, and she was sure they laughed at her.

Toby Dolan was nowhere in evidence.

She stopped a waiter. "Which way to the dressing rooms?"

He was carrying a tray of drinks and twisted his head in the general direction. She found the stairway entrance, a flight of narrow steps placed against a wall that led upstairs. She stumbled going up, and the heel of her shoe broke. It did not come off entirely and she limped up the rest of the way.

At the top of the stairs was a narrow, green hallway, with paint peeling to show white plaster beneath, and printed signs in Portuguese amid scrawled crayon messages.

"Toby!" she called.

She knocked on the first door she came to; it was locked. A small fear knotted in her stomach.

"Toby! Toby, goddamit, where are you?"

No answer. She tried the other doors in the corridor. At last one opened. A slim Negro stood there wearing striped shorts. She recognized him as the one who had raped Mrs. Sabine.

"Oh, I'm sorry. I'm looking for someone."

"That's all right, miss." He moved toward her. "Maybe I can help you."

"No. No, I'm sure you can't. Thank you."

"Just a minute . . ."

She turned to go. In quick, silent steps he caught up with her.

"Please! I just want to get out of here."

"Not yet . . ."

His hand seized her by the elbow. She recalled too vividly that terrible moment, before the lights went down, when this savage struck Mrs. Sabine and climbed into the tub, naked, with her.

She fought down the scream. It would infuriate him. Perhaps if she tried to reason with him . . .

"Don't hurt me. I'll do anything you want if you will only be nice."

His hand released its grip.

"You're Jacquelyn Stuart, aren't you?"

"Yes."

"I thought I recognized you." The dark good-looking face broke into a white grin. "I'm an old admirer of yours, Miss Stuart. I wonder if you'd mind giving me your autograph? My wife and kids would be awfully pleased."

CHAPTER EIGHT

She had felt safe in bedrooms all her life. She was not especially tidy, but she kept her bedroom neat—her clothes in the closet, her negligees hanging behind the door, her shoes neatly arranged in the rack, her jewelry in the jewel box on the dresser top. Surrounded by intimate possessions, she never felt a stranger in a bedroom.

She sat up in bed, feeling secure, feeling safe, and laughed at her panic earlier in the evening. She hugged her knees. What a fool I am. But the evening had seemed to be building toward some sort of frightening climax. The way Toby abandoned her had been shameful. She did not intend to forgive him easily for that.

The telephone began ringing, and rang four times before she answered. She identified the caller's voice at the first syllable and carefully screened annoyance out of her own voice.

"Hello, Mother. Are you calling from New York?"

"No. I'm up here at the school." Mother's voice sounded as though she were practicing self-control. "I came up to visit Gene."

"How is he?"

"Jacquelyn, dear, you mustn't get excited."

"Why should I get . . . ? Is he sick?"

"No, it isn't anything like that. He just . . . isn't here."

"What? Where is he?"

"You promised not to get excited, dear. It seems that Charles came up to visit him yesterday."

"Charles! I thought he was in England."

"Apparently he flew in yesterday and came up here. He's taken Gene away with him."

"He's done *what?*"

"Dear, you really must try to be calm."

153

"The sneaking bastard! Where? Where has he taken Gene?"

"I'm sure nothing is wrong. Charles is his father, you know, and he wouldn't let any harm . . ."

She thought of Gene sitting with her in the off-campus soda shop, balancing a chocolate milk shake on the table. She had watched him grow up like some strange sort of tropical plant unfolding. She never should have left him in that school with no one to love him or care what happened to him.

"Where has he taken him?"

"I talked to the headmaster. All he knows is Gene won't be back to school this semester. Charles told him."

"That's kidnapping."

She felt as though she had swallowed a scalding hot liquid. If she was half a mother, she would have taken Gene with her. After all, nothing is more important to a mother than her son. Nothing *should* be more important!

"I'll sue the school, Mother. They never should have let Gene go with him."

"You can't blame them. After all, Charles is the boy's father and—"

"I have custody!"

The air about her seemed fragmented, reflected disconnected images. A succession of governesses had been better mothers than she was. Once, she came back from several months abroad and Gene (barely two years old) clung to his governess when she tried to take him into her arms. When he was four, she asked him, "Did you know that your mommy is Jacquelyn Stuart?" He looked at her with wide, wondering eyes. "What is a Jacquelyn Stuart?" She had neglected her son shamefully. Shamefully!

"You really must try to control yourself, dear," Mother said.

"I'm taking the first plane back."

"You can't!" Mother said increduolously. "You're starting an important picture. Why, it would cost hundreds of thousands of dollars. We're doing everything possible. I've got a call in to Arthur Eakam. I'm sure he's competent to handle this. After all, we don't want a lot of messy publicity."

"I don't give a damn about that. If Charles has kidnapped my son . . ."

"I'm sure there's some perfectly logical explanation."

Jacquelyn took a deep breath, and let the air escape slowly and evenly.

"I'll wait until I hear from Arthur Eakam, Mother. Then I'll take it into my own hands. Whatever Charles's reason for doing this, he's not going to get away with it."

She paused, half hearing words that buzzed over the receiver like the drone of a mosquito.

"I'll wait here, Mother," she interrupted. "Have Arthur call me as soon as he's spoken to you."

She replaced the telephone receiver with a deliberate motion and closed her eyes. When she opened them the telephone was standing there as though to assure her that she had actually heard what she had heard.

It didn't seem possible. Not Charles. Well-mannered, civilized, urbane, gracious Charles was not capable of such abrupt and decisive action. Had she missed something that was in the essence of the man—something that prepared him to act in an unforeseeable way? Had time canceled out some truth in their relationship? Episodes from their life together came back as though to answer the question. Time past shifted to time present and the outlines of remembered reality were blurred. Charles? No, it was not possible . . .

It began the night of the party for *Pont Royal.* The party had quickly turned to pandemonium, with shouting, leaping, laughing dancers shedding clothes as they circled the disordered living room. Jacquelyn sat in a chair, a little terrified by the wild behavior of these people, having failed to rise to their pitch, and feeling terribly out of it. She looked around for Toby, and Toby was nowhere to be found. Someone clutched at her arm, tearing the silk. Someone else tried to get her to join the naked conga line, now in full career around the room. The dancers knocked over a high table lamp with a Buddha-figured base. It fell and glass bulbs broke not far from where Jacquelyn was sitting. A small incident, not worth noticing, but her nerves were at such knife's edge that she shrieked. She seemed to go to pieces, holding herself in with her arms and elbows defensively.

Then that tall man with the gentle voice and charming French accent found her. He was wearing a tuxedo and had not divested himself of any clothing or joined in the exuberant goings-on in the room.

"Is there anyone in particular you're looking for?"

"Toby. Toby Dolan."

He pursed his lips ruefully. "I am afraid I do not know where he has gone."

"Will you take me out of here—please?"

He didn't say a word, but got her wrap from the closet, put it around her and somehow got her out in the hall. The tumult was still going on behind them, but what a relief it was when the door closed and the sounds faded, and she found herself walking along the hallway with the tall man's arm about her. The starched front of his dress shirt crackled with the pressure of her cheek tight against it. She was so grateful to him for having rescued her, and still so frightened and bewildered, that holding close to him was like being in a haven of security and peace.

"Where do you live, mademoiselle?" he asked. "I will take you home."

"No, no, I can't go home."

She could not face the prospect of her empty apartment.

Charles hesitated. "Would you care to come for a while to my place? You can rest and freshen up. Perhaps then you will feel better."

She was apprehensive and a little excited by his offer. Charles divined her mood and smiled.

"It's all right. I am not such an ogre as I seem."

Charles Laurent lived in a small stone house on a rocky cliff above the ocean. They drove out in his car with the top down. The night was cloudy, and when they neared the shore the salt air began to clear her head. She stole glances at the elegant man at the wheel beside her. His profile was patrician, with high, white forehead, long, narrow nose, firm chin, and well-sculpted mouth. His hands on the wheel were casually graceful, with long, narrow palms and long, delicate fingers. She had never met anyone like him before, impeccable, courteous, a real man, not like the boys she had known.

What a child I must seem to him, she thought.

Charles obviously lived alone. The house was small, but the interior was bright and warm, with large framed canvases of bold colors hanging on its walls, with masks and small, primitive, stone sculptures. The floor was of stone too, with scattered Aztec throw rugs. In one corner of the room there was an easel.

"Do you paint?" she asked.

"I dabble," he told her.

She was glad that she did not ask him then what he did for a living. A bit later she found out that he was an actor, rather well-known in his native France, and had been signed to appear in a movie in Hollywood where he would play the other man and lose the girl to Mark Vaughn.

"That's a terrible piece of miscasting," she said.

He had been pouring a glass of wine and tilted the bottle up to look at her with curious amusement.

"I don't think you could ever lose a girl to Mark Vaughn," she explained.

"What a charming thing to say," Charles answered. He finished pouring the wine and brought it to her. "I hope you are feeling better."

"Oh, yes, much better."

She sipped her wine, looking over the rim of her glass at Charles crouching at the fireplace, stirring up a fresh log. Sparks flew. He swung the black iron grate back into place.

"Would you care to hear some music?"

He played a Brahms quartet, and a trumpet concerto by Vivaldi, and "Carmina Burana," an exciting arrangement of medieval chants that pleased her. She tapped her feet to the abrupt wild rhythms. Then he put on a record of someone singing French songs. She did not understand a word, but the man's voice was deep and pleasantly sexy.

"You look tired," he said. "Perhaps I should take you home."

"Not yet," she said. "I'm enjoying myself so much. Who was that singing?"

"I'm afraid it was me."

"Oh, dear." She sat up. "Really?"

He was smiling. "Yes. I am also a singer. Not of the stature of Yves Montand or Jean Sablon but with a small following."

"Can I hear more?"

"Do you really want to?"

"Oh, yes, please."

He turned the record over and she listened now with interest. She liked his masculine voice and the easy, beautiful, tumbling sound of the French language.

"I'm afraid I don't understand French very well. What were you singing about?"

"Love. A man's memories of how beautiful Paris was when he was in love and how everything changed when love was gone." He smiled. "The French don't sing about very much else."

She thought for a moment. "That's true here too. I think all of our popular songs are about love."

The record ended on a rather plaintive saxophone. Charles got up and turned off the hi-fi set.

"Songs do not tell the truth about love," he said. "They pretend it is some kind of magic that solves all problems. It is not like that in life."

He is so wise, she thought. He knows that love is difficult and cruel and somehow always seems to get tangled up with sex. Sex is what the songs leave out.

Charles suddenly said, "You do look tired. Would you like to sleep here tonight? I'll drive you home in the morning."

She hesitated, intrigued but a little afraid because she was sure his invitation was really a cool, understated way of asking more, and she did not know how to respond.

"The guest room is very comfortable." He smiled, almost teasingly.

She liked Charles Laurent. Being with him here was like finding a quiet oasis in the frenzy of this evening, an oasis where fear suddenly vanished.

"Yes, I would like to stay tonight."

He showed her to the guest room behind the foot of the staircase, a small softly-lit room with a fringed Chinese red throw on the bed and a furry black rug underfoot. There were two framed watercolors on the wall, abstracts, and she thought Charles might have painted them.

"The bathroom is that door on the left. Do take a bath if you feel like it. It won't disturb me because my bedroom is upstairs. There's a robe hanging in the closet over there, and you'll find pajamas in the top dresser drawer. They're men's pajamas and much too large for you, but please feel free to use them if you like."

She looked up into his eyes, questioningly, expectantly. In the hush in the room she thought he would lean down to her. She loved that moment before the first kiss. Everything up to that moment is a pavane and then the lovers silently agree to come together. It is a moment heavy with unasked questions.

He turned to leave. "Sleep as late as you want. I'm not an early riser myself. Good night."

He smiled and closed the door behind him.

She had been prepared for a crisis in which a decision

would have to be made that would affect her whole emotional life. Now she was let down, disappointed.

Surely if he hadn't wanted her to stay with him he would not have asked her. Then why did he leave her like this? She decided that he was shy and his courtliness was, in part, a way of disguising it.

She was too tired to take a bath. She undressed quickly, found the freshly laundered pajamas and put on only the top part; they were so large, the pajama jacket fit her like a nightshirt, the bottom reaching halfway down her thigh. The pajamas belonged to Charles and the cool touch of silk on her naked body was almost like his touch. She washed her face and climbed into bed. Just before falling asleep she thought of Charles Laurent sleeping alone in his room and decided he was the nicest man she had ever met.

Sunlight streamed through the windows. At the door to the bedroom she remembered and went back and got her pajama bottoms and put them on. She rolled up the pajama legs into an oversized cuff above her ankles.

She found Charles Laurent in the kitchen pouring coffee into the serving pot.

"Good morning. Did you sleep well?"

She stretched. "I must have. I don't even know what time it is."

"Quarter past ten. I've had juice and was putting up coffee. What would you like? I can make sausages and eggs."

"That sounds lovely. Can I help?"

"You can set the table."

She felt gay and carefree, padding back and forth in morning sunlight to the table on the porch. She carried out tablecloth, napkins, and utensils. In the kitchen there was a delicious odor from the browning sausages in the pan. She felt as though she were playing house, but was pleased that Charles was doing the cooking. She would not have liked to confess that she did not even know how to turn on a gas range.

Before they sat down to breakfast, Charles brought her a robe, a fuzzy brown garment that somewhat overwhelmed her. The sleeves hung down, and she had to be careful to keep them out of the plate of sausages and scrambled eggs when she reached for her coffee. Charles laughed at that and at the picture she made in his robe, and she laughed with him. She felt warm and contented and as though she belonged here.

"How long are you going to stay in Hollywood?" she asked Charles.

"As long as a welcome exists for me. I've only signed to do one picture."

"You'll be wonderful in it."

Charles smiled. "I'm not ambitious. I became an actor because I discovered it was such a ridiculously easy way to make a living."

She was impressed by his nonchalant attitude toward Hollywood, career, stardom. She had been brought up to think of these as ultimate goals, and Charles's ability to accept ultimate goals as only a part of some larger perspective of living made her feel how terribly wise and knowledgeable he was. He must be very talented also.

"Would you mind if I ask a favor?"

"Not at all."

"I'd like to hear your record again. The one you played for me last night. I was too sleepy at the time to appreciate it."

Charles did not answer. He appeared to be listening to something else.

"A car just stopped on the road."

She peeked beyond the projecting wall of the porch and saw who was coming down the rocky path to the cliffside house.

"It's my brother!"

"How did he know you were here?"

"I don't know."

Richard came along the walk beside the wide picture window. She thought: Richard shouldn't find me like this. I ought to go and get dressed. A moment later the doorbell rang.

"I suppose I should let him in," Charles said, with a sigh.

She barely nodded, incapable of any further reaction.

Richard entered the living room.

"Hey, Sis."

"Good morning." She turned to Charles. "Charles, this my brother Richard."

"How do you do," Charles said.

Richard's face seemed devoid of expression. "Mother's hysterical because she wasn't able to get you on the phone all night. I checked with some people who were at the party and they saw you leave with Mr. Laurent. I've had quite a time tracking you down."

Charles said, "She did not want to go back to her apartment. I offered her a place to stay for the night."

"It was an awful party, Richard," Jacquelyn said. "I can't tell you how awful it was . . . and Charles was so kind."

"I'll wait for you here," Richard said. "You'd better get dressed. Mother thinks you've been raped or kidnapped. Or both."

"You have my word as a gentleman . . ." Charles began.

"Listen, what went on here is strictly your business and hers," Richard said, looking at Charles for the first time. Then, to Jacquelyn he said, "Shall we make up a story for Mother, or do you want to read her the Declaration of Independence?"

Jacquelyn hesitated. There was something to be said for telling Mother that from now on she would live her life as she pleased. Yet Mother still controlled her income and could cut off her allowance any time she wanted.

She began to stroke the side of her neck with nervous despondency. "I'm not sure," she said slowly.

"We'll talk about it in the car," Richard said. "You'd better get your clothes on now."

Jacquelyn nodded and hurried to the guest room. When she returned, fully dressed, Richard was standing in the living room, pretending to examine one of the paintings on the wall.

"I don't think Jax appreciates your taste in art," he said. "She goes more for conventional types like Andrew Wyeth."

Charles said, "Wyeth is so accepted that there is nothing for a real artist to do but rebel against him."

"Yeah. He's so well accepted I hear there's a movement afoot to have Congress declare him an official landmark."

Charles chuckled. "I do prefer the moderns. There is such a sense of dash and excitement in their work, if you know what I mean."

"I'm no art critic. I like what I know. Sometimes these modern painters make me feel as though I'm talking to a complete stranger on a crossed telephone line." Richard turned. "Ah, there you are, Jax. Ready to go?"

She came into the room. "Thank you," she told Charles. "Thank you so much . . . for everything."

Charles gave a small bow. Jacquelyn went out the door with Richard, up the walk to where the car waited at the cliff.

"I'm going to tell Mother. I don't care what she thinks, I don't have to explain anything," she said as she got into the front seat of the car.

"You certainly don't," Richard asserted.

Jacquelyn looked at him, startled by something odd in the tone of his voice.

"Our behavior was completely aboveboard, believe it or not."

"I believe it."

"I'm trying to tell you that nothing happened."

"I know."

"How can you?" She was bewildered by his attitude; it didn't make sense.

"I've met Charles."

"He's a perfect gentleman."

"He is that."

There it was—the slightly muffled cynicism she didn't understand.

"You try to make everything sound as though I've been acting like a child."

"Do I?"

"You don't know Charles, how fine he is."

"I can truthfully tell Mother your virtue was in no danger," Richard said, grinning widely. He turned the ignition and shifted into gear.

As the car started forward, Jacquelyn turned for a final look at the slanting roof of the cliffside house, barely visible above the rim of the curving road.

"It might interest you to know that I would have gone to bed with him if he asked me."

"Better luck next time, Jax. You'll have to pick your next . . . seducer . . . a little more carefully." Richard bent forward slightly against the wheel and she saw laughter shaking him as he drove carefully.

She had never been so angry with Richard in her life. She heard herself say an outrageous thing. "I intend to marry him!"

That stopped the laughter, sobered Richard quite as she might have expected. He braked the car to an abrupt halt. "You've just made that up, haven't you? To see if it sounds like fun."

Suddenly it was a lovely idea to be engaged, to be

faithful to a man who would in turn be faithful to her. They could be engaged for as long as they liked, and then break the engagement. It lent a kind of legitimacy to lovemaking and she was quite sure what making love with Charles Laurent would be like. He was so gallant, such a gentleman, yet so sophisticated and experienced.

"Don't you believe people can fall in love at first sight?" she asked.

"I find it pretty hard to understand how Charles Laurent could kick up a dust storm in your libido."

"I don't like you making fun of the man I'm going to marry—or about my feeling for him."

On the brown hillside, clusters of low yucca, greasewood, sumac, and dwarf oak grew on the scorched dry earth. She felt a sympathy with those tough-fibered, water-starved plants, fighting to grow, storing up in their branches the highly combustible oil that was necessary for them to survive. After a time they became like tinder, and the smallest lick of flame could set them blazing.

Richard scowled. "Don't start being contrary, Jax. You can probably get any man you want. You're beautiful enough. But marriage isn't a game. You have to be awfully sure of what you're doing."

She stared ahead. "I'm awfully sure," she said stubbornly.

She was married to Charles Laurent three months later. When Charles proposed, he was very serious, not like his usual, ironic, detached self at all, and his sincerity brought tears to her eyes. She desperately wanted to marry him. On the few occasions he had made physical overtures he had shown himself to be well-versed in the art of arousing a woman, but each time he brought her to the brink, willing and shamelessly eager, he drew back as though frightened. He knew that she was a virgin and even in the midst of her frustration she appreciated the limits he set on gentlemanly ardor. There was something reassuring about a man who had himself under such control.

They chose a small Episcopalian chapel for the wedding. Jacquelyn wore a simple dress and a mantilla, both of white lace. She had every reason to wear white, she thought. Mother wept because she looked incredibly beautiful. Outside the chapel thousands of spectators waited, flowing across the street and into fields and driveways of

houses like a patient black lava. There were police barricades and hordes of policemen on duty. Within the cleared-
off area before the chapel a police car waited, and
occasionally a mounted officer rode up nervously. The
limousines bringing the wedding guests crawled in through
the close-packed multitude with a motorcycle police escort.

The roar as Jacquelyn emerged from her limousine
swelled in volume and cascaded from walls and roofs of
adjoining houses, multiplying until the noise was deafening. Jacquelyn smiled and smiled, full of love for all.

She remembered clearly only the moment when the
minister asked, "Do you take this man . . . ?"

"I do," she said, and repeated the vow to Charles later
that evening in their hotel suite, after a quiet dinner of
cold capon and champagne. Her heart was beating rapidly
in expectation of the long night of love before her. She
was cuddling in his arms, and Charles kissed her as expertly as always, long, deep, searching kisses that left her
feeling almost paralyzed. The soft pressure of his hand on
her body, here, there, started the hot ache mounting.
Clinging to him, she had never felt such excitement. She
wanted to be ravished. She was prepared to cast off shame
and even to know pain within the pleasure to come.

Then, with relief, she felt him move, saw his lean,
muscled, tan nakedness above her, and thought how shattering it was to be so at the mercy of a man.

At last he entered her. It hurt, but the pain did not
surprise her; she was ready for it. She made a small
sound, and spread her legs apart to receive him. She
closed her eyes and waited. Her back felt rigid with
expectancy. It was going to strike now, that overwhelming
feeling. She was ready to be rent by it, to contain an
experience that would be a revelation and a release.

It was over.

Curled close beside him, his arm laxly beneath her and
over her shoulder, she could not help feeling that the thrill
must still be hovering somewhere near. It had escaped
her. The vibrations of recent passion were dying along the
pathway of her nerves but were not quite gone. She was
not even much changed. She was deadened, then filled
with a sharp anguish. What had she done wrong? Charles
did not seem dissatisfied. He was lying with his eyes closed
and a slight smile on his face. Was this all? She had felt

almost nothing. It could not be all. There seemed to be so much feeling left in her. So much.

A thought jumped out of her mind: *Next time it will be different.*

After a brief honeymoon in La Jolla, they moved into his house. Jacquelyn wanted a home of her own and could not become used to a place where all the decisions of decorating and planning had been made. Charles had exquisite judgment, but she was not happy to rely on it. When she made new suggestions, for a different nubby kind of drapery at the windows instead of the heavy silk, for a new tub-shaped living room chair, or tall vase-shaped lamps instead of the colorful pottery type that Charles had, he was very kind to her, almost fatherly. On the occasion when, in a fit of temper, she insisted on bringing in a period sofa to replace the severely functional one in the living room, he let her have her way. It was a mistake. The sofa didn't go with anything. She put up with it for two days, trying to persuade herself she would get used to it, and one night she simply broke into tears. Charles comforted her. The following day the period sofa was gone and the old one was back.

Often standing in the kitchen (where Charles did the cooking) she would stare out the window toward the beach and think how dear he was. Sitting across from him at the dinner table, she felt comfortable. At parties, he was the perfect escort, attentive, handsome, intelligent, amusing. She knew that many women envied her. Only at times did the fleeting thought enter her head, usually on those evenings when they were going to make love, of how another man, less considerate, less tender than Charles, might make her feel. Most of the time she doubted there would be any difference. Sex was an overwhelming experience only in books, or in the extravagant tales of liars.

Charles took over as her financial and business adviser. When the lawyers or accountants called, they always spoke to Charles and later he would explain the intricacies of the deals being offered to her. Fortunately he had plenty of time for her business affairs; his own career seemed to have hit an air pocket. After his first movie, there were no other offers. It was a little strange, because she found Charles by far the best thing in the movie, although he did not appear as handsome on screen as in real life. His chin seemed a little weak, and he did not quite fit the established mode of Hollywood leading men. Also, his manner was too light and his air of ironic sophistication too cool for women who preferred more soulful lovers. It didn't help Charles that his one movie was a dismal box office failure.

For the most part they lived quietly, enjoying the company of only a few close friends. Toby Dolan came often to see them, and he and Charles got on famously; one evening during the week before Christmas Toby brought Christopher Leigh with him. They all draped tinsel on the sixteen-foot tree and hung holly and pine cones from Tiffany glass chandeliers. Christopher was an intense, very handsome young man with a rooted antipathy toward Hollywood and all its ways, a devotion to his Art, and a personality that generated a peculiar moody kind of electricity. He was on the launching pad for a spectacular rise to stardom. Everyone agreed nothing could stop him. His very first movie, a high-budgeted Western, made him famous, although he did not know which end of a horse was which. He had even forced a fine performance out of the huge, ramshackle, aging star, veteran of a hundred Westerns, whom people in Hollywood affectionately called The Mountain because of his immense size and granite appearance. Playing opposite Christopher, whom he hated, The Mountain projected a kind of smoldering antagonism which fit perfectly into the story of the rivalry between an old cattle baron and a young gunfighter. The movie made millions, and Christopher Leigh promptly left Hollywood to appear in a dolorous Broadway tragedy which became box office because everyone wanted to see him. The heads of every Hollywood studio offered him fabulous sums to come back for another movie. While Christopher was visiting them, he was considering half a dozen offers and was continually making insulting remarks about the level of Hollywood creative talent. Charles found him delightful, Toby roared, but Jacquelyn resented Christopher's easy assumption of superiority and his disdain for the standards of excellence she had been taught to accept. It made her feel inferior. She was not articulate enough to argue with Christopher, and she became withdrawn, almost silent in his company.

When she was offered the starring role in *Furious Thunder,* a Civil War romance, Charles read the script and advised her to refuse it.

Henry Orrin called the next day. "You're making a mistake, dear. Take my word for it—*Furious Thunder* is going to be one of the big grossers. It'll make millions. Have I ever lied to you? It's a wonderful role."

"Charles thinks I ought to have a chance to show what I can do as a dramatic actress."

"Does he know this business better than me? Besides, you can't win a fight with the studio, Jackie. No star is that big."

"I don't want to fight with anybody. But I have to do what I think is best for me."

Henry Orrin's voice lost its friendliness. "If you don't take the script, I'll have to suspend you from salary."

"You can't force me to do anything I don't want to."

Jacquelyn had never learned to limit her spending, always lived up to the dollar whatever did not go into the trust fund set up by Mother. A few weeks after the studio suspended her, her cash reserves dwindled to the danger point and Charles was unable to help because he was not working.

One evening she went to a party at Chasen's where Charles got into animated conversation with a tall, lean, distinguished-looking man. Jacquelyn drifted over to hear Charles recounting her current difficulties with the studio.

"Jacquelyn, dear," Charles said, introducing her, "I'm sure you've heard of Meyer Whitney."

"Of course." Jacquelyn smiled at him even as she studied him with dislike. One of the famous Whitney brothers, the best looking, and the one with a reputation as a bon vivant. He had the arrogant manner of a man too sure of his power and attractiveness. Probably cut quite a swathe with the ladies. She tried vaguely to recall a story she had heard about this youngest of the powerful Whitney brothers. Oh, yes. He and the wife of a leading symphony conductor. It had happened before Jacquelyn was born, but the romance had been rather notorious in its time. The wife was a woman in her fifties—and young Meyer scarcely more than twenty. The scandal ended when the husband was chosen to be the permanent conductor of the Berlin Symphony—a post, rumor had it, arranged for him. Afterward Meyer went on to a succession of romances, frequented the races, and became known for hosting the most fashionable parties in London and Paris.

Charles continued with his discussion of the script's failings, but Meyer now seemed interested in Jacquelyn.

"It does seem a shame," he said to her finally.

"What does?"

"That you're being kept off the screen. I've only seen you in one picture, but yours is the kind of beauty no one forgets. I'm sure your fans miss you."

"I'm not sure how long they will," Jacquelyn said candidly. "Movie fans are famous for their short memories."

Charles said, "I gave the script to Christopher Leigh to read. He called it a giant marshmallow, a *Gone with the Breeze.*" Charles laughed. "It's a magnified soap opera. Christopher even suggested a title for it. *Abraham Lincoln's Other Wife.*"

Meyer Whitney smiled politely. "It's sometimes difficult to estimate a motion picture's value from reading the script. You can't allow personal taste to rule. I wouldn't be surprised if *Furious Thunder* makes a lot of money."

"Why do you think so?" Jacquelyn asked, surprised.

"It has everything the public likes," Meyer turned to Charles. "I'm having dinner with Henry Orrin tomorrow. If you like, I'll recommend a settlement to him."

"On what terms?"

"Jacquelyn will agree to appear in the movie. And she'll get a new contract, with a much better financial deal."

Charles hesitated. "Do you think Henry Orrin would agree?"

"I can't guarantee it. But I am the largest stockholder in Mammoth Studios."

"We'll think about it," Charles answered dubiously.

When they arrived home that evening, Jacquelyn and Charles quarreled because she thought she should accept Meyer Whitney's offer immediately. They needed the money, and Meyer Whitney was probably right about *Furious Thunder*'s box office potential.

"The trouble with you is you think you're smarter than anyone in Hollywood. Well, I've seen those foreign pictures you like and I think they stink. Arty-farty little pictures that look like they were made in a closet! I don't blame people for not going to see them. Why should anyone pay to see a bunch of degenerates sitting around analyzing each other?"

Her voice, as usual, became shrill in the upper registers. She was unable to control it when she became angry.

Charles answered mildly, "Darling, there is no reason for anyone to get excited."

"You ought to have learned by now that Hollywood can get along without you a lot easier than you can get along without Hollywood!"

She wished she could say more cruel and cutting things— oh, the damnable poverty of the words she knew!—but she could not trust her voice. She hurried out of the room.

A few minutes later, when Charles joined her, she was lying face down on the bed with fingers clutching a pillow. Charles sat beside her.

"Something is troubling you. What is it, darling?"

She turned on the bed to face him. "I went to the doctor this afternoon."

Instantly concerned, "You're not ill?"

She shook her head, partly to deny and partly to keep tears from starting.

"You don't mean that night, a few weeks ago . . . when . . . ?"

She nodded bitterly. "It's my fault. I didn't want to be careful. I made you do it."

Charles put his arms about her and held her. "This is wonderful news, darling."

"No, it isn't. I don't . . . want . . . to have a . . . baby . . ."

The final words became elongated on the breath preceding tears. Why had she done it? She had secretly hoped it might bring Charles and her closer together, untie them in a mystic way. What an idiot she had been!

Charles kissed her hair. "It's going to be all right. You'll see."

She began sobbing, and Charles, vainly trying to soothe her, said that they would, of course, accept the terms that Meyer Whitney suggested. But by then she was not crying about their financial difficulties. She bitterly regretted that she had allowed him to make love to her without precautions. A baby was in the making. I'm only twenty years old, much too young. She imagined herself as she would appear, months from now, swollen and ugly, carrying out the final act of a hateful schedule. She would become a dowdy woman, smelling of milk and urine, curdling with hostility toward the mewling pink bundle of life she had created. She had been so unencumbered, so perfect—and now all that was over. She could no longer pretend to be a young girl. She would suffer the nearly total obliteration of motherhood.

Charles sat up with her until three o'clock in the morning. She cried all the time.

On the morning after the telephone call from her mother, while getting dressed in her villa at Rio, Jacquelyn came to exactly the same conclusion she had before. It was not in Charles Laurent's nature to take hasty impulsive action.

But he had kidnapped their son. Something had obviously provoked him to do this unimaginable thing. What was it?

A soft knock on the door.

"Come in."

Janet looked in. "Oh, you're awake!"

"I can't sleep. I've been going over and over this whole terrible thing in my mind and I just can't make any sense out of it."

Janet came in and sat down in a chair near the bed. "Have you thought that Charles might have done it simply for publicity?"

"Never. There've been too many chances for that over the years. The furthest he went was to allow a book to be ghostwritten for him. *My Life with Jacquelyn Stuart*. It was a flop because he couldn't bring himself to say anything indiscreet."

"He must have had some reason."

Her whole body was pounding until she was sure she would explode. "I keep trying to imagine where Gene is this minute. What he's thinking."

"He's probably not worried. He's with his father. I'm sure Charles made up some reasonable excuse for taking him out of school."

"I always call him. Every week. When I don't make my regular phone call, he'll begin to wonder. He'll ask questions. He'll demand to talk to me. Or Brian. He loves Brian so. More than he ever loved Charles. How will Charles react to that?"

Anxiety, born of self-inflicted suspense, began to take full possession of her.

"Something has to be done," she said, pacing the room. "It has to be done *soon!*"

"Isn't your lawyer going to call?"

"Yes. Yes, that's right." When Arthur Eakam called with definite news, she would act. What could she do? It would accomplish nothing to fly to New York. Gene wasn't there. Charles would never have taken him to New York.

"I don't know what to do," she said. "If I stay here waiting for the telephone to ring, I'll go mad."

"You know what? Finish dressing and be ready when the car comes to pick you up at seven thirty."

"What's the point? I can't work."

"It's the best way to keep your mind off things."

"Suppose someone calls with news?"

"I'll have the call put through directly to you at location."

Jacquelyn moved about the room restlessly.

"You're right," she said finally. "I'll feel better being around people. Just be sure to relay any calls to me as soon as they come through."

All that morning, waiting for shooting to start on *Death of a Peacock*, Jacquelyn felt a terrible constriction in her throat. She was playing the wife of a Brazilian general who falls in love with a fiery young revolutionist who later turns out to be a homosexual. In a climactic scene, her revolutionist lover, played by Ross Hamilton, leads an attack on the general's home in which her two children are killed. This had overtones for Jacquelyn that did nothing to quiet her nerves.

They had chosen a hilly region outside the city for the first day's shooting. The first day of a motion picture production was like the opening night at a theater. Everything that went before was a rehearsal in which problems were talked over, solutions proposed, and the action blocked out, planned.

She listened abstractedly as H. T. Wallace, wearing a khaki shirt and white duck trousers with open sandals, flipped through mimeographed pages of the script to talk about scenes he hoped to complete that day.

The first scene to be shot, number Forty-one, read:

Medium-Long Shot—New Angle
Diana and her lover Philip slowly mount the hill
to the spot where they first met.

While Jacquelyn discussed the scene with Wallace, an assistant director nearby was writing in a hard-covered notebook. Every detail of the day's shooting, from the first trip by car to the location, to the placing of equipment and unloading of the trucks, and to lining up the shots would be entered in the notebook which would be submitted to the producer, and forwarded by him to the headquarters of Mammoth Studios in Hollywood.

"We'll run it through without film just to see how it looks," H. T. said. "Okay, Jacquelyn?"

She didn't hear him. When he raised his voice, she jumped a little. "What?"

H. T. repeated himself with elaborate patience. "Okay? You got it this time?"

"Sure. Fine."

The people on the set were all known to her, familiar faces, but nothing allayed the fear that had localized as a tightness in her throat. She had a foreboding about the next telephone call. She looked nervously over toward the trailer that was H. T. Wallace's office and that contained a portable radiophone. There was no sign of anyone coming out of the trailer with a message.

They rehearsed the scene of climbing the hill. H. T. Wallace told her to pause at the top, and look down at the view. Then he moved to the camera and watched as she and Ross Hamilton, playing her lover, began the climb. At the midway point, an assistant with a loudspeaker box on his shoulder brought a microphone to Wallace, who continued to give instructions through the mike.

"All right," he called as they reached the top, "that looks fine. Come on down again and we'll start shooting it."

"Better tell the prop men to move some of that cactus out. It's sticking me right in the crotch," Jacquelyn told him when she came down.

The prop men hurriedly complied, moving up the path with clippers to snip the offending cactus, and after that the scene went smoothly. They moved on to scene Ninety-four, in which she discussed with the village priest whether she should continue to see her lover. In the middle of the first take, H. T. called "Cut!" because there was a shadow on Jacquelyn's chin. He moved her about two feet to the left. On the second take H. T. was dissatisfied because he wanted a new angle on the dolly. On the third take, he thought that Jacquelyn looked too perspiry, and then objected to putting too much white powder on her face. The fourth take went through without interruption, but H. T. thought he liked the second one better, reserving decision until he could look at them both in the projection room. Scene Eighty-three followed—some footage of cars arriving from which, in later shooting, Jacquelyn, her lover, and the village priest would be seen to emerge. These car arrivals occurred at widely separated places in the script but would later be spliced in where necessary.

While the car scenes were being shot, Jacquelyn retired to the sidelines to soothe her nerves with Scotch and a game of gin rummy with H. T. and the still cameraman, while they discussed the kind of photographs that should be taken for publicity purposes. These included poses in which she would wear a revealing, partly unbuttoned white blouse and would be full length on the grass with her skirt carefully hiked to an interesting angle and a long stalk of grass between her teeth.

"I've done that one a thousand times," Jacquelyn said. "I'm getting grass stains on my teeth."

All photographs taken would be approved by her before publication.

Jacquelyn asked H. T. what time it was.

"Nearly ten thirty. You've got the next hour off, sweetie. I've got to give the crew some idea of what I think the big confrontation scenes are in this movie. Helps their morale if they figure out how some of this footage we're taking fits into the finished picture."

She spent most of the hour hovering near the trailer truck, waiting for the telephone to ring. Nothing happened. She waited until the last possible moment. She was the star and didn't have to appear on the site until everyone else was ready.

When she returned, H. T. Wallace set up the cameras for shooting scene Thirty-nine, in which the village priest would notice a jangly bracelet Jacquelyn was wearing which was a gift from her lover. H. T. explained briefly where she should move and where he was going to cut. The camera would finally swing around in a closeup of Jacquelyn's face.

"Another closeup!" Jacquelyn sighed. "Having that camera on my face all the time is like getting raped."

"That's what the customers pay for," H. T. said. "Your face and your mammary glands."

"I ought to make a picture in Cinerama sometime and really give them their money's worth. Two-hundred-foot tits," Jacquelyn said.

She was weary of the old, old tricks. They seemed to have a special meaninglessness today and she could barely restrain her venom. Her mood didn't improve during repeated takes of the scene, one because of a bad angle of sunlight and shadow, another because Jacquelyn muffed a line, a third because a rabbit raced across the field in back, a fourth because a plane appeared in the sky. On the fifth, H. T. Wallace finally nodded and said, "Okay. Print it."

At twelve thirty, the temperature was hovering around a hundred degrees, and H. T. called a lunch break. Over cold cuts, potato salad, and soda he sat with his cheek cupped in one hand.

"It just occurred to me," he said, "that the cost of the half day's shooting we just finished is about seventy thousand dollars. Enough to support the average American family for nearly fifteen years."

"It seems a terrible waste of money," Jacquelyn remarked.

H. T.'s small, round, apple-hard face squinted at her. "Not at all. My dear, did you ever attend a rehearsal by Toscanini?"

"No."

"Fortunately I did, about ten years ago. I can't remember how many times he went back over a single passage. Made the orchestra play it again and again until he found the sounds he wanted. It was a great experience. Since then I've figured that if Toscanini can go back so many times in search of perfection I could do it too."

There was no overestimating the egocentricity of movie directors, and Jacquelyn could forgive their frequent posturing and strutting. But she was in no mood for it today. Her son Gene was missing, she knew not where, caught in some spider's web. Oh, it was easy enough to tell herself Charles would not harm him. But how did she know? Charles had surprised her with this rash action—could he not surprise her with another, even more desperate and dangerous? She blamed herself—because if it had not been for her neglect, none of this could have happened. How she regretted it! How many times she had berated herself in the past few hours! An awful, awful thing had happened and the worst was that she could see her own role, her guilt, all too plainly.

"Oh, for Christ's sake, H. T.," she said bitterly. "You're not comparing yourself with an artist like Toscanini, are you?"

There were shocked faces at the luncheon table. Jacquelyn was doing the thing which, by common consent, no one in this business ever did. It was too easy to strip off the skin of a fellow worker and show the nakedness of his creative bones.

H. T. said weakly, "Well, we're working in different mediums, but . . ."

"You're not in the same class."

H. T. managed a sickly shrug, as though to reconcile himself to the attack, to limit the damage, and to recoup the loss as gracefully as he could.

"Well, my last movie grossed seventeen million dollars. That's a lot more than Toscanini ever took in for a concert."

His last movie, *Town Without Shame,* had to do with a small New England town that was practically a volcano of incest, rape, sodomy, sadism, murder, mutilation—with a little necrophilia thrown in for good measure. It had a Moral. A young boy, a cripple, became the focal point around which all the forces for good in the town gathered, forces that eventually rid the place of incest, rape, sodomy, sadism, murder, mutilation—and even necrophilia. The one hundred and eight minutes of the movie bulged with the sort of incident that would never have been allowed on the screen except for the Moral.

"You call that movie artistic?" Jacquelyn asked.

H. T. nodded in a way that seemed to ask her not to go any further.

"Toscanini could do better by sticking his baton up his ass," Jacquelyn observed.

H. T. sighed unhappily and gave Jacquelyn a wounded look. It was clear that he would not be rude in return. He looked at his watch, and in a quiet voice told his technical advisers and the head cameraman that they would leave directly after lunch in order to scout the countryside to find a place to put up a standing set.

"Why don't you go home and rest?" H. T. suggested to Jacquelyn. "This heat is terrible. You've been a good trooper but you don't want to overdo things. Frankly, sweetie, you've been looking down in the mouth all day."

Twenty minutes after the car deposited her back at the villa the telephone call came through from Arthur Eakam.

"I know how worried you must be. I didn't want to call until I had something definite to report. I think I have some good news now."

"You've found Gene!"

"We know where he is. Charles has taken him back to London. They're staying at the Grosvenor House."

"London!"

"I tried to get Charles on the phone there to find out what this is all about. He either isn't in or he won't talk to me."

"I don't care about Charles. I want my son back. He didn't have any legal right to do it. I was awarded custody of Gene, and Charles knows that goddamn well."

"I will point that out to him, very forcefully. Leave this to me, Jacquelyn."

"What are you going to do?"

"Everything must wait until I talk to Charles. Until I know why he took the boy . . ."

"I don't want to wait. Charles may be planning anything. I'm not going to feel safe until I've got Gene back, either in school or here with me."

"If necessary, we'll bring legal action . . ."

"How long will that take?"

"Hard to say. I hope it won't come to that. I think I can persuade Charles to listen to reason."

"What's going to happen to Gene in the meantime?"

"I'm sure he'll be safe."

"I want my son back."

"It isn't quite that easy, Jacquelyn. In the first place, Charles is in England and beyond the reach of our laws. I don't say we can't bring pressure to bear, but then there's the publicity to consider. I'm sure we want to avoid that, for your sake and for the sake of young Gene. It's best to take a little longer and to work behind the scenes, quietly, to get the result we want."

She waited, stiffly resistant, staring at the mouthpiece.

"Arthur, you don't understand. Get him back any god-damn way you can!"

After she hung up, slowly, very slowly, her temper began to subside.

Charles was in London with Gene, beyond the grasp of the ponderous machinery of law in which Arthur Eakam put his naïve faith. If Charles was adamant there were doubtless measures that Arthur would undertake to bring him to some sort of accounting. But those measures would take time, and there were other things Charles might do in the meantime. He might leave England, and take Gene with him.

She thought of calling Charles directly, and went as far as to lift the telephone to do it. She held the phone in her hand as she considered the possibilities. Charles had refused to speak to Arthur Eakam, and would probably do the same to her. If she did speak to him, whatever reason he gave for his rash act would undoubtedly cause her to lose her temper and threaten him. Threats would only cause him to take alarm.

Whatever was done had to be done quickly, surreptitiously, dramatically. Gene had to be taken away from Charles, if necessary by force. . . . But how? She knew no one in England willing to undertake such a venturesome assignment.

Or did she?

The operator's voice was inquiring impatiently, "Do you wish to place a call?"

"Yes, please. I'd like to make a long distance call to London. To Mr. Brian O'Neal."

CHAPTER NINE

It's no wonder the horse and jaunty cart have survived so long in Ireland, Brian O'Neal thought bitterly, when you consider the way the trains run. He had been traveling for hours and the train would get into Dublin at six thirty-five in the morning. He would never have taken a bloody train in the first place if it were not for fog blanketing the airport at London and the dampness at Dublin. The Irish always called it dampness when it was a downpour and a soft mist when the heavens poured down wrath.

Meanwhile, sitting in a first-class compartment all to himself, with the blinds drawn on the corridor, Brian was whiling away dead time in a manner Irishmen had done for centuries. He was getting drunk and reading poetry. He was, to be truthful, also getting a little drunk on the poetry of Stephen Innis. A blastit wonner. The mad way the man used words was enough to make the stomach growl and the head empty itself out with delight.

Brian would have liked more than anything else in the world to be a sad, mad, bad, glad poet like Stephen. But there was no sense grieving over what was forbidden to him. The poets were the great men. It was a bit difficult to think of future generations worshiping a lecherous bard like Stephen, his friend and fellow drinker, but that would happen. Stephen, the real Stephen, would be lost in his own poetry. Ah, there's a tomb worth cirrhosis of the liver. Brian emptied his glass and reached down to get the bottle from the floor.

He read aloud in a booming voice:

"Lovers spawn by the sea, joining green solemn
Life as they burrow deep from gulls

178

And hollow quicksand with the salt imprint
Of hard bodies."

When the train pulled into Dublin he was barely able to weave onto the platform. He left the luggage for the porter, and the porter brought the wrong luggage and had to go back; then the porter lost him; then he lost the porter. Everything was going as usual in Dublin.

By the clock it was seven forty-six when he left the terminal. That was not half as alarming as it seemed. The clock was at least forty minutes fast.

"It's a soft day," said the taxi driver, a fine upstanding bald man named O'Rourke, who had the build of a wrestler and a handclasp like an ironworker. He crushed Brian's hand and wrestled the luggage onto the rack atop the high-riding black taxi which doubtless did double duty at many a fine funeral. He covered the luggage with oil skin.

A barn flashed by, high-piled with hay, with cattle grazing in the field beyond. O'Rourke began to sing. After a minute Brian sang along:

"My mother said that I never should
Play with the gypsies in the wood,
The wood was dark; the grass was green;
In came Sally with a tambourine."

A round pile of stones loomed. The home of fairy folk who disappeared somewhere within the circle whenever their enemies showed up. Probably they were Druids, if the legend had truth (and all legends had some truth), but to the Irish they would always be the fairy folk. He knew himself that there were such creatures, for Old Billy had seen with his own eyes a thatched hut, reputed to be their home, that was marked for destruction, except the bulldozer kept going off the road as it approached the house to do its leveling work. Finally driver and machine ended up in a ditch. If that was not the fairy folk's doing, Old Billy asked, what was it? Brian had no answer for him. Either you had faith in the fairy folk or you did not.

The Druid's circle was about four miles south of the one-street village where his father lived, a slender, white-haired old man with serious blue eyes and a gravely comical expression on his thin, well-boned face. Brian felt his anticipations rising to a high point.

"About ten minutes to go, sir," O'Rourke said. "Aghalee is the next village."

"Yes," Brian said. "I know."

He was an exile, but not that much of a stranger. Aghalee was home, and would be home no matter how far he roamed. He thought of explaining that to O'Rourke and decided it was not necessary. O'Rourke was Irish. The O' before his name meant descendant of, even as a Mc would mean the son of, and it was not needed to tell an Irishman about home. Brian was about to ask O'Rourke if he was related to the O'Rourkes who lived near Kinvarra, who once owned the McDraik castle on the banks of the Dunkellin River. But the softness of the day lifted and he saw in a flash of sun a narrow stream that ran down by Clondalkin, speeding between muddy banks. As a boy he had taken up his stand on that stream and waited for fish that hardly ever came. He had stood for hours then and hardly been aware of it. Now his legs felt cramped just from riding in the back of the taxi.

Oh, what a cold wet morning. A pull and a caress on the heartstrings.

One hell of a glorious day.

"Brannigan is dead," Old Billy said. "Went down of a thundering stroke last week on a Monday. I tell you, boy, when the years rain down, a man gets up to meet each new day with a prayer of thanksgiving."

Old Billy wore a faded red houserobe over pajamas and had on a pair of scuffed old slippers. His thin face seemed thinner and the cheeks were sunk in, but the blue eyes still snapped.

"You've got a number of years yet, Old Billy."

"I wouldn't count on it. You know Kevin McGrath? He was taking his grandson to school a few weeks back and toppled right off the cart into the road. Frothing at the mouth, they say. Gone in a twinkle of an eye."

Brian spooned up oatmeal from the bowl on the round wooden table. The floor of the cottage was of stone, and peat was burning in the fireplace. Nothing had changed.

A strong gust of wind keened at the windows and the glass pane rattled.

"Isn't it a soft day?" Old Billy asked.

"You don't have to sound so damn cheerful about it," Brian said, and finished up the dish of oatmeal.

"It's fixing up to be a real fine afternoon," Old Billy predicted.

"Is Stephen Innis in town? I heard he might be."

Old Billy said, "I saw him at Flanahan's pub last night. He had a sober expression on his face. It was the only thing sober I noticed."

"I was reading him on the train. He's a better poet than Yeats."

"Ah, lad your taste is all in your feet. But no matter. I'm too old to argue with the vulgar as I used to. By the bye, while I was in Flanahan's I'm told there was a phone call for you from London. They left a number for you to call back."

"I'll have a drink there later on. It's probably from my new lady friend."

"Tell me something about her. Is she as pretty as the last?"

"They're different." He told his father about Merrill Yeaton, enlarging upon her qualities.

"And how is it between the sheets?" Old Billy asked. "The last one seemed right in that department. A man could attempt astonishing things with a woman like that and bring them off. She had the proper proportions—a physical intelligence, y'know? Plus the face of the Virgin Mary and a look in her eye that promised a good deal of technical virtuosity."

"You're a dirty-mouthed old man, Old Billy."

"I am," Old Billy replied with satisfaction. "We have a lot of despicable qualities in common, eh lad? We like jolly cuddly girls who indulge a man and know exactly how to behave when working on a new part. Your other one was like that. This one may need a bit of instruction. Make her do her exercises faithfully in bed half an hour each morning. It's essential to stoke up her faith in her own equipment. And it kills both the bird in the bush and the bird in the hand." Old Billy whinnied.

"You've gotten worse, I think."

"No worse. No worse. I am as I was. Age encourages a quiet withdrawal into the obscene intimacy of thought."

"I'll bet you can still hold up your end with women."

"Maybe so. But the lasses don't want an old man. They look for young bucks like you. Take it where you can, boy, and without too much thinking. Go straight at it, on instinct, and women will thank you for it. They like a clever man to talk to, but in the bedroom they want muscles. Don't ever let this Merrill woman get the upper hand of you. Pay no respect to her money. She'll use that to castrate you. You'll sing falsetto before the first year of marriage is over. Don't turn against your sex. We're men, and we have to play the part of men."

"She won't get the better of me, Old Billy."

Old Billy shook his head and pulled his red robe close about his narrow chest. The peat fire had dropped low, and a chill invaded the low-ceilinged room.

"I wish I were twenty years younger," he said. "I'd have a go at the other. I've a part I could play to the dear girl's entire satisfaction. You're a woolly lad, Brian, with horn enough for a goat, but you have all this bother in your head that gets into the way of your loving a woman. It gives you terrible doubts as to what you want. This Merrill woman may have all the other things you're after and be deficient in the arts the other one knows. Such a woman is dead from the word go and will only play live until she gets her hook in your mouth."

In Flanahan's pub, Emmet McCluskey, the bartender, said he had heard nothing of a telephone call.

"Long distance, was it?" Emmet asked, with his head on one side.

"That's right. From London."

"Michael Casey was on duty then. He'd know."

"Where can I find him?"

"Home asleep."

"A lot of good that does me."

"He has five children," Emmet said. "The poor man needs his sleep."

"Did he leave a number for me to call?"

"He never told me anything. Whiskey?"

"Jameson," Brian said.

"Did you find out who called?" Stephen Innis asked when he brought the drinks back to the table.

"It was probably Merrill."

Stephen shook his head. "Breathing down your neck already? Poor lad." He hoisted his glass. "I don't think Old Billy will approve of her. Not after Jacquelyn."

"You may be right."

"Your dear father was fair gone on Jacquelyn. Especially after the episode in the Cuchulain burying ground. He told me once it proved that you were getting ahead in the world if you'd earned the right to bed down such a handsome colleen. I had the clear impression Old Billy would have liked nothing better than to bed down Jacquelyn himself."

"My father's a monster. I never denied it."

A soft day. Beyond the streaming windows of the pub Brian could see nothing at all.

"There was a lot of the peasant in her," Stephen mused. "There isn't much of that in Merrill. She's a person of consequence and knows too many people of consequence. Strikes me as the sort who would take an interest in world news."

"She does."

"Her worries will show. Pretty women should never read newspapers. It makes wrinkles."

"Do you read newspapers?"

"I don't need to be told what to think of governments, the army and navy, diplomats, or moneychangers. All I ask of grafters is that they have a bit of style."

"Let's drink to that," Brian said.

They finished their glasses together.

"I'll stand another round." Brian signaled to the bar.

Emmet McCluskey came over with two Jamesons on a tray.

"Would this be what you're looking for?" he asked, and showed Brian a slip of paper with a number. "Michael Casey left it stuck in the cash register."

"It's a London number."

"You might as well try it," Stephen said.

Brian called the number and got Lester Mitchell who told him that Jacquelyn had called the studio.

"She sounded worried. She asked me to get in touch with you and to have you call her."

"Thanks, Lester. How does the weather look?"

"Still pouring. Enjoy your holiday. There won't be any outdoor shooting for another day or two."

Lester gave him Jacquelyn's telephone number, and Brian called the local operator and repeated it to her.

"Glory to God," said the operator. "A call to Rio de Janeiro in Brazil. I don't know for certain that there are lines up. I'll have to look up the charges."

"Make it person to person," Brian said. "Collect."

There was a good deal of fluster for a few minutes. He heard voices dimly as the operator conferred with other operators.

Then she came back. "The circuits are busy. It'll be forty minutes."

"Call me back. I'll be at Flanahan's pub in Aghalee."

When he returned to the table Stephen had disappeared and the door to the men's room was swinging. He recalled the time he had brought Jacquelyn to Flanahan's pub and they had argued politics with that Protestant blackguard from Ulster. They had laid the Ulsterman waste with Jacquelyn firing eyes from the north and him cross-firing logic from the south. Jacquelyn used her trick of seeming to listen attentively while leaning slightly forward and letting the Ulsterman have a view of her boobs. The poor fool's tongue had grown sticky and Brian had descended on him with the full force of his socialist convictions. It had been a rout.

Of course they had quarreled too. She had a stubborn streak in her and wouldn't give in even if she shook the pillars of matrimony. There had been wild battles about his staying married to Fabia. Jacquelyn felt she wasn't being properly appreciated. She didn't care about the ring or the ceremony, but she resented the presence of Fabia in his thoughts. Once when he happened to remark that a pretty woman in a white coat looked like Fabia, Jacquelyn struck back in a fury. She went to the hotel and got her things and set off in a jaunty cart for the airport. It happened while he waited at the pub with Old Billy for her to lick her wounds and come back to apologize. What a damn fool he'd felt when the jailkeeper, Paddy Brennan, had come into the pub to ask if it wasn't his girl friend he had seen take off from the hotel in Purlie Higgins's cart. There was no mistaking Jacquelyn from the poetic glow with which Paddy described her. But he called the hotel to be sure, and damn, she was gone. He vacillated whether to have a pint and forget her, but Old Billy, pouring at the bar, would have none of that. He wouldn't serve anyone, Old Billy said, who was such a blithering donkey as to lose a good woman for lack of disciplining. She'll never learn by running away, Old Billy argued, whereas you go and bring her back and give her a good hiding and she'll never open her mouth to you again unless it's for something you want to put in.

"I've got my jeep outside," Paddy Brennan volunteered. "She's running, though she won't budge out of second. Take it if you want."

He pursued her in the jeep as far as the Greenbrier

Tavern where the jeep balked and would run in nothing but reverse gear. He could not see himself backing all the way to cut her off. He had a pint at the Greenbrier with one or two cronies, and that caused him to feel gloomy and morose because he began to talk about women and how any man who had anything to do with their damnable fickle temperaments would never have his mind free for a day's work. There was general agreement. Tommy Shea dropped in then, and it turned out he had seen Jacquelyn in Purlie Higgins's cart pass him on the way. Tommy did not know who she was, never having been in a motion picture house in all his life, but her beauty had become a star in Tommy's personal heaven. He could hardly talk of her without removing his hat. While Tommy blew the froth off a pint in her honor, it made up Brian's mind for him, and he abandoned the jeep and took after her with Tommy Shea's team and hay wagon. A rough bouncing ride it was since he had to take a shortcut across the meadow to be sure of heading her off. His teeth were fair jarred loose in his head.

When he caught up with her, thundering out across the road so that Purlie had to haul in the horses, and then jumping down and running over to her, she looked at him, frowning and preoccupied.

"All right. I'm sorry," he said.

She came down from the jaunty cart into his arms. He sent Purlie Higgins home alone in his cart while he and Jacquelyn climbed into the back on top of Tommy Shea's hay wagon. What a time there was. The team of horses found the way home and they were picking straw out of their clothes and their hair for days afterward.

"I think I may buy a farm and settle down," Stephen Innis announced.

He came up to the table to sit opposite Brian.

"What's for an Irish whiskey?"

Brian said, "I'll have an Irish with you. Now, what were you saying about buying a farm?"

"I'm serious. I can live anywhere I like. When you're as poor as I am, there's no place that's off limits. Poverty does not recognize geography and makes all places equal. And poetry makes all poets equal in poverty."

"If I could write two lines like yours, Stephen, I wouldn't ask for any more riches."

"What's wrong with being an actor? That's an art too."

"A mimetic art—nowhere near the same thing. Besides

there's too many riding sidesaddle on my back. Producers and directors and all that bilge who have trashcan lids for heads. Not to mention the jingle men whose brains are stuffed full of coins. They're the ones who tell a poor actor if he can act or not. It's to beg their favor that I have to be off to America and if they don't give me the money, then I'll be sucked down and have to do my acting in the street like an organ-grinder's monkey. Do you call that sort of doing an art?"

"I'd rather walk naked wearing a green sash on my behind through every pub in Dublin. You're too good a man for such carryings on, Brian."

"I do not wish to excoriate myself further in this matter. I cannot afford to regard myself lightly before supper. But I still wish I could write poems like you."

"I'll teach you all I know. It's a fine game, Brian. Usually I put it down in a rush so the words will get jumbled up and sound dirty. Afterward I model it until it's all done up lovely and looks gorgeous. That's when you feel good, when a poem shakes you off and says, 'No more. I don't want touching up. I look beautiful the way I am.' Then you have to send it off to be published immediately, so you won't tinker the heart out of it. And you sit back and relax, and you just love yourself because you can do anything, invent things, a poem that swings along like the hips of a willing girl."

"It's a great gift," Brian said enviously. "Believe me, Stephen, there's nothing in the world to equal it."

"Then I'll make a poet of you and we'll get drunk together every night."

"It wouldn't work," Brian said, "except for the drinking part. We do that well enough."

"A sweet comfort," Stephen said, examining his glass with approval.

"It'll put us both in our grave before our time."

"Aye."

"We're a pair of fools is what we are. Why don't we swear off?"

"There's a race of burly men who shoulder their way through the world, Brian, and have no need of the sauce. They drink or not as they like. They're damn self-satisfied. They want no more. Just nothing at all."

"We could be like that if we tried."

"We're not cut out for the burly race."

"What's wrong with us?"

"Self-doubt, in there so tough and hard that no one can get it out. The burly race are not self-doubters. But we know there ought to be more to us than there is, and if we tried harder there would be. When a man gets to thinking that way, he's in need of a bit of distraction. That's what the bottle does. Puts the warming glow to the cold places inside, and for a while we don't think we ought to be better keepers of our talent. We settle to make love like goats to all the girls in Ireland."

Brian smiled and lifted his glass sadly, and they sat looking at each other.

"Ah, green grow the lasses, oh," Stephen said.

The telephone rang.

"That's for you," Stephen announced. "It has the sound of your name. *Bri-an*. You hear?"

He picked up the receiver with a not quite steady hand.

"Brian O'Neal, is it? We've got your party at the other end of the wire. She's in Brazil," the operator said with a clear note of triumph.

"Hello."

"Brian, is that you?"

Damn. Moments like this made him wonder if his feeling for Jacquelyn was quite entirely dead.

"Jacquelyn."

"Brian . . . It's about Gene."

His heart lurched. As for his qualities as a father, there was much to be said against him, but there was no doubt that he loved the boy. It was his truest emotion and the one he could most easily display. He was not a shy man with children and had a knack of appealing to their acute sense of the ridiculous, making up marvelous senseless make-believe, or truthfully answering their questions with no embarrassment on either side and with absolute respect for their intelligence. Only an insensitive person would ever condescend to a child.

"What about Gene?" Brian asked.

"Charles took him out of school. He took him to London."

Charles Laurent. The donkeyhead she'd once been married to. Incidentally, the boy's father.

"He's all right then." That was his first thought.

"I don't know how he is." Her voice cracked as she came near tears in the familiar way. "Brian, Charles had no right."

"How'd he do it?"

"It was kidnapping!" The voice was suddenly seized with fury—and that was familiar too. "The son of a bitch flew to New York, went to the school, and took him out. And flew off with him! I could have him hanged."

"He won't do the boy any harm."

"Everyone says that. But what is he up to? He won't even talk to my lawyer."

"A bit peculiar."

"Brian, when Gene finds out that he's not going back to school, and there's no way he can talk to me . . ."

"You don't know what kind of a story Charles told Gene."

"I don't care. I could kill him. If Gene suffers in any way . . ."

Silence ensued. What a wonderfully perceptive boy. Knew exactly when to leave you alone, or to come over and put his arms about you when your whole head was raw with a hangover.

"Where are they?" Brian asked.

"Grosvenor House. Brian, you're the one I can depend on. Will you go up there? Get Gene back. Will you?"

Taken feature by feature, eyes and nose and mouth and jaw, Gene was not good-looking. But there was such life in his face when he smiled. And the eyes had the same terrible impact as the mother's. He did not resemble the father.

"I'll look into it and do what I can."

"I trust you. I can't tell you how grateful . . ."

"I love Gene too. Aside from the dubious point of legitimacy, he's my son."

"Call me as soon as you know anything?"

"We'll call you together," Brian promised, "the boy and I."

He went back to the table where Stephen brooded over an empty glass.

"Do you think they're taking any planes out of Dublin today?"

Stephen cocked an eye at the window. "Could be. The day's brighter."

"I'm going up to London."

Stephen nodded. "Good. I'll go with you."

"No, you won't. This is personal business." Brian put a pound note on the table. "Explain to Old Billy, will you? Tell him I'll be back to visit him in a while."

"There's a set to your jaw, Brian, that I think bodes ill for someone."

"It might," said Brian.

On the way to the airport in the antique taxi, Brian did not join in the driver's singing. He saw the murky gray rush of farmland and heavily wooded country, broken by gently rounded hills that were assuming form and substance in the strengthening light. The air was gentle with mist. He tried to guess where he was—just past Murphy's Hill, or the Giant's Corner—but nothing in the landscape gave him a clue. Not too many years ago he would have been able to identify every part of this country he had known when he was young. He would have remembered the very shapes and colors of the land.

Gene had been six years old when Brian went to Madrid to play Nero, and met his mother for the first time. The lead role in the picture was Jacquelyn's, as the courtesan-mistress who became a convert to Christianity and helped in Nero's overthrow. From the first, Brian made no distinctions between Gene and Sean, who was eleven, or Doreen, who was nine. They were his children by his marriage to Fabia. He saw them as frequently as he could, between chores of picture-making, until Fabia took the children off with her to keep them out of the scandal. What happened during the filming of that movie was newspaper history, but amid the turmoil of public declarations and private griefs he thought of the effect on Sean and Doreen with real regret. He did not expect either of them to forgive him, but he looked forward to more understanding when they grew to be adults and judged him as a man rather than as an errant father. He hardly saw them now, but still dropped them wildly humorous notes when the fancy overtook him. In the years of marriage to Jacquelyn, Gene became his new son and filled that place in his empty heart.

As they neared the airport the sky thundered with planes circling in for a landing.

"You're in luck," said the driver. "The airport is open."

Brian sat back and smiled. He would be in London soon enough.

It would be great to see Gene again.

In the large central room of the Grosvenor House, surrounded by glass walls, people sat on upholstered chairs and settees, enjoying their tea and cakes. Brian turned right to the room clerk's desk.

"Mr. Charles Laurent," he said.

Watery eyes met his. "Is Mr. Laurent expecting you?"

"I want to know his room number."

"I'm sorry, sir. We cannot reveal that information."

"Put me on the phone to him. He's expecting me."

"I'm sorry, sir. Mr. Laurent left quite explicit instructions that he did not wish to be disturbed."

Brian crossed the short side-lobby and got into the elevator. "Close the doors," he told the elevator man in a tone which persuaded him to close the doors. "You and I are going to do business together. You know Charles Laurent?"

The operator was a grave courtly man, with white hair that stuck out behind his ears.

"Did you ask at the desk, sir?"

"I asked at the desk. Now I'm asking you."

"I'm not sure I know any of the guests by name."

"A Frenchman. He's staying here with a small boy about eleven years old."

"A rather tall gentleman. Very handsome."

"That's him."

"I've taken him up once or twice, sir."

Brian took out a five-pound note. "What floor?"

"I believe the tenth."

"Good. Take me to the twelfth." He gave the operator the five-pound note. "I'll walk down. In case the room clerk is watching to see where you took me."

On the tenth floor Brian went to the laundry room. A maid was storing linens. She almost dropped the pile of folded sheets.

"Brian O'Neal!"

"Would you do me a favor, lass?"

She turned brick red. "Oh, Mr. O'Neal . . . !"

"I'm looking for a friend of mine." He produced another five-pound note. "I want to play a practical joke on him. I know he's on this floor, but I'm not sure of the room."

"A gentleman friend?"

Brian nodded. "A small boy staying with him. His name is Charles Laurent."

"Room Ten-Twelve. I was cleaning in there just a while ago. He's a sweet lad. And a fine-looking gentleman."

"And you're a dear lass." He gave her the five-pound note.

When he found the room he knocked on the door.

"Who is it?"

"A message for you, sir."

The door opened slightly, and Brian opened it the rest of the way. He was in a small wide foyer, with antique mirrors and side tables and chairs.

"What do you think you are doing?" Charles Laurent brushed back his hair with his hand.

"I've come for Gene."

"Gene isn't here."

"Gene," Brian shouted.

An excited treble responded, "Brian!"

Gene bounded into the room, and Brian swept him up in one arm. The boy hugged him and burrowed in his shoulder.

"Brian, I didn't know you were coming! Why didn't you tell me?"

"I wanted to surprise you. Are you surprised?"

"It's great! It's super!"

"What do you think you're going to do now?" Charles inquired.

"Have a drink with you," Brian said, "and listen to what you have to say."

"I'll have you thrown out unless you leave quietly."

Gene lifted his head from Brian's shoulder, looked at his father inquiringly, and then back at Brian.

"Aren't you friends?" he asked.

Brian stooped and allowed the boy to stand on his own feet. "Even friends have disagreements once in a while. You'd better go to your room and wait there until we settle this."

"But Brian . . ."

"I said go."

Gene glanced briefly at his father, turned and left without a word. He accepted discipline from Brian that he would not have accepted from anyone else. A good lad.

"He's my son," Charles Laurent said. "I intend to keep him."

"You practically kidnapped him. You don't have a shred of law."

Brian followed Charles into a living room furnished in dark wood that had a comfortable old-fashioned look.

"I believe any court would recognize that a father has responsibilities to his son in certain circumstances."

Brian thought irritably, people who talk with a French accent should not use jawbreaking English words. "Responsibilities" came out with too many long-drawn eeee sounds, and even with an extra syllable thrown in for good measure.

"What circumstances?" he asked.

"They should be clear enough."

Charles sat down in a chair and crossed his legs. He wore blue ribbed socks over his thin ankles.

"Well, they're not."

"The boy has a right to know who his parents are. He can't be tossed around from one man to another."

"Who says he has been?"

"Did you read Marta Moran's column the other day? Now everyone knows. You and Jacquelyn are being divorced and she has her next waiting. Meyer Whitney."

Brian felt the climate of the argument warming. "What business is that of yours?"

"Meyer Whitney will be the third father Gene has known—since Jacquelyn and I were divorced. Not to mention a few others whose status was never confirmed by a legal wedding."

The light in the room seemed to grow brighter. He saw Charles in a kind of glare, the more so because what the man was saying had a certain plausibility.

He said, "What you say is full of holes and dirty. If you open your mouth to utter one more foul word I will close it for you with a fistful of your teeth."

Charles Laurent seemed about to reply, and did not. He closed his mouth without assistance.

"Gene," Brian called.

The boy emerged promptly from the bedroom.

"Pack your things. You're leaving with me."

Gene began to smile and looked uncertainly in his father's direction. Charles came slowly to his feet.

"Are you coming, Father?" Gene asked politely.

"No, he is not," Brian said. "Hurry now. We'll have time to visit Trafalgar Square. I'll let you throw pebbles at Lord Nelson."

Gene hesitated long enough to observe the amenities, then turned and ran joyfully back into the bedroom.

"You're not taking my son out of this hotel."

"Someone will have to stop me."

Charles struggled with indignation and resolved the struggle in favor of another attempt at reason.

"Gene is my son. He's as much my responsibility as Jacquelyn's. He's all I have—all I can show for the years that Jacquelyn and I were married. I'll be more a father to him than Jacquelyn has been a mother. All I ask is a chance for us to get acquainted again, to know each other as a father and son should. Is that too much to ask?"

"Yes," Brian said. Triple damn the man. He had no right to sound reasonable. Brian had a job to do and, besides, though Charles happened to be the boy's father, it would do Gene precious little good to live with him. The boy has his rights too, and that's for sure.

Charles moved toward the telephone.

Brian said, "That would not be advisable."

A grimace tightened on Charles's lips. "Gene is going to live with me. He needs a home. Jacquelyn is not able to take care of him, and I won't have him turned over to a long procession of substitute fathers. I should have done this long before. Certainly when she married you."

"I can't hear you. As far as I am concerned, you are extinct."

"How can you be a real father to Gene when you shamefully abandoned two children of your own?"

"Ah," Brian said, "I hear you now."

He moved forward, holding his hand clenched so tight that nothing could have squeezed through his fingers. As he moved, Charles moved back and his eyes flickered away.

"I'll call the police. You will be charged with assault," he said.

"Put up your hands."

"No."

"You've no worry. I'll let you have the first whack."

"If you think that would settle anything, you're mistaken."

"I'm for trying it."

"I won't."

"You have the advantage. I can't hit a man who won't defend himself."

Charles picked up the telephone. Brian quickly slammed the phone down while Charles's hand was still on it.

"Not playing the game," Brian chided.

"This is ridiculous. If you take Gene out of this room, I

will telephone downstairs as soon as you go. You won't go farther than the lobby of this hotel."

"Then we'll have to make sure you don't telephone," Brian said.

Charles stared at him as though trying to divine his purpose. His eyes widened . . .

When Gene returned five minutes later to announce that he had packed his valise, Brian was alone in the living room.

"Good," he said, and accompanied Gene to the bedroom to take the packed valise. "You sure you have everything?"

"I even packed my toothbrush," Gene affirmed.

As they were going out the front door, Gene stopped suddenly. "I should say good-bye to my father."

"He's gone out," Brian said. "He told me to say good-bye for him."

"He didn't even wait?" Gene asked. "Gee."

"He doesn't like sad partings. I don't like them much myself. Do you?"

"I guess not," Gene said.

Brian closed the door quickly because thumping sounds from the closet were getting louder. Even allowing for the fact that Charles could, in a reasonable time, work the handkerchief out of his mouth, there was small likelihood that any shouts would be heard. They built these old hotels out of solid soundproof materials. It would take a good while longer to work out of the towels binding his arms and legs. By then he would be fair exhausted. Charles was not a very strong man. It was quite surprising how little resistance he put up.

They stopped at the stationer's on the corner to make a telephone call. The operator at the London exchange was not particularly impressed by a long distance call to Rio de Janeiro.

"Jacquelyn, there's someone here who wants to talk to you."

He put Gene on.

"Hi, Mom . . . Sure, I'm fine . . . Brian came and got me . . . We're going to Trafalgar Square and throw pebbles at Lord Nelson. He *promised* . . . Didn't you promise, Brian?"

"Scout's honor," Brian said.

CHAPTER TEN

The next afternoon, at half past three, Meyer Whitney arrived at the location. Jacquelyn was in the middle of a scene with Ross Hamilton, one of those blond, good-looking, young, screen lovers whose current popularity with millions of teen-agers was destined to last no more than the customary three or four years.

A chauffeured Rolls pulled up on the road below the encampment, and Meyer came up the trail alone. His arrival was accompanied by a drone of excitement. H. T. Wallace halted the shooting and beamed indulgently while Meyer and Jacquelyn embraced. Then he came over to introduce himself and to shake hands. When others of the cast and crew also came over to be introduced, H. T. decided to accept the inevitable.

"That's all for today," he bellowed over the loud-speaker.

His assistant made a final entry in the log, and the company began to get ready for the trip back to Rio.

Jacquelyn went over to H. T. to thank him for his consideration.

"That's all right, honey. The head cameraman tells me he's been fighting shadows on the set all day, so we won't lose much by it. Have a good time with Mr. Whitney."

Descending the trail with Meyer, a few minutes later, Jacquelyn said, "That's the first time I've ever heard H. T. call anyone by his last name."

Meyer chuckled. "Should I be flattered?"

"I think it's because all movie people are intrigued by men like you."

"Why?"

"It must have something to do with your money."

"They make money too."

"It's different. Everybody in movies feels that the party

can't last very long. Your kind of business seems built on bedrock."

They reached the car, and the chauffeur opened the rear door for them.

Meyer said, "I'm just more diversified. If it's a poor season for apples then at least I've got money in peaches and pears and oranges."

"Or your brothers have."

"We're a close family," Meyer agreed.

They settled back into deep gray, upholstered seats.

"I've been having a bit of family trouble," Jacquelyn said. "Thank heavens it's all settled now."

She told him about Charles, and his taking Gene out of school and away to England. She tried to convey some of the anxiety she felt on that day before she called Brian. Before she finished, she realized that she was making a sort of forehanded apology.

"I'm surprised you didn't call me, dear," Meyer said.

"Brian was in London, and I was sure he'd know how to handle it."

Meyer's finely chiseled features remained immobile. "I have my own methods. I can assure you they're quite as effective as Brian's."

"Everything worked out for the best. Brian has been a father to him. I don't think Gene would have gone with anyone else as readily."

"The problem seems to have been a simple one."

"My lawyer didn't think so. Anyhow, it's over now and everything's all right. Gene is back in school. I told the headmaster that if anything like that happens again I'll hold him personally responsible."

"How is the boy?"

"A little puzzled by how quickly everything happened, but he accepts it. I called him a couple of hours ago. I think he's glad to be back, and delighted to have seen Brian again."

In a perverse way she was insistent on having Meyer acknowledge her obligation to Brian. Instinct told her that the only way to do it was to keep going forward, through unstated opposition.

"Just the same, the next time a problem of any kind arises, dear, I hope you'll let me handle it."

"I hope you aren't offended. I asked Brian to help and I think he behaved magnificently."

"You were lucky. There might have been complications."

"Why should there have been?"

"One can't go pushing into a man's hotel room and practically assault him. Not even in a good cause."

"He got Gene. That's all I care about."

"He might have landed himself in prison and accomplished nothing except to get a good deal of unfavorable publicity. Fortunately, that didn't happen, but I do think I could have achieved the same result with less risk."

"At the time I wasn't concerned about the risk."

"In any event this sort of question won't arise again. Once we're married, I'll always be around to call on when there's a problem. And I'm here to speed that day. Specifically, to find out what happened to the arrangements I made with Hernan Ramirez. Have you seen him?"

"He's called twice since our dinner, but I've been too busy."

"I thought Hernan and I had a clear understanding. My lawyers in Mexico City assure me that the delay is at his end. But don't worry. I'll get it straightened out."

"I'm sure you will."

"Is anything wrong?"

"No, of course not, darling."

Something in her expression must have led him to think so.

Meyer was in excellent form at dinner. He was polished and sparkling, self-contained and hard as a diamond that has not shown its cutting edge. Jacquelyn had dressed carefully for the occasion to make Hernan aware she was a prize well worth contending for, even against Meyer Whitney. She was wearing a black and white striped, floor-length silk gown, very Grecian, falling away in folds from one bare shoulder. A hairpiece of long curls was pinned to her dark, almost black shoulder-length hair. With her eyes half closed, her cheeks flushed, she knew exactly how beautiful she was. Hernan was hardly able to keep his admiration from showing; his attention kept wandering to her during the conversation at dinner.

As brandy was served after dinner, Meyer said abruptly, "I confess, Hernan, that I'm a little surprised."

"Surprised, Señor Whitney?"

"At how long it's taking your consulate to arrange for Miss Stuart's divorce."

Hernan, attired in a maroon evening jacket with cummerbund and dark trousers, tapped a well-manicured fingernail on the table before him. "You understand, Señor Whitney, that this is a very complicated affair."

"We're friends. You may call me Meyer."

"Yes. I most humbly assure you, Señor Meyer, that I am doing my best."

"Then what accounts for the delay?"

"There are highly placed persons in my government who do not approve of such an ... er ... unorthodox procedure."

"Why?"

"They believe it would set a harmful precedent."

"Do you have their names? I'll talk to them."

Hernan flushed. "I have already done so, Señor Meyer."

"If the bottleneck is in the higher echelons of government, the proper thing is for me to take it up with them."

"This is a delicate matter. Such things take time. One must move through the proper channels."

"I've never done that, Hernan. Proper channels are always fouled up with red tape. No one gets anything done by going through them."

"Nevertheless, Señor Meyer, there is sometimes no alternative."

Meyer smiled. "My specialty, Hernan, is discovering alternatives. I know what a difficult situation this is for you, so I am prepared to be as much help as I possibly can be."

"Señor Meyer, I cannot see ..."

"The next time you talk to your superiors in government, the ones putting roadblocks into the way of this divorce, remind them that there is a deal pending between the Mexican Government and the United States Potassium Company. I believe it involves a sum of something close to eighty million dollars."

"I do not see, Señor Meyer, what that has to do with—"

"Perhaps I can make it clearer. I am associated with American Potassium. Whether that deal is approved will depend largely, if not entirely, on my attitude. My attitude, in turn, will depend entirely on how cooperative your government is going to be in the matter of Miss Stuart's divorce."

Hernan sat still. Indignation and fear were struggling

equally behind his almost impassive olive countenance, revealing the struggle only in the intensified glitter of his dark eyes.

"The honor of my government, Señor Meyer, is not for sale at any price."

"I'm not proposing to buy it. We are both accustomed to dealing in facts, Hernan, and these are facts. Your superiors might not like it if they were not informed in time about these facts."

"I can, of course, Señor Meyer, understand your impatience." Hernan gave an oblique glance at Jacquelyn. "As I have said, I am eager to assist you in any way within my power."

"Then we'll have no problem. My attorneys will be in town tomorrow. If you'll be kind enough to devote most of your day to them I'm sure we'll get all the details ironed out."

Hernan Ramirez seemed to be searching for some inoffensive way to make a further negative reaction. His glance flickered once again to Jacquelyn, as though imploring her to understand his dilemma. Then he shrugged, and in the slight movement of his shoulders there was the quintessence of defeat.

"I will cancel all my other appointments, Señor Meyer. I will be at the service of your attorneys when they call."

Even in the midst of the realization that she could no longer count on Hernan Ramirez as an ally, Jacquelyn could not help admiring Meyer Whitney's forthright masculine use of power. Hernan Ramirez was doubtless a man of some strength of character when confronted with an ordinary opponent, but he could not stand up against Meyer. She was looking straight ahead at the candlelight, and a faint crease touched the corner of her mouth. It had been a hopeless scheme. What would she have gained? A few weeks of delay, and what then? Now it was over. Meyer was going to have his way. If the truth were told, she felt relief mingled with her disappointment.

That night, in the dark bedroom at the villa, with Meyer asleep beside her, she watched the tiny radium hands on the dial reach twenty minutes past four. The hands of time moved on, whether powered by electric current or injured pride, and nothing could turn them back. Brian was gone. The Beautiful Couple were two separate people. She stared into darkness. She was realist enough to accept it. Meyer Whitney was far more than a mere substitute. Since she had to marry someone, the fact that it was Meyer Whitney was something to be proud and happy about. He was the most important person she had ever met, and a woman's life was not all of a piece until she was married. If a woman stayed single there were too many loose ends in her emotions—bits and pieces of feeling that did not fit anywhere because she did not belong to a man. Marriage was the guiding motive—even for hatred, even for infidelity—and the legal sanction for childbearing. There were women who planned their lives around having children, using the family as a goal and setting their sights on it. She had not been like that about having a child with Charles, though. She hadn't wanted Gene. She couldn't imagine herself with his baby, cuddling and nursing it. Of course he wasn't Gene then—only Charles's child, a struggling sexless nothing in her body.

The white-faced clock seemed to waver, and the sensation of dizziness it caused reminded her of an evening, years ago, when she had just returned with Charles from a concert at the Hollywood Bowl. She had been so dizzy that the gravel walk seemed to rise up on end. Charles had had to steady her, help her into the house and bring her a brandy. She felt hot and tingly all over, and Charles was assuring her that some pregnant women often felt that way, when the telephone rang and it was Meyer Whitney.

"I'm sorry to say that Henry Orrin didn't accept my suggestion for a settlement of your dispute with the studio."

"Oh. Well, thank you for trying. Did he say why?"

"He says that to give you a new, better contract would simply be rewarding disloyalty at a time when the studio has every right to expect loyalty from its biggest stars."

Jacquelyn didn't know how long she would be able to hold out. Her bank account was scraping bottom, there was no money coming in, and they owed everyone, including an overdue mortgage payment on Charles's cliffside house.

"The funny thing is Charles and I talked it over and agreed that I would do *Furious Thunder*—if you persuaded Henry Orrin."

"Don't give up yet, my dear. The studio will eventually agree to a new contract."

Meyer Whitney did not know that she was three months

pregnant. If she had to wait until the baby was born before starting another picture, her fans might forget her. And it would be a year after the baby before the picture was even released to theaters. In Hollywood a year can be a very long time.

Jacquelyn sat up. Her dizziness was gone.

"I don't know," she said. "I'm tempted to agree to appear in *Furious Thunder* on any terms."

"You won't have to crawl to him. Mr. Orrin and I have had several disagreements, and matters will come to a head at the next meeting of the board. That will be in two weeks. I'd strongly advise you to wait until then."

Two weeks later Henry Orrin resigned as head of Mammoth Studios. His successor at the studio was Dan Reed, a successful producer of TV spectaculars, and one fabulously profitable TV series before he moved over into motion pictures and produced two money-making films. He had a reputation as a loudmouth and an aggressive, noisy self-publicist. In Hollywood the changeover was regarded with suspicion; Henry Orrin was a veteran of motion pictures who knew everyone in the cinema colony. And Hollywood, writhing in the python coils of TV and of diminishing box office grosses, resented and feared anyone who came over from this alien medium.

Shortly after he took office, Dan Reed invited Jacquelyn to the executive dining room at the studio. He was already at the table when she appeared. As he stood up, she was surprised at how short he was, a stocky, broad-chested man with a high, dark shock of black hair and a square face notable for a belligerent thrust of chin.

He pulled out a chair for Jacquelyn at his table. It was a deep-cushioned velvet chair with a gold nameplate on its back.

"How thoughtful," she said. "It has my name."

Dan Reed grinned; his dark face lit when he showed his capped white teeth. "I hope it makes you feel this is where you belong. Right back here at the studio."

She looked around the dining room, a large walnut-paneled room with heavy sound-deadening draperies at the windows. She recognized the studio treasurer and one of the studio's top producers, and Henry Margate, the English director. The treasurer was dining alone, the other two shared a table. There was no one else in the room.

"I've never had lunch here before."

Dan Reed edged her chair in toward the table.

"I'll keep your chair here in case you should ever want to again."

She smiled up at him. "Don't you think your other guests might object?"

"Screw them," Dan Reed said.

She blinked as he sat down opposite her. It was either his ordinary way of speaking, or he was deliberately attempting to shock her. Well, she was not easily shocked.

"Is that your philosophy?" she asked lightly. "Screw all but six and save them for pallbearers?"

Dan Reed heaved with laughter. "We'll get along fine. You're my kind of broad."

She did not really like Dan Reed, but she knew how to handle the straight-Scotch locker-room type. She turned languorously toward him and gave him the full impact of her emerald eyes.

Dan Reed swallowed. "Have you met our studio treasurer?"

"Oh, yes."

"And Harvey Fellows, the producer? And Henry Margate?"

"No, we haven't met."

In the course of lunch, all these gentlemen came over to be introduced. She remembered Henry Margate clearly, a fat man whose weight had begun to sag into his stomach and lower abdomen, but who had thin, knobby legs and long, slender arms. He stared at Jacquelyn soberly.

"I'd like to do a picture with you sometime. I have an idea you'd be wonderful in something sexy. You could get away with things that Rita Hayworth and Marilyn Monroe could never do. A woman who looks like an angel and acts like a nymph in the bedroom, that's every man's ideal. Do you agree, Dan?"

Dan Reed smiled widely. "You'll have to get in line if you want her for a picture. Right now, I'm going to con her into starring in *Furious Thunder*."

Dan Reed said he had invited her to talk to him without agents or lawyers around because he hoped they could get right down to brass tacks. She was sure that he thought he could outmaneuver her because she was a woman, but she had been carefully briefed for the interview by Charles and her lawyers. He came up to six thousand a week and fifty weeks minimum, but she had been warned not to accept a regular contract because it would carry protective clauses against such contingencies as pregnancy or prolonged illness. As soon as the studio discovered she was pregnant she would go on suspension again until she could return to work, so the six thousand a week would only last five or six weeks. Then she'd be back in the same dangerous financial shoals.

Finally Dan Reed lit up a cigar without asking her permission and blew a smoke spiral toward the ceiling. He tipped far back in his chair. "I'll lay it on the line for you, sweetheart. There isn't a studio in town will pay the kind of money you're asking. Not these days. If I agreed to it, they'd boot me out of this office and I only just got here." His Adam's apple bobbed. "What's your absolute bottom-of-the-barrel price?"

"What's your best price?" she countered.

"You want it straight? Here's the deal. Ten thousand a week. A guarantee of six weeks work. You can't have script approval. I agree the script is a turkey. I'm having it gone over by two new writers. It isn't in any condition to show the janitor, much less the star I'm trying to con into appearing in it. But take my word for it, when the cameras roll, *Furious Thunder* will be right. It'll be more than right. It'll be great. You know who we've signed as your co-star?"

"I haven't heard."

"Joel Page. You can't get a hotter box office name than that."

Joel Page was a moody, intense, rebellious young man who had made his initial screen appearance playing a moody, intense, rebellious young man. He had instantly captured the younger generation who were now assiduously copying his black leather jacket, wrist band, drooping cigarette, mumbling manner of speech, uncombed look, passion for motorcycles, and general contempt for the Establishment. In a subsequent picture, playing the role of a fanatical rabble-rouser in a southern town, Joel Page widened and deepened his hold on his audience. In a frankly unsympathetic role he was so bitter, so uniquely anti all accepted values, so unregenerate, that his young admirers acclaimed him as not merely a personality but an actor of the first stamp. He carried over his surliness into his offscreen behavior, having an open liaison with one of the screen's first ladies and then openly jilting her, refusing all fan magazine interviews and winning the Sour Apple

award of the society of press photographers by not posing
for pictures, and at a premiere breaking out of line to
grab a cameraman, seize his camera, and break it over his
knee. A volatile, dangerous, unpredictable young man—
these were qualities that spelled box office.

"You and Joel Page will be an explosive team,
sweetheart. Real dynamite. Conservatively, I figure that a
picture like *Furious Thunder* will gross twenty million.
It'll outgross *Giant*."

"If you believe that, then you can afford to give me
what I want. You're saying sixty thousand. I'm saying a
hundred. There ought to be room for compromise."

Dan Reed waved his cigar. "It's not negotiable,
sweetheart. That's the top of the mountain."

She smiled her prettiest smile at him, disliking him
thoroughly.

"I'll gamble with you if you're a gambling man."

"Me? Spin the wheel and I'll push my last chip onto the
table."

"Fifteen thousand a week. No guarantee at all. If you
finish the picture in less than five weeks, you'll save money. If it takes more than five weeks I'll get the price I'm
asking."

She liked the urgency of a deadline. If the picture took
longer than six weeks, her pregnancy would start to show.

Dan Reed squinted at her from beneath straight black
bushy brows. "You're a blackjack dealer, you know that?
But I'll go along. Fifteen a week straight and God help me
if the movie runs over schedule. I'll tell the boys to draw
up the new contract. One thing I insist on. Your lawyers
can check details, but they can't reopen negotiations. Not
any more."

"All right."

Dan Reed removed his cigar and held it between thumb
and forefinger. "I said you're my kind of broad, didn't I?"

He laughed. His laughter had a harsh, jarring quality.

She threw herself into her work on *Furious Thunder*
with a drive and dedication that left her little time for
anything else. It was an emotionally complicated time. She
was racing the clock, watching for the first betraying
bulge that would reveal her pregnancy, and at the same
time trying to cope with the demands of her role as Lena
Morgan, impassioned daughter of the Confederacy who

marries her young lover and sends him proudly off to war. The role would not have been difficult in itself, but it was made so by the terrible intensity and absorption of Joel Page playing opposite her. Joel infused his own smoldering personality into the romantic young husband who hated war. Even the most casual lines of dialogue seemed to flame with his suppressed hatred and hostility. In trying to match his high-pitched mood Jacquelyn was draining herself of all her reserves. At the end of a day's shooting she could hardly drag herself to her dressing trailer to change costume and wait for Charles to come and pick her up. He arrived promptly at the close of each day, and drove her home to the cliffside house where they had a quiet dinner and went to bed early. In the third week of shooting she began to have dizzy spells on the set and had to ask for intervals of rest.

Everything reached a climax during a scene in the movie which took place at a dinner given for her young husband on his return on leave after the battle of Antietam. The festive proceedings were to be interrupted by a furious argument with her husband when she tried to justify the deaths of so many of his friends. Even in reading the manuscript, she envisioned Joel Page playing the angry young man for all it was worth, his rangy body shaking with the high-voltage current of simulated fury. There was such a terrible conviction about everything Joel Page did that every scene with him became a raw and bleeding slice of real life. She would as soon have had a genuine argument with Joel as contend with him on the movie set. His spare and haughty face became cavernous and inhuman with a genuine wrath. It was frightening to see him, frightening to hear him at close range. She did not even have the comfort of reminding herself at such moments that he was merely acting, because in order to immerse herself in the action, she had to become a part of it and live, as far as she could, in the jungle of passions Joel created. His implacable stare and hissing tongue sometimes reminded her of a cobra about to strike.

When the day arrived for the dinner scene to be shot, she had worked herself into a highly nervous condition. She was trembling when the makeup woman applied her eyeshadow. The woman asked if she was feeling all right. Yes, yes, I'm fine. On the set, the dinner table in the mansion was ready and the guests were waiting. She

presided over the table with the Old World grace of Lena
Morgan, forcing everyone to ignore the shabby condition
of the linen, the tarnished silverware, the absence of
servants. War was taking its toll in Lena Morgan's world
too. Joel Page sat subdued and quiet in his place at the
other end of the table; then the conversation turned to the
course the war was taking, and with tears in her eyes
Lena Morgan spoke of the gallantry of the men who
fought and died at Antietam. Joel Page became as pale as
gray ice.

"Only a fool thinks there's anything gallant about dying
in war," he said. "Only an idiot fights in one. We're all
idiots—wearing different-colored uniforms."

She glanced about the table at her guests, who were
annoyed, unpleasantly shocked and puzzled. Then she replied, not in anger or reproof, but in coolness and detached, forgiving pride. Joel become frankly exasperated.
In the light of tall candles his figure rose, impossibly tall
and ghostly in the wavering shadows. In a moment the
evening was spoiled—too late to save it with polite words
or move the party elsewhere, too early for everyone to go
home.

"If you were half a woman," Joel was saying, "if you
had any gentleness in your blood, you'd weep for the
living, not the dead. It doesn't matter about the dead.
They're out of it."

She fluttered for a short time like a moth about a
flame, then, singed by him, flared back. In no time the
battle was on. It seemed to annihilate space. She reeled
under the pure savagery of Joel's assault. Guests gathered
near, made their excuses and their departures. Now they
were alone. She was defenseless. The words she had to say
were inadequate poor things against the onrush of his
passionate and searing tirade; could these words be written by the same author? He was shouting at her, out of
control, mouth distended, eyes garing. Oh, no. . . ! Oh,
no!

She came to in her dressing room. The wardrobe mistress was applying ice-cold packs to her eyes. She sat up
suddenly.

"I'm all right," she said impatiently, brushing the woman's hand aside.

This was too silly. What a fool she must have made of
herself.

"You ought to rest a while, Miss Stuart."

Miss Stuart. That queer unchangeability of a star's name, a name worth more than a marriage. Mrs. Charles Laurent was still called Jacquelyn Stuart. *Miss*. A very pregnant Miss.

She forced herself to continue sitting erect, although she was beginning to feel dizzy again.

"What happened? I fainted, didn't I?"

"Yes, Miss Stuart. Joel Page carried you in here. He looked almost as pale as you did."

"It wasn't his fault. Will you tell him I'm all right? I'll just rest a little while, then finish the scene."

"They're shooting around you, Miss Stuart. Mr. Page said you shouldn't try to work for the rest of the day."

"That's kind of him. But I intend to."

"They've started on the new scene already. It'll be too late by the time they're ready for you, Miss Stuart. You might as well go home."

The wardrobe mistress leaned toward her and patted her with a fumbling hand.

She telephoned Charles, but there was no answer at the house. When she left the trailer, Joel Page was passing near. He had changed out of his Confederate uniform and was wearing his familiar black leather jacket and narrow corduroy trousers. He had abandoned the erect military stance of the young Confederate soldier, and moved with his usual careless slouch.

When he saw her emerge from the trailer he came over.

"You feeling better?"

The careful diction of the southerner had vanished into the slurring rough-edged New York accent.

"Yes, I am, thank you. I don't know what came over me. It must have been the heat of the lights."

"Sure," Joel said. "You'll be okay tomorrow."

"You're not working. You've changed costume."

"They weren't set up for any of my scenes. They're shooting minor stuff. We'll go back to the same thing tomorrow. Fairchild says it looked pretty good up to the point you conked out, so maybe it won't take too long to wind it up."

This was the longest consecutive speech she had ever heard Joel Page make off-camera. Conversation with him was usually conducted in staccato monosyllables, almost like Morse code.

"I thought you were wonderful."

Joel Page looked down at his boots. "It isn't much of a script. We gotta give it everything."

"It may turn out better than we think."

"Nah. Manure is still manure when they call it fertilizer. How're you getting home from here?"

"I tried calling home but there's no answer. I'll take one of the studio limousines."

"I'll go your way, if you don't mind riding a bike."

She had never ridden a motorcycle in her life, and had no particular desire to. But she didn't want to offend Joel Page either.

"Well . . ."

"Don't do me any favors. Just say no."

"I wasn't going to say no."

Joel had no noticeable reaction. "Okay. Meet you at the gate in ten minutes."

He slouched away. She watched the indolent movement of his body with resentment. She didn't want to go home with him on his silly motorcycle. After the burden of this day she wanted to relax quietly in the deep-cushioned interior of a limousine instead of having this unruly man bucketing along the highway with her. It was both undignified and dangerous. But how could she say no?

Later, speeding on the motorcycle, she began to feel better about it. She sat astride the small seat behind him, her hands clasped about his waist. The stiff leather of his back was against her body. He drove, as she expected, unreasonably fast. The highway was slightly wet in places, and each time they came to a curve her grasp on his waist tightened. He barely seemed to flick the handlebars as the motorcycle roared on. He was wearing goggles and she saw the glint from time to time as he turned his head. There was a wildness about him; all his physical reactions seemed to be coiled into a spring that was going to snap at any moment. As the wind whipped through her hair, she squinted behind the shield of his body, intensely aware of herself as arms and breasts and legs. They seemed to be flying free, traveling through a dimensionless space at an incredible rate of speed. There was the unmistakable promise of danger, and the unspoken exhilaration.

She looked out from the protection of his shoulder and recognized where they were. A few moments later the motorcycle coasted to a stop near the entrance to her house.

She got off, reluctantly. Joel sat on the motorcycle, which was tipped at an angle, while he supported himself with one foot on the ground.

"That was exciting," she said. "I enjoyed it. Wouldn't you like to come in?"

Joel pushed his goggles up onto his forehead and looked beyond her.

"Isn't that your husband's car in the driveway?"

"Yes."

"I'll take a raincheck."

He stepped down hard on the pedal, and the motorcycle roared off down the road.

She had meant the gesture to be polite, but his refusal made it seem something more. She was annoyed at him. Did he really think Charles would be jealous? Or that if her husband was not home the invitation might have included something more? His arrogance was shattering, positively shattering. For a brief time during their ride she thought she might want to explore further the tantalizing excitement of Joel Page. She was glad now that he had declined her offer. There would not be another.

She passed the car in the driveway and entered the house. It seemed to be empty.

"Charles?"

She spoke quietly, afraid he might be asleep. But how could he be? He must have returned in the last few minutes or he would have been at home to receive her telephone call. Then she noted the whiskey glasses and the empty bottle on the patio table, and a second later she saw Charles's jacket hung over a chair in the living room.

"Charles?"

No answer. She looked more closely at the jacket and didn't recognize it. She had never seen Charles wearing it. But somehow the jacket looked familiar. Then she remembered it belonged to Christopher Leigh.

Where the hell is Charles, she thought angrily. The last thing she wanted tonight was company. She was too tired, and feeling mildly nauseated.

She climbed the stairs that curved up to the gallery bedroom she shared with Charles. It was her favorite room, with an immense skylight that at night allowed them to lie abed and look at the stars. She thought she might take a nap, if Charles and Christopher did not return from their stroll too soon and waken her.

As she turned the knob of the bedroom door, she heard

a scurrying movement. A flurry of quick human sounds, not quite voices.

She opened the door.

At her first glimpse of the two naked figures on the bed her initial impulse was to slam the door shut to close out a vision that quickly became larger than life and more malignant. But it was too late. *My God! Oh, my God! ...* She remained standing in the open doorway, as though nailed there. There was nothing to be said, no explanations. In a play the curtain of the final act would go down when she opened the bedroom door and saw Charles vainly trying to protect Christopher. But life was not a play, and the action kept going on endlessly, meaninglessly. There was no way to escape from subsequent minutes. Or from the house. Or from the days, weeks that would follow.

Charles had a pleading expression. What did he want from her? There were no lines on his smooth face. He looked vulnerable, like a plucked chicken, on all fours in the tangle of bedclothes. Christopher had turned on his side until she could see only the bare shoulder and the side of his face.

Along with her revulsion she felt a twinge of pity. There was a smell of tobacco in the room. They must have been smoking a little while ago. They had no time to put a decent face on it. Charles was not expecting her to arrive on a motorcycle or at this hour of the afternoon. Even if he had not been too ... engaged ... to hear. She leaned back against the doorjamb. It's been silent too long and I'm getting silly, beginning to find ways for Charles in which he might have escaped, in which I might have been spared.

"Jacquelyn ..."

Charles's voice sounded deeper, a moaning as if he was enduring unendurable pain. Poor Charles. He had so little, and pride had been a part of it.

He got out of the bed, and looked even more ridiculous, framing his face to say ridiculous things.

"I didn't expect you ... Christopher and I lay down to take a nap ..."

In the angle of the bedroom mirror she caught a flash of her image in the doorway. It seemed a wonder that the mirror hadn't cracked. All of her world had shattered, so the mirror would only be giving a true reflection of what it saw.

"You . . . damned . . . *pervert!*" she said.

"Jacquelyn, you have no right to talk to me like that. You don't understand . . ."

He came toward her, his organs dangling, swaying. Horror overcame her. She didn't want to look at him, and didn't want him to look at her. There was intimacy even in eyes meeting.

"Don't touch me. Don't you dare!"

Christopher had not moved. From the bed she heard choked stifled sobbing, like a boy, a truant boy who's had his shameful secret exposed.

Charles stopped and looked uneasily at her.

"You have no right to take this attitude, Jacquelyn. If you have a vicious dirty idea in your head . . ."

She had a physical fear of any contact between them. Her fists were clenched, and suddenly she became aware of something wet and slippery in her palms. She looked down, surprised. Her fingernails had bitten deep enough to draw blood. In her right hand she was clutching her handbag.

Her damn voice went shrill in the upper register.

"Oh, for God's sake," she cried, "get some clothes on!"

As he came nearer she began to beat at him, swinging her purse. She pounded him on the head, and he tried to fend off the blows, muttering, "Please . . . please." The metal buckle caught him in the mouth and bloody spittle dribbled down his chin. "Please . . . please . . ." and she still continued to pound at him, cutting his nose, his cheeks. "Please . . . please!"

She turned and ran, down the winding stairs, past the stark black and white painting, with its jagged edges and tones and textures, stumbling across the gray carpet, past the bright yellow and blue and red abstraction by Léger with its broad stripes around a white dot in the center. In the foyer was the painting Charles favored— "The Sea of Hair"—with all the waves tossing up hair that looked thoroughly substantial, only the phenomenon of light and dark connecting the pigment to the title, showing the slow, heaving, congested mass of hair floating out like dark scum on the sea's surface.

The car waited in the driveway.

She got in and started the engine and threw it into gear. An astonishing thing happened. The car did not go into reverse as she intended. It shot forward. What had she done? In a panic, she jammed down hard on the brake.

The car zoomed forward. She had hit the accelerator by mistake.

The end of the driveway loomed, with its short, concrete, protecting barrier at the cliffside. The car sped forward, and there was a loud thump. She screamed as she felt the car rising up up, and then a sickening halt, a suspension in air, before the plunge. She screamed again. Her head struck the windshield. Steel buckled and glass cracked around her. This is it, she thought. This is death and I'm experiencing it. This minute. I didn't mean to.

Oh, God. There was no pain at all. That was surprising. She had really expected pain.

Certain episodes remained vividly in her mind but did not seem connected to any other episodes by a lapse in time. She was eight weeks in the hospital all together, but she might have been there eight days, or eight months. She was aware that the summer had come, in the way that summer comes to southern California, with imperceptible new warmth and morning fog from the beaches. When they moved her out of the hospital room to lie on the terrace for part of each day she became aware of the heat and how reluctantly the sun departed later and later in the afternoons. In the glare she forgot Charles's look as he had tried to explain away his guilt in that house by the cliff that now seemed so far away, both in distance and time.

She was lucky to be alive; she knew that. The car had gone over the barrier and started down the cliff but had caught in the tangled mass of chaparral, where it hung on the edge of doom.

In the second week at the hospital she browbeat the nurse to bring her a mirror. And for the first time she was not so sure she was lucky to be alive. Her head was swathed in bandages for her fractured skull, and a strip of bandage covered the long red slash on her shoulder that had required forty stitches. That was going to need plastic surgery, and so was her nose, swollen and discolored from its torn septum. Her cheekbones were turning a nasty purple color, and one eye was nearly shut. Worst of all was the displaced vertebra in her back; she could not get up to walk, or even sit up to see her reflection in the mirror.

She thrust the mirror at the nurse. "Take the goddamned thing away. I don't want to ever look in one again!"

There was one miracle, almost as great as the miracle of her being alive. She had not lost her baby. The fetus had clung to her womb as desperately as she had clung to existence; they were one in their need to survive.

Mother and Richard had been to see her. Mother looked at the bright side: her face had not been permanently injured. "You know, dear, your face is your fortune. As long as you've got that, you'll be all right." Richard spent hours with her, talking of the world outside. He told her of the boat he was building, the people he met, read some of the messages that poured in from fans all over the country. He did not seem to be concerned when she did not answer. He knew those were the moments when waves of pain crashed over her and turned the world black. Richard did not know about moments that were worse than pain, when she felt as though she were drowning in memory. During the day she could will herself to not think, but at night she would wake up, shouting, seeing again white, naked, male bodies imprinted against the dark walls of her hospital room.

In the fourth week she was allowed visitors. One of the first was Dan Reed. She heard his harsh, loud voice in the corridor, and the excited giggling of the nurse. Then Dan Reed himself entered, grinning widely, a dead cigar jutting from his mouth.

"When the hell are you coming back to work?"

She smiled wanly. "Dan, I don't want to hear any fake pep talk. We both know I may never be able to work again."

"What kind of attitude is that? I never had you pegged for a quitter. Listen, I got projects lined up that are gonna keep you busy for the next five years."

She sat with arms folded on the coverlet and shoulders hunched, and wished he would go away. She did not think she could listen to his high-voltage enthusiasm.

"I'm pretty tired, Dan. They don't allow me to talk to people very long."

Dan Reed pulled a chair over beside her bed. "Trying to give me the old brusheroo? I've been flaked off by experts, but I don't stay flaked. I'm dandruff. Every time you turn around, there I am on your shoulder."

"That's a lovely image." She leaned her head back against the pillow. Obviously she was going to have to insult him to make him leave. Still, he meant well in his gruff, unaware fashion.

"Okay, I don't have a great way with words. I can't act either. And I can't direct. But did'ja notice? All them other talented people work for me."

"Well, I don't! At least not anymore." So that means I don't have to listen to you either, she thought.

"That's what I came to talk to you about. How about a new contract, starting right now?"

"Do you always make jokes in such bad taste?"

"You say the man is joking. I say the man isn't joking."

"It would be a very bad gamble. I might never be able to get out of bed."

"That's my worry. You want the contract? You got it."

"Suppose I say yes, and sign, and you pay me for years while I just lie here."

"I'll bring a camera crew in, and shoot the way you look against that pillow. I could sell glossy photos for ten bucks apiece and make millions."

She laughed, and for a moment *was* pleased. She could not say exactly when it had happened, but she was enjoying his visit. There was an elemental vitality about him which swept her up into its excitement. In an attempt to discover what it was about Dan Reed that gave her this feeling, she found herself staring at him. He smiled at her and, embarrassed, she partly averted the directness of her stare.

Her voice was gentler when she said, "You're a nice man, Dan Reed."

"You're not hard to take yourself. Don't think I was kidding about those glossy photos. They'd be a bargain at a sawbuck." He pointed to the door. "I understand they're going to put up a new plaque over the door when you leave. 'Through this portal passed the most beautiful woman in the world.' They won't even put your name after it. Everybody'll know it means you."

Warm blood flushed upward through her cheeks and into her scalp.

"Listen, did you hear how we got lucky on *Furious Thunder*? I hauled in a top writer to fix up the screenplay so we could go on with what we've got. We're even using the dinner scene right up to and including your passing out. It works great. If you ask me, it's better this way than before."

"How could you do that?"

Dan bit off the end of his dead cigar and spat it into the wastebasket. "All it takes is guts. We made the dinner scene the point at which you break up with your husband. Then we rang in a new dame for him and a new curtain that makes it look as though he's going to be happy with her. We're using some of the old stuff you'd shot for the fadeout to indicate that you end up back in the old mansion, without your husband, carrying on in the old genteel tradition. It cuts out a lot of the slop. This way it's a character study with a bittersweet ending. The critics are gonna love it."

"It sounds ingenious."

"Wait'll you get a look at the new property I've got lined up for you. This script is better than anything I've read since *Birth of a Nation*. You remember Henry Margate? He's going to direct it. And he'll have a chance to test out a theory of his. That you can play sex better than the bimbos that are being paid to project nothing else but."

"Dan, the doctors say I need another operation before I can walk. And even then it may take months."

"Do I think of everything? This script has you an invalid three quarters of the way. You're a lady with a past, see, and you get racked up in a skiing accident with this married guy you'd gone away for the weekend with. While you're lying around, you've got a chance to think back over your life and all the affairs you've had with men. This current guy is the real love of your life . . ."

She turned her head away. "It isn't going to happen."

"Who says so?"

"I do. For one thing I'm pregnant."

Dan Reed grinned. "Babies don't take forever. Nine months is the limit."

"For another thing, we both know I'll probably never walk again."

"Are you nuts? I've talked to the doctors and looked at the X-rays—the sexiest goddamned X-rays I ever saw. There's no reason you can't be up and around as soon as they shove that vertebra back into place."

"Stop it, Dan. I know you're trying to paint lovely pictures, but it's no use. No cripple gets to be a movie star."

Dan Reed leaned over her; he had something on his breath that smelled spicy as cloves.

"You heard about that psychiatry they use in Japan?

They lock up somebody in a room with absolutely nothing to do. No reading. No nothing. At the end of a week of biting his fingernails the patient is ready to go back to work at anything. Ready? He's practically climbing the walls. That's how it's going to be with you when you get through with this hospital routine."

"I don't want to hear any more. I really don't. Just leave me alone." She rolled over and pressed the button to call the nurse. "Go away!"

Dan Reed said, "Okay, sweetheart. Call nursie to come and give you a nice sympathy rub. I could have been wrong about you. Maybe you *are* a quitter! I'm going to keep the Henry Margate picture open for you for a month. If you say no then, Gerda Andersen gets it."

"Gerda?" Her face, until then averted, turned to his. "She's all wrong for that part. Gerda can't even stand up on a pair of skis."

"I wouldn't let her schuss down a mountain even if she was Olympic champion. She's too valuable a property—and she'll be even more valuable after she gets the full Henry Margate treatment."

"You're making a mistake. Gerda can't even pretend to be the athletic type."

"Funny. I talked to her before I came here and she kept telling me *you* were wrong for the picture. She also passed along a hot rumor—right out of Buckpasser's feedbox."

"A rumor?"

"That your doctors said you'd never walk right again. I checked with the doctors and it isn't so—but I understand Gerda's busy spreading the good word."

"That bitch!"

"You two love each other, huh?"

"I haven't spoken to her since we appeared in a movie five years ago. She showed up for a promotion party wearing a bikini so small she kept popping out. All the newspaper people were there to interview me. She was just playing a supporting role in the picture. My kid sister! But she wound up getting all the publicity."

"She's telling everyone who'll listen that even if you get to walk again, you'll be off the screen so long you'll be washed up."

The nurse entered and stood by the door, starch white.

"Well, I hope she's wrong, sweetheart. You know I'm rooting for you. But in this business you can't play sentimental favorites. If you say no in a month, Gerda's going to take over."

During the next three weeks of her recovery, huge baskets full of flowers arrived each day, always with the same card: *Dan.* One morning a small potted plant arrived in brown paper and she opened it to reveal orangey-red and scarlet poppies. There was a note in a tiny envelope: *In case you want to make your own opium.* The handwriting was large, sprawling, almost childish in the formation of letters. It was signed *Joel Page.*

The next morning when the new baskets from Dan arrived, the nurse wanted to throw out the little plant by her bedside. Jacquelyn refused to let her. Each morning she watered the poppies until they were thriving, showy flowers.

Before the end of a month, during one of Dan Reed's regular visits, she was able to walk down the corridor with him.

"Well, honey, you beat the deadline," he told her. "You're walking great. The hip action is spectacular."

"The case of the sexy cripple, that's me."

"You don't qualify, sweetheart. You're going to be back bigger than life and twice as natural. When can you start on *Call Me Anytime?*—that's the picture with Henry Margate."

"The doctors say I can go back to work a few weeks after the baby is born."

"Furious Thunder went into general release last month and it's cleaning up. Your fans are going to be drooling at the mouth to see you in a new picture."

"I still have ... a personal problem to settle, Dan. I don't know what to do about it."

"Charles?"

She nodded.

"When would you like to see him?"

See Charles? At the thought her chest seemed to constrict.

Dan said, "Good. That's what I wanted to know. It's over, isn't it?"

"Yes, it's over."

"The sooner you wind up the details the better. When the past is dead you gotta bury it."

She looked at Dan Reed and then couldn't look at him. She couldn't even breathe ...

On a warm, cloudy day Charles came to sit beside her

on the hospital terrace. He smiled his gentle smile while she watched him with almost blank eyes, feeling nothing. He began by saying that he supposed what had happened to them was his fault, although he did not say what he meant by fault, and he kept implying that nothing had happened that afternoon with Christopher Leigh except in her mind. He agreed that he had been unable to live up to her expectations of him, and that in many ways he was weak, although he had done his best both to try to hold their marriage together and to forge a career for himself. He could not honestly say that his failure was his own doing, but certainly it was not hers; fate had conspired against them. He had been unable to contribute to the support of the household and the entire burden had fallen on her. Of course, he had intended to make it all up to her when the winds of fortune stopped blowing so unfavorably. But then . . . this other thing had happened and he supposed it was now too late to talk about a future together.

"Yes, Charles. It's much too late."

"Well, then, if we can't be married any longer, I suppose there is nothing left but a divorce. I am willing to wait until after the baby is born . . ."

"That would be months. I can't wait that long."

Charles shrugged. "I will not ask for custody of the child. I would like to have visitation rights. As for a property settlement or alimony, I have nothing but the house, which is mortgaged . . ."

"I don't want anything from you, Charles."

His lean, handsome features turned mournful. "Jacquelyn, these months with you have been the happiest of my life. I am trying to say something I mean. I know I have been no help to you, but perhaps if we tried again . . . with the child . . . "

"No, Charles." She wanted to close her ears against the appeal of humility.

"Do you blame me?" he asked, as he was ready to leave. "I blame myself. It is only, you see, that when someone is left in a vacuum he must grab at anything he can find . . . anything that he believes will make him happy again."

That was the closest he came to a confession, and perhaps it was better. He was so terrified, and he had to be left something. Odd, she had never noticed before what a frightened man Charles Laurent was. It came to her now as a revelation and she felt sorry for him.

All she managed to say was, "Where are you going to go now?"

"I am going home. To France." His eyes appeared slightly wider and open to pain. "If you would come . . ."

"No, Charles."

He managed a rueful smile, and for an instant she saw again the wistful gallantry of the man.

She held out her hand. "But I do hope you'll be happy."

"Jacquelyn, I am sorry—for everything."

Mercifully she could banish the memory of him with his going. His image did not long survive his departure and was gone almost as swiftly as the reflection in a mirror. Another image was about to replace him . . .

I will watch television, she thought. Just to pass the evening. She had watched all the television programs she had heard about and always wanted to see and somehow never had the time. She had all the time she wanted, now. She went into the living room of the small apartment and turned on TV and watched an old movie with Humphrey Bogart, a woman's cooking program, a soap opera, a contest game with a panel and contestants, a science show, and when another old movie was beginning, also Humphrey Bogart, she finally gave up and ate the dinner of roast lamb and baked potato that the nurse had prepared. She mashed the brown oval of baked potato with her fork and spread it out and then piled it high. It was a lovely evening, and outside she heard the laughter of young college students on their way to night classes at the nearby community college. She began to wonder when the night would pass. Another thought struck with a cruel, sharp little blow in the center of her forehead: What am I going to do tomorrow?

The telephone rang.

This is Joel. What're you doing tonight?"

"Oh, nothing much. Having a baby, I guess. It's nearly over, though."

"You ought to be well enough to go out for a drive. How about it?"

She hesitated.

"Why don't you come over for coffee?" she suggested.

"Not me. I can't be cooped up at night."

"I'd have to be crazy to ride a motorcycle in my condition, Joel . . ."

"Who said anything about a motorcycle? I got a brand-new Ferrari. Fireman's red. I'm going to try it out tonight for the first time."

"I'd love to go. When?"

"Twenty minutes. And you be ready."

The red Ferrari was waiting at the dim end of the walk when she emerged from the house. Joel reached over to swing the door open.

"How marvelous," she said and her eyes lit up with excitement. "This is gorgeous. I love it."

She got into the car and they flashed away, with the engine making a deep roaring sound and the car incredibly swift, flowing, almost voluptuous. The night air made her feel drunk. When he reached the open highway, Joel opened up, and the wind twanged around the windshield as though about to break through. The speedometer inched up past ninety, moved on toward a hundred.

"You're going to have the cops on your tail before you know it," she said.

"There's one back there now. Watch me leave him in the dust."

Joel pushed down on the accelerator and the Ferrari really swung out. Nobody could match that rhythm, and when the engine seemed thrumming at its top level it swung still higher. The car angled around long, swinging curves. She risked a glance back and the police car was a distant speck of trailing headlights. Then the headlights vanished. Abruptly Joel swung the wheel over, and the red Ferrari cornered sharply and writhed rapidly down a country road. He stopped and switched off the lights.

In a minute the police car zoomed along the highway behind them.

"Prob'ly radioed ahead. Someone's coming the other way to meet him. Closing a vise. Only there ain't nothing in it."

He began to laugh. She didn't join him because something was happening to her.

"Joel."

"What is it? You look kinda pale."

"You better get me home as fast as you can."

"Is it starting?"

She nodded. I'm a mess. I just broke water. I want to go home and change. Will you take me to the hospital?"

"Okay. But you hang on, hear? I don't want you having the baby all over the front seat of my car."

Now you just bear down, honey. You bear down as hard as you can."

Her hand locked in the nurse's hand. She tensed against the returning spasm of pain and remembered to bear down, the way the nurse told her. So far, so good. She was an old dead woman gradually growing rigid with rigor mortis. Then she began to feel trembling and faint and cold all over. As the spasm passed, she leaned her head in her arms to conquer nausea, swallowing the spittle that came to her mouth, holding herself in against pain.

The door opened quietly.

"I think she's ready now, doctor."

"All right. I'll give her a shot."

The hypodermic came toward her. The doctor bent over.

"Don't touch me," she said sharply. "Go away."

Something touched her, and she felt the needle sting. Tears came to her eyes. She had wanted to go the whole way without anything.

Suddenly she was emptying out and she felt her body leaving her. The doctor swung up a tiny pink bundle, head downward.

"A boy," he said.

She could say nothing. She clung to the edge of darkness, feeling her way around its outer edges . . .

They walked toward each other in bright sunshine, beneath trees heavy-laden with bright yellow oranges. The sunlight came down through the branches and cast a dramatic white light in places, but he was dappled in shadow as he walked toward her. It seemed to her that his steps became more deliberate and that his gaze became fixed on her. She looked straight into his eyes until they were close to each other, and then he removed the basket of oranges from her arm and put it on the ground.

"That's enough," he said.

"Yes," she said, too quickly, too brightly.

Half slouching, he looked at her, almost coldly. There was a day's grizzle of beard on his face and a faint dark moustache. His hair was tousled and looked dirty. This was the man who had raised such an emotional storm in her these past weeks. She appraised him, the tall slender

figure, sturdy wrists with the black leather band, smoldering gray eyes, insolent shoulders. His thin mouth was set
in an ironic smile. She stood and looked at him, and he
kept on smiling.

"Don't you think it's about time?" Joel Page asked.

"For what?"

"I'm not a kid and neither are you. When are we going
to make it with each other?"

She looked down. He tried to meet her eyes and when
she wouldn't, he held her by the shoulders to compel her
to look up at him. "You've been wanting it to happen. I
didn't push you because I figured you needed time to get
over having a baby. Now what is there to stop us?"

Again, she managed not to meet his eyes. There was
really nothing to say, yet she was filled with words, words
that meant nothing. *Joel, I'm not even sure I like you
when you act like this.*

"I'm not hanging around to play games with you in
orchards or go for long moonlight drives or any of that
crap. I can take you right here, and get it over with.
That's what we're all about."

She felt as though she were standing on a fence, balancing precariously, and he was the truant boy who had come
along to give her a push.

"I want to go home," she said.

He stared at her. "Is that the truth?"

"Yes."

He shrugged. "Okay. We've sure wasted a lot of time."

In complete silence they started back along the row
between the orange trees. It was a quarter of a mile back
to the house with the sign that had made them stop: "Pick
Your Own. A Basketful For Two Dollars." She had not
bothered to pick up the basket.

"Oh," she said, and stopped. "I forgot the basket."

He started back, and she caught up with him as he was
stooping to pick it up.

"Joel . . ."

He straightened up slowly, warily. She thought, I will
never see him again. The quarter of a mile will end and
how will I live afterward? I want to go away with him
and lie late in bed and have breakfast in the sun and make
love all the day and the night with no bad conscience. But
that isn't Joel's way, and it's too late for that now.

"You goddamned tease," he said as he took her roughly
into his arms and thrust her back against a tree trunk.

She felt his fingers, hard and probing.

"Don't do that," she said.

He did not bother to answer. His lips forced down and his beard scratched her. Slowly his hand crept up. Overhead the oranges glinted in the sun and she smelled their fragrance and saw a white cloud in the sky. He was against her and between her thighs. She saw herself as a young girl, naked and free, displaying her body in innocence, breasts and hips and thighs. She was aware of the bruising contact but had a feeling that she was floating, tumbling, as in a dream.

Joel twitched violently in the stillness, in the silence in the orchard. His hands were digging into her shoulders, and she could hear his breathing. Then he gave a moan and clutched her, held her, lurched against her, fought her. Oh God, she thought, dear God.

Restlessness was the key, she decided. He never liked to follow any pursuit for a long time. He had worked as a circus roustabout, a soda jerk, a bronco buster in a rodeo, a book salesman, a clerk in a liquor store, and even put in a one-year stint in the peacetime Army from which he had been discharged under something of a cloud after a run-in with a drill sergeant. He had a terrible aversion to being tied down or settled in one place, and this extended even to owning things, which somehow gave him the unwanted feeling of permanence. He sold the Ferrari after a few months, and went back to his motorcycle which he accepted not as a possession but as a necessity to prevent him from being located too firmly in any given place at any given time. He enjoyed acting because he didn't work for more than a few weeks at a time and could earn enough money to indulge himself in any new thing that suited his fancy.

His fierce independence kept him from being allied with any political causes: he was neither of the right nor the left, but looked on politics and politicians as though from a long distance off, with a knowing indifference. He liked women because they gave him something, but he could never accept them as equals. At best, they shared with him a momentary pleasure and after he had his fill of them, he became tormenting and even insulting, contemptuous of their absurd devotion to him.

He had been born and raised in the tough precincts of New York's Spanish Harlem, dropped out of school and went traveling with a circus. During his late adolescent years, first with the circus, then the rodeo, or working at odd jobs in strange towns, he became a solitary hanger-on, learning the bitter lesson of self-reliance in harsh and uncaring relationships. After the Army he joined a little theater group in Sausalito, mostly because the girls in it were the prettiest in the town. An agent saw one of the productions, signed him, and the dim years vanished in an overnight blaze of sudden fame. He was only twenty-three when it happened.

Jacquelyn thought she understood Joel, and while she could not enter his tight, self-enclosed, hostile world she hoped, gradually, to bring his world into some sort of congruity with her own. After the first few months of their affair she began to sense how sentimental this hope was. Joel enjoyed humiliating her. He would show up to escort her to a party wearing faded sailcloth trousers, raveled sneakers, workshirt and black leather jacket. The first time that she refused to go with him, he simply took off on his motorcycle, and she did not hear from him again. Finally she called him. When she went with him to a social gathering, he would likely as not sit alone in a corner, discouraging conversation and drinking himself into a sullen temper. At one party, given by the director Henry Margate at the conclusion of *Call Me Anytime,* she got into an argument with Joel. The quarrel began when he accidentally spilled part of his drink on her lap and ended when she slapped him and he promptly slapped her back. Several men in the room invited Joel to step outside with them and settle the matter. Joel accepted one invitation and five minutes later they found the man gasping on the garden walk. His nose had been broken and he had been kneed in the groin. Joel was nowhere to be seen.

Talk was going around about Jacquelyn and Joel, and she was omitted from the guest list at several large functions to which she would ordinarily have been invited. She declined others. Gossip about them invaded the fan magazines and the columns, but only succeeded in enhancing their standing with the public. Joel's admirers believed their idol had made it big with the best-looking broad in cinema land. For Jacquelyn's fans, *Call Me Anytime* completed the transformation to a new public image. In the role of Harriet, the rueful girl of many affairs, she was better than even Henry Margate had foreseen. Margate claimed credit for bringing out in her a hitherto suppressed sexy quality which contrasted effectively with her angelic beauty. But a good deal of the credit for teaching her how to portray a woman who knew about love belonged to Joel Page.

She was passionately in love with his body. She lay with him in bed and ran her hands over his lean nakedness, over the ribs showing in the flat chest and the nipples small and blue-colored. He had a narrow waist and a perfectly flat stomach and long, slender, muscular legs. His organ was fascinating even in repose, lying on its side like a flail, long, powerful, and supple. In moments when he wanted to make love, it hardened and rose in a tower, smooth and flushed, with a pale circumcision ridge near the top. *Sure, I was circumsized. My old man was a bug for cleanliness and he thought clipping it was a clean thing to do.*

Though Joel never fully satisfied her, she was pleased by his brusque forcefulness, the hasty way he finished and then pulled away as though ashamed of his passion.

She knew Joel was not faithful. She heard stories of what went on in the large, ramshackle, frame house he had rented on the outskirts of Pasadena. It was said that he held orgies there that rivaled those of the Fatty Arbuckle era. There was one story going the rounds of a coursing in which Joel played the greyhound and five young starlets nude except for bunny tails were the rabbits. One girl was only seventeen, and only a great effort by the studio's public relations department and a very large check kept the parents from filing suit.

One day the phone rang in her apartment and she heard a hesitant, young, female voice at the other end.

"Is this Miss Jacquelyn Stuart?"

"Yes. Who is this?"

"I'm a . . . friend of Joel Page. I have to talk to you, Miss Stuart."

"What about?"

"It's . . . personal."

"Did Joel tell you to call me?"

"Oh, no, Miss Stuart." There was a pause, a tremulous hesitancy. "He certainly would never tell me to do that."

"How did you get my phone number? It's not listed."

"I got it from Joel. He . . . well, he doesn't know I have it. He'd prob'ly kill me if he knew. I just had to talk to you, Miss Stuart."

"I'm afraid I can't. If Joel doesn't know about this . . ."

"It's about Joel. It's something you ought to know."

"I'm sorry."

She hung up and the girl called right back. She said she had known Joel for some time and what she had to say was important not only to Jacquelyn . . . but to Joel Page as well.

"He can get into a lot of trouble, Miss Stuart, if you don't agree to help him."

"Well, all right. But I won't meet you at my home."

She named a place, a drive-in hamburger palace on Sunset Boulevard. She dressed in casual clothes, told the nurse she was just going out for a drive, and kissed baby Eugene good-bye.

She took the nurse's old Chevrolet from the garage and drove to the hamburger palace. A blonde waitress with a vividly painted mouth took her order without giving her a glance. A few minutes later, after the waitress delivered hot coffee, a dusty white Studebaker Lark entered the parking lot, circled, then pulled into the lane adjoining hers. Jacquelyn made out a pale, misty face behind the windshield. After the girl got her order, she brought her tray over to Jacquelyn's car and got into the front seat.

"I wouldn't have recognized you, Miss Stuart, in this car and that get-up and all."

"I prefer not to be recognized. What did you want to see me about, Miss . . . ?"

"Call me Sue." The girl, a wispy, frail, dark blonde, timidly pretty, wore a blue denim wrap-around and sandals without stockings. She wore no makeup except for heavy eyeshadow which accented her pale face by making her eyes seem huge and dark. She waited for Jacquelyn to call her by name and when nothing happened, she continued: "I know you're a good friend of Joel's. He's told me a lot about you."

Jacquelyn winced. She didn't like to be a subject of discussion between Joel and his other girls. She was also a little disappointed in Joel's choice of female companions; this shy, defenseless creature would hardly have been a worthwhile challenge. Perhaps her very helplessness had appealed to him.

Jacquelyn drank her coffee. She didn't really want it, but she felt this was as good a way as any of avoiding the necessity of talking.

"Joel sent me the money to come out here from New York," Sue said.

Jacquelyn would have guessed from the rapid slurred accent that the girl must have grown up in much the same background as Joel. She waited for her to go on.

"I've been staying at his place in Pasadena. My room is upstairs, and I don't know anything about what happens in any of the other rooms. I'm not a bad girl, Miss Stuart, and what Joel does is his business. That's how I look at it. He's good to me. He gives me money when I need it, but I don't ask for much. Just enough to buy a few groceries and for a couple of dresses. I don't like to be a sponger, if you know what I mean."

"I know what you mean," Jacquelyn said. "But I'm afraid I don't see what you're driving at."

"I've got to do something, Miss Stuart, and I don't want Joel to know anything about it."

"What do you have to do?"

"I need a doctor."

Jacquelyn knew what was coming and she didn't want to hear it.

"I'm pregnant, Miss Stuart."

Jacquelyn's voice sounded surprisingly calm to her own ears: "I see. I suppose you're trying to tell me that Joel Page is the father."

"It's got to be him, Miss Stuart. I haven't had anything to do with any other man for weeks and weeks."

"Then why not tell Joel about it? He's the logical one for you to talk to."

"I can't," Sue almost wailed. "I just can't do that to him. It's all my fault. I should've been more careful. Joel thought I was using something, but I wasn't, and when he wanted to, I just couldn't say no to him."

Jacquelyn felt the last of her energy being drained from her, and she could not assemble her thoughts. She sipped at her hot coffee while Sue watched her.

"You know how Joel is, Miss Stuart," Sue said. "He gets around a girl. I'm not saying I shouldn't have been smarter seeing what time of the month it was and all, but when he started . . ."

I'm going to be sick, Jacquelyn thought. She swayed gently in her seat, her eyes closed, sure that she could feel the hot nausea beginning.

"I don't want to hear any more of it," she said finally in a clenched and determined voice. "This is between you and Joel. If it really is his baby, then he'll have to decide whether he wants you to have it or not."

Sue stared at her in shock. "I can't have it, Miss Stuart. Nobody would say that's the right thing to do. I've got to have an abortion and I don't know any doctors, and I don't have the money to pay for it."

Jacquelyn answered angrily, "Why come to me? Do you expect me to give you the money to get rid of your damned baby? Have it, for all I care!"

Sue began to cry. "I can't, Miss Stuart. I can't. It wouldn't be right. It'd be against God."

"Isn't it against God to murder an unborn infant?"

Sue covered her face with her hands and began sobbing in misery. "Not if it's a child born out of sinnin'. I can't tell Joel I'm having his baby because he'd think I was crazy to let anything like this happen. It's not as if I was just one of his girls."

"Aren't you?"

Sue slowly lowered her hands away from a tear-stained, desperate face.

"No, I'm not, Miss Stuart."

Jacquelyn had heard all she could. But as she turned the ignition key and the engine roared, she was still straining, with an odd sort of dread, to hear what Sue had to say.

"I've been trying to tell you. My name is Page. Susan Page. I'm Joel's sister."

The Chevrolet swept up the concrete driveway toward the ramshackle frame house. Through the drooping leaves of a eucalyptus tree she saw a light on the verandah and another square of light from an upstairs room in the house. She stopped the car and went up onto the verandah where there were two old wooden rocking chairs and a magazine rack with gay-colored covers. She found Joel lying back on the sofa in the living room, bare-chested and wearing faded-blue sailcloth trousers. His feet were bare. There was a drink on the low table beside him, and he was looking at photographs and laughing.

He was surprised when she entered.

"What are you doing here? I didn't expect to see you tonight."

"I've just come from a meeting with a friend of yours."

He slipped one photograph behind the pack, and examined the next one. "A friend of mine?"

"Your sister, as a matter of fact."

"Sue?" He slid another photograph behind the pack. "I didn't know you two were acquainted."

"We weren't—until tonight."

Joel sighed, shuffled the photographs into order, and put the pack down on the table.

"Something bugging you? You want to spill it or you want to play games?"

"I don't care what you do with other women. But I always thought you had enough common decency to draw the line at doing it with your sister."

Joel's mouth tightened. There was silence.

"Sue tell you that?"

"Are you going to deny it?"

"I don't have to deny nothing. Sue's got a terrible reputation for making up stories."

"She isn't making up the fact that she's pregnant!"

Joel sat up slowly and rubbed one hand over the hairy center of his chest.

"You two really got pretty chummy, didn't you?"

"She came to me because she needed money for an abortion. She was afraid to go to you."

A car passing on the street outside made a shifting circle of light on the wall of the room. Joel waited until the noise of the passing motor whined away.

"Did you give her the money?"

"Of course I did. I found the name of a doctor for her to go to, and bought her a train ticket. I've made all the arrangements."

"You're a goddamn bossy female, you know that?" His voice had taken on a low, almost whispery tone.

"I had to do something for her. Mostly, I had to get her away from you."

"Why?"

"I think that's obvious."

"You believed everything she told you, didn't you?"

She opened her mouth to reply and didn't. I don't know why I came here in the first place, except to make Joel face up to what he has done. To make him see himself for what he is.

She managed to nod her head.

"You goddamn fool. Sue wouldn't know how to tell the truth about anything if she tried. She's my own sister and I tell you she's never told a truth in her whole life. Now, what have you got to say to that?"

"I don't believe you."

"You ... don't ... believe ... me?"

Joel got up from the sofa in a lithe, springy motion. As

he came toward her, he looked as though he intended to walk through her.

"Where has Sue gone? Where did you send her?"

"I'm not going to tell you!"

"You're going to tell me, sweetheart. You're going to tell me every damn thing I want to know."

As she tried to pull away, he grabbed her wrist and turned it until she felt a sharp stab of pain.

"Let go of me!"

"Where's Sue? Where have you sent her?"

"You can break my arm. I'll never tell."

Joel gave her wrist a further wrench. Then he pushed her away, and reeling she fell down.

"You better get something straight. I don't know how much of this crap you think I'm going to take. You're a jealous bitch, but you ought to know I'm a normal. N-o-r-m-a-l. And that doesn't mean I go around screwing my sister."

She had fallen back against the low-lying table and dislodged the packet of photographs. They slipped to the floor. Her attention was caught by the overlapping squares of color. She picked them up and riffled through the lot.

Then she began to laugh. She had an impulse to put her hands over her mouth to stifle hysterics.

"Oh, you're a normal all right. You've even got pictures to prove it. In color."

He came at her with a fury that made it seem his legs were short and he was running across a distance with only hatred to shorten the space between them. His hand raised and she saw it coming down a moment before the jolting impact struck her.

"You shut your bitching mouth, you hear? *You hear?*"

"Go ahead. Tell me how normal you are. I could take these pictures into court and . . ."

Again the heavy hand struck. The room blurred, and she tasted salt in her mouth.

"What I do with other women is my business. Sue's a different matter. *Where has she gone?*"

"I promised not to tell you. She doesn't want to see you."

The next blow caused her to fall, bruised and breathless, face down on the carpet.

"I'll ruin your face so you won't show up before a camera for the rest of your life. You know I'll do it. And I don't care what happens to me later."

"You crazy son of a . . ."

He bent to grab her hair and yank her upright. She clutched a heavy glass ashtray from a table and hit him on the temple. Blood spurted. He put his hand to his head, and it came away red. The sight infuriated him. He came back at her in a frenzy. Back and forth her head turned under the stinging impact of backhanded lashes. She was trying to catch her breath, dazed and bleeding and crying. Everything was spinning, and she willed herself to go under. But she stayed conscious, while in the center of a whirling vortex a quiet, insistent voice demanded: "Tell me. Where is she?"

Tell me. Where is she?

"Goddamn you!" she screeched. "I'll kill you if I get the chance!"

He grabbed both her breasts and pushed savagely. She staggered and tripped and fell heavily. She crawled to where the phone was, and when he caught her she struck out at him with the receiver. His hands closed on her throat and his voice cracked.

"I swear to Christ, you're asking for this."

He was in a maniacal fury. He'll do it, she thought, he'll kill me, but the need to defy him was greater than her fear. Her breathing became labored. She could hardly see. She heard a croaking voice that seemed like a stranger's until she realized it was her own voice.

"Go ahead! Go ahead!"

His fingers loosened. "I ought to kill you. I ought to crack your lousy neck."

"Go ahead!" She was becoming aware that she had won. She pressed her hands against the wall, struggling to breathe, struggling to rise. She gagged. Her legs were too weak to support her and she slipped and lay weakly, in triumph "You dumb bastard. You can't do anything. She's in Mission City by now."

In the silence she pursed her lips, testing her ability to do it. Something began dripping down the corner of her mouth, rolling and gathering into drops and falling. He kept his promise. He ruined my face and I'll never show up before a camera again. But I've won. He couldn't make me tell.

The silence began to alarm her. With infinite care she turned her head.

Joel was sitting deep in a chair, his legs splayed out, and his lean body shaking with soundless laughter. One side of his face was streaked with blood. She watched him, dazed, uncomprehending.

"Mission City," he said. "Mission City!"

She held her head steady with an unasked question, bewildered, sensing dimly that something had gone wrong.

"Stupid," Joel said, standing up. "That's all I need to know. I can be in Mission City when her train gets in. It won't be hard to find her. I'll get the cops to help me do it. Tell 'em my sister ran away from home—and she's underage. Tell 'em she's booked for some quack abortionist. When they put a missing persons' bulletin on the radio no doctor in his right mind will touch her for any amount of money." He drew in a wheezing breath of satisfaction. "Stupid, stupid," he said.

The feeling of triumph that had been sustaining her began to ebb, and with it went the last of her strength.

She managed to ask, "Why? Why do you care so much."

"You really want to know, don't you? All right, you nailed it, baby. It's my kid—and I want her to have it. Now I hope you're happy." At the door he stopped to look back at her. "You went through all that for nothing. What a dumb bitch!"

He seemed to stagger a little as he went out the door. Then the door slammed, and she slid down beside the wall and lay crumpled, with her head cradled on her arms.

She never heard the roar of the motorcycle start up in the driveway.

From the time she recovered consciousness in the living room of the great sprawling frame house in Pasadena, she felt as though some giant boulder had rolled out of the pathway of her life. Even as she went up the stairs of the house, swaying a little and holding to the banister, sure that she was going to be terribly shocked at what she would see in the mirror, she felt somehow cleansed of an old poison. It was right that her affair with Joel Page should end in this way. It was like a fever, and its natural end was delirium. In the bathroom in dim yellowish light, she took a moment to muster her courage before looking at her image. It was a ridiculous grotesque portrait of herself that she saw, her right eye puffed, and dried blood staining underlip and chin, bruises making her face look as though her skin was caked with dirt. But in that first calm appraisal she knew a great relief. There was no permanent damage. Nothing broken. She touched the bruises, wincing at the hurt, but found nothing that bandages, cold packs, and iodine would not repair.

She smiled lopsidedly at herself. "My dear, you look absolutely beautiful."

She washed her face and dried it, and did the minor repairs that makeup could accomplish, before she went downstairs to the living room. Marks of the struggle were still to be seen in the scrunched-up carpeting, overturned lamp, telephone on the floor with plastic black coils leading to an endlessly buzzing receiver. She placed the receiver carefully back in its cradle and lifted the phone onto a table. Over there on the sofa he had lain when she entered the room, and the vision of him bare-chested, barefooted, sniggering over his obscene photographs returned vividly to her mind.

"Oh, you're a normal all right," she said to herself. "N-o-r-m-a-l."

She did not see the photographs anywhere; he had been careful to take them. On impulse she picked up the telephone and dialed her apartment.

"Hello, Patricia?"

"Is that you, Miss Stuart?"

"Patricia, I'm not going to be home for a couple of days. If anyone calls, just say you don't know where I am."

Patricia would not be surprised. There had been other occasions when she did not return to the apartment for a few days, when she was stealing away with Joel to a rendezvous. She remembered a motel near Big Sur which they particularly liked the looks of; it had been booked when they applied for a room. There might be vacancies now, and it would be a good place to hide out from the prying world.

As she was leaving she glanced back at the living room where so much had happened in the last hour, so much that changed the direction of her life. She tried to endow inanimate objects with the significance they deserved, but it was useless. She could not confer emotion upon a place or change this large bare, somewhat chilly-looking room into anything but what it was.

The Chevrolet was waiting in the driveway. She hesitated before she got in. Joel's motorcycle had been parked nearby. He must have taken it, and even now he was speeding toward Mission City to intercept his sister. Well, she had tried. From now on, the problem would have to be resolved between them. No matter what happened, she was queerly grateful for what had happened. It had set her free.

While she was at the motel, she saw a copy of a day-old newspaper. Joel Page had been killed when his motorcycle skidded out of control on a country road and plastered him into a tree.

CHAPTER ELEVEN

At seven o'clock in the morning, a caravan consisting of cars, trucks, and a horse van straggled up a rocky mountain road past groves whose deep, tangled leaves kept out the sunlight. The cast and crew and equipment of the production of *Death of a Peacock* were underway to a new location site. The road narrowed and ceased to be asphalt and became strewn with pebbles, and they passed a cataract pouring down white thunder over a jutting lip of rock. Jacquelyn, riding in the second car of the caravan, could feel the vibrations of the cold torrent around which yellow and brown giant butterflies soared, glistening, and clung to the long wet grass that grew down on either side of the gorge. When sunlight touched the butterflies they seemed to ignite and burn in air, great throbbing veins of color. From the height of the mountain she saw the rawness of the sea below, the waves surging in over ponderous earth.

It was a long drive, and in the rear seat of the car she passed the time studying the script. In the car ahead, H. T. Wallace rode with his chief assistants, and in the car behind was her co-star, Ross Hamilton, with the writer and photographer team from *Glance* magazine. *Glance* magazine had assigned the team to do a picture layout on the movie, and their presence in the caravan was a source of irritation to Jacquelyn. While their assignment was supposed to cover everyone, she would be the focal point. That meant interrogation about herself and Brian, which she did not welcome. She had managed to seem aloof this morning when introduced to the two representatives from *Glance*, a garrulous, masculine-looking Frenchwoman of about fifty, somewhat bitter about life, whose face was held together by a network of wrinkles, and a powder-white photographer, whose body was so slender and wiry it seemed to have been distilled and whose head bobbed loosely on a neck so long and thin that he looked decapitated. After minor pleasantries she turned aside their questions and quietly arranged for them to ride with Ross Hamilton on the trip to the new location site.

Riding along now, she thought briefly of the samba she had listened to with Meyer Whitney last night. *Quero chorar, não tenha lagrimas.* I want to cry but I have no tears. Strange how popular songs sometimes caught at the truth of feeling. Brian claimed that folk songs did that because they sprang from the people. She frowned. The thing she had to do, simply had to, was stop remembering what Brian said or thought or did. Ever.

On the top of the mountain, a plateau of five acres had been miraculously transformed into a village of storage sheds for props and costumes, bungalows for dressing rooms and living quarters, long barracks for infirmary and dining quarters, and a couple of standing sets which included one of a popular but sleazy nightclub, and another which was part of a small town with cobblestoned streets and old baroque houses with gilded wood and plaster that seemed to lean upon each other for support.

The presence of the writer-photographer team was good for the morale of nearly everyone working on the picture. There was a new crispness, a sense of importance. Everyone was more alert because a great international news magazine had decided their activities were worthy of coverage. They were under surveillance by a different medium.

After the filming of a crowd scene, a bitter quarrel broke out between Ross Hamilton and the director concerning the use of a stand-in for him in the scene in which he was supposed to go horseback riding with Jacquelyn. Originally, the scene had simply called for a stroll in the countryside, but Wallace decided to use horses, which had been brought along in a special van, to give the scene a little more color and movement.

Ross said, "I'm scared to death of the beasts. I turned down a very good Western script because I had to be on a horse."

H. T. Wallace pointed out that these were well-trained saddle horses and that he would have to do nothing more than jog along for the closeup scenes. In the long shots, doubles would be used.

Ross said plaintively, "I break out in goose pimples when I get near one of them. I had a cousin who was killed riding a horse. She was just cantering through the park and the dumb animal took her right under a branch. Broke her neck. I've never wanted to even look at a horse since."

"Look, this is costing seven thousand dollars an hour. We can't afford to stand around arguing. Give it a try. Once you get up on the horse you'll find out you're not as scared as you think."

The presence of the *Glance* writer-photographer team was the decisive factor. Ross suddenly envisioned how his cowardice in getting on a horse would appear in print, possibly with photographs and captions. He approached a placid brown stallion as though the animal were intent on killing him. The head propman cupped his hands and gave him a boost into the saddle where he sat as unsteadily erect as Robespierre in a tumbrel on the way to the guillotine. Robespierre probably looked happier.

"I'm worried about this," he said, indicating the saddle pommel. "It's liable to stick me in the wrong place. I could be castrated."

"Okay," H. T. Wallace said to Jacquelyn, who came forward, followed by her make-up man, holding a mirror and making a few final adjustments, and by her hairdresser. "We're ready for a take."

Jacquelyn handed her tall glass of Scotch to the hairdresser. There was tissue around the glass to keep if from dripping on her costume. She wore a tight blouse, open to the third button to show cleavage, and well-fitted jodhpurs.

She yelled, "Carmella!" to the continuity girl who hurried over to confirm a line of dialogue. Then she nodded.

"I'm ready, H. T. What do you want me to do?"

"Cross to that tree over there," H. T. Wallace indicated. "Just ambling along, and talking. At the tree, stop while Ross leans over a little and you embrace. Nothing passionate. This is your first kiss and there's got to be a yielding but tentative quality about it. On your part, Jacquelyn, because you're in love and don't know how to handle the situation. On Ross's part because . . ."

". . . because if I really try to grab her, we'll both fall down," Ross said sourly. "And probably get trampled on."

"Concentrate on kissing Jacquelyn and forget the horse," H. T. advised him. "If you've got that kind of anxious expression on your face when we let the cameras roll, it'll just mean retakes. You want to get it over with as soon as possible We all do."

Jacquelyn took the bridle of her horse and started to swing up to the saddle. As she did, something snapped in her back, and a fork of pain shot through both her legs.

Frank Perrone, the head cameraman, was the first to notice.

"Hey, something's happened!"

H. T. Wallace was quickly at her side.

"It's too ridiculous," Jacquelyn whispered. "But it's my back. You'd better get the medic."

They eased her down out of the stirrups. What a curious thing, she thought, out of breath and a little shocked, I'm really going to pass out . . .

Night shooting. Giant arc lights surrounded a large, open, marble-floored room. The time was half past ten, and the setting a room of a palace at Thebes. Brian O'Neal playing Oedipus the King, was meeting with the blind see Tiresias in the white marble and plasterboard set that was the palace.

The ancient Tiresias, cowering in his ragged garments before the richly appareled King, was too meek and humble to suit Lester Mitchell Lester ordered another take. He seemed to be in a trance from which he would suddenly emerge to flip about the set, changing a vase here, moving a piece of statuary there, muttering to himself and puckering his lips around an unlit cigarette. He acted out the roles of both Oedipus and Tiresias, making minor suggestions. He asked Tiresias to lean a bit backward before denouncing Oedipus, and asked Brian to move over slightly so as to be framed in an archway. Suddenly he yelled, "We blew another light. Hank What the hell's the matter with everybody?" Finally he retreated with a curt, "All right. Let's get the cameras in there now."

Brian and Tiresias again spoke their lines, building in anger to the point at which the King accuses Tiresias himself of the murder.

"Thou art thyself the unclean King," Tiresias said.

"Cut," Lester Mitchell said wearily. "Not unclean King, Harry. Unclean thing."

"I'm sorry, Lester. I guess I'm a little tired."

"We're all a little tired. Let's try to get it right this time."

They went through the scene again, and the dialogue went well until Tiresias delivered his awful warning that Oedipus would one day return "beggared and blinded, the brother and the father of his own children, the seed, the sower and the sown, shame to his mother's blood and to his sire a murderer and committer of incest." In the middle of the denunciation Tiresias began blinking, and finally tears ran out of one eye.

Lester Mitchell called, "Cut."

He walked over casually, smiling gently, but with the air of a man counting to himself.

"What is it this time?" he inquired pleasantly.

"These goddamn contact lenses," Tiresias said. He was holding his lids apart and trying to squeeze out the lens that gave his eye its blank, blind look. "I'm always getting something under them. It's murder."

Tiresias removed the piece of grit, replaced his contact lens, and they tried the scene for the fifth time. It was completed without a hitch.

"That's great," Lester said. "Two more pages of immortal rubbish into the can."

The still photographers leapt in for a shot. Merrill Yeaton came onto the set from behind the floodlights.

"You were wonderful, darling," she told Brian, and kissed him approvingly on the cheek.

There was a general air of relaxation among the crew and the grips.

"It's been a long night," Lester said, stretching. "See you at eight tomorrow, Brian. Same place, same story."

Brian took Merrill's hand and walked off the set.

"I think Lester is something of a perfectionist," Merrill said. "That's why everything is taking so long. You're way behind schedule, aren't you, darling?"

Brian said, "We're all working our bloody asses off. This isn't an ordinary movie, you know. It's the first major film ever made about Sophocles' famous old chestnut. We've got to keep the tempo right, the action flowing."

"The people who go to it won't go for that reason. They'll go for the incest."

"Another moral barrier falls. Nothing left but cannibalism. I have a great idea," Brian said. "Maybe we can work cannibalism into *this* script. We'll get a new title. How about changing it from *Oedipus Rex* to *My Mother, My Supper?*"

Merrill chuckled dutifully. Jacquelyn would have

roared, a fine girl with a loud, long laugh when he amused
her, and that was often. My God, in that white sweater,
her arms, the soft pattern of her breasts, the dull woolen
nipples. Not dull beneath the wool, though. Lovely dark
circles. Sex is a great joy, Brian thought, a whirler of
blood through the veins, a cleanser of the brain, and a
boon to the heart and the intestines.

He was tired, but it was nice to know he would not be
alone tonight.

Merrill stirred. As she slept, her long, silky flank
touched him in bed. He liked to bed her, but she couldn't
stay just the girl who made his cock rise. Oh, no! That
would never do for a lady like Merrill. He could have
fucked her until her acne went away, but she wouldn't be
content with that. So here he was, making a sure money-
losing picture in London, and the wedding plans were all
set as soon as he got word of the divorce. That should
have been Merrill's occupation, making plans. When the
new world comes, and everyone is equal and no one is
poor and peace reigns everywhere, Merrill will be indis-
pensable. She will never let anyone forget how much
better off he is.

Tomorrow evening she had a dinner party planned. For
a good cause. Raising money for state nurseries for children of low-income workers. Lord Harrow, the newspaper
publisher, was going to be there and was particularly keen
to meet Brian, the son of a poor Irish pubkeeper. As an
existentialist socialist who prided himself on his hatred for
all marks of caste, Brian could not have cared less if all
the lords had been hanged by Oliver Cromwell. He was
going because Merrill had planned it. Suddenly he was
shaken by a desire to get away from Merrill and all her
rich, liberal friends. There are some things I don't have to
accept, Brian thought. I am going to hate some things
until I die. I can't jingle in tune, and I will always have a
desire for some nook or corner in which to hide myself.

To be honest, he was also anxious to get away from the
poisonous cloud of failure that was gathering about
Oedipus Rex.

At breakfast he told her about the new financing for the
movie and deliberately mentioned that the deal was arranged through Margot Wesley. He got the reaction, a
slight widening of the eyes, a fixity of smile that became
more emphatic as he added Lyle was out of the country

and he had gone to Margot's house to conclude arrangements. Her brain received the message as though it were a letter, folding it carefully and slipping it back into an envelope for filing away. Not quite forgetting. It would become something she forgave him. Margot became an advantage she had over him because she rose above it. Merrill was forever rising above things.

When he asked for the newspaper, she gave him a slightly twisted smile.

"I don't believe they delivered it this morning."

"Ring them up. I've got to have the paper. I can't put any food down unless I pour print after it."

"It's past seven. You're due back at the studio at eight."

"I'll not go uninformed. Where is my paper? Call Scotland Yard."

"Brian, I didn't want to upset you this morning."

"You have it?"

She nodded.

"Good. I'll get my glasses."

"Brian, I'm afraid you're going to make more of the news this morning than is necessary."

"Look, I don't feel like toe-dancing around with you at this hellish hour of the morning. Just where is the newspaper?"

"You don't have to be abusive."

"I'll be as stinking abusive as I want."

Merrill's eyebrows rose. From the drawer of a sidetable she produced the newspaper.

He stood there, in maroon pajamas and a brown wool, ribbed sweater, and read that Jacquelyn had been thrown from a horse during the filming of a scene in *Death of a Peacock*.

"It says here that she's in a bad way."

"You know how newspapers exaggerate."

"No, I don't know how newspapers exaggerate," he mimicked.

"You don't have to act annoyed."

"I have to if I am."

"I don't understand why."

"You could give people the newspaper when they ask for it instead of acting so damn coy."

"Well, now you know. I was only trying to spare you. You can hardly blame me."

He had to blame someone, and was irritable because

she was shutting herself off as an object of blame. It was not her fault, but what the hell.

"I have to find out what's happening to her. I'm going to Rio on the next plane."

"Brian! You don't mean it."

He started to wrestle the brown sweater up over his head.

"For sweet Mary's sake, don't get me started. I know well enough what I have to do."

"I've already sent a cable."

He stopped with the sweater up beneath his armpits and stared at her out of the neckhole.

"When did you do that?"

"As soon as I saw the newspaper this morning. I knew you'd want to know. You were in the bathroom."

"A man can't accommodate his bowels without things going on behind his back. What did the cable say?"

"I asked the American consulate for further information. They will call collect or cable. I'm sure we'll have an answer in a few hours."

"That's too long. The newspaper says she's going to have an operation."

"You can't do anything about that. If you want to call the hospital directly . . ."

"Hospitals never tell you anything."

"You're not serious about going?"

He pulled the sweater over his head without replying.

"Why?" she asked. "You know I don't want you to."

"Because," he answered sourly, "as a child I was chosen by the fairy folk to be a wanderer. They put their mark on me in the shape of a butterfly on the right side of my neck." He indicated the very place near the collarbone. "This kind of stigmata marks a man who is not born to be enslaved of women."

"Brian, I'm trying to be understanding, but you must try to be reasonable too. You won't arrive there until long after the operation is over. Even if there is one. If you do go, what will Jacquelyn think? I'll tell you. That you still love her and don't want a divorce."

"I don't want any more talk about it."

"All I'm asking is that you wait a few hours. Until there's an answer to my cable."

"Is *that* all you're asking? Well, it's too much."

Merrill stood stock still. He knew she was mentally

counting off, and she got to six or seven before temper showed through.

"Go ahead! Do what you want! You don't have to take me into consideration."

"Don't give me your Mary in the manger. That's a bitch way of getting what you want."

"This sort of fighting is going to get us nowhere, Brian."

"It's a damn sight not going to get you anywhere."

He flung off the top of his pajamas, turned and strode flatfooted to the bedroom. He picked up a splinter in his bare foot along the way and that added to his indignation. Damn women try to tie a man into a knot and slip them over their finger as a remembrance.

In the end she apologized and came to the airport and stood there crying and waving as his plane took off for Rio de Janeiro.

The silver jet banked and began the long descent to the airport. Brian lay stretched out, his face turned sideways into a pillow away from the hot sun that streamed in the window beside him.

"Are you awake, Mr. O'Neal?" the stewardess asked.

His head moved slightly. "Yes."

"You asked me to tell you when we were arriving. We should be at the airport in a few minutes."

Brian turned his face up. The stewardess was a tall darkhaired girl with a lovely smile.

"Thank you." He sat up and then noticed the stewardess staring and looked down at himself, following her eyes. "I guess I was asleep. I was dreaming."

She turned scarlet. "Yes, Mr. O'Neal."

"What's your name?"

"Maria Carvalhos."

"Brazilian?"

"Oh, yes."

"How can I reach you? Through the airline?"

"I have an apartment in town."

"Would you write down the telephone number and address?"

The stewardess glanced around to be sure no one was listening and she fluffed up his pillow.

"I'd like that very much, Mr. O'Neal."

"So would I."

She would enjoy it enormously, Brian thought, because

what she wants of me is exactly what I am prepared to give. I am quite suited to the role of a lover because I'm a peasant and only the working class has an absolutely satisfactory knowledge of how to behave with women. They do not waste time in the oily art of seduction, nor puff the thing up to a melodrama, nor cover up with good manners what feats they will be able to perform. A working-class lover goes about the business with a hearty natural air, gives as good as he gets, and does not waste a woman's time with malingering preliminaries. If he wants something extra, he asks for it, and if he feels like fooling around for a while before taking her he does so with uncalculated zest.

Maria Carvalhos moved off, giving him a sample display of hips rotating. He would probably not call her. But he had to show some interest when he caught the poor girl staring at him as though his peter was a magnet. The heat from his dreaming brain had permeated his loins. She thought the hard-on might have been for her.

It hadn't been. It had been for Jacquelyn. He had been dreaming about Jacquelyn in the oddest way. She was sitting on a throne like the Queen of Sheba, wearing nothing but a tiny jeweled breastplate and a narrow circlet of jewels across her deeply tanned body. It was an image that embodied much of his feeling about her beauty, strangeness, and perversity—how she disturbed and excited him.

The plane touched wheels down on the runway. Brian offered a silent prayer to a God in whom he did not believe but whose power he feared: Let her be all right.

As he got off onto the landing platform, Maria Carvalhos smiled brilliantly. They shook hands and he felt the rustle of paper in his palm. That would be her address in town.

Brian shrugged as he put the paper into his pocket. Time passes, but a man comes up against the same problems and somehow manages to make the identical mistakes.

The receptionist behind the grilled window of the hospital office was an interesting blend of the Indian and Portuguese that constitute so large a part of the Brazilian population. She had very black hair, almond-shaped eyes, and high cheekbones, and there was something dark cream about her complexion that suggested Africa was somewhere in the amalgam.

"I'd like to see Miss Jacquelyn Stuart, please."

The girl's eyes widened. She wore large golden circle earrings that swung as her head moved.

"Senhor O'Neal. Oh, yes. I'll give you a pass to her room." She began to fill out a small white slip. "That part of the hospital has been closed to visitors. So many people are trying to get in to see her. Reporters and people who say they are important. The photographers are the worst."

"Photographers are always the worst," Brian said. "If they could get there with a camera, they'd take pictures of her sitting on the john."

The dark cream darkened. "You go to the third floor, Senhor O'Neal. As you go off the elevator turn right." She handed him the slip of paper. "Give this to the guard."

As he got off the elevator he saw a desk placed in the middle of the corridor, and a bored guard reading a newspaper. The guard put down the newspaper as Brian approached. His dark Negroid face was that of a street urchin, prematurely aged. He even carried a gun in a leather holster with a flap. He was a small man with a full head of hair turning gray.

"What do you wish, Senhor?"

"I'd like to see Miss Jacquelyn Stuart."

The guard was already starting to shake his head when Brian presented his pass.

"I will have this checked out, Senhor. You wait here."

The guard went down the corridor and turned off into a corner room. Brian glanced at the newspaper, but it was in Portuguese. There was a small picture of Jacquelyn on the front page, and he deciphered enough of the caption to know that the story was about her accident. He did not want to let his thoughts dwell on that.

The guard returned.

"I am sorry, Senhor. Senhora Stuart is not having any visitors today."

"Is her condition that serious?"

"I cannot reveal any information, Senhor. Those are my orders."

"Has she been operated on yet?"

"I cannot reveal any information."

"Look, I'm her husband. If you won't tell me, I'm going in there to find out for myself."

The guard took this as a jab at his authority.

"No one may go in without permission, Senhor."

Brian indicated the gun in the holster. "If you want to stop me, you'll have to use that."

The guard moved to oppose him, offering his small body as a barrier. Brian moved through him. The guard tried to hold him back but Brian forced him along the corridor by the sheer forward momentum of his body. The guard's hands clutched at Brian's arms and, unable to keep his feet, he slid to the floor.

Lying on the floor he looked thinner, like a small, crumpled old man. His mouth moved like a puppet's.

He undid the flap of his holster. "I warn you, Senhor."

Brian looked at him with exasperated amusement.

"In a country ruled by a military dictatorship," he said, "everyone goes crazy.

The guard looked off down the corridor, and following his gaze Brian saw a man emerge from the corner room.

"Is anything wrong?"

As the man approached, Brian recognized him.

"You're Meyer Whitney."

"And you're Brian O'Neal."

There was thunderous silence in the corridor, the sort of absence of noise that, translated into sound, would make a prodigious musical score. They shook hands, prolonging the handclasp and getting the feel of the other's grip.

"I suppose you gave instructions just now," Brian said, "that I wasn't to get in to see Jacquelyn."

Meyer nodded. "I don't want Jacquelyn to be upset. That's all a visit from you could accomplish."

"How is she?"

"She's fine."

"What about the operation?"

"She isn't going to have one."

Brian's eyes crinkled with satisfaction. "Well, that's a relief anyhow."

"There was never any question of operating. You must have read the first stories. You can blame those on a couple of reporters from *Glance* magazine. Brainless wonders who didn't wait for the diagnosis before they sent off cables announcing that her spine was badly injured and she was facing a major operation. Unfortunately that story was picked up by the major newswires."

"What's wrong, then?"

"Well, really nothing but a sprained back."

Brian glared at him. "You're joking."

"She wasn't thrown. She sprained her back while she was getting up into the saddle."

Brian looked Meyer over as though he could tell from the man's appearance whether he was putting him on. Everything about Meyer Whitney was in faultless good taste, from the black moccasins to the chaste gold of his cuff links, the thin gold watch on his wrist, the perfect fit of his custom-made silk shirts. He was very elegant.

Brian wore a rumpled sports jacket, gray trousers, and a lightweight green turtleneck sweater.

"You mean I've come all this way from London because Jacquelyn sprained her back?"

"I'm afraid so."

Brian smoothed out a slight bulge in his sweatered midriff. "What you're telling me is that I've been God's own green fool."

"I wouldn't go that far. You may have been a little impulsive."

"Impulsive?" The humor of it finally got to Brian. He burst into laughter. "All those thousands of miles for nothing!"

"It's understandable," Meyer said kindly. "You thought she was seriously hurt."

Brian's expression became thoughtful. "Did I? Or was that just my excuse?" He slapped his unpressed trousers. "It puts everything into perspective, doesn't it?"

"I'm afraid I don't understand."

"If she'd been hurt, operated on, crippled even, I would never have discovered the truth of why I came. I'd have thought it was honest human concern. Merrill knew better ... Well, I'm here now, and not sorry, and that shows me up for the pitiful liar that I am."

Meyer Whitney stared coldly at the ceiling. "I don't see what this has to do with anything."

"Oh, but it does. Jacquelyn will agree."

"You're not going to see Jacquelyn."

"You're wrong about that."

The little guard sidled up. His hair was mussed. He seemed to be hoping this argument would amount to something.

Brian said, "He'll have to shoot. That would make an interesting scandal, wouldn't it? There wouldn't be anything else on the front pages for quite some time."

"Suppose I tell you Jacquelyn doesn't want to see you? That she's told me so herself?"

"I'll believe that when I hear her say it."

He started down the corridor. As the guard started to intercept him, Meyer Whitney shook his head. Meyer followed Brian, walking casually, not hurrying.

At the door to the corner room Brian stopped and saw Meyer following, and smiled. Then he opened the door on a sitting room with a small couch and chairs, a rug, and a television set. On the right an open doorway led to the bedroom of the suite.

"Is that you, Meyer?"

She had been leafing through a script, sitting up in bed with pillows fluffed behind her back. Her poise forsook her when Brian entered. She dropped the script.

"My God! Brian!"

"You're looking well," he said, "for a hopeless invalid."

"Brian, what in the world are you doing here?"

"I read a few scare stories about what happened to you. I had to come and make sure you were still all in one piece." He eyed her admiringly. "Everything seems in place. I never saw any of it looking lovelier."

"Don't practice your blarney on me, Brian."

He noticed that she smoothed the bedcovers about her waist. Meyer Whitney stood in the doorway.

"Do we have to talk with him around?" Brian asked.

Jacquelyn said, "It's really all right, Meyer. There isn't anything to worry about."

Brian added, comfortingly, "If I have a go at her, she has a powerful pair of lungs. You'll hear her in the next county."

"I told him you didn't want to see him," Meyer said.

Jacquelyn shook her head. "I'm sure Brian didn't come here to make trouble."

"I don't suppose a few minutes can do any harm," Meyer conceded.

"Alone," Brian said.

Meyer Whitney went over to kiss Jacquelyn. "If you want me, push the button for the floor nurse. I'll be just down the corridor."

"I'll be fine," Jacquelyn said.

Meyer Whitney walked out as though Brian were not in the room.

Brian indicated the huge basket of flowers standing in the corner. "These from him?"

"Yes."

"Are you going to marry him?"

"Yes."

"When?"

"As soon as I get the divorce."

Brian sat down on the edge of her bed. "It'll be queer, you married to Meyer Whitney and me married to Merrill Yeaton. That will take getting used to."

"We came to believe a little in our own publicity. The Beautiful Couple. The perfect marrieds on screen and off. Our divorce may set the public relations industry back a hundred years."

" 'My dear, in the contest of life, the love of women is a hindrance.' "

" 'Oh, Nero, thou art cruel. Thy very soul is corroded by lust for power.' "

She began to giggle and he tried vainly to maintain a straight face, the countenance of power, before it broke up.

"Do you remember?" she asked, laughing with him.

"How could I forget? Those would have been the worst lines delivered in a movie since poor Anne Baxter in *The Ten Commandments* had to look Charlton Heston right in the eye and say, 'Oh, Moses, Moses, you blind, stubborn, adorable fool, you.' "

It had been on the third day of shooting on the super-spectacular *Nero* in which they co-starred. As Nero's young mistress, she was pleading with him against his decision to light up hundreds of tarred Christians as burning torches to illumine a parade. Brian balked at saying those lines aloud. When Sir Ogden Lewitt, the director, tried to make him do it, he deliberately fluffed the dialogue, and on the eighth take Sir Ogden gave up and canceled shooting for the rest of the day.

"That's when I began to appreciate you," Jacquelyn said. "Until then I thought of you as just another leading man . . . But that impressed me."

"I'm glad. I was mainly trying to impress you at the time."

That was the simple truth. He furthered his campaign by helping her with her acting. At first he taught her the little tricks. He showed her how to find her marks on stage by staying near the heat of the lights. This allowed her to move about without having to worry constantly if she was in correct camera range. Then he taught her the more complex business of interpreting a character. He was so intense about his work that he both impressed and frightened her. She didn't know then that often he had to drink to recover some of the sheer nervous energy he poured into a characterization. He kept picking away at his emotions, analyzing them, measuring them, intensifying them, projecting them into the skin of a character, until he got a bit emotionally depleted himself.

Jacquelyn was appreciative because he understood the disoriented feeling that came over her when she was trying to submerge her personality into someone else, the need to anchor herself down firmly to the role. All right, let's try to see this woman you're portraying, he told her. Say she's about twenty-two. Beautiful enough, spirited enough to attract a narcissist like Nero, ambitious enough to want to stay with him even when she learns he's really a madman. He helped her to find a voice and a walk, to figure out how this woman laughed, what she laughed at, and what made her cry. As Jacquelyn got more into the character it became somehow easier to be herself, for when she had the mannerisms down pat, the problem of the role no longer dominated her.

By then, she had fallen in love with him.

Matters were somewhat complicated by the omnipresence of Lora, a statuesque strawberry blonde whom Brian acquired somewhere in his travels and brought along with him to location at *Nero*. Lora never missed a chance to make clear her position as Brian's good and constant companion. She sat on a canvas chair nearby during the shooting and watched Brian emote, staring with soulful eyes. One afternoon, when Brian invited Jacquelyn for a drink with him in his trailer, he thoughtfully disposed of Lora first. He had her driven back to the apartment in his limousine. However, Lora had the wind up about Jacquelyn and came back to the location alone. When he entered the trailer with Jacquelyn, there was his strawberry blonde, big as life and twice as naked, waiting for him on the couch. Jacquelyn flounced out in proper indignation. A moment later Lora followed, shrieking and hurling insults back at Brian as he tossed her clothes after her. He never let Lora come back to the set and never answered her phone calls, but it was a whole week before he persuaded Jacquelyn to talk to him again.

"Do you know when I first knew I had you?" Brian asked.

"When?"

"When I burned the calf of my leg, the time I got too near the flames I was setting off before I began fiddling. You stood by, wincing and horrified, while all the bandages were put on."

"I was feeling sorry for you, that's all."

"Ah, it was more than that. I remember thinking to myself: the next move and she's mine."

It took a bit longer. Jacquelyn was still annoyed with him and tried to get revenge by upstaging him and getting every foot of film focused on her. Brian was an old hand at such tactics and when he saw what she was up to, he simply outmaneuvered her. There was hardly a shot in which he did not somehow get the better camera angle for himself, and when she had to be in the foreground he was always inventing some piece of distracting stage business to draw attention to himself. She wasn't aware of how successful he was at this devious game until one day she went to see the dailies in a projection booth. After about twenty minutes she stood up and hurled her shoes at the screen and stalked off.

The next morning when she appeared on the set, Brian offered his hand.

"Truce? That wide-angle lens is big enough to include the two of us."

She tried to be stern with him, but a sense of the ridiculous overcame her. As she recalled the intricate, exaggerated maneuvers of the silly contest they had been engaged in, she broke into laughter. Finally, still laughing, she collapsed into the tall lavender-colored deck chair with the white fringe and the letters JACQUELYN across the back. He stood beside her, and while the electricians were lighting the set they roared together.

No one understood what was going on.

The final move in Brian's campaign—what he later called seductio ad absurdum—came two days later during a scene in which Jacquelyn kept blowing her lines. Sir Ogden was at the boiling point before Jacquelyn finally confessed that she was upset because she'd been getting obscene phone calls from a mysterious caller. She was nervous when shooting ended for the day, so Brian took her back with him to his trailer and gave her a drink. The calls had been coming for a week and she didn't know how to stop them, because whoever was calling knew her private number and even when she changed it he always got the new one.

A few days later they caught the offender. He turned out to be a young Italian electrician on the set who had been mooning about Jacquelyn. Brian and Jacquelyn celebrated by having dinner together. And that night, instead of going back to his apartment, they went to her villa . . .

It was easy, too easy, to slip into this kind of reminiscence.

She asked firmly, "How long are you going to be in Rio, Brian?"

"Now that I know you're all right, I'll go back tonight. Tomorrow at the latest. I still have a movie to finish."

"How is it coming along?"

"Oh, it's going to be one of those arty masterpieces that will make critics die and draw dutiful audiences."

She was looking at him with those astonishing emerald eyes. Memory fastened on him like a barnacle. They used to do it in that bungalow atop the rock at the end of the spit. Their hideaway was soon discovered by photographers who came in small boats round the bend of the inlet to aim their telephoto lenses.

"Why are you staring?" she asked.

"I was remembering," he said.

Quick matinees in his trailer on the set, and long nights in bedrooms. Ah, what marvelous breasts she had! There was a sort of spongy second flesh beneath and in the full flush of the phenomena, with her dark hair loose and her eyes shut, she was a perfect wonder. A man sets out to do something else with women, be something else, and before the bedclothes are straightened he turns out to be something he never meant to be. A lover. God loved women and why couldn't they let it go at that? Why did they need husbands? They took all the gifts the Deity gave them and used them in a mean narrow way to ensnare creatures of the same Benevolence who are entitled to their freedom.

"Ah, the wicked craft of you. I've been undressing you there in the bed."

"Stop it, Brian."

"Life is all a matter of undressing when you come right down to it. You take off clothes and illusions, ambition and titles, and in the end you are nailed into the wood with nothing left but a crown of thorns and an autopsy report. Do you remember the first time?"

"If you don't stop, I'll call Meyer."

"It was in the villa and we drank champagne. I knew you were excited when you were in the chair and I kissed you. That delivered you into my hands."

"I know what you're up to, Brian. It won't work."

But she heard his call in her inner ear. It brought the look into her face that drove out bitterness. As for himself, he felt that he was laid open to her as he was, a "poor, bare, forked animal."

He moved toward her.

"Don't," she said.

The sunlight of late morning came through the windowpanes and was purified within the antiseptic hospital room.

"I dreamt of you on the plane. You were the Queen of Sheba."

"I'm warning you."

There was no man of such unmalleable stuff that he could resist her. If she had been a thousand miles away he would have found her steering by the compass of the cock. He had loved her so well he might have died of it. Other women didn't matter. He picked them up on a cocktail fork, as an appetizer. He sniffed them, like toasted nuts at the martini hour. It was Jacquelyn he wanted.

"Brian, if you touch me . . ."

Their matings always had the true tiger in them. She leapt to meet him in the bed. He had gone deep like a cormorant after the prize in her belly.

His skin burned. "Remember the days at the beach?"

Their elbows and knees were crusted with sand scabs and their bodies chafed like pink bark. When they put their clothes back on they were putting on a disguise to resemble normal human beings.

Now he was drawn to her with an intensity that was becoming painful, even menacing.

"I remember everything," Jacquelyn said in a chill and penetrating tone, "including Merrill."

He shook his head as though his face had been slapped. "Why did you say that, love?"

"I thought you might be forgetting your grand new lady. She is a lady, isn't she?"

"She is indeed."

"You've always been attracted to that kind. You have such a yen to be accepted into high society. You want to be one of them and not what you are—a performing ape, a clown. A still harder slap. He could almost feel his nose start to bleed.

"I took up with Merrill on a business matter. That's all there was to it in the beginning. Just business!"

She shrilled laughter. "Business. Is that what you call that money-losing antique? *Oedipus Rex!* Nobody who puts a dime into that turkey will ever see a penny back."

"You can't stretch your precious money-ruler to cover everything. Your little computer mind doesn't understand anything at all about art!"

"*Aht!* I'm sick of hearing you talk about it. If you ask me, it's pretentious crap. C-R-A-P!"

The hospital room began to smell to him of burning sulfur.

"How would you know, love? All the pictures you make run at intermission in burlesque houses."

"At least I don't make failures. None of my movies lose money. How about the ones you did before you met me? You could have exploded a bomb in the theaters at night and never hurt anybody."

"I'd rather act in *Oedipus Rex* than a thousand of your superspectacular stinkers. Like *Nero*. Or the one we were supposed to be in next. *Black Ivory!* That would have been a real epic to throw up by. See Jacquelyn Stuart make it with an elephant in Darkest Africa. Tusk, tusk!"

"At least people would pay money to come into the theater."

"To see you naked, love, with a python ripping off your panties. That's what your public loves. You play the same scene in every picture."

"But they come to see me. ME! No one would pay Confederate money to see you posing in Greek robes and spouting all that gibberish you love! What do you want to be—a phallic symbol for all the phony intellectuals in the world?"

He had never been able to figure out where any of their quarrels started, or for what precise reason, but they were all rooted in jealousy.

"I'd rather be a phallic symbol than a garden-variety all-purpose whore. You only draw the morons who want to watch your breasts jounce. You won't even be getting laughs on the late late show in another couple of years."

"Try to convince yourself of that, won't you? You and your Sophocles. You can't just be a movie star raking in money and being famous. No, that isn't good enough for

Brian O'Neal, The Actor! You have to convince yourself you're something better. That's important to you. You want to know why? Any good psychiatrist could tell you! It's because you never got over being the son of a poor Irish pubkeeper who had to work part-time in the fields like a drayhorse. You've tried ever since to get yourself a toehold among the Upper Clahsses—to be respected as some kind of a genius instead of what you are. A *freak*! A freak just like all actors—*a freak like me!*"

His shoulder muscles ached with an undelivered blow.

"You irascible, exasperating bitch! I wish everybody could see that famous face all contorted to look like a shrieking Medusa. You'd freeze up the blood in the veins. But that's the real Jacquelyn. You compare yourself to someone like Merrill? Why, for sweet Jesus' sake, you couldn't even *act* a lady! I wouldn't cast you for anything better than Merrill's scullery maid!"

Her voice went up the scale to a piercing whistle.

"Get out!"

In her wrath she became a roarer of the first magnitude. The room had a live atmosphere and sound behaved queerly in it. Even the walls bellowed.

GET OUT! GET OUT!

Meyer Whitney hurried in. "What is it, dear?"

Jacquelyn underwent a slight convulsion. "I can't stand him. Make him go!"

"I have no reason to stay," Brian said. "I wish you all the happiness you deserve. And that's as much misery as any human being can stand."

Meyer turned to Brian. "Enough of that," he said. "You're leaving now."

Brian could feel a switch being turned in his brain. The air pulsed with violence.

"Someday," Brian said, "someone will make a movie with Jacquelyn as she really is. It will be a revelation. The Queen of Shrews crowned with pure bitchery!"

Meyer's cheeks mottled. "I'd rather not have to throw you out."

"Repeat that."

"I'd rather not have to throw you out."

"Come. You're showing off. You don't owe that many wounds to chivalry. Let it go, man, and live long."

"Step outside with me."

"My pleasure."

He went out with Meyer following a pace behind.

Meyer took himself as seriously as a school monitor ushering a truant pupil to the principal's office.

In the corridor Meyer said, "I don't expect to see you around again. I am going to leave orders—quite explicit orders—that will prevent you from getting back."

At that moment, if Meyer read the warning glint in Brian's eyes, he might have avoided further trouble. But Meyer Whitney's experience with opposition had taught him to ride roughshod over it, and the habits which success teaches a man are difficult to break.

Meyer Whitney's voice lowered to a near basso as he added: "You will catch the very first plane out of Rio."

That was exactly what Brian intended to do, but he was not to be warned into it.

"I'll go when I damn well please," Brian said. "Give orders to your flunkies if you like, but don't try it with me."

The guard moved nearer.

"What are you worried about, Meyer? That I'll come back in the middle of the night and sneak into Jacquelyn's pants?"

In a buoyant, detached way, with joyous anticipation, Brian saw Meyer Whitney raise his arm and fist. Meyer's reflexes were slow. Brian went underneath the punch and came up with a fist solidly into the solar plexus. Meyer grunted. His mouth sprang open and his face turned white. Brian brought his right hand over in a cumbersome but effective way. Meyer's cheekbone crunched and he went down.

Brian lifted the guard a foot clear of the floor. He dangled in Brian's grip like a squawking chicken.

"Now, you don't want to get me mad, do you? I might have to wring your neck."

The guard struggled with the flap of his holster, kicking his feet and flailing with his free arm. In the end, regretfully, Brian had to fetch him one. The guard ended up on the floor with his arm stretched protectingly across Meyer. As a precaution Brian undid that holster flap and took the gun and dropped it down a laundry chute.

As he was waiting for the elevator, Brian put his hand in his pocket and found the slip of paper with Maria Carvalhos's address. He was feeling a little weary from lack of sleep and the emotional din of the past few minutes. He would spend the rest of the day in sleep and when he awoke, if Maria was in the same mood, they would spend a lovely night. In the morning he would be aboard a plane and head for home, a rested and wiser man. Coming so far had not been without purpose. He felt a real sense of accomplishment, having rid himself forever of the vision of Jacquelyn as succubus and goal.

The elevator arrived with a sliver of light showing beneath its metal door. Brian looked down the garishly-lit hospital corridor; the fury of the storm had passed and everything was at still center. He was not aware that, in falling, Meyer Whitney had broken his collarbone.

Both men lay in sprawling graceless postures. The white linoleum resembled a strand covered with bones and wreckage.

CHAPTER TWELVE

In her living room at the villa, Jacquelyn reread old letters from her son Gene.

Dear Mom ... yesterday we had a soccer game. I'm on the Cherokees. We walloped the Mohawks 8–7 ... When are you and Brian coming to see me?

It was Brian her son wanted to see. Brian was closer to him. He included her merely out of politeness.

Dear Mom ... I've been busy studying for my exams so I haven't wrote in some time. But I miss you and Brian a lot. How is Brian?

She had carried Gene inside her body for nine long months. That was their last true intimacy. He was eleven years old and should have been an anchor that tied her down to real goals. Instead he floated somewhere on the periphery of her life. What was wrong? Why couldn't she be a proper mother? It was a costly failure. Children endured through other forms of love and were still there when youth faded and career was a memory. Gene sees through me and knows that I'm acting when I'm being his mother: I'm always Jacquelyn Stuart.

"Am I intruding?"

She looked up, holding the letter. Hernan Ramirez was in the doorway of the living room, dapper, swarthy, with a gleaming white handkerchief in the breast pocket of his powder-blue jacket.

"Come in, Hernan."

"I have had a most interesting talk with Señor Whitney."

"Is he feeling better? I was going to see him later this evening."

"He appears in excellent spirits, Doña Jacquelyn. He was, of course, delighted with the news I brought to him."

"What is that?"

258

"If you will appear at the consulate tomorrow, we can proceed immediately to grant the divorce."

Hernan, preening himself with satisfaction, seemed to have completely forgotten that he had once been trying to delay the divorce proceedings.

She folded Gene's letter and put it on the coffee table. "Meyer must be pleased with you. You're a very willing—and effective—aide-de-camp."

Hernan started to smile and then, like a man who has bitten into a sweet and unexpectedly come on a hard core, he changed expression.

"I have tried to do what is best for everyone. I do not fault myself."

"How about the others? The ones against granting the divorce because of the honor of your country. Do they now fault themselves?"

"Everything has been arranged without illegality."

"Meyer usually gets what he wants."

"I extend to you a wish for your very great happiness, Doña Jacquelyn. If the divorce is accomplished in time, Señor Whitney wishes the marriage to take place at four o'clock in the afternoon of tomorrow."

"Do the doctors say it is all right? Meyer is still recuperating from his accident."

"He has permission of the doctors."

"I'm sure he is grateful to you, Hernan. After all, why not? You are such an efficient . . . servant."

Hernan's teeth showed, although he was not really smiling. "I do what I can, Doña Jacquelyn. Señor Whitney is a very good friend and a very bad enemy. My government prefers to have him for a friend."

"So do you, I imagine. It must be even harder to stand up against Meyer than, say, against your father-in-law. Or even your wife."

Hernan removed his handkerchief and touched his temple. "We wish you to appear at the consulate as early as possible. Will ten o'clock of the morning be too early?"

"Of course not, Señor Ramirez. I'll be there at ten."

"I hope all goes well with you, Doña Jac—" He checked himself, hearing the significance of how she had addressed him. "Señorita Stuart."

"Good-bye, Señor Ramirez."

"Hasta la vista, Señorita Stuart."

Hernan bowed out, teeth and handkerchief gleaming.

Jacquelyn sighed and retrieved the letter.

... Would you tell Brian that the new first baseman's mitt is working in swell. I wrote him about it but he hasn't answered. I would like it if he wrote me. Hoping to see both of you soon. Yr. loving son, Gene.

Sports was a topic that brought Brian and her son together. She had tried to join in their interest and finally learned to memorize the names of the Los Angeles Dodgers' players and to enjoy watching Sandy Koufax pitch. Gloom descended upon the household when Sandy retired with bursitis in his shoulder. It had been one of the minor griefs that bind a family together. On the day they heard it, they were sitting at dinner in the house in the canyon. It was a pleasant time of day, with no work to be done, and just the three of them at supper. Afterward Brian had promised to teach Gene chess. Brian loved the game and was always spotting Jacquelyn both castles and a queen. He had hope for Gene, though. The boy was eager to learn, Brian said. Gene would have been eager to learn how to walk through fire if that would win Brian's approval.

That night, the radio announced Sandy Koufax was retiring. Brian and Gene finally went outside to toss a baseball back and forth for an hour, just to forget. When she went out to visit them the innocent game of catch had turned into a World Series with Brian as the Baltimore Orioles and Gene as the Los Angeles Dodgers, and it was the bottom of the ninth, two out, with Sandy Koufax pitching a no-hit, no-run game and Frank Robinson coming to bat. With Brian, nothing remained casual recreation. An innocent game of roll the hoop on the back lawn became a polo match in which half the neighborhood kids were involved. Brian translated everything into terms of conflict. On their trip to Washington, traveling on the underground car through the passage to the Senate Building, Brian kept Gene goggle-eyed by pointing out in his most portentous tone that it was through this very passageway United States Senators went on their way to declare war. Brian was full of resounding tales of valor, from the impossible feats of Irish heroes to the ringing rhetoric of Napoleon Bonaparte—*If your standards fail you, rally around me; you will find me on the road to victory and honor!* Some quotations sounded in her memory as they would probably sound in Gene's memory for the rest of his years. No one could listen to Brian's magnificent voice—and oh God! how well he knew it was

magnificent—without unconsciously mouthing the words
to discover whether the magic was in the words or in the
voice that spoke them. When she spoke to him on the
telephone, she could without the least effort bring back
every line of his face, every movement of his mouth. And
seeing him again, at the hospital, she realized that she had
not stopped loving him. Somehow his extravagant passion
for her had abated. Everything changed, grew old, with-
ered, died. It wasn't fair. *Damn Merrill!*

They had met Merrill Yeaton at a party to raise funds
for a newly organized chapter of something called the
Workers Political Educational Committee. With a painful-
ly acquired instinct, Jacquelyn became aware that Merrill
had joined the Legion. The Legion was her name for the
numberless, nameless horde of Brian O'Neal worshipers.
These fated women all acquired the same blank, intent
look shortly after meeting him and wrapping themselves in
the deep timbre of his low, strong voice, responding in an
almost electrical way to his animal mating call. Her fears
were allayed when at home, later that evening, Brian
waxed poetic about the soufflé au Grand Marnier and
spent a few minutes coldly analyzing the character of
blonde rich girls who are liberals because, he said, the
shadow of the future is there for anyone to see and their
connection with the working class will have value when
the rich must seek asylum. A week later, Merrill played a
larger part in conversation, for there was talk of filming
Oedipus Rex in which Brian had scored a personal success
on the stage some years before. Merrill, with her father's
indulgent backing, was interested in providing the financial
support. Jacquelyn did not say anything because she knew
Brian resented any display of female jealousy, but she did
manage to question Merrill's qualifications as a film mag-
nate. Brian was testy in his answer.

And then he stopped talking about Merrill, and she
knew it meant the affair had begun. Even at that point
Jacquelyn managed to remain unworried, though wary,
because Brian never let things go beyond the bounds of
prudence. He was discreet because he loved her and did
not cause unnecessary wounds. A month later, against all
odds, *Oedipus Rex* was actually scheduled to go into
production.

Brian announced that he was going on to London
without her because there was no part for her in *Oedipus*

Rex, nothing but the role of the aging Jocasta, who was both wife and mother to Oedipus.

"I don't think you're ready to play mother roles yet, Mrs. O'Neal."

"If you go to London, Brian, I'm going too."

"Now that would be a waste of your precious time. A waste staggering to think on. Why, your time must be worth nearly a hundred dollars a minute. You can hardly afford to sit down and have your coffee in the morning, for—poof! there goes a thousand lovely dollars."

"It's no use turning me off with words, Brian. I know that trick too well. If you go to London to make this movie, I'm going with you."

Brian's grin wavered. "Why? To sit around and wait for me to finish work every day? It'll take months out of your schedule. They've got projects waiting for you lined up six deep like pensioners on the dole."

"I'm not going to let her have you all to herself while I'm six thousand miles away."

"Her?" The grin faded.

"You know very well who I'm talking about."

"I know very well who you're talking about." The lilt left his mimicking voice; it was gravelly and bass, like a grizzly at the mouth of his cave, warning off intruders.

"Are you going to deny what's been going on between you and Merrill Yeaton."

"Merrill, is it?"

"I'm not blind. I've watched the signs for some time."

"You've watched the signs for some time, have you?"

"Don't talk that way. You don't frighten me."

"Oh, I think I do. I think you know me well enough to be frightened. I've never let a woman get her meddling hands into my life and I'm not beginning with you. I married you, but that doesn't mean I agreed to the chains."

"Did you think I would stand by and let you have your fun? You're crazy! I've been quiet before because I knew those cheap tarts didn't mean anything. Merrill's different. She's a *high-class* whore."

"You always have a foul mouth when you're angry."

"That's all she is, for all her education and breeding. Her and her fine liberal airs. Always prating about freedom and civil right. All she's interested in is free love! Staying out all night screwing with other women's husbands."

She caught a glimpse of herself in the mirror. Lovely girl with startling green eyes, fine-textured porcelain skin, and the face of an angel. Oh, the ugly depths of her. She *liked* to use the sort of language that made other ladies gag.

"Well, you've left this house for the last time, only to come reeling back with the smell of her well-bred cunt on you!"

"God damn it! Are you going to shut up?"

His strong hairy hands fixed on her throat with thumbs extended over the jugular.

"Go ahead. Hurt me! How low are you going to sink, you rotten Irish whoremaster!"

With a groan he flung her away. She stumbled, fell on the sofa, and her skirt flew up. She lay there. Oh, I would have been a good tavern wench, lolling about with coarse loving men and fine bawdy gentlemen out for a spree, ending up with someone new each night in a straw-lined cot above the tavern.

Brian stared at the bare white flesh above her stocking tops.

"You've done it this time," he said. "This time you've driven me mad. I'm going out of this house, to London, and never coming back. But before I go . . ."

He had never made love to her in such a sinister way, tearing at her clothes, and all the while staring into her eyes as though to see through the angelic image. He knew what she was like beneath the skin. A highly physical woman, who demanded a lot of attentive lovemaking. He had never put her up on a pedestal because he knew her feet were clay. Or mud. Then she forgot all that. He was playing with her. That damned control of his. She raised herself for him and he wouldn't come in. He kept at her and at her until she was pleading, crying, sobbing. She rolled on the sofa and clawed at him. A highly physical woman. Bet your fucking life! She cursed him in his ear and reached down to tug and yank him. He evaded her. What are you—a fucking pansy? Oh, Christ, I don't know what I'm saying. What I'm thinking. Do it. Do it. DO IT. Oh, please, please, please. Why are you torturing me? Bastard. Dirty dirty bastard. I love you and you should love me. You should help me. No, you can't. You can't do that. YOU CAN'T LEAVE ME LIKE THIS! She tried to haul him back. Please come. Anything. I won't quarrel anymore. She couldn't even say it. I'm ready. READY! It can't wait. I don't care about Merrill! It's me you want, I know that. You can't go away and leave me. Not ever, but especially NOT NOW!

She lay crumpled on the sofa, curled up against need, and heard him moving about in the room while she cursed him deep in her stomach.

And then he was gone. . . .

It was an hour before she could bear to look at herself in a mirror. She looked ghastly. I should never have given Brian an ultimatum. I should have known better. He is not the sort of man who will accept ultimatums. But I knew I had waited too long and put too much blind faith in our love. Merrill is different. Entirely different. And now Brian has left me.

She spat at her image in the mirror. I hate my face. I hate myself. I hate myself for losing Brian.

She had to beat her mind to drive him from her. She would do it. Brian was not going to break her on the rack of memory.

She would begin by burning out the part of him that was still with her. She gathered Gene's letters . . . *Where is Brian? Tell Brian . . . I miss you and Brian . . . I wrote to Brian, but . . .* and put them into the large ceramic ashtray and lit a match to a corner. The paper edges blackened and curled, and small leaping flames went from word to word.

Fire was the best cure, the lovely, dry, white and yellow fingers reduced everything to ashes. She had learned that lesson a long time ago. Dan Reed finally vanished from her life in a puff of smoke and flame, fourteen months after Dan himself had gone with vile worms to dwell. All his memorabilia survived him. There were letters, photographs in the album, scribbled notes, even the razor he shaved with on the last morning, countless items which had meaning to no one except her, even the varnished cover of the theater program for *Voyages of Sinbad* which bore the imprint of her lipstick wishing him luck. She saved all these as though they somehow conferred life upon him. . . .

Dan Reed had a harshly masculine laugh. When he threw back his head the neck muscles corded, and there was a small gold cap on one molar.

She couldn't help smiling back at him. "What's so funny?"

"That you're still worried about playing a steamy babe in *When the Dog Bites!* Honey, haven't you seen the first grosses on *Call Me Anytime?* Haven't you read the notices? That's the best testimony to sex appeal since Samson pulled down the building for Delilah."

"Just because I was successful in one sexy role doesn't mean I should keep doing them."

They were sitting in the small study of Dan Reed's office. The room consisted of a desk, two chairs, and several rows of books the studio had made into motion pictures. In the larger office rooms outside, the usual uproar was going on, with secretaries busy on several phones at once, but in here silence reigned.

Dan Reed's face bore the faintest of smiles. "Would I let you wear out a rut, honey? This is the top-budget movie in the house. It's got great possibilities. It's based on the number-one best seller and it's about this social worker who's supposed to be helping a young gang of adolescents and how her beauty makes problems for them until one day they gang up on her and she ends up getting pregnant . . ."

Dan Reed went on telling her the plot of the book. It was easy to understand why Dan thought it would be a big grosser. All the built-in exploitation values of juvenile delinquency, explicit sex, crime, and violence had caught Dan's attention, but he was shrewd enough to realize that in order to get more than a merely sensationalist movie he needed the right approach. That's why he wanted to emphasize the socially useful aspects, the study of social work among depressed classes, the sympathetic portrait of a young woman devoting her life, and as it turned out, sacrificing her virtue, to her ideals.

"We've signed Homer Graetz to do the screenplay. He's a solid writer. You know his credits. He's got taste. All the values in the book will come through with him and that will help us beat off the censors. *When the Dog Bites* is going to be a real social documentary."

As he finished talking, Dan Reed leaned back and lit a fresh cigar.

"Well, what do you think, honey?"

"I like the way you want to treat it. And of course I'm glad to hear about Homer Graetz. But it still sounds pretty steamy."

"This is a big project and it's going to take time. Homer Graetz has been working on the screenplay for ten weeks already, and it'll be another month or two before he's got it right. When he does, I promise you *When The Dog Bites* is going to be a hell of a lot more important than the book. I don't just mean at the box office. It's going to be the kind of movie we'll both be proud to have been associated with."

She sighed. "You're a good salesman, Dan. I don't know how anybody resists you."

Dan Reed shifted the cigar in his mouth. His answer had an undertone of sadness. "You don't seem to have a lot of trouble in that department."

"What do you mean?"

"I was talking about me. Dan Reed, personally. You do a pretty good job of putting me off."

"I wasn't aware I was doing that."

"Maybe not. That's one reason you're such a good actress. You've got all the intuitions about yourself, but you don't register too much what other people are thinking. That's what gives you that slow quiet look on the screen—you're thinking about yourself and your emotions all the time. That's what suggests hidden depths in you. And you never go right at a thing, even if it's something you want. You take a guy like me, I see something I want, I lunge at it like a trout at a fly. But you sort of go around it, testing your emotions all the time, figuring out what it is and what it's likely to mean in your life. You're hard to figure, mysterious. That's the quality that's made you a star. But now I want you to do me a favor. I want you to forget you for a few minutes and look at me. Like I wasn't just a producer, or the head of a studio, but a man who happens to think you're the top of the mountain, the most desirable creature that God ever put onto his green earth."

He must be in his late forties, she thought. He was neither bad-looking nor good-looking, but he did have one asset: he was unquestionably male.

"This isn't just some new idea I've got, honey. I've had this thing for you ever since the first day we met. You were married to Charles Laurent then. When that busted up, I thought I could move in. But I missed my chance when you were in the hospital. Sending flowers didn't get the message across. I should've been there in person, but I was taking it easy with you because your marriage was busted up and you were rocked around from the accident. That was my mistake. It gave Joel a chance to beat my time."

She recalled a sunset evening on the beach beneath the blankets with Joel. That surly, handsome face with the dark, uncombed hair and malevolent eyes. The lean rope body with all its physical energy. She could still hardly believe that Joel was dead.

"You could have been his number one girl for a long time, probably as long as you wanted, but that wouldn't have suited you. Because whether you think so or not, honey, you're a marrying woman."

How about you, Dan Reed? You've been married three times; first, to a nice young Italian girl who gave you a son almost my age, and after her to that hardened facial mask who ran a famous cosmetics concern, and, oh yes, the third was a bounding buxom blonde a-twinkle in diamonds and pearls. The last two gave you their all, literally, because you damn near bankrupted them before you were finished.

"Would you call yourself a marrying man?"

Absently Dan Reed picked up a letter opener and ran his finger along the smooth, polished mahogany edge.

"I've gone around with a lot of women, baby. I wouldn't kid you about that. But there's always been one I was faithful to, and she was usually my wife."

He went with her to the door of his office, and as she was leaving, he impulsively bent over and kissed her forehead.

Two weeks later her agent, Morey Bloom, called.

"Listen, pumpkin, are you interested in attending the premiere of Dan Reed's new super-epic?"

"No."

"It would give the opening a shot in the arm—and it couldn't do you anything but good. This is the picture of the year—and there's a lot of TV coverage. The picture has a twenty-million-dollar budget and all the production values. Practically every big star in Hollywood is playing cameo roles. It's Dan's last shot to save the studio from going under."

"Going under? I don't understand."

"Dan's overreached himself. Started too many new features at a time when grosses are declining and TV is a big competitor. He caused fireworks for a while, but he finally fizzled out."

"From everything I've heard things couldn't be rosier at the studio since Dan took over."

"That's his publicity, pumpkin. Don't fall for that. The studio is going to report the worst loss in its history, nearly forty million. Dan Reed may have been talking up a tempest, but the movies he's made aren't drawing a teacup. He and the whole studio are against the wall and the squad is already calling, 'Ready . . . Aim . . .' "

"I'm sorry to hear that. I like Dan."

"Everybody likes him except his creditors. That's why everyone pitched in to help make *Voyages of Sinbad* the biggest epic ever. It may bail him out of that hole he's dug himself into. But whether it does or not, the premiere's a great showcase for you, pumpkin."

"I just don't feel up to going out in public yet, Morey."

The next day a delivery wagon pulled up to her door from the Adze Galleries and a uniformed messenger carried a large, square, flat package to her door. She opened the wrapping and saw it was an original painting by Andrew Wyeth, a lovely farmhouse setting with a breeze blowing curtains at a window. She had gone to a Wyeth show at the gallery a week ago, loving again his cool, disciplined mastery, the sense of calm and serenity, and for days afterward her eyes had been full of Wyeth wherever she looked.

The messenger also gave her a card. It was from Dan Reed.

Personally I don't dig it, honey. But I hear you like it, so you got it. How about having dinner someday?

She would have returned any other present, jewelry or furs or anything, but she could not bear to part with her Wyeth. She dropped a thank-you note into the mail, and Dan Reed called the next morning.

"How about Chasen's? They got a good lobster thermidor and I got my own bottles in their cellar."

She laughed. "You're incorrigible."

"Don't use big words on me. I never got out of fourth grade. Does that mean yes or no?"

"It means yes," she said.

The lobster thermidor was as good as Dan predicted it would be, and the wine was better. Dan Reed was a perfect dinner companion, amusing, admiring, making every effort to please. He revealed how he learned about her admiration for Andrew Wyeth—the owner of the Adze Galleries had mentioned her visit there to Dan at a cock-

tail party. Long before they finished the coupe aux mar-
rons she had decided that she would attend the premiere
of his *Voyages of Sinbad*.

When she told him so, Dan Reed simply stared at her.

"Do you think that's why I asked you out?"

"Isn't it?"

"Hell, no. It was to give you this."

He took a small case from his pocket and handed it to
her almost casually. But his hand trembled slightly and she
received the secret message of his nervousness.

She opened the case on the most spectacular diamond
ring she had ever seen.

"Do you like it?"

"It's fabulous. I can't accept anything like this."

"Why not?"

"It's too much."

"It's for our engagement and it's thirty-eight carats. I
don't want any wife of mine going around wearing
Woolworth's."

"Dan, you're crazy."

"About you, sure. I've been trying to tell you that for
some time. The trouble with you is you don't listen."

He was smiling at her with such a comforting tender-
ness. She blinked back tears, and a moment passed before
he returned clearly to her field of vision.

"Dan, I appreciate this very much, but we don't know
each other well enough to . . ."

"I know everything about you I need to know. You
want to know me better? Fair enough. For the next three
weeks, we'll see each other every night. By that time,
you'll know me well enough to get married."

"Things don't happen this way, Dan."

"They do with me. Listen. I can't afford to wait around.
You're not getting any younger. How old are you? Twenty-three? I'm only forty-nine. In another six months you'll
be a wrinkled old lady and nobody'll want you."

He was still smiling, but his eyes remained fixed on her
a second longer as though trying to divine the answer.

"Dan, I can't say yes. Not like this. Not now."

"Okay. I'll be around for the rest of your life. But the
sooner you say yes the better. I've got big plans for you,
baby. You're not going to be just a star, or even a big
star. You're going to be THE star. You in the spotlight
and everyone else in the shadow."

"You paint pretty word pictures, Dan."

"You've got it all coming to you. You're not getting a bargain in me, baby. I'm not the top prize in the cracker-jack box. I'm a little tin dictator around the house, and I'm loud. I don't mind arguing in front of people. I'm also pretty damn jealous, and when you're mine I won't let you take second looks at any man. I might give your fanny a good swift wallop if you try. But that'll do you good. Every woman has to be told how far she can go." He grinned at her; there was something compelling about his sureness. "But we'll be very good for each other. Wait and see. If I'm wrong, you can be honest in twenty or thirty years and tell me it's all been rotten and I made an awful life for you."

She started to reply and stopped because he had taken something else from his pocket. It was a plain gold wedding band.

"My mother's," he said. "She passed on a year ago and I inherited it. Just in time, too."

"Just in time?" She was starting to feel mesmerized, repeating what he said as though she no longer had a will of her own.

"You'll be married in it. It's only worth a few bucks, but my mother stayed married for forty-one years. That's a good omen. Why do you think I'm giving you that big hunk of an engagement ring?"

She shook her head numbly. "I don't know."

"I don't want you to think I'm cheap because I'm getting married to you with a plain old ring like this."

She did go out with Dan Reed for two of the promised three weeks. Every night was something of an adventure. He might call up to ask her if she liked Chinese food and when she said yes, he would rent a helicopter and fly her up to San Francisco to Sheila Chung's. Or they would spend an evening gambling on a yacht anchored just outside the Coast Guard limit. Dan was ahead forty thousand dollars at one point but then lost a fortune. When she asked why he hadn't stopped when he was ahead, Dan answered simply, "I want everything or nothing, baby. That's the name of the game. It's why I'm so crazy about you. If I couldn't have you, I'd probably become a monk."

She never heard him speak of money troubles. The studio's financial report had just been issued and, as Morey Bloom predicted, it was disastrous. A stockholder's revolt was underway, and Dan Reed was freely rumored to be on the way out. Poor Dan, they said. Almost everyone claimed to like him although some were heard to wonder openly how Dan had managed to con his way so far, even granting that he was a highly persuasive salesman. Anyone could tell with half an eye that Dan was not a businessman; he was a reckless high-flyer, a robber baron, an adventurer, and a gambler who never knew when to stop. She picked up these messages out of the air, overheard at parties, dropped on the telephone, mentioned out of context at meetings with such people as Morey Bloom and Arthur Eakam and all the well-meaning acquaintances who supposedly had her interests at heart. The knives were out in the open. The feast of the cannibals was soon to come.

"They don't worry me, baby," Dan Reed said, when in tearful rage she reported some of the things people were saying about him. "I figure that's how people are. They like to ride with a winner, and until I get me a winner I'm going to have to keep on the move so somebody doesn't put a bomb in my pocket."

When *Voyages of Sinbad* opened there was no doubt that Dan Reed had found his winner and doubled it in spades. Jacquelyn would never forget the night of the premiere. Like any of the spectacles that Dan stage-managed, it was a costly and glittering affair. Prince Philip was on hand, handsome, tall, well-spoken.

"Your Highness," Dan Reed said, introducing her. "I'd like you to meet the most beautiful woman in the world."

Prince Philip murmured, "Oh, yes, Miss Stuart. I saw you in *Furious Thunder*. We played it one evening at the palace."

Dan Reed raised skeptical, black, bushy eyebrows. "The Palace? I thought that house went back to playing vaudeville."

It was an inside, show business joke, but Prince Philip laughed.

Voyages of Sinbad itself was a hugely entertaining movie. As one critic put it later, it was "the only super-epic in Hollywood history that has managed somehow to retain the grace and nimbleness of an adroit light comedy. Even the top-heavy roster of stars are maneuvered into the complicated plot in a completely ingratiating way. If, as production values are measured in Hollywood, *Voyages of*

Sinbad must be considered an elephant, it is certainly a most beguiling beast."

Jacquelyn saw *Voyages* at a private screening a few days before the premiere, and while she thought it might be a success, she was not prepared for the ovation that the premiere audience gave it. No one left their seats until the final cast credits were flashed at the end of the movie, and then they began an insistent rhythmic clapping that forced the writers to go onstage for a bow, and many of the stars, and last of all Dan Reed. Dan's appearance almost brought the house down in tumultuous uproar. Everyone stood while shouts of Bravo rang through the auditorium. The Hollywood cannibals were intent on proving they had sheathed their knives.

Darryl Zanuck was in the audience, and later in the theater lobby he and Dan Reed met for a moment.

"How'd you like it?" Dan asked.

"Don't ask silly questions. It's going to run for ten years and make a hundred million dollars. I'd give half my studio just to participate in the profits."

Jacquelyn was so excited that she kissed Darryl. His tiny moustache tickled her slightly.

Jacquelyn also planted her lipstick imprint on Dan Reed's souvenir program "just for luck and because this is the happiest night I can remember."

But there was something that night that kept her from being happy, which ran through all the brightly colored triumph like a black thread in the woof. She did not hear whole passages of dialogue. At first she thought the sound track was at fault, but she realized she was wrong when the rest of the audience burst into laughter at the conclusion of speeches she had not heard. In the lobby, she was not aware that Dan had spoken to her until she noticed him looking at her and awaiting an answer.

"Who do you think you're staring at?" she asked testily.

"I asked you a question, sweetheart."

"How do you expect me to hear in this uproar? I have a headache, Dan. I want to go home."

"There's a big party after the show. We gotta be there."

She had to follow the movement of his lips to be entirely sure of what he said. Her panic was quickly translated into anger.

"I don't feel well. I don't give a damn about the party."

"But Prince Philip——"

"Are you going to take me home? I can go without you."

"Okay, okay. You don't hafta scream!"

In the limousine, going home, she told Dan what was troubling her. The next afternoon he went with her to the office of a leading ear specialist, who told her that her deafness was not temporary.

"It's the result of the previous injury to your skull. The hearing in the right ear is not too badly impaired, but it's almost totally gone in the left."

"What can I do, doctor?"

"Hearing can be restored by an operation. We call it a fenestration. We simply reopen the hearing canal."

Dan Reed went with her to the hospital and waited through the hour-and-a-half operation. He slept that night in a room across the hall, and in the morning was back at her bedside. Flowers began arriving an hour after he left for the studio, and kept coming every hour on the hour. He sent telegrams on the half hour between. One telegram would say, *I love you madly,* and the next, *Why are you neglecting me like this?* and the third, *Haven't seen much of you lately. So what's new?* When she learned that Dan had been putting off an important trip to London to close the international distribution deal of *Voyages of Sinbad* she insisted that he must go. He called her from the airport in Los Angeles, and again from New York during his brief stopover, and a few hours later on the transatlantic telephone from his London hotel. He spoke to her that evening for three hours, and called back at ten o'clock California time (it was seven A.M. in London) just to say good night. The next morning at eight he was on the telephone again, and got off only long enough for the Beatles to sing their latest hit song to her on the phone; he hired them especially for the occasion. That afternoon (it was midnight in London) he called again. This time he had gathered in his hotel suite a score of her friends. The phone call lasted for two hours while everyone got on to say hello. She was dizzy, overwhelmed, laughing and crying at Dan's mad extravagance. But she was happiest of all that she could hear every single word spoken to her. The operation had been a complete success.

When she gave Dan the doctor's report there was a long silence. She heard him struggling for words through a choke in his throat. All he managed was his invariable sign-off in the usual brusquely affectionate tone.

"I'm mad about you, kiddo."

Only this time she replied, mimicking his tone: "I'm mad about you too, kiddo," and they both knew that she had accepted his proposal of marriage.

He answered, "You don't have such big eyes. They just look that way because you got glandular trouble."

Dan planned the wedding as though by staging the biggest extravaganza of all time he could prove to the world how happy he was. He hired the Hollywood Bowl for the evening, with Andre Kostelanetz and his orchestra to play "The Wedding March" and "I Love You Truly." There were nine thousand invited guests. Most of the biggest names in Hollywood were on hand as bridesmaids and ushers. An invitation to the wedding became a mark of status in Hollywood. It was said that those who couldn't wangle an invitation to the wedding were afraid to go out that evening for fear of being labeled "outsiders." Dan and Jacquelyn's telephones rang constantly with imploring speeches from acquaintances who felt they were being unjustly ignored. Matters began to get out of hand. Invitations were peddled by speculators at two and three hundred dollars apiece, and there was a report by a columnist that a has-been director attempted suicide when his name was omitted from the invitation list. A helicopter service offered flights over the Bowl at triple its usual rate on the evening the wedding was to take place. There were offers from all three major television networks to carry the ceremony live, or on tape, and they were ready to pay half a million dollars for the privilege. Dan Reed, after some consideration, declined the offer. At a press conference on the evening of the affair, he pleaded, "Give me a break, will ya? This is my wedding. It isn't opening night at a circus." The remark gained a certain amount of currency as a masterpiece of unintentional double entendre.

On the evening of the ceremony, Jacquelyn arrived at the Hollywood Bowl shortly after eight o'clock. She was wearing a voluminous pink silk and chiffon gown, pale as the first touch of dawn, which unfurled about her in swirls light as air, and from the folds a chiffon scarf, in paler pink, was caught up and draped over her head. For blocks outside the Bowl, crowds had gathered, a black and threatening flow over sidewalks and streets, into parking lots, and cresting on roofs of any buildings that command- ed the approach. There was a curiously menacing and hostile air about these uninvited onlookers. Perhaps they resented being mere spectators or perhaps the dry poverty of their own lives made them envy and hate the ostentation and display of someone like Dan Reed. Whatever the reason, their enmity was apparent as the limousine moved through the streets. Jacquelyn saw threatening and even obscene gestures. A tomato smashed against the windshield of the car, and later she discovered that eggs had splattered the roof. Crowds blocked the car off at the entrance and motorcycle police had to clear a narrow passage. A group of teen-agers, pressing in close, got hold of the fenders and began to rock the car. Jacquelyn screamed in fright. A bearded prophet lifted a sign proclaiming the end of the world and calling on her to repent before it was too late. Two youths of college age clambered atop a knoll to unfurl a banner "Here's Hoping Dan Scores His Hole In One!" This caused a great deal of laughter in the multitude. A few seconds later a string of firecrackers went off almost like a machine-gun volley. Several people jumped onto the rear bumper of the car and began jouncing back and forth until a policeman arrived to shoo them away. Another man, a rather wild-looking fellow in a brown suit, was arrested when he deliberately dropped his trousers as the car passed.

Inside the Bowl, the scene was pandemonium. The guards and police assigned were not sufficient to keep out gatecrashers. The interlopers swarmed over the gallery seats and raced in clusters down the aisles toward the stage, pursued by guards and police and upsetting vendors' trays on the way. The ushers, most of whom were volunteers, were unable to direct guests to their proper seats, or handle altercations when the wrong people took the wrong seats. There were even a few fistfights. The loudspeaker system worked intermittently, apparently because of sabotage, and the famous entertainers on hand could not be heard beyond the first ten or twelve rows. This set up a further uproar among the crowd. Shouts grew so loud at one point that even when the loudspeaker system came back on, the entertainers could not be heard above the noise. Dan Reed had ordered champagne instead of soft drinks, and the vendors could not serve more than an aisle or two before their supplies were exhausted. Paper cupfuls were guzzled down quickly and then there were requests for more. When a fresh supply arrived, it was often warm and flat. Paper cups and debris littered the steps, the aisles. When Kostelanetz struck up "The Wedding March" he was met by hoots of derision and a chorus of off-key singing from the crowd. The minister, more than a little overcome, rushed the ceremony when a hail of debris began to litter the stage. Reporters and photographers stormed forward before the final words were spoken and Dan fitted the plain golden band onto Jacquelyn's finger. Their final vows were exchanged in a blinding battery of flashbulbs and against a chorus of insistent badgering questions. Dan put his arm about Jacquelyn as the ceremony ended and with the aid of friends forced his way through the mob. Jacquelyn was in tears when their limousine finally cleared the fringes of the crowd. They reached the speedway and headed north toward their honeymoon hideaway.

Certain things she would remember all her life. The details might become stiff and discolored like an old newspaper, but what was said by the pages of memory would always be true. She remembered the drive up the coast road, with fog rolling in, and the radio playing, and Dan Reed serious and intent at the wheel. He was driving the little Fiat Spyder, the car she came to love above any other she ever owned. The limousine and chauffeur had only taken them as far as the parking lot where Dan had left the Fiat with all their baggage packed into its trunk. Never before or since had she gone away with so little luggage. Nowadays, on a trip to Europe, she carried hundreds of pounds of extra weight in luggage, and was followed by trunks and trunks. On that honeymoon trip she had only a single bag and a Valpack with dresses and a coat. Dan had only a valise with an extra suit and underwear and shirts.

The cottage stood at the highest point of a cliff above great brown rocks on the shore where shattered waves beat in with unwearying power. She had not been with any man since Joel Page. Probably everyone assumed she had been having an affair with Dan Reed, but it wasn't true. She would have gone to bed with him if he asked, but he wanted something else. He wanted her entirely for his own and, knowing this, she did not try to placate him with sex. She sat in the car outside the cottage while Dan Reed took the bags to the door. Then he came back to the window at her side.

"We're home, baby."

She followed him like any good child, willing to do

whatever he might ask. She had prepared herself for what would happen and was determined not to let any disappointment show. It was easy enough to pretend. She had pretended often with Charles, until near the end when she stopped because she didn't care enough. Dan was much more experienced, of course, and she couldn't help fearing that he would find her out. She didn't want him to be hurt or angry. Lies became useless when they ceased to give comfort. Dan Reed lived truthfully. Having created himself by one big lie, he had no further use for anything but honesty. He had already established the self that he cared about, and that self was too important to need sustaining by minor lies.

The cottage had an electric heater in each room. Blue fire glowed in the coils with a steady silence. Except for a single standing lamp in the corner there was no other light. From the windows they could look out on the rocks and the dark silver sea. Dan helped her to unpack, and smiling shyly (she had never seen him smile that way before), put her nightgown over the heater to warm it. Later, he moved the nightgown into the bedroom and spread it out on the bed like a deflated, thinned-out person.

He helped her undress. Her back was toward him when she was naked and he put his arms about her in a fond embrace. It was not going to be difficult, she decided. In the roaring dark there was a salt smell from the ocean. In a single move, he turned her around. On the bed he moved the nightgown out of their way. There was no need for it.

She turned her face as his kisses left her lips and moved down the length of her body. She seemed to hang breathless with waiting, until the last of her defenses was penetrated. From there it was straightforward, a long mounting flight. She was exhausted, wrung out with passion. She kept going ahead, into more and more, out of a numb and broken curiosity to see how long the feeling could last before it would vanish. My God, no. It was beginning again, a sharper ascent than before. She could not allow it. She would not survive. Her last breath was torn out of her. Her throat split with a hoarse cry.

When it was over she fell asleep in his arms without a word. In her dreams her hungry thoughts circled like wolves, and when she awoke some time later she was again in his arms.

In the morning, while she slept, Dan dressed and drove into the village and bought newspapers. He came into the bedroom and dropped them over the bedspread.

"Everybody hates us, baby," he said. "They hate us all over the front pages."

What he said was literally true. The newspaper reports of the wedding were written with typewriters that must have been dipped in bile. Dan Reed was accused of having produced a "saturnalia of bad taste," an "orgy of violence and a general public nuisance," and a "witches' sabbath of defilement that included a sickening travesty on the sacred institution of marriage." Accompanied by photographs of the rioters and lurid accounts of the general uproar, there were bitingly satirical reports on the wedding ceremony and the two principals, Dan Reed and Jacquelyn.

Dan grinned at her. "As a wedding, baby, it was the biggest fiasco of all time. And it cost a bundle. But it was worth it, and then some. We're married, kiddo."

It was the beginning of the exciting time. To live with Dan Reed was to share his incredible zest. There were moments when his happiness almost exploded out of him. A week after the wedding they were in Paris, and Dan threw open the window of their fourth-floor hotel room to shout to people passing on the street below: "I'm married to the world's most beautiful broad!" No one appeared to understand what he was shouting, but most people looked up and smiled and waved. They understood that the man at the window was bellowing his joy at being alive.

Every night he was insatiable. His ardor compelled her to match him, and they became more inventive with each encounter. Do you like this, he would ask. Or do you like the other more? She had not known there were so many different avenues to pleasure. No matter what they did on a given night, they tried some variation the next. As a lover she was obedient, devoted, like a child a little ashamed of how naive she had been. She was not acquiring knowledge so much as shedding old ways—becoming less encumbered as she moved toward some ultimate goal. Tenderly she explored him, while he touched her, traced the slow awakening circles of love. She would stop for a breath, and then let him start again. Afterward there were solemn moments in which she lay with her head on his belly, and playful moments in which she made a circle of her fingers and slipped them, cool as a wedding band, around him.

As the shape of her own desire became clear, she became distracted by a fear that this could not last. The frequency of their sexual unions was frightening in a way, evidence that lovemaking like this could not go on. Yet she did not want it ever to change. She wanted to lie exhausted, disgorged of passion like a great distended dying fish on a beach. Each time was the best, the best ever. Sometimes, staring in the dark, she would remember how much older he was and this must have an ending in time, sooner than she knew, certainly sooner than she wanted. With such thoughts, the atmosphere in the bedroom seemed to become colder, quieter, piercingly clear. She had the terrible foreknowledge a child has when during the night the concept of death becomes real and everything on earth mocks the morning light.

Dan Reed behaved as though the world was one huge carnival show in which he had to visit all the attractions before closing time. She completed only one movie, *When the Dog Bites,* after their marriage because he kept her so busy she couldn't promise to be in any one place for the required two or three months. They went everywhere, met everyone, did everything. In the first year they traveled over two hundred thousand miles in Dan's personal jet. They flew over to attend the opening of the new Givenchy collection where he bought her fifty thousand dollars worth of dresses at a single showing. They flew to attend the opening of *Voyages of Sinbad* in Tokyo. They were in Hollywood when the London Zoo announced the acquisition of a new prize panda. Dan packed up Jacquelyn and young Gene and flew over; he persuaded the keeper to let Gene give the panda its first midday feeding. A short editorial in the Los Angeles *Times* denounced Dan for such extravagant indulgence of a child when there were so many under-privileged children who could not even afford the price of a ticket to the circus. Dan promptly issued an invitation to one thousand orphans to attend the circus as his guests. Because there was no circus in town when he issued the invitations, he paid for the Ringling troupe to come in to Los Angeles on the next train, and guaranteed a weekly gross while they were in the city. During the week, orphanages sent their kids free, and circus performers visited the children's wards at all the hospitals.

Although she fully understood that flamboyance was a necessary part of his makeup, Jacquelyn occasionally

fought with him about it. No matter how spectacular his
grandstand stunts were, she said, at bottom they simply
proved that he was a show-off. They fought about many
other things also, roaring battles in which no limits were
set and both of them said the most damaging, hurtful
things that came to their minds. But even at the worst
moments they enjoyed the brawling because the sheer
intensity of battle promised an exquisite catharsis in the
reconciliation to follow. They spent every possible moment in each other's company. When he was at work at
the studio, Dan called her ten and twelve times a day,
often to report on what he had been doing and who he
had seen during the past half hour. She was offered a
starring role in a glossy tale of modern young lovers with
Brian O'Neal, the sensational Irish actor, as her leading
man. She turned it down because it would have meant
going on location for a month and she could not bear that
long a separation from Dan. To celebrate her decision,
Dan bought a diamond tiara worth at least a quarter of a
million dollars and that night she wore the tiara to bed
with him. Nothing else.

When she missed her first period she did not tell Dan
but went alone to have the tests made. Because she loved
Dan and had never really loved Charles, it was different,
entirely different, this time. She wanted Dan's child with
all her heart and she was exultant when the tests were
positive.

That evening they attended a testimonial dinner for the
Grand Old Man of the motion picture industry, a crusty,
illiterate, arrogant, thieving little man who was one of the
pioneers of the industry and upon whom age had conferred a dignity he never earned. Tickets were sold at a
hundred dollars apiece for the benefit of the Arthritis
Foundation, and everyone in Hollywood was in forced
attendance. Jacquelyn sat with Dan on the dais, reserved
for Very Important Guests; the master of ceremonies was
a television star imported from New York for the occasion, whose slightly waspish humor was leavened by a
sudden alteration in tone when he addressed himself to the
Grand Old Man. Then he became sentimental, projecting
the boyishly sincere quality the Grand Old Man had hired
him to project in a new motion picture. The television star
got some laughs when he talked about Dan and Jacquelyn, seated on the dais near him. He understood, he
said, that Dan and Jacquelyn had been signed to appear in

a new television soap opera to be called "Marriage *Can Be Beautiful*." They proved, he said, that George Bernard Shaw knew what he was talking about when he said marriage would always be popular because it combined the maximum of temptation with the maximum of opportunity. The Lord knows, he added, that for millions of American males Jacquelyn Stuart represented the maximum in temptation—if they ever got the opportunity.

While the television star was talking, Jacquelyn leaned over to Dan.

"I went to see the doctor today."

"What for?"

"To make sure we really have a second Dan Reed on the way. Or would you prefer a daughter?"

Dan's war whoop of triumph caused everyone on the dais and in the packed ballroom to turn toward him. The television star, in the middle of a story, recovered to say, "Say, I didn't realize I was being *that* funny!"

Dan called out, "Sorry, Jimmy. I just got some good news, that's all."

The television star indicated the crowded ballroom. "Why don't we share it with the good folks out there then?"

"Okay. You might as well be the first to know. I'm going to be a father!"

Dan put his arm about Jacquelyn while celebrities were rushing over to wish them well. She was flushing crimson. It was undoubtedly, she thought, the earliest public announcement of a pregnancy ever made.

The next day's newspapers hardly mentioned the Grand Old Man at all. All featured Jacquelyn's pregnancy and how Dan Reed, the proud father, had broken the news to the world.

Her pregnancy was the most publicized in history. As though on signal, every fan magazine came out with supposedly exclusive stories revealing plans for the new baby, what they intended to name it if a boy or a girl, how Dan was worrying about whether Jacquelyn's injuries would cause trouble during the delivery. There were even minute-by-minute accounts of "Jacquelyn's Terrible Three Hours," those in which she knew of her pregnant condition and feared how Dan Reed would react in view of his being so much older, etc. All of these stories had the tone of intimate chatty memoirs that sounded as though written by people who virtually lived in the house with Dan and

Jacquelyn but, in truth, the accounts were made up entirely out of news clippings and the writer's own imagination.

The one interview that Jacquelyn did grant during this period was to Marta Moran. Marta had pulled every string she could get hold of, exerted all the pressure she was capable of exerting, and finally resorted to blackmail by printing a few unfavorable items about Dan Reed and his mismanagement of the studio and then passing along the word that she would become more explicit if Jacquelyn didn't give her an exclusive. Jacquelyn never told Dan the reason why she decided to give Marta her interview.

Dan was in the house when Marta arrived, and he stayed for the interview. Marta began innocuously enough, with general talk about how Jacquelyn was feeling in the fourth month, when they had informed four-year-old Gene he was going to have a new brother or sister, how they were fixing up the house for the new arrival, and whether the baby might change their free-wheeling style to a more domestic life in the future. Then, for no reason except Marta's interest in controversy, the talk turned to religion. What denomination did Jacquelyn belong to?

Jacquelyn said, "I was brought up as a Presbyterian. I suppose that's what I'd still call myself."

"How do you feel about it, Dan?" Marta Moran asked. "Will the baby be brought up as a Protestant?"

"The baby will be brought up as a boy or a girl."

Jacquelyn laughed, but Marta responded with a patient smile that indicated that she had not yet hit pay dirt.

"Of course you're a lapsed Catholic, Dan, with all your marriages and divorces. But you still have to bring up the child in some religious faith. Which one is it going to be?"

"I don't know, Marta."

"You don't know?"

"Let's put it this way, Marta. I've got a lot of questions to ask and I haven't run into a religion yet that's got *all* the answers. Maybe we shouldn't expect a religion to be that all-wise. After all, religions are started by men, and we've only been on earth a thousand generations. If we're lucky, there's going to be a couple of hundred thousand generations to follow us. If we had all the answers to everything, what would those coming generations have to do? Just sit around and twiddle their thumbs?"

"Then you won't insist that the baby be raised as a Catholic?"

"No."

"When the child is old enough to pray, will you send it to a church?"

"Marta, it can pray anywhere it gets a mind to. I do some of my best praying on the toilet. Where do you do yours?"

"Aren't you being sacrilegious?"

"You got something against toilets? The way I look at it, God gave us bowels, so He couldn't be too surprised if we use them once in a while."

"I'm trying to ask a serious question."

"No you're not. You're trying to stir up trouble. Jacquelyn's entitled to her belief and I'm entitled to mine, and when our child grows up it'll be entitled to its own belief. You're even entitled to yours, Marta. Just don't come around here sticking your nose into matters that don't concern you."

Dan Reed was afraid of nobody, and when angry he never failed to speak his mind. That was the reason that he had almost as many good enemies as good friends. There were people who feared him, and people who were jealous of his success, and people whom he let know all too clearly that he disliked them. Marta Moran belonged in the latter category. After the interview, Dan Reed moved to the top of her hate list. Marta swore to drive him out of Hollywood if it was the last thing she ever did.

Dan wasn't worried. He laughed off the scurrilous attacks which began to appear in her column, a spate of stories which reflected on his mismanagement of the studio.

"When the chips are down," Dan said, "they pay off on the winner. If I make money, I'll stick. If I lose money, they'll throw me out. There's nothing Marta can do either way."

Jacquelyn knew that Dan was worried about how things were going at the studio. The titanic box office success of *Voyages of Sinbad* made the financial picture look better than it really was. Most of the pictures on the schedule were continuing to lose money, and Dan spent a lot of his time running around to plead with bankers for production loans for his future enterprises. As he put it, the studio was nearly tapped out on credit and owed the skin off its bones.

In June, three months before the baby was due, an important meeting was scheduled with the New York executives and bankers. Dan was the key figure in the negotiations. He agreed to fly to New York in his personal jet on twenty-four hours' notice.

"I'm going with you," Jacquelyn said.

"Nothing I'd like better, baby. But the doctor says you have to take it easy. We don't want anything to happen to our kid, do we? And without your health, you ain't got nothin'. Remember that, kiddo."

"We've never been separated. I want to go with you, Dan."

"It's only for one night, baby. I'll be back before you know it. I'll call you as soon as the conference is over."

Sunlight filtered into the room, painting light squares on the carpet's figured scroll which seemed to contain a hidden message. She could not explain her uneasiness. It might have been merely the impending separation, or the instinct of a mother-to-be to keep the protector male near her, but she believed the cause lay deeper, in the difference in their ages. Dan was so much older than she, and lived at such a furious pace, that she had begun to worry about him of late. He looked haggard, and even his restless energy seemed to have reached its limit. He complained, for the first time since she had known him, of feeling tired and of vague pains in his chest and arms. But he put off going to the doctor; he was too busy, there were too many other appointments to keep. To provide quiet intervals, she tried to limit their social activities, pleading her own indisposition, but on those evenings when she succeeded in keeping Dan at home, he spent hours with a telephone cradled at his ear, puffing at his cigar. He might as well have been in his office.

On the night before his departure for New York, Dan stayed at home and they made love. Somehow the act was different. In the intricate apparatus of her emotions, like tiny chiming bells that after climax shifted their tones and interaction, there was a change she did not welcome, a change that underlined her fears. Afterward Dan felt chilly and weak. He lay in bed and grinned at her when she returned from the bathroom.

"What's the matter?" she asked.

"Nothing. I was just thinking how much I like your ass. Round, firm, and fully packed. You're the only woman I know who looks just as good going as coming."

"Never mind pretending to be lecherous. You have to leave early tomorrow. Go to sleep."

"Pretend? Come here."

"Oh, Dan, no."

He pulled her naked into bed beside him.

"Dan, please . . . I don't want to. I don't feel like it."

His hand moved over her navel, over the swelling of stomach that was rounded now like a huge balloon of flesh. She reacted to his touch; she couldn't help it.

"Come over me, baby."

She moved, slightly cumbrous, like a plump older woman, but the thrust of his body was familiar and exciting. She shivered and tried to hold him tight. All of a sudden, she began weeping.

"Are you all right?" he wanted to know.

"Yes, I'm fine. It's just . . . I like it. I don't want to, but I can't help it. I like it so much."

"I like it too."

She put down her arms to hold his face, and then put her lips on his, bending over with difficulty . . .

In the morning, wakened by the alarm at five thirty, she felt clean and refreshed, smiling because she was content and in love and very tired. She got up and dressed and sat in a chair, still smiling and a bit remote. She wore only a white dress over her naked body, and her hair was tied back.

Dan, coming out of the bathroom in his undershirt and trousers, with lather on his face, looked at her admiringly.

"One other thing I didn't mention," he said. "I like your eyes, too."

"Thank you, sir. I'd better fix you something to eat before you go. It's too early to wake the servants."

"Why don't we grab something at the airport?"

"No. I want to fix you something. At least I've learned how to make boiled eggs and coffee. Let me."

In the kitchen she felt really free, watching the water boiling in the pot and the white eggs seeming to move in bubbling froth. The coffee gurgled in the Silex, and her unhurried thoughts seemed to flow upward with the black liquid.

Dan came in, freshly shaved, wearing an unbuttoned white shirt. He embraced her from behind, his hands cupping her breasts.

"How about it. Do you love me?"

"You're all right," she said.

It was still dark but she could see the horizon line of dawn clearly, like the thin edge of light beneath a window shade. She relaxed against him. He untied the ribbon that held her hair and let it fall below her shoulders, dark against the white dress. As he began to stroke her hair lightly she felt a little frightened.

"Please," she said, "we haven't time."

He didn't listen. Desire came over her, sudden and bursting. She felt weak and helpless as a child. His body was her master. She forgot the eggs bubbling in the pot and the coffee boiling and ready to serve. He kissed her hair and the back of her neck while his hands gently moved along the curves and the soft swell of her belly. Then he began to pull the zipper at the back of her dress.

"Dan," she murmured. "This is crazy. Not after last night."

But he was discovering her with his hands. She felt as though nailed to the floor of the kitchen, and the bubbling sounds were no longer on the stove but somewhere inside her where her need was simmering. Her legs were heavy and bound and her pulse was beating as though counting off the minutes until it would happen to her. Her fingers reached behind to touch him. He took off his shirt and then helped her out of her dress. Her skin was tight and shone like ivory in the fluorescent light. She thought of asking him to stop, but he wouldn't stop and if he did she would only ask him to begin again—her need was strong, strong. When his lips touched her breast she held him to her as though he was her baby, and her nipples hardened. They moved into the bedroom, and the moment they came together she felt as though seized out of her body, drawn upward out of her envelope of skin. She went up, scattering in the ignited air and falling in charred brown sticks of silent sound. And then he came out and she rolled off him. He lay with his hands at the side of his body. She put her head on his chest; his breathing was labored and the slow beat of his heart sounded like a blind man's stick tapping, going forward, hesitating, moving sluggishly.

"Dan?"

A second passed before he answered, "Yes?"

"Why are you lying with your eyes closed?"

"It feels better in the dark, baby."

"What does?"

"Nothing. I got a little dizzy."

Alarm surged. "We shouldn't have done it. I've made you sick."

"Me sick?" He rumbled laughter in his chest. "You know me better. I never get sick."

But he kept his eyes closed, and after a minute complained of a tightness in his chest.

"I'm going to call the doctor," she said.

"Just give me a minute to rest. I'll be fine." He repeated, as though it were a command to himself, "I'll be perfectly fine."

He opened his eyes to prove it, then shut them again.

"Dizziness?"

"Yeah. Everything's rolling around like a ship at sea. Maybe I did pick up something. A bug in my system. I'll shake it out of me before I go."

"You're not going anywhere until the doctor says you can."

Dawn began to invade the bedroom, a sad, gray light. Dan kept his eyes open as though by an act of will, but seemed to be having trouble with his breath. And he could not get his tongue to curl properly around words. "Don' you worry, baby. I'm gonna be all righ' . . ."

She eased his head back against the pillow and as she did so, got the terrible message of urgency from his body. All his muscles seemed to gather as though for a great effort, an attempt to leap an impassable wall. His neck set powerfully into his shoulders, and he shifted his weight as though some crushing weight were pressing down on his wide, stocky chest; his expression seemed a bit quizzical, a bit amused, as though not quite sure what was happening to him but aware that it was nothing to worry about. Then the line of his mouth changed, twisted as though a hammerblow had struck. A startled look came into his open eyes. His throat muscles worked as though he were going to heave, but only a little bubble forced its way up out of his mouth.

After a minute she discovered there was no expression in his eyes at all.

CHAPTER THIRTEEN

Everyone told her that it was the punishing pace that had killed Dan Reed. They said she certainly had nothing to reproach herself for; she had tried to get him to slow down. They told her this during the brief moments when she came out of the fog of sedation that kept the fact of his death from getting through to her. Nothing but sedatives worked. She couldn't talk to friends or read or watch television or even go out of the house. There was nowhere to go. There was no safe place to be now Dan was gone. When she tried to eat, food wouldn't stay down. As soon as she began to ease up on the drugs and became aware of her surroundings, it was unbearable again. When she finally asked, she was told that the funeral was the next morning. But the doctor forbade her to go.

"I have to," she said. "I have to see Dan. It's the last time. I have to see him."

Her mother had been hovering about her for days, murmuring and anxious. *My poor child, my poor baby,* she told anyone who called, *I don't know what's going to become of her. She's half mad with grief.* Mother enjoyed being back in the center of things.

Richard came the night before the funeral. He had been sailing in his schooner and there had been no way to reach him. When he turned on the radio to get a weather report, he heard the news, changed course, and sailed in to the nearest marina where he took a taxi directly to the house.

When he came into Jacquelyn's bedroom, she was sitting before the dressing table mirror, just staring vacantly as she combed out her loose, dark hair. She smiled dreamily at the image that appeared in soft focus at the far end of the room. A man wearing a V-necked shirt and windbreaker and white duck trousers with rope sandals.

288

Richard? Richard was not real. He was just part of her daytime dream in which Dan Reed was alive and would soon be entering the room.

Richard walked slowly across to her. His image was tall above her in the mirror.

"Jax?"

She swirled and flung her arms about him and held on. He pressed her head against his side.

"It's my fault! Dan is dead, and it's my fault. I killed him."

"You know that isn't so."

"I don't know. I don't." She deliberately did not look at him. "He was so tired, so worn out. And that last night I . . . we . . ."

"Jax, there's always a reason we can find to blame ourselves."

Something strange in his voice, something faded. She thought she had not quite conveyed the intensity of her despair.

"You don't understand what I'm trying to tell you," she said. "We made love, do you understand? Several times."

"What's so terrible about that?"

He was offering ritual comfort, not bringing his attention to bear on what she was saying.

"And then he died . . . I kept calling to him and shaking him, but he didn't answer. I killed him!"

"Jax, that isn't true."

She sensed what was lacking—the power of will to grapple with her problem. He let his hand fall away from her head. That was unlike Richard, who knew how much she needed the physical reassurance of touch, a man's touch.

"Now he's dead." She grasped his hands. "Oh, God, I *killed* him! Do you understand?" She had to keep giving words to the terrible burden of guilt.

"Jax, you've been through a lot, I know. But you'll find the strength. We all find the strength or break. And you're not going to break."

She did not believe it possible, this remoteness at a time when she needed him close. There was a part of herself that she could never share with anyone but him. Didn't he know how much she needed him?

"Richard, what's the matter? You're not listening."

"Yes, I am, Jax."

"What did you mean, there's always a reason we can find to blame ourselves?"

He touched fingertips to his forehead. "There are little ways we hurt people we're supposed to love. The little ways are worse than the big ones."

She guessed: "You're not talking about me and Dan."

"I'm tired, Jax."

"You're talking about Mady."

"This is no time to tell you my troubles," he responded dully.

"It is Mady, isn't it?"

He turned away uneasily.

She had been frightened by his weary indifference. He was always her guide, a lighthouse on a rock, and when suddenly he was not there she was relieved, actually relieved, to discover Mady was the reason. The horrid woman! Oh, why hadn't he listened when she tried to warn him?

"Whatever has happened, I know it isn't your fault."

"I haven't been a very good husband. She has a right to expect more. I'm a failure Jax—worse, I haven't tried to succeed. The pharmacy is a bust. I'm going to have to sell it, for less than half what I paid."

"You're meant for bigger things than being a pharmacist in a small town."

"I haven't even been a good father to my kids. I'm always running away when I've got a weekend. I spend more time on my boat than I do with my family."

She gave him a tender look. "I'm sure they don't have anything to complain about."

"I try to be the right kind of husband and father, but then a feeling comes over me—that I'm killing myself for the benefit of others. And I go looking for something and I don't know what."

Richard had never confided in her so deeply before. There had been a distance between them, other persons between, but the distance wasn't there any longer. Mady with her bright red hair, strident poodles, and two squalling children, were put back into perspective.

She put her head against Richard's chest, and began to cry. He put his arms about her.

"It's all right, Jax. I'll make it up to you—to everybody. It's going to be different from now on."

"You're always the one I can turn to. That can't change, ever."

"Everything changes, Jax. If you remember that, it may help you face the fact that Dan is dead. Everything changes, and there's nothing to do but go on living."

Her eyes felt queerly concentrated as she looked up at him. "I want to go to his funeral, but I won't be able to make it. All those people."

Once she had climbed on top of a car to wait until policemen rescued her from frantic autograph seekers. Another time she had crawled under a table to avoid a horde of photographers in a restaurant. She couldn't go through that sort of thing again. Not now.

"If you want to go, you will. It's the first step back, Jax."

"Back to where? I have no place to go."

"We'll figure that out when we know what you really want. There's a different answer for everyone, Jax."

Through grief's darkness she saw a steady, saving beam. The Richard she knew.

She whispered, "I want to see Dan again. I do."

In the morning, Mother laid out a black dress and a hat with a short black veil. She began to dress. Richard came by half an hour before the time to leave, and they had breakfast sitting in the kitchen while Mother fussed at the stove making scrambled eggs for everyone. Jacquelyn could not touch food. She drank a little lukewarm coffee.

Richard smiled at her and touched her hand. She began to believe she could make it, after all.

As she was starting toward the front door, Richard stopped her.

"No, the side entrance. And in my car."

"Why? The limousine is waiting out front. I saw it."

"So did everyone else. Did you notice the police cordon at both ends of the street? The crowd is going to break through the minute the limousine pulls away."

"I don't believe it. On a day like this? People don't behave that way."

Richard said, "They won't look for you in my car. And we won't take the main route. A police escort is going with the limousine to throw them off—they've even got a policewoman dressed up to resemble you." Richard put his arm about her. "Here we go."

They drove off in Richard's three-year-old Buick, and as they turned the corner a block away from where they would ordinarily have emerged, a huge swelling sea of people spread out across the avenue, blocking all south-bound traffic. Why are they here? She wondered. Do they think even this is some sort of entertainment?

At the entrance to the cemetery Richard moved the Buick into a line of cars waiting to have credentials checked at the gate. Accredited limousines with stickers on the windshield were passing through without check at the gate, but were having a hard time with the crowds before getting there. Each time a new limousine rolled up, a throng surged forward to have a look at its occupants. On the sidewalks outside the cemetery, vendors were selling hot dogs, soda pop, and ice cream, and others were doing a brisk business in studio photographs of Jacquelyn. Movie magazines that featured Jacquelyn and Dan on the covers, and which had gone to press long before Dan's death, were being hawked to the spectators at premium prices.

They passed through the gate at once; the gatekeeper had been told they would be in his line. They began a slow circling trip inside the cemetery grounds. Hundreds of people had somehow gotten inside and were sitting around on the grass near tombstones. Some had spread tablecloths and were having picnic lunches. The narrow roadway was littered with empty boxes and soda bottles, some already broken.

Near an impressive-looking mausoleum, one large family had set up a portable table with hampers of food. Two boys were throwing a large striped beach ball high in the air. On the roof of the mausoleum an older boy had planted himself with a camera to take pictures of the cars as they passed.

Suddenly the boy stopped, lowered his camera, and began shouting to the family below. The mother, an ample woman, looked up at first with annoyance and then, getting the message, turned to stare directly at Richard's car. Her husband, wearing only undershirt and trousers on his skinny frame, threw aside the sandwich he had been eating.

"They've spotted us," Jacquelyn whispered. "Hurry!"

But there was nothing to do. The car was almost touching bumpers with the car ahead and there was no way to get past it on the narrow roadway.

Richard rolled up the windows and locked the door. In a moment they were surrounded. The mother came to the car window, moving along with them and gesticulating and shouting. The father rapped sharply on the pane beside Richard as though commanding him to stop. Richard ignored him, staring straight ahead as they approached the area ringed off by police. The two boys who had been playing beach ball climbed up onto the fenders of the car. One of them began pounding on the fender, sending vibrating sounds through the car body.

The uproar began to attract the attention of other spectators. They began to converge on the car. Jacquelyn put her hands over her face and bent her head, but could not shut out the increasing commotion all around.

"HEY, JACQUELYN!"

"Jacquelyn, what are you hiding for?"

"Dan's dead, Jackie. How about me? I'm livin'!"

"You ain't gonna be a widow long, Jacquelyn!"

"Oh, Jackie, YOU'RE BEAUTIFUL!"

"Give us a kiss, will ya?"

She held her breath until she felt a warning catch in her throat. Too much had gone out of her with Dan, too much hope and too much feeling. She hated her fellow creatures, irrationally, because they were here and Dan was gone. He had been a strong man, strong enough to make his mark and to disobey their rules, but now he was weaker than any of them. He was in no way their equal.

The rear window of the car cracked. Someone must have thrown something against it. At that moment she no longer wished to participate in the ways of the world. She was living through the precise instant in which she learned for all time to hate the obscene squawking of so-called admirers.

The car had stopped and began rocking to and fro under the pressure of the crowd. A chant began.

"GET OUT, JACKIE ... GET OUT, JACKIE ... GET OUT!"

She began sobbing. Oh, God, please, she thought. Oh, God, please get me away.

The police arrived to clear a space for the car. When she reached the gravesite she was trembling and had to remain inside the car for a few minutes before she could trust herself to get out. Then she did, and stood with the others to watch the coffin lowered into the ground. She was sorry not to have been at the chapel because this way she could not see Dan again and it was very hard to convince herself he was actually inside the box that was now disappearing from sight forever. A newspaper blew across the site, stirred by a mild breeze. One of the watchful men from the funeral home intercepted the newspaper before it went down into the pit with Dan. Something for him to read, she thought, with a ghastly inward chuckle that broke to become tears. Richard moved closer to her. Everyone was staring. Mother came over too: My poor child, my poor dear baby.

Suddenly a photographer aimed his camera, took a picture, and then another, before several funeral home attendants hustled him out. A small argument about the camera nearly turned into a physical struggle. But everything was hushed as the minister, standing on a green knoll beneath artfully drooping eucalyptus trees, began to deliver a short sermon to the gaping brown-colored rectangle in the ground. She could not hear any words. The minister was a fleshy, broad-nosed, red-complexioned man, who mourned without love, in a ritual whose ceremony had a sick life of its own, independent of love.

Jacquelyn could not stop crying, but she did so silently until the minister finished and spoke a few words to her, and people began to drift away, turning back to stare.

"Can't we go now?" she asked Richard.

"In a few minutes. The police want to make sure there'll be no interference this time."

A spasm swept over her body. "Why can't they leave me alone? What kind of . . . animals . . . are they?"

The landscape before her wavered in a convulsion of pain. She felt daggers pierce her abdomen.

Her fingers dug into Richard's arm. "You have to get me out of here. Now!"

"What's the matter?"

With an immense effort she kept her voice in a tightly controlled whisper: "The baby . . . I think something's wrong."

She drew her hands in against her body and began to crumple. Richard half carried her from the gravesite, while she tried to hold herself in against the onrush of agony. Then she ceased to struggle and let it all wash over her, and the darkness came on quickly, lit by red spears that seemed to thrust deep into her intestines. Richard swung her carefully up into his arms and she lay there, her face feeling hot against the cool bristle on his neck. They kept moving, and then the swaying movement slowed and she managed to look up and saw a crowd gathered, watching like a somber jury.

All right, she thought with a kind of fury, I hope you're all satisfied! I hope you've all got what you came for.

She felt and heard the impact of hard-shod feet approach her bed.

"How are you feeling?" the doctor asked.

"Better, I think. Stronger."

"You've lost quite a lot of blood and had a rough time. But you're going to be all right. All you need is rest."

"And my baby?"

The doctor looked at her for a moment, as though trying to figure out whether he should tell her, then he shook his head.

Losing the baby and Dan was such a perverse double cruelty that she could not even feel resentment after she left the hospital. Or perhaps the miscarriage caused such a deep physical weariness it muffled her emotional responses. In the end she simply wanted to be alone and not think, to shut out the horror that confronted her in every waking moment. She was tired of seeing people, and this not only included people in crowds (she would never feel quite the same way toward crowds), but individuals too. Her mother was always telephoning or trying to come by to visit. All her friends—she did not know there were so many—were trying to call. Each one seemed to want a private word with her, as though that would somehow assuage her grief or give her a kind of support. They meant to be kind (or did they?), but when they came they covertly scrutinized her and gauged how she was coming through the crisis. *Poor Jacquelyn*, she could hear them say later to friends, *I saw her alone the other night and she looked terrible*. They sat with her and said the same things over and over—the mindless repetition of a television commercial trying to implant a single message. *You're going to be all right. This will pass and life will be worth living again.*

The only real person in her life was Richard who came to talk or not to talk, simply to be with her. He talked to her about what was happening to him, and somehow that proved there was someone in the world whose love belonged to her. Someone she could love. He had sold the pharmacy and put the money into a big, three-masted schooner. His plan was to take out deep-sea fishing parties, which he had already begun doing; it looked promising. She thrilled to his tale of a sudden storm and how he sailed the swift boat close to the wind on a perilous journey home. She felt as though she were battered by waves, and gathering strength from him to meet the next shock.

She knew the next shock would come when she tried to return to a new way of life. Her other life had begun to seem a dream of happiness. Dan, always Dan, appearing to her vibrant and alive with a peculiar ability to triumph over everything, even death. She believed she would always love him. On certain mornings she felt that she spoke to him, exchanged words that made everything different and restored her to the dreamland. Nothing else mattered. It was herself and Dan, and that was all, and never mind the rest. Too much had happened to her in a few weeks, and the spillover of anguish flooded her with memories that made any sort of future life appear impossible.

But somehow she began again, tentatively, taking her son Gene out, going for a walk or a short drive, or spending the day at the beach. She was nervous about going out alone after the incident with the crowds at the cemetery, but every day the pressure on her to do so increased. She talked it over with Richard, who had volunteered to take her on a shopping excursion or to sit among people at a restaurant. But she had to do it by herself. Making a real effort, she broke the spell of her fear by going to lunch at the Brown Derby, driving most of the way and walking the last few blocks. She sat alone at a luncheon table, smiling and signing autographs.

"Oh, there's Jacquelyn! . . . Hi, Jacquelyn! . . . Hi, Jacquelyn . . . Oh, she's just gorgeous . . ."

Her agent, Morey Bloom, called her twice a day with news of what was going on in Hollywood. One afternoon he called her in a frenzy of excitement. She had just been nominated for an Academy Award for her performance in *When the Dog Bites.*

"That's ridiculous," she said. "I wasn't even good in it. Penelope Ardrey should win this year, hands down."

"She's nominated too. But the tradewinds say that you're going to get it."

"Why?"

"It's your year, pumpkin. Everyone's in your corner and looking for a way to show it."

"I don't want to win because people feel sorry for me. That isn't even fair, for God's sake."

"Fair schmair. The main thing is, get a pretty new dress and show up for the countdown. Whether you win the Oscar or not, you're going to be the big attraction at this year's show."

On the night of the Award dinner, Richard was her escort. Up to the last minute she was sure that she would not be able to go. Even though she had bought a magnificent new Givenchy, a high-waisted Empire gown of sunbeam yellow, appliquéd with white flowers, and elegantly simple in its long sweep, even though she had promised that she would attend, she did not really think she could go through with it. She would plead illness, she thought, and it would be true in a way because her fear of the curious mob penned behind wooden barricades, waiting to overwhelm her, was a terror that bordered on phobia. She hated the idea of the entrance way ablaze with light, thousands of tiny, prying little bulbs. She hated competing with the hordes of glamorous women and their perfectly groomed male escorts, glittering celebrities moving out of the darkness beneath the lights to vanish in the auditorium after their brief moment.

But in the end she went, for many reasons: because Richard expected her to go, because she had promised and it was easier to keep the promise than to get out of it, because a part of herself did look forward with anticipation to the evening; but most of all because she had a conviction that the only way to finally end her fright was simply to act as though it was behind her.

A thin nervous man, in a full dress suit, greeted her as she stepped out of the Rolls at the entrance. He looked uncomfortable and was perspiring freely; his scrawny neck swam so loosely in his wide collar that his head seemed to be in imminent danger of slipping down and vanishing out of sight.

"Miss Stuart, I'm delighted to see you."

From the crowds on either side of the protective barricade there came a collective indrawn exclamation:

"JACQUELYN!"

"Look—it's her! Who's that man with her?"

"Jackieeeeee!"

As she emerged from the shadows into the cold brilliance of the lights, Jacquelyn grasped Richard's arm. She was wearing the yellow gown and a sable wrap thrown with artless artifice across her gleaming bare shoulders.

A tremendous burst of applause was punctuated with shrill screaming. Her grip on Richard's arm tightened. At the cemetery they had crowded in, thirsty eyes shining with anticipation.

A young man wearing a zippered jacket over a wild-colored madras shirt and very tight, checked jeans and boots ducked beneath the barricade. He almost reached Jacquelyn before a policeman caught him.

"Jackie, tell him to lemme go. I gotta talk to ya!"

Flustered and perspiring, the thin man in his dress suit led the way beneath the marquee.

"You're an angel, Jackie," the young man called after her. "You're gorgeous!"

A fat young woman with high-piled dark hair and harlequin sunglasses held out her arms toward Jacquelyn in an empty embrace.

"You'll win, Jacquelyn. We all love you so!"

When Jacquelyn glanced in her direction, the plump young woman burst into tears. Her two young friends, on either side, tried to comfort her, but they began crying too.

Inside the lobby, flashbulbs exploded and photographers circled each other for a better position. Richard shielded her and got her past the waiting TV camera and into the tight-packed auditorium. Her hand was through his arm and he pressed it reassuringly to his side. She turned to smile at him. It was going to be all right.

She saw an attractive, tanned older woman precede her into the auditorium. The woman had an interesting bony face, a lovely wide mouth, and dark hair that hung down beside her face. An expensive gown was draped rather loosely on her gaunt frame.

Jacquelyn caught up to her. "Penny?"

Penelope Ardrey turned. "Jacquelyn."

"I want you to know that whatever happens tonight, I think you deserve to win. You were wonderful in *The Last Mistress.*"

"Thank you, dear. But I have a feeling that when the roll is called up yonder your name is going to lead all the rest." Penelope flashed a smile at Richard; she had a beautiful smile. "And who is your escort?"

"Oh, Penny, this is my brother Richard."

They chatted for a few moments before Jacquelyn

turned to talk to a producer who took both her hands in his and stared at her with rapt sincerity.

"This is going to be a night for you to remember, Jacquelyn. And I want you to keep in mind that when they call your name, it isn't just because you're a great actress. It's because you're a great person."

"Thank you, John. I really don't deserve all the fuss that's being made over me."

The producer's eyes filled. "You say that because you're the kind of person you are. Sweet and humble and ... Jackie, I've got to say this. You're a credit to us all. You make me proud to say I work in Hollywood."

The producer was swept away into the crowd. When Jacquelyn turned back, Penelope Ardrey shrugged her shoulders.

"You see what I mean, darling," Penelope said. "You've joined the Hollywood hagiology."

"What?"

"You're one of the accredited saints. Beyond the reach of us ordinary mortals."

"I don't understand what it's all about."

"You've suffered, darling. You've known a great love, lost it, and now you're ready to rise above it. You're Hollywood's version of the Virgin Mary. There's no sense fighting it. It's your image from now on and you have to live with it."

Richard took her into the theater and as they went down the thickly carpeted aisle, heads turned to stare, row after row. A tall usherette in a red uniform with brass buttons preceded them reverently, and made the most of a brief moment showing Jacquelyn her place and giving her a souvenir program.

The moment she sat down, everyone around her began turning to speak, to shake hands, to smile at her benevolently. From farther away, others in the audience seemed to follow her every gesture. Penelope was right. The great ingenious Hollywood publicity machine had received one of its indecipherable orders. Mammoth gears had begun to turn, and a new image of Jacquelyn Stuart was forming in thousands of press releases and handouts, in planted stories in newspapers and magazines which, in turn, had unpredictable repercussions in other newspapers and magazines, in television shows and late-night interview programs. Of course, the first victims of the new publicity were its makers; Hollywood believed more implicitly in its myths than anyone outside of the industry. When the deed was done, there was created a Jacquelyn Stuart larger than life, magnified out of her identity into the heroine of great tragedy, a universal symbol.

Richard held her hand while Jacquelyn thought: I'm going to have to do something to reestablish contact between the real me and this image. *You're an angel*, the boy in the madras shirt and tight jeans had shouted. Enough was enough. She was not going to be crucified by their need for a saint. The crowds breaking through the barricades to surround her, to touch her, were not going to possess her also.

The Awards ceremony rambled on its course. There were minor awards to the people who made movies semi-anonymously, and then major awards to the people the public thought made the movies. At last the moment arrived to choose the best actress of the year. Bobby Randall, this year's master of ceremonies, turned the microphone over to Mark Vaughn and Gerda Andersen, who read off the various nominations.

"And the winner is . . ." Mark Vaughn began.

She never heard her name above the tumult that began with the very first syllable. A roaring torrent crashed over her head like the long boom of a surf roller. She looked about her, dazed and bewildered.

"It's you, honey," Richard said.

She got to her feet and started down the aisle. She was trembling. The cheers went on and on and on. All the seats she passed were occupied by agitated white faces, waving hands, people shouting unintelligible messages. In each aisle people stood up, and began applauding. As she passed Henry Margate, the roly-poly British director was blubbering like a jowly infant, but he managed a "Bless you, child, bless you."

Quite suddenly she was frightened to her marrow. If Henry Margate could react this way, this was no temporary new image, a transient phenomenon, but something that would become accepted along with such firmly established Hollywood legends as that Rudolph Valentino was the world's greatest lover, Charlie Chaplin was the world's funniest man, Marilyn Monroe was the world's sexiest woman, Gary Cooper was the world's truest American, and *Gone with the Wind* was the finest movie ever made. Jacquelyn Stuart was about to be enshrined as the world's greatest widow. Lovely, suffering, almost virginal, saintly.

As she mounted the steps to the platform, with cheers and applause ringing in her ears, Jacquelyn knew that if she did not do something drastic to change the course of events, there would be no getting rid of her new image.

Bobby Randall bounded across stage to greet her. He hugged her and then, suddenly recalling the limits of *lèse majesté,* drew back, and holding her hand at almost arms length, crossed the stage with her to the podium where Mark Vaughn and Gerda Andersen also waited. Gerda was dissolved in tears. Mark's lips quivered handsomely while, without seeming to, he kept his right profile aimed at the audience.

"Oh, darling," Gerda bawled, "I'm so happy for you!"

She flung herself onto Jacquelyn. Mark waited his turn patiently, then holding her pinioned by the elbows, he said, "You're a great human being, Jackie, that's what you are. That's why you deserve this award."

Several minutes passed before the uproar in the auditorium ceased. With one hand, Bobby Randall held the gold statuette close to his heart. He seemed about to confer the Congressional Medal of Honor.

"Jacquelyn," he finally said into the microphone, and with the magic of that name, pacified the last rebel outposts of applause and cheers. "Jacquelyn," Bobby went on in a louder tone, "I want to say a few words before I give you this. Because with it goes not only an award as a great, great actress, but something I know you value much more: the heart and soul of everyone in Hollywood who has ever worked with you and has come to know you for the wonderful person you are. You've been an inspiration to us all, Jacquelyn, because you helped show us the kind of courage that we all will need sometime or other in our lives, and because no matter how badly life dealt you the cards, you played them the way you got them, with never a complaint. And you've ended up by beating the odds— winning without any tricks or pretense—because trickery and pretense just aren't in your nature. Great people like you always win because the rest of us need you to come through for us, so we can keep on believing in all the wonderful, warm human virtues that you represent." Bobby paused for exactly the right dramatic emphasis (he was a master of timing), and added in a choked voice, "God bless you forever, Jacquelyn Stuart."

Then it was Jacquelyn's turn. As she stood at the podium, the silence that fell upon the awestruck audience was like the hush in a great cathedral before High Mass. The gold Oscar was slippery in her slightly perspiring fingers.

"I want to thank everyone for this, and I realize what a great honor it is. But listening to some of the things that have been said about me here tonight, I'm reminded of a story."

The worshipful atmosphere in the hall lightened; people smiled at her and at each other with relief and gratitude. She was going to strike a light note; what good taste, their attitude now seemed to suggest, what a truly great lady.

"It's the story of a Presidential candidate who was making a short stop in Indian territory. He promised if he was elected to get the Indians better food and housing. The Indians set up a great cry: Hoodah! Hoodah! Then he went on to promise that they would no longer be second-class citizens, and again the cry: HOODAH!"

She heard expectant rustling, a collective leaning forward so that no one of them would be late in laughing at the punch line.

"Later, when the Presidential candidate was leaving, he came to a pasture where a herd of horses had been kept for some time, and his guide pointed to the places in the pasture where the horses had relieved themselves. 'Please, sir, be careful not to step in the hoodah!' "

There was something a little strange, even impressive, in the spectacle of all those hundreds of people holding in a single stunned breath.

Jacquelyn's voice rang clearly across silence: "I would ask all of you, all my friends, to please remember that I'm no different and no better than I was ... so let's not get any deeper into hoodah than we have to!"

Bobby Randall's face had gone white and unbelieving, while his mouth made gaping motions. The silence in the auditorium lasted seconds longer. The reactions of a crowd are the sum of a million infinitesimal phenomena. Just as a thousand atoms of a certain type produce lead, so a million of another kind will produce quicksilver. In the midst of the prolonged silence, laughter sprang up, first from a small group who were genuinely delighted, then from a larger group that swiftly translated shock into an equivalent volume of laughter, then from a still larger group who were glad to find any escape into a reaction that would help them surmount this difficult moment, and soon the entire audience was laughing in a huge burst of what appeared to be spontaneous merriment.

Jacquelyn held her Oscar, waving and smiling at the crowd. Nearby, Bobby Randall was bent double with a fit of laughter that left him purple and gasping for breath.

Jacquelyn's scabrous remark became famous in the annals of the Academy Awards, but, more important, it smashed finally and forever the burgeoning legend that she was some kind of saintly tragedienne. When Morey Bloom called in the morning he was his usual cheerful self.

"Pumpkin, you got more publicity than Abe Lincoln got for the Gettysburg Address. It's sensational. It's historic. Everybody's talking about you. You've been denounced by every ladies club east of San Diego—and letters and telegrams are still pouring in. Last I heard, the ratio was about eight to one against you."

"Is that good?"

"Why worry? The people who write don't go to the movies. It's the young people who don't write or send telegrams who go to see movies, and they respect you because you leveled with them. You called crap crap, right on television with thirty million people looking on. And the press is with you. They say it was real womanly of you, and that you're an honest gal without an ounce of phony. That's all good. It's a sellable image."

"There you go with the image."

"We sell the sizzle and not the steak, and your sizzle is a message every man gets right in his groin. You made a smart move last night, pumpkin. If you'd let them put you up there as a saint, you'd have been dead on the shelf. Everybody would love you and nobody would go to see you in a theater. Who needs that?"

"That's not why I did it, Morey."

"Sure, pumpkin, I know. You're a real broad. I'm just spreading out the form sheet for you to read. You're still holding the title as leading sex goddess."

During the weeks that followed her appearance at the Academy Awards, there were times, returning to a lonely house at night, when Jacquelyn thought she would trade all that indiscriminate love from a multitude for just one night in the arms of a man she loved. There had been no one for her since Dan. When he died, she made a promise to herself that there would never be anyone else. But that had been in the depths of sorrow at losing him. Before long, she felt the ache begin. In her new movie, *Fallen Woman,* she played a promiscuous lady heiress who cut a wide swathe through the young, handsome junior executives in the department store she inherited from her father. She had to enact a number of passionate love scenes with some very attractive men, and each time it happened she could hardly eat or sleep when she went home. Her need was not sublimated in either her work or her duty as a mother to Gene.

Gradually a feeling of depression came over her. When her drive became too hard to control she began to wonder if she was becoming a kind of nymphomaniac. She went for a few sessions to a psychoanalyst who assured her that her physical requirements were perfectly normal for a woman her age and that there was really nothing wrong with satisfying them, as long as she acted with reasonable discretion.

Reasonable discretion, however, was what worried her. Hundred of men were anxious to have an affair with her, and she was flattered by their attention. But she knew only too well that they wanted more than an affair; they wanted everyone to *know* about the affair. If she yielded, her reputation as a wanton would soon be spread on the fleet wings of gossip. On the other hand, the nicest men, who might have shared with her a discreet yet meaningful emotional relationship, were too defeated by her fame, by her beauty, and by what they imagined the competition must be. These men never asked her out.

The first man to really interest her came along almost a year after Dan Reed's death. Ralph Terry was a boyish Senator from New Hampshire, happily married, with four children and a highly promising political career. There was some talk that he might be the next Republican candidate for Vice President. They met at a party, and when their eyes locked across the room he came over to sit beside her, and showed her pictures of his wife and children. He told her quite honestly how lonely he was. He had come to Hollywood as part of a subcommittee to examine the possibility of a system of classification for films that would head off passage of stricter laws on censorship.

For Jacquelyn, the young Senator seemed an ambassador from a more interesting and consequential world. Her own fame seemed frivolous and transient beside his. When he told her about his work in the Senate she sensed in him the essence of political power, the real seriousness of leaders in Washington who were shaping the destinies of a world. She could almost hear him orating in the halls of Congress, swaying minds with sincere idealistic eloquence; returning to a fine old Georgetown mansion on a narrow dignified street, and dining there with the leaders of foreign countries, as mighty decisions hung in the balance.

The die seemed cast. She would become important in his life. She envisioned herself as a sort of Madame Pompadour, or at least a *maîtresse légitime*, playing a mysterious but meaningful role in great events.

She didn't rush things. There was plenty of opportunity for them to get to know each other. At the end of two weeks, she arranged for them to spend a night at Bobby Randall's house when he was away for the weekend. It was a lovely country house, built on a rise overlooking a lake, and surrounded by a long stone wall covered with ivy. Ralph was enchanted with the house and the view. The two beds in the master bedroom were double-sized and their heavy, white, textured covers seemed to fill the room like a carpet. She undressed alone in the bedroom, while Ralph used the bathroom to disrobe.

Much later, in bed, his face was flushed and shining with sweat and his mouth had dropped open slightly with exertion. Then he stopped; everything stopped. She felt his small stiffness crumple like a coat taken off a hanger.

"I'm so sorry, my dearest."

"It's all right."

"It's all my fault."

"You mustn't blame yourself."

He was guilty about betraying his wife. He drew an increase of virtue from his guilt: it fortified his belief in himself. She remained friendly with him for some time, but when she read of his later political troubles she shrugged over the inevitability of his fall. A man who was not able to create in himself enough passion to overcome moral scruples was not strong enough to go far in political life. She was not surprised when he failed to get the Vice Presidential nomination.

Not long after the Senator departed, the telephone rang in her home. It was Christopher Leigh. She had not heard from him since the day she caught him in bed with Charles.

"Jacquelyn? Chris Leigh."

"No!"

"I'm just in town for a few days. On my way to do

some location shooting in Honolulu. I thought we might have dinner."

She was no longer angry with him; she doubted she had ever been. And he *was* amusing, one of the most intelligent men she had ever known.

"That sounds lovely, Chris."

"Tonight?"

"Of course. Yes."

"Shall I come for you at eight?"

"Whenever you can. I'd love to see you again."

While they were dining at the Alhambra that evening, Seth Rosen stopped at her table.

"You're looking wonderful, Jacquelyn. Really wonderful. It's good to see you back in circulation again." He dismissed Christopher Leigh with a glance. "Would it be all right if I called you one evening?"

"I hope you will," she said, and he took her private telephone number.

She and Christopher went to a favorite hangout of his, a dark, low-roofed place called Nell's Tavern. Everyone seemed to know Christopher and to accept him as a regular, not as a movie star. Jacquelyn herself drew reserved but polite attention; the others all seemed to take for granted that she was with Christopher and therefore not to be bothered.

"I like this place," Jacquelyn said. "How did you find it?"

"A friend of mine took me here the first time. Listen, do you really want to get loaded?"

"Like what?"

"Have you ever turned on? You're really missing something if you haven't."

"How long have you been using it?"

"Oh, a year at least. I'm sorry I didn't get the kick earlier. Some people have a hard time getting high, at first, but I was with pot from the very first time. It was made for me."

That night, when he took her home, she tried it for the first time. She simply sat and giggled helplessly. She didn't understand Christopher when he told her he visited different worlds when he was on a high.

On their second date, however, she really got on a kick. After a few puffs, a sensation began, over which she had no control. Everything stretched out in a very interesting way. The cigarette flame was not a simple flame but a conflagration in which each individual strand was burning like a separate tree in the forest. She watched fascinated as the fibers blackened and turned gray. This seemed to take several hours, and she found it not only fascinating but funny. All her impressions, of things, of colors, of sounds, were breaking down into tiny little pieces. She discussed this with Christopher. He was, she suddenly discovered, beyond any doubt the most interesting man she had known. The goddamnedest conversationalist! They spent what seemed to be days talking about everything from Flaubert to trout fishing, and yet it all took less than an hour. When Christopher left, she was very hungry; she raided the refrigerator and ate everything she could find. Nothing ever tasted so good.

After that, she spent many evenings getting high. As soon as she lit up, she began to find her way into that sharply enclosed but welcoming world. Suddenly everything became charged with interest, especially listening to music. She was able to hear in a way she never had been able to, hear separate instruments in a band playing solos, and weaving their separate melodies together into *thrumm-thrumm* rhythm. Stoned, she understood music.

Christopher was her usual companion on these jag parties, but she was never quite clear about what else he wanted from her. One evening, they were alone on the terrace of her home, in the coming-down stage of a high, and he began talking to her quietly. The conversation slowly began to make sense, because she was falling out of a high, and he came through in little bursts and snatches of meaning. Darkness was settling in on the hills, and a chill wind made her wrap herself in her coat. He told a long disjointed tale of frustrated love, and there was no doubt Christopher was the frustrated one and the party of the other part was not feminine. He was suffering one of those periodic bouts of absolution that overtake men who realy have no interest in women. When she discovered he was crying, silently, her nerves began to feel ragged. It reminded her of something inherently revolting, of that moment when she had surprised him with her husband. Pain struck, terribly, sharply, then slowly faded.

By the time Christopher left that evening, she had made up her mind not to see him anymore. When he called to ask her out, she refused. He must have suspected that some decision had been arrived at, for he did not call again. The end was not surprising. Their relationship really had nowhere to go; he had merely been tantalizing himself with the hope of a heterosexual affair.

Seth Rosen telephoned the next evening. She accepted his invitation joyfully. When Seth brought her home after their date, she asked if he would like to come in for a brandy. She slept with him that night, and every night for the next two weeks.

Their affair was a success that more than made up for the abortive afternoon on the beach so many moons ago. Seth ended her fear that she might not have a satisfying physical relationship with anyone after Dan, and there were unexpected benefits. Her interest in smoking pot vanished, and she no longer made the round of night spots, drinking heavily in the company of two or three strange men. She didn't even need her customary sleeping pills to go to sleep at night. With her deepest craving satisfied, lesser hungers did not get through.

There was never a question of marrying Seth. Seth was essentially a nihilist with no faith in any of the virtues, and he considered love to be what it seemed, and it seemed to be sex. On the other hand, Jacquelyn believed it dangerous to believe in sex exclusively. While her conscious self agreed with Seth, there was another, more demanding person underneath who rejected Seth's conclusion about the central place of sex. She wanted a long-term enduring communion with a man, and not a succession of moments allowed to continue only as long as they were pleasurable.

Nevertheless, her affair with Seth ended only when she became interested in someone else.

This one became known to her diary as The Professor, although actually he was not a professor but a columnist who specialized in heavy-browed interpretation of current news for a newspaper syndicate. She met him when he interviewed her for an article he was doing for the *Atlantic Monthly* on the social stratification in Hollywood. She became fascinated with him. He was not at all the pompous thinker his writings indicated, but a lively warm man, married three times, who had a great gift for humor. His deep-chested fifty-year-old body had astonishing vitality, and their affair, while short-lived, had many satisfactions. When The Professor left for an extended journey through the trouble spots of Southeast Asia she was genuinely sorry to see him go. But as she stood at the airport, watching his plane taxiing down the runway, she was fully aware that he had left no deep impression on her and that they were free of each other forever.

By then she had learned she couldn't live without a man. Sheer physical hunger caused her some alarm. At night she would throw off blankets, then pull them back. Her body glistened with sweat. She would sit up in bed and in darkness struggle against an overpowering need. When she touched her forehead she felt flushed and feverish.

The roster of her lovers during this period ranged from her six-foot-five leading man in *The Joshua Tree* to five-foot-tall Bobby Randall, from suave and world-weary John Marks, the director, to the friendly, nice-boy-next-door Jimmy Blane, who wrote the avant garde songs of social protest that were the rage on college campuses. For two weeks, while she was vacationing in Majorca, Meyer Whitney became her constant and devoted escort. He followed her back to Hollywood, and something might have happened if he had not been appointed a member of a Presidential trade commission and sent off to Brussels. During the month he was away the whole course of her life changed.

One night she was invited to go with friends to the famous Café Algiers to hear Ugo Tarelli. Ugo was the new sensation of the Hollywood thrill-seekers, a bitter dwarf whose savage wit spared no one and who took particular delight in raking over the celebrities in his audience. She agreed to go, largely to escape the importunities of love-smitten Jimmy Blane who was calling her several times each night to plead for some explanation as to why she would not see him again.

The Café Algiers was in a dismal side street in one of the least attractive sections of Los Angeles, really a narrow building that had carved out a seamless space for itself between a garage and a wholesale furniture outlet. The building had at one time housed a bar and grill, then was renovated to offer burlesque entertainment to bar patrons, and finally closed down for several months. Then Ugo Tarelli came to town, preceded by advance publicity about having been indicted for obscenity during a nightclub act in New York, and having been banned in Philadelphia, Boston, and Baltimore. Naturally, no respectable club or theater would have him and, just as naturally, everyone turned out to hear him.

Most of the wooden tables in the sordid dark interior of

the Café Algiers were occupied by leading figures of the film colony. It had become, in a matter of weeks, a question of status to be seen at the Café Algiers, recognized, and hopefully insulted, by Ugo. His insults, moreover, were not the comparatively genial thrusts of a Don Rickles or the mumbling verbal assaults of a Lenny Bruce. Ugo was filled with a genuine perverse hatred for mankind and specifically for the specimens who could afford to come to a nightclub to hear him. The source of his waspishness wasn't hard to find; it sprang from his physical deformity. Ugo was a real dwarf, and not one of the well-proportioned, fair-haired kind who sometimes look like Dresden images of children. He was very dark—his mother had been a Negress—and his face was like a gargoyle's, full of malevolence. His act consisted of sitting or squatting on a chair, his hands gripping the back of it almost as though he were about to spring out at the audience. His shortness of stature was emphasized by the high-ceilinged room—a Lilliputian in a world of Gullivers. As he cast his venomous glance about the room, choosing a target, his forehead became furrowed with deep wrinkles, and when he spoke, a guttural raucous voice grumbled out of his misshapen chest.

Jacquelyn feared him, and was fascinated by him. When he visited their table after the performance, Ugo chose a seat next to hers, hauling himself up onto the chair with his hands and greedily sampling food on everyone's plate while making grunting cries of pleasure, smacking thick lips, and rolling his eyes. The others laughed at everything he did, but Jacquelyn could hardly force a smile at his antics. She had never experienced such an instant physical distaste for anyone. To calm herself, she ordered another drink and still another. She was wondering if she could persuade the others to call it an evening when suddenly, in a quavering way, Ugo began to sing. The effect was extraordinary, like the wail of a lost child, or like the surprising loud sound made by a squeezed doll. All the while Ugo sang he kept looking at her, with a silly half grin on his ugly face, and it struck her that if Ugo were crawling across the floor of her bedroom in darkness she might well step on him and would probably crush him beneath her weight. She shuddered.

Before he returned to give his final performance of the evening, Jacquelyn was quite drunk. No one had wanted to leave while Ugo was at their table, but now the others felt it was time to go home. Jacquelyn insisted on waiting for Ugo to perform again.

"It wouldn' be nice," she said. "Walking out'n him just as he's gonna go work again."

"We've already seen the show, Jacquelyn. Other people are waiting to be seated for the next performance."

"You go, then. I'm staying."

She waved them away. After a while when she was alone, everything became a little mixed up in her head because it seemed to her Ugo was again at the table. He was watching her with moist bloodshot eyes. Then she left the club with him, and went home in a taxi. She recalled clearly going up the walk to her house when the taxi dropped her off, Ugo trotting beside her, and his voice seeming to ascend from some impossible depth.

"I was glad when I saw you and your friends walk in, Miss Stuart. I've always been an admirer of yours. I always liked you, if you know what I mean."

She laughed. "I didn't think you were suppose' to like anybody."

She reeled, and little hands helped her by holding her at the waist.

"Oh, that's just an act. I like some people. But it's pretty hard to find people who like me."

"Oh, I wouldn' say that, Ugo. I like you."

"Do you really? Do you really, Miss Stuart?"

His tone was pathetically grateful, like a hurt little dog that had found speech to thank the hand that caressed it.

" 'Course I do." She yielded to impulse and actually did pat his head. "I like you a lot, Ugo."

"I'm really a nice man. People just don't look into what I'm like. They just see the outside of me, and I'm not handsome." Ugo cackled while his eyes rolled and seemed startlingly white in the darkness.

"Good looks aren't ever'thing," Jacquelyn assured him. She fumbled for her key and it dropped out of her handbag. Ugo recovered it as quick as a flash.

He gave her a sidelong glance as she found the lock and opened the door.

"Thanks f'r taking me home, Ugo. I'm all righ' now. Look, I'd ask you in but it's awfully late, and the governess is asleep . . ."

"I understand, Miss Stuart."

He didn't understand. He stood there, calm and smiling slightly, and it made Jacquelyn sick at heart that he should think she was treating him badly because he was an ugly little dwarf. That wasn't the reason. Ugo was human, like anybody else, and had feelings. As far as she was concerned, all the dwarfs should marry all the tall people of the world and produce a new race. Of course, in order to achieve this, there would be some monstrous matings between enormous men and tiny little women they would force open, and strange little men would scarcely be able to achieve useful penetration in hugely welcoming vaginas. But it could be done. It might be done.

In the middle of the night she wakened from restless erotic slumber. She made a distinct effort to forget the mad and voluptuous images that had haunted her unconscious hours. When the imagination was seriously infected one had to post signs reading "Off Limits," exactly as the authorities did in certain sections of a city that were not fit for decent folks to visit.

Still the images returned: a drunken woman, dancing naked on bedsheets in an orgy of gaiety—the kind of gaiety that exists only when one has broken through former bounds of inhibition and learned the wild delights of pure revelry. This was followed by a macabre celebration of the most grotesque acts of copulation.

It was all part of her dream. Her nightmare.

She rolled over in bed, waking, banishing the forbidden thoughts. Then her hand touched something, a human body, a thigh, different from any human thigh she had ever felt, smaller, but not a child's exactly.

She sat up suddenly. Ugo was asleep, lying on his back in the bed beside her, and breathing heavily as though he had catarrh.

A few days later, in a panic of self-revulsion, she accepted an offer to go to Madrid to star in the multimillion-dollar production of *Nero,* co-starring Brian O'Neal.

CHAPTER FOURTEEN

Lester Mitchell, in dungarees and a faded blue work shirt, wearing a cap pushed back on his head, was preparing to shoot a scene in which Oedipus attacks and mistakenly kills his own father. He was discussing with the head cameraman how the coach carrying the father would come along a narrow stretch of dirt road.

Brian wandered over. "How many feet have we shot so far, Lester?"

"About five thousand. Why?"

"I dunno. I'm just trying to act like a producer. A producer is always supposed to come around to ask questions, isn't he?"

Lester laughed, a trifle uneasily. He knew that Brian took this production seriously and was always talking with technicians, cameramen, studying how the lights worked, talking with the set designers, and even working with the grips. Brian's question was not as idle as it seemed; it meant he was impatient with the progress they were making.

Brian went back to stand on the road and watch.

They filmed the coach clattering up. Lester Mitchell wasn't satisfied. He wanted more dust as the coach jolted to a stop. This was partly to symbolize the confusion in which the slaying takes place, Lester explained. Finally they decided to have the coach drag several tree branches in order to raise the required amount of dust.

Dame Sara Thomas, who was playing Jocasta, came over to watch with Brian.

"One thing I admire about Lester," she said, "is that he seems to know exactly what he wants."

"He can't get dust in this part of the country. The ground's too wet," Brian observed.

Dame Sara said tartly, "You're an Irishman. Don't complain about English weather."

"Everyone knows Irish rain is different. It's softer."

Dame Sara smiled faintly. It was apparent she wanted to talk about something else.

"I suppose you're the one I should ask," Dame Sara said. "I realize that everything is a little chaotic around here, but there must be someone I can talk to about money."

"A fascinating topic."

"I haven't been paid in two weeks."

"You're looking striking today, Dame Sara. Really striking."

She wore cinnamon-colored slacks, a green V-neck sweater, and a kerchief about her head. She was fifty-two years old, looked forty, and was the only voluptuously haughty woman Brian had ever known.

"When I signed to do this movie, I was to be paid promptly at the end of each week. It was in my contract. I've insisted on having that clause in my contract since I was on tour with a play that closed in the hinterlands and left me stranded without bus fare."

"Time you got over that silly neurosis. You will never find yourself without bus fare again, I promise you."

"You are quite mad, you Irishman," Dame Sara said casually, "and I find you almost irresistible. But not quite. Especially not quite when it comes to my being paid."

"Everything will be straightened out soon. We're negotiating a deal now for a big studio to take over the production."

The demands of business were more than Brian could bear. Plans and deals and investments and profits and percentages and rates of return and capital gains and all the trumpery that goes with being a Corporation rather than just an actor. Between takes, he was always busy with staff meetings, board meetings, story conferences, production, administrative, and financial meetings.

"I talked with my agent yesterday. He said that they want me for a new production of *Antony and Cleopatra*. Technically, he assures me, I am not under contract to you because I have not been paid. Failure to pay me for two weeks breaches my contract."

"You'll be paid," Brian told her. "I'll talk to whoever is in charge of the money myself. As soon as I find out who he is."

"I'll wait until tomorrow." Dame Sara said, and drifted away.

Lester Mitchell called off filming the coach scene a few minutes later. The air had turned cooler and it began to rain.

Back at the studio lot, rain was still falling when Brian and Lester Mitchell met in an office reserved for the *Oedipus Rex* company. The office was deserted, with gray covers on the typewriters and neat stacks of typing paper arranged alongside on the tables. Lester strode back and forth dispiritedly, holding a sheaf of papers in his hand.

"What a nightmare," he said. "We have enough unpaid bills to make an artificial snowstorm. We owe everyone. By that I mean, quote, *everyone.* The situation is out of control, Brian."

Brian leaned back in a swivel chair and folded his arms. "I told you Runnymede Studios is going to back us. I have Margot Wesley's word."

Lester chose a telegram from the sheaf of papers he was holding. "I wired Lyle Wesley on the day you took off for Rio. I tried to explain how urgent our situation is, and that we need an advance payment simply to keep production going. This is the answer I got this morning."

Brian read the yellow crinkly paper carefully. It expressed concern at the predicament in which the *Oedipus Rex* producing company found itself, but no final decision had been reached on the vital question of Runnymede taking over, and in the absence of such a decision it should be quite evident that any advance payment was out of the question.

"What do you make of it?" Lester asked.

"The ponderous wheels are turning," Brian said, handing the telegram back. "Nothing happens overnight. Not where big corporations are involved."

Lester thrust another sheet of paper at him. It listed over one hundred people associated with the production, including four on the camera, three on sound, six on lighting, eight propmen, a set decorator and assistant, a script girl, five secretaries, a production man and two assistants, three assistant directors, three makeup men, two hairdressers, a body makeup girl, a still photographer, a press agent, a dramatic coach, a controller, an assistant controller, six chauffeurs, two watchmen, a wardrobe mistress and assistant, two seamstresses, and three film editors.

"There's really going to be a mob scene if those people aren't paid. We can't keep putting them off with promises."

"Is there enough in the till to pay them all tomorrrow?"

"We can squeeze by if we skip you and me and Dame Sara."

"Do it. I'll tilt the cornucopia in the morning and see what happens."

"I didn't know we had one."

"Margot Wesley. I'll ask the dear girl to pour out enough coin of the realm to pay off our debts."

Night had fallen over the city of London and the Thames when he crossed the bridge and after a few minutes drive came to the Georgian house of the Wesleys. He stood hesitating at the door. They had parted quits, and it would have been better to leave it so. He had been taken into her confidence as well as into her arms, and liberating moments make poor memories. One either has to move forward and build them into a future or leave them behind, abandoned places along a rocky coast.

He knocked.

Margot answered the door herself. She was wearing a light blue dress with white ruffled collar, and her hair was softly brushed.

"Brian. It's good to see you again." She offered him her cheek. "Lyle's waiting for you in the den."

"Aren't you coming?"

"No—a woman's place is behind the scenes." She took his arm and walked with him to the open door of a comfortable book-lined room. "I've done all I can, Brian. Believe me," she whispered and was gone.

The den was lighted by a single standing lamp over a comfortable black leather chair in which Lyle Wesley sat reading a book. He got up to shake hands.

"Have you read that?" he asked, indicating the book he put down.

It was a novel called *Town Landing,* and was supposed to be a sharply satirical portrait of life in a beach colony.

"No, but I've heard good things about it."

"It's a beautiful book," Lyle Wesley said. "Really beautifully written. Good characters. I've been thinking of taking an option on it. But I don't think I'm going to."

"You might be passing up a bet if it's as good as you say."

"It isn't box office." Lyle picked up a humidor to offer Brian a cigar. "It hasn't got the elements, the spice, the sensationalism, that made *Peyton Place*. There's hardly any sex. Everyone in the book is married—and stays that way."

"Ah," said Brian, "a fantasy."

Lyle chuckled. "Married people are still in the majority, Brian, even the ones who stay that way. That's why they get their kicks reading about the other kind." He closed the humidor and returned it to the table. "I suppose you've come to talk about *Oedipus*."

"Margot's spoken to you about it."

Lyle nodded vigorously. "She likes the idea. Even thinks it might make a little money."

"It's being made for minimums. Everyone's in for basic pay and a percentage. If people pay to see the Royal Ballet at two-a-day prices, why not *Oedipus Rex?*"

"You're very close to Margot's reasoning."

"I can promise you that we'll keep a very sharp watch on costs. But the fact is at the moment we're hard up for cash. That's why Lester Mitchell wired you . . . ."

"Runnymede never actually made a commitment," Lyle answered with a slightly sharper tone. He bit off the end of a cigar. "Brian, I'm sorry to say that the board met yesterday and voted against undertaking a co-production deal with you."

Lyle did not meet his gaze. Brian kept staring.

"I'm damn sorry," Lyle said. "But there's really nothing I can do. It's the board's decision to make, you understand."

"Margot led me to think it was your decision to make."

"She shouldn't have. I'm head of the studio, naturally, and they allow me a certain latitude. But I have people to report to, too."

"Why would the board turn it down? You recommended the deal, didn't you?"

"Off the record? Yes. Partly because Margot was so strong for it. I'm frank to say I rely on her judgment pretty heavily. I wasn't confident it would be a money-maker, but the industry can use good pictures that have a limited audience appeal." Cigar smoke partly obscured his face with its deeply engraved cheek lines. "But I can't say the board is wrong. *Oedipus Rex* doesn't have the elements, Brian. You had a personal success with it on the stage a few years back. But that's different. The stage and the motion picture. One is for a very small group of people. New Yorkers mainly. The rest of the country likes entertainment. Good wholesome entertainment, something to take their minds off their troubles. You can't blame them for that."

"Lyle, I need backing or the whole production will have to be abandoned. I can't stop now. I've put too much into this."

"I wish I knew what to do," Lyle said.

"Call a special meeting of the board. Let me talk to them."

Lyle shrugged. "You know I can't do that, Brian. I'd do anything for you, within reason. But I can't challenge a decision taken at higher levels. They wouldn't consider me a very good executive if I did. A good executive has to accept decisions as well as make them. That's the position I find myself in, Brian."

"I'll sign a contract to do another movie for you as soon as I finish *Oedipus*. I'll even sign a two-picture contract."

"We'd be interested in talking to you, Brian. Right now we don't have any suitable properties. In any event we couldn't tie that deal in with our taking over *Oedipus*."

"I'll put my future in hock. If *Oedipus* doesn't pay off, I'll take less money for my next picture. I'll work for nothing to make up the difference."

He only wanted to move his bag and baggage away from the trouble he was in.

"I do wish I could help, Brian. I just can't. The decision of the board is final."

Brian burst out suddenly, "The hell with you and your damn board! I'll find the money someplace else."

"There are rules I have to live by just like everyone else, Brian. Please try to understand that. If it had been any other property than *Oedipus Rex*—something more commercial . . ."

"I want to act in a film in which I speak lines that won't cause me embarrassment. That's why I picked *Oedipus*. I could have co-starred with Jacquelyn in an epic filmed in Africa and called *Black Ivory*. It features an ersatz Lord Jim and an ersatz Sadie Thompson and a love affair that's supposed to lead to their spiritual regeneration. Plus elephants and tigers. You'd have backed that, wouldn't you? You'd have rushed in to put money in that."

"All your pictures with Jacquelyn made money," Lyle pointed out sadly. "We're in business to make money, Brian."

As Brian was leaving, Margot emerged from the room to the left of the foyer.

"Brian, I can't let you go away thinking I let you down. I tried my best. Lyle was ready to do it. And then . . ."

"I know. The deal fell through."

"It wasn't quite that way." She paused, as people do who want to summarize in a tidy way. "When you flew down to Rio to see Jacquelyn, you had a quarrel with Meyer Whitney."

"We had a difference of opinion."

"You knocked him down."

"If I hadn't, he'd have knocked me down."

"Did you know you broke his collarbone? He had to go to the hospital. And you dealt an even worse injury to his pride."

"I can't weep for him."

"Lyle couldn't tell you, but Meyer Whitney is behind the decision of the board not to co-produce with you."

He stared blankly at her. She decided he had not heard and started to repeat it, but he made a slight gesture that stayed her.

"You're saying Meyer Whitney sabotaged my picture?"

"He's not the sort of man you should have for an enemy, Brian."

"I shouldn't have just smashed him. I should have trampled him. Well, now that I know who has his thumb in my pie, I'll have to do something about it."

"What can you do, Brian?"

"Raise the money elsewhere. Meyer Whitney doesn't guard all the gates to Fort Knox. There are other men with coins to jingle, and if they see a chance to make them multiply they'll fart at Meyer Whitney."

"Brian, you don't have a really good deal to offer. No one expects *Oedipus Rex* to make money."

"I'm not going to fold up, love."

He began withdrawing into a secret compartment of his mind, a burglarproof, windowless place no one could penetrate. Sometimes he could not find his way there without drink, but he was able to find it now.

"You may think bloody Meyer is too much for me to

handle. But he isn't all that powerful. He doesn't brood over all with great invisible wings. *Oedipus* is important to me. I intend to finish it."

Margot reached up suddenly to kiss his cheek. "I hope you do, Brian. With all my heart." She seemed close to tears.

She turned quickly and ran through the doorway to the adjoining room.

Brian stood looking after her in puzzlement. There it was, something he had noticed before, softer and gentler this time. She was feeling sorry for him. Well, the walls of his private burglarproof room had to be strong enough to keep pity out. Defeat is for those who can afford it. Not for the likes of Brian O'Neal.

As long as a man goes forth to battle, he will never lose.

Lester Mitchell met him at the entrance to the projection room. He was wearing crimson flannel slacks and a gray blazer with crimson buttons.

"We're going to look at the last of the rushes. Come in and watch with me."

Lester preceded him into a large dark room with six rows of seats. In the room Brian identified and nodded to a woman of forty whose generous makeup did not conceal the crowsfeet at her eyes or the wrinkles forming in her cheeks. She was Louise Thompson, the press agent for the movie. Seated beside her was a thin woman with a bony face whose hair was dyed to a slightly orange tint. She was Paula Welch, the chief cutter. Also in the room was Pete Hendrickson, one of Lester's assistants. On the wall at the opposite end of the room was a screen, now blank. Lester found a seat for Brian beside him and then snapped his fingers. The room darkened and the projectionist in the booth behind them began to unreel the last scenes filmed of *Oedipus Rex*. Brian saw the coach jostling up the narrow road, followed by a scene between him and Dame Sara, playing his wife and mother, Jocasta. In this scene Dame Sara wore a green Grecian robe, and her arms seemed white and flabby. When the rushes were finished, and the lights came up, Lester told Paula Welch how he wanted them trimmed. Louise Thompson came over to congratulate Lester and Brian. She told them that all the rushes looked magnificent so far.

"This is going to be an easy movie to sell," she said.

"It's a classic, and it's a masterpiece. The public is hungry for culture."

"Keep whetting their appetite," Lester said.

"You know I will, Les darling. The thing is, I believe in this picture. I really believe in it."

Smiling, Louise Thompson left the projection room.

"That's what we need around here, eh Pete?" Lester asked his assistant. "A little more faith."

"We could use more hope too—and lots more charity," Pete Hendrickson said.

"Good old Pete," Lester said, clapping him on the back.

Pete Hendrickson left the projection room.

"Getting old," Lester said. "A good man, but he's turned sour. He depresses me. I'm not going to use him anymore."

"You can't blame him for being cynical after all the years he's spent in this business."

Lester gave him a shrewd look. "So it didn't go well with Margot Wesley yesterday?"

"I have to go to New York and shake the money tree. That's where the dollars are."

Lester shook his head sadly. "It would be a useless trip."

"Why?"

"If Lyle Wesley can't make the deal, what other distributing company can? The New York people don't even talk your language, Brian. All they're interested in is how to meet that terrific studio overhead."

It was true, and Brian knew it. Movies had become an international business and international financiers were in charge of it. It was enough to give a plain actor a headache.

"I've got something to sell," he said stubbornly.

"Sophocles?"

"Me."

He was used to thinking of himself as an asset, a human commodity that could be bought, sold, traded like a share of company stock, inanimate, unresisting. Sooner or later, all motion picture stars reach this conclusion about themselves. There is no missing the irony of a final confrontation between lawyers and accountants for your side with the lawyers and accountants for their side; even your champions implicitly accept the premise that you are a property and only argue about the real value of the property. Once he had stood up in the middle of a wrangling to declare, Listen, you bastards, I, Brian O'Neal, am a person. It achieved nothing. The human computers merely clicked off a new equation allowing for the factor of temperament, and the consequence was a subclause having to do with the fact that he was entitled to a month's vacation at the completion of any movie.

Lester said, "You're a name, Brian, but you can't carry a movie single-handed—or at least there's no track record to show it. I'd lay a thousand to one against your pulling this off. It's practically hopeless. There's no salvation in sight for *Oedipus Rex*. We've had it."

"Then so has Brian O'Neal as an actor. And I won't admit that."

"You'll go on to other things. So will the rest of us. Dame Sara has already served notice. She wants to leave to play Cleopatra, and if we skip another salary check she's pulling out. Even if you get the money we'll need a new Jocasta and have to shoot all those scenes over."

"She won't go. If she does, we'll find somebody else."

"As soon as word gets out we can't meet next week's payroll, the rest of the company will be making tracks. Most of them have offers pending."

Brian shook his head. "I'm not going to give up."

"There's Merrill, of course. She *might* be a way out. She could go to her father."

"If she came back with the money she'd carry the manacles with her."

"We're at the end of the line. If you're not willing to go to Merrill . . ."

Suddenly Brian was sick of business, and the net closing in.

"I'll go on to New York," he said, "but not for another day or two. I'm going back home."

"To Ireland?"

Brian nodded. "A man has to restore to himself a sense of who he is."

"If you want to tie one on and forget your troubles, you're entitled. Don't put other names to it, Brian."

"You're a shrewd man, Lester Mitchell," Brian told him. "But you're not a wise man by half."

In the hall adjoining Jacquelyn Stuart's bedroom in the villa outside Rio there was a large standing clock almost five feet tall. Inside the bottom half of its violin-shaped casing a gold-painted pendulum swung to and fro on a long rod. The clock's face was gilt and the hands elaborately shaped. She liked best the large hole in the center of the clock face where she could look in and see the mainsprings at work. At the quarter hour the clock gave a hollow *dong* and at the hour it struck the number with portentous tones. In a way the clock seemed almost human, calm and regular and full of significance on the surface, with much hectic activity going on beneath. The clock moved on irrevocably, a record and a testament, changing nothing, only wearing down the gears and the machinery a little more every year until finally all action stopped.

The clock was striking seven in the morning when, over breakfast, she opened a letter that had just come from her brother Richard in the morning mail.

Dearest Jax,

This will come as something of a surprise to you. I've left Mady and have taken off for points west, as far west as sails will take me. I don't know if I can explain why. All I know is that it's a wild ocean and I'm going to find or lose myself on it. I have spent most of my life trying to contain my disorders, and all the while disorder may be the truth of what I am.

Jax, I've never been more miserable. Probably none of this makes any sense, but maybe this will: Don't let anyone make you the embalmer of your own life. While you're alive, fight for what you need to live. That's all I wish for you.

> *My best love,*
> *Richard*

Suddenly Janet's voice broke in: "Meyer Whitney is here."

Jacquelyn looked up, holding Richard's letter in her hand. "I can't see him. Perhaps in a few minutes. Tell him I have to get dressed."

Janet, disapproving, said all right, and left.

Jacquelyn held Richard's letter tightly. She was confused, like a child who has taken apart an intricate piece of machinery and now is sitting on the floor with no idea of how to put it together.

She had no idea how much time passed. Her memory was teeming with past conversations, incidents, jokes and secrets shared with the brother she loved and admired. Then Janet was back in the doorway again, looking impatient.

Jacquelyn said, "All right. I'll see him now."

Meyer entered, stylish as ever in a canary-yellow sports coat and powder-blue slacks. His arm was in a sling. When he saw her, something in her expression seemed to stop him for a second; then he came forward. She kissed him, carefully avoiding the black shoulder sling.

"All ready, darling. This is our big day. We'll pick up the divorce decree at the consulate. We can be married immediately afterward."

Beyond the bright living room the pool shimmered deceptively ice-blue in the tropical sun. In a little while Brian O'Neal would be filed away, and she would be Mrs. Meyer Whitney.

"Is anything wrong, darling?"

"No, nothing at all."

She kept thinking she had forgotten something, some sort of paper or document. Richard's letter? *While you're alive, fight for what you need to live.* She expected this thought to mean something to her—what, she didn't know. She waited with the patient abstractedness of someone who has stumbled on a new kind of food which has to be tasted, sampled, digested, before a verdict can be rendered.

Meyer said, "Actually, I want to talk to you before we go. It's about Brian."

"Is he all right?"

"I imagine by now he's beginning to regret his rashness the other day."

His voice was soft, but when he had something important to tell he often made it appear casual.

"I wish you wouldn't doubletalk, Meyer. If you have something to say, say it."

"Brian is getting a double dose of misfortune. He's not only losing you, but losing that artistic masterpiece of his."

She winced at the satisfaction in his tone.

"Are you talking about *Oedipus Rex?*"

"The production has suspended. It's finished."

"Finished? What happened?"

"I suppose you could say that *I* happened."

There was an expression in his eyes she couldn't read, and then she could. It was gloating.

"Meyer, did you do anything to really hurt Brian?"

"Someone had to teach that wild Irishman he can't assault people at his pleasure."

"What have you done?" There was quiet menace in the question.

He smiled slightly, and his reply became more deliberate. "Brian may be a good actor but he's a calamity as a businessman. Let's just say I pulled the rug from under him."

"How?"

"It wasn't hard. He was badly undercapitalized and no one associated with the production seems to have much financial sense. They turned to Runnymede Studios for help. My brother Samuel and I have several friends on the board of Runnymede. The board turned the proposition down cold."

"What does this mean—to Brian?"

"Simply that he has no distributor—and no money to finish his picture with."

She said quickly, "You can't do it! What Brian did was in anger. It could happen to anyone. What you've done is . . . cold-blooded."

"If by that you mean deliberate, it was. I received an injury at the hands of Brian O'Neal and I repaid it in my own way."

"Ruining a man is a high price to put on a broken collarbone."

"Not when it's my collarbone."

"Why didn't you sue him for assault?"

"That would be degrading."

"You can't be this big a bastard, Meyer. It isn't too late to change your mind. You can still persuade Runnymede to back Brian."

"There's no reason to make this a personal matter between us. Meyer's voice had changed; there was an edge. "You can hardly expect me to let what Brian did pass as though nothing happened. You should know me better."

She took a long breath before she answered slowly, "I've known this part of you for some time, Meyer. I'm always going to hate it."

He turned toward her awkwardly because of the sling on his shoulder. "I can't allow you to interfere with my business decisions. The Brian episode is finished. It's a closed issue."

"I won't accept that!"

"Neither of us will refer to it again."

"Am I finding out what sort of a husband you intend to be?"

"I love you and I'll make you happy. I won't cheat on you, or get drunk, or abuse you. That's what's important for marriage—that kind of consideration. It may seem the obvious thing, but it's what most marriages are built on. It's what makes them last."

"Is that what you believe, Meyer?"

"Yes, it is."

She took a deep breath, smelled the fragrance of many bouquets of flowers in the enormous airy living room.

"Brian never had that kind of consideration," she said. "He was incapable of it. He did cheat on me and get drunk and even abuse me. He never had consideration for anything but his own needs."

"You can't compare me to him."

"We were very happy. Oh, I know you'll say it didn't last. But that isn't the test of everything."

He cut in sharply, "Are you still in love with him?"

"Maybe I am."

In a dazed second of silence his shoulders seemed to draw together. Then slowly, consciously, the tension eased out of him.

"You're saying that out of anger. How could you possibly be?"

"I remember the first night we made love. It was in a villa outside Madrid where we were doing *Nero*. You know what happened afterward? I burned all the things I'd saved of Dan Reed's. Burned them right there in the fireplace."

"You'd better consider seriously what you're saying. If you're trying to offend me, you're succeeding too well. If you go on, you may go too far. There won't be a second chance—not with me."

He spoke softly and she listened with a curious feeling of hallucination. She understood the meaning of her almost sensual attraction to a line in Richard's letter. *While you're alive, fight for what you need to live.*

"I don't want a second chance, Meyer."

"What?"

"I don't want your kind of consideration. I want a sense of being alive. And that's something you can't give me."

He looked at her with a slightly bewildered expression. "Do you think Brian can?"

"Right now, he doesn't know how to cope with what you've done. He'll probably go off and get drunk. And you know, that isn't a bad idea, Meyer. If it's what he feels like doing. When he feels like getting drunk it's usually a wonderful idea."

He stared at her. "I can't believe you're serious. You had a rotten marriage."

"When Brian drinks, it's to forget. How about you, Meyer? If we had a quarrel, would you drink to get over it? Or would you keep a drawer in a filing cabinet with my name on it and every offense listed, waiting for the right time to deal with it?"

"A little late to be talking like this. We'll be married in a few hours."

"Meyer, I'm sorry, but I don't think we could be happy."

He had not expected that. He sat as if frozen, until he reached up with one hand to stroke the side of his jaw.

"You're hysterical. I'll give you time to think it over. I think you'll want to apologize for some things you've said today."

"You'd better go now, Meyer."

"What will you do?"

"I thought I made that clear. I'm going to take the first plane out of here to find Brian."

Anger showed through his bafflement. "To that womanizer, that weakling, that human sponge? He won't give up Merrill to fly into your arms."

"If I have to fight for him, I will."

"So he can drag you downhill with him? Is that what you want? In heaven's name, why?"

"I don't suppose you'd understand. It's because with Brian I can live each moment. Not scheme for the future and wake up one day to discover the future is already in the past."

"Quite the philosopher, aren't you? What you really want is to jump into bed with him."

For a moment she thought she had hurt him. But the expression in his eyes remained distant, rebuking, impervious.

"You'd be surprised how good fucking can be, Meyer, with a real man. You'd be very surprised."

His face turned very pale. "You've always been cheap, Jacquelyn. It's the one thing that worried me about you."

He spoke without the appearance of anger, but in the

pale depths of his eyes a look told her he would never forgive what she had said. Never in this world.

Later that afternoon Toby Dolan came to call. He entered the bedroom at the villa to find her with Janet, packing.

"What's all this?" he asked, indicating the clothing spread out on the bed and draped over a chair.

"I'm leaving."

"Where to?"

"It's all right, Janet. I can finish by myself. Thank you." She waited until Janet left the room. "The plane ticket says Dublin so I suppose that's where I'm going."

Toby found a chair not occupied by clothing and sat down with affected nonchalance.

"You're going off on a wild Irishman chase. I'm surprised, Jacquelyn. You've always had such pride."

"Pride is a pretty useless trait, isn't it? When it keeps you from having something you want, I mean."

"Are you sure this isn't just the result of some quarrel you've had with Meyer Whitney?"

She smiled and shook her head. "Toby, let me ask you the sort of question I have never asked you before. Do you like being a homosexual?"

Toby's voice turned sibilant: "What are we playing, darling? Truth or Consequences?"

"You don't have to tell me if you don't want to."

"I don't mind. It's nothing I'm ashamed of. I wouldn't have minded being born something else. It would probably have been a lot simpler. But I am what I am, and I wouldn't change it now. So I suppose the answer to your question, darling, is yes, I like being what I am."

"So do I, Toby, only it's taken me longer to discover what it is. That's one advantage of being . . . different the way you are. You're put off in a special category and you know where you belong. It's clear-cut. For someone like me it's a question of finding a right direction. It's as though I'd had cataracts over my eyes, and then suddenly they're removed and I can see again. The light is half blinding."

Toby was watching her with a distant, slightly reproachful smile.

"So you're going to pack up, leave an entire production,

the best movie role of your career, and a highly desirable fiancé in the lurch, and take out after a drunken actor who is currently expecting to divorce you so he can marry someone else?"

"That's one way of putting it," Jacquelyn said.

CHAPTER FIFTEEN

The pub was smoky, and there was blue tobacco haze curling along the edges of a long mirror behind the bar that was so old it looked as though there were faint white streaks of paint on it.

"She was pockmarked," Stephen Innis said, "and to tell the truth I think she fell in love with my striped suspenders. I had taken off my coat because it was so damn warm in the place, and she took one look at my suspenders and was done for. I talked it over with her a bit and then we went home together and went to bed and never slept a wink. I swear to you, Brian, I had a steel prick that night. In again, out again, until I fetched such piteous cries from her you'd have thought her heart was breaking."

"Stephen," Brian O'Neal said, "you were always a gorgeous liar. Do you ever tell the truth sometimes just to clear all the cobweb lies out of your brain?"

"I always tell the truth," Stephen said with dignity, "except when I'm drunk."

"I've never seen you sober."

"How would you know, you blatherskite? You're always up to your eartips in Old Bushmill."

"That's a foul canard. Old Bushmill is North Ireland. I'm a Jameson man."

Noise eddied around them. In a corner an old piano tinkled, and several men, gathered by the piano player on his stool, joined in song. They sang "The Wild Colonial Boy" and "I'll Go No More A-Rovin'."

"That's a kind of poetry I wish I could write," Stephen said. "It's as good as three whiskeys. The girl was soft as the underside of a pigeon's wing, Brian, and clean as a sun-washed clam. I never loved anyone as I loved her. I

330

would even have given up drink to keep her. I could have
written her poems that would have mastered the secret of
the age."

"What ever did happen to the dear creature?" Brian
asked.

"She left me."

"She fell out of love with your striped suspenders?"

"She did."

"And with your steel cock?"

"That, too. I am but a man, after all, Brian. I could not
compete with her new infatuation."

"Who was he?"

"It wasn't a 'he' at all. She conceived this mad infatuation for a candle."

One of the group gathered about the piano now got up
onto the bar and began to do a jig. Everyone in the pub
clapped hands in rhythm. There was hardly room to move
one's hands enough apart to clap.

"I haven't taken a breath in twenty minutes," Stephen
said. "Let's find the door before I start to drown."

They reeled into the street, supporting each other.

"Would you take me with you to America?" Stephen
asked.

"Why would you be wanting to go there?"

Stephen plunged both hands into his pockets and turned
them inside out. "Do you hear a rewarding jingle? None?
Aye—I haven't had a ten-shilling note to call my own in a
fortnight. And I've a weird woman at home and two
weird little babes."

"Will a fiver help?"

Brian drew out a five-pound note. Stephen took it
shamelessly and stuffed it into his vest pocket. Everything
given to Stephen was dropped down a bottomless well.

"I still want to go to America," he announced. "I'm sick
of being in restraint. I want money enough for drink and
high-skirted girls and for my weirdies at home, too. I live
in fantastic poverty in Ireland. I want to go to America
and be rich."

"You wouldn't like it, Stephen. What would an Irish
poet do in America? You'd be ignored or made too much
of. Either way would be the ruin of you."

"I'd rather die of adulation than honest poverty."

"Stephen, you're a great man because you write of
things you know and feel. If I took you out of here it'd be
like pulling you up by the roots. You'd never grow again."

"I want to be like you, Brian. You could have been a great actor. But you went off and made your fortune. Now you have everything a man wants."

Nothing Stephen said could have hurt him more. In recent years he had been circling his talent warily and only now had he begun to realize there was no one but himself to possess it.

"I sold myself off at the auction block. I'd be cursed forever if I let the same thing happen to you."

"Take me on the plane, away. I want to ride the range in Chicago and climb the mountains of Detroit and canoe the canals of Los Angeles. What will I do here, Brian? Live out my days in a churchly, ignorant land? I want to go to Cincinnati. I've never been to America, Brian, and if I'm ever to be a great poet I have to see the world."

"They have no room for poets in America, Stephen."

"I'll write for the cinema. I've always wanted to write for the cinema."

"You couldn't do it. You're a poet. One of the few real poets alive in the world today."

"I can write big or small. I have this idea for a film about a rebel boy who owns an alligator. The alligator is all of life to him. He defies the whole town for it, but one day the alligator breaks loose and eats up a policeman, coughing up the badge. And the town rises up in a fury and lynches the poor amphibian. Whereupon the boy rides off on his scooter and crashes and kills himself. It won't be a tragedy. It'll have all the action of a Hollywood Western. Quick, quick, quick. There'll be all sorts of wonderful touching scenes I can improvise, showing how love develops between the boy and his alligator. It will be done slightly tongue-in-cheek. A mixture of sadism and healthy violence, with a lot of sex thrown in."

"I don't think they'll buy it."

"It would be terribly good. The sheer beat and drive of it, the naked power, will win the public. The whole thing will be shot in a crazy rhythm like modern beat music."

Stephen slipped until one knee touched the ground but held on with this arm to Brian's neck, forcing Brian to bend over him. Stephen whispered in his ear.

"Don't leave me, Brian. Good friend. Sweet fellow. Take me with you to pick up girls at the amusement parks in Vermont and to hear the seals bark in New York harbor. I have a great love for history, Brian. I want to go."

"We'll see, Stephen," Brian said, dragging him back to his feet.

"I want to die of drink and Protestant women in a hospital with clean white sheets. I want my ears to go deaf from the popping of champagne corks."

"You know you can't drink that stuff."

"I'll pour it over me and hang the bottles on a shelf to show what a great rich man I've become. Oh, how can you go off to America and leave me here at the bottom of the pile?"

"I'm only going to try to get money enough to stay here and work as honestly at my trade as you do at yours. I haven't the gift for making words as you do. Only for saying them. I've ignored that poor talent too long, Stephen. That's why I'm going off to America to shake the money tree."

Stephen said now, "Will you look who's coming down the road? Legs pumping and potbelly shaking. The ghost of Old Billy."

It was Old Billy himself, with damp, wet hair flying and cavernous face gasping on broken teeth.

"He looks a bit put out," Stephen said. "Well, I'll be toddling home to my weird ones."

Stephen Innis weaved off as Old Billy braked his bicycle to a halt near Brian.

"I went to Flanahan's," Old Billy said accusingly. "You and Stephen always get drunk at Flanahan's." He grabbed one leg and pulled it over the handlebar.

"We tried Red Dog tonight. I felt in the need of crowds. And Dougherty has a fine hand at the piano."

Old Billy approached suspiciously. "Look at you now. That comes of the Irish without a dash of relievin' soda. You've had sufficient for the burying of three. Is that a condition for to be leaving the country in the morning?"

"Did you pedal all this way just to jabber at me?"

"That I did not. I have a cable." Old Billy reached into his shirt as though scratching himself and produced the yellow sheet mildewed with perspiration. "It's from your wife."

"Jacquelyn?"

"For Jesus' sake, you know your own wife's name, don't you? She's coming here."

"Jacquelyn coming here? Why?"

"I forgot to put the question to Western Union."

"She's heard what happened," Brian said with new bitterness. "She's come to crow over me."

"If you're after the prize for being the worst booby in the hatch, you've got it. Why would she want to do that?"

"Because she thinks I'm on the toboggan, and she's on top of the hill. She thinks I'll crawl to her and lick the sides of her shoes. Well, she's wrong. I'm no trumpery man to caw at. She's not even my wife—no matter about the final papers. Everybody knows a divorce isn't in the law—it's the result of other things. Jacquelyn and I are divorced. That door's closed."

"Aye," said Old Billy. "But what have you got locked away in the room behind that closed door?"

"Nothing," Brian said defiantly. "Nothing."

"Then what's to worry yourself? Come home and get a shave and sober up, and when the blood color is out of your eyes, you'll tell her that in so many plain words, I have no doubt."

Brian looked at the smiling face of his father, and suddenly he felt the kind of fear he had only felt once, when as a boy of fifteen, he had first been about to make love to Molly Kinsella. Such an extraordinary thing about to happen, to lie naked with a girl, he had been sure he would be shocked into impotence. To keep himself from going mad he had kept repeating, "Well, there's nothing else to do but do it, is there?"

He cut himself shaving, his hand was shaking so. The trouble is fidelity has never been a temptation to me. It would drive me mad to spend all my powers in one sad little dark hole. The cut was a nasty one, a long thin line along the underside of the jawbone. When a man's skin is dried to the brown color of a leather shoe, and you can play thump on his rib cage, there's time enough to be faithful. Meanwhile, let copulation thrive. After I die, I promise I'll cuckold thee only with worms.

He dried his face and wiped the ooze of blood from the thin cut. His black hair, which he wore longish and thick at the sideburns, was flecked with gray and curly from the steam of hot water in the basin. He peered at himself in the hazed mirror. That haunted, troubled, staring look which drove women wild was due to weak eyes. How sexy to be shortsighted.

He had never been able to make friends with a woman. Isn't that strange? Never. Why do they never plumb my emotions and my mind? Sometimes they start out that way, but their interest keeps descending. No complaints, lad. We've got as good as we gave.

A car pulled up in front of the house. A door slammed. She's here.

Ah, I wish I had a God to pray to, now and at the hour of her coming. Let me pray to Mother, dead of tuberculosis, or to dear Timothy who died at Dunkirk when he was only nineteen and not for Kiltartan Cross. A foolish thing praying to the dead, when your faith is agnostic, but who is there to pray to among the living? Sisters Kathleen and Bridget, thoroughly married, and with children of their own who pray to them? Or youngest brother Patrick, who lives so sedately in London? It would be blasphemy to pray to a chartered accountant.

He went downstairs in the small house, curving along the narrow stairway whose bare wooden steps he had climbed as a boy and man, through poverty, hard work, study, and religion. An unfrivolous life he led in childhood.

Jacquelyn was in the living room, in the narrow room with the brown wooden cabinets and horsehair sofa. She was sitting at the round table with Old Billy.

Old Billy was carrying on in his senile flirtatious way. Old Billy Goat. Jacquelyn turned her head to smile at Brian and turned back to hear Old Billy out. He finished in a cackle of glee, striking his kneecap.

"This is a surprise," Brian said. "I thought you were in Rio de Janeiro."

"No. I'm here."

"So you are." He saw Old Billy watching with one arched white eyebrow. "Would you care for a drink?"

"No, thanks. I had a cocktail with dinner on the plane."

Brian drew up a chair. "Good to see you again. There's nothing wrong, is there?"

"I just want to talk to you, that's all."

"Oh?"

"God's own fool," Old Billy interjected. "Well, I'd better leave you two. It's past bedtime. I don't sleep anymore so I go to bed early to make up for it."

Old Billy kissed Jacquelyn on the cheek, rested a hand briefly on Brian's shoulder, and departed up the narrow stairs.

"He hasn't changed," Jacquelyn said.

"A year older. So are we all."

"A pretty eventful year."

Brian said with ironic amusement, "Shouldn't we have done with small talk? You were never very good at concealing something when it was in your mind. Why did you come all this way?"

"Because I heard you were in trouble."

"Good of you."

"I wanted to help."

"It's nothing I can't handle. I'm going to the States in the morning. I'm going to get the money I need." A brittleness in his voice betrayed anxiety—that was the trouble, he had trained his voice too well as an instrument to record emotion. Another thought came to him strongly as he downed the last of his tumbler of whiskey.

"Because I'm an actor, you see, a real actor, not one of your silly men. If I only wanted to make money I could've sold mutual funds to nervous widows. Do you know I was once considered fit to hold the stage with Olivier and Scofield and Burton? I've been throwing it away on heavy-breathing epics, and next thing I know people aren't talking about Brian O'Neal as an actor anymore. They're talking about Peter O'Toole and Albert Finney. I've been letting the sand slip through my fingers and it's time I called a halt. It's time I fell back on what I began with—and added to it a spot of self-discipline."

His anguish was real. Self-discipline was a quality he had never been able to achieve.

"I'd like that too, Brian," Jacquelyn said.

"Tell your fancy man for me that *Oedipus Rex* is going to be made if I have to finish filming it on used condoms."

"I can't tell Meyer Whitney anything. You see, I've left him."

His heart expanded with a convulsive motion. "Jilted him at the church?"

"Something like that."

"A last-second reprieve, isn't it? Is it definite or a lover's spat?"

"I'm not going back. I don't think he understands why or accepts it. But I'm not going back."

"Because of this?"

"Partly."

"What's the other reason?"

"Do I have to tell you now? It's a little hard to explain."

He nodded, watching with interest the slow flow of color into her neck.

"I discovered I'm not in love with Meyer and I can't be."

"And the reason for that?" He wanted to hear her say it.

The emerald color of her eyes startled him to disbelief.

"It may have something to do with you. And with something I want, something I need. But mostly it has to do with what and who I am." There was a silence; they both seemed to be waiting for her next words, while expectation built slowly, very slowly. "Can I stay?" she asked.

The enlargement of his heart had gone on so that words choked off down in his chest.

All he said was, "You'll need a place to sleep tonight."

His back was stiff when he awakened, and his head tight with aching. Another damned migraine. He never was able to get enough sleep after one of his drinking bouts. He felt cold, and his face was yellowish in the mirror. Liver turning to sawdust, the doctor said. You'll have to choose between drink and living to a ripe old age. Not much of a choice. Old age held no attractions.

He brushed his teeth with a nylon brush. Brushing sideways. One of the vanishing minority who will not push up and down. A man has to keep his habits against the whole weight of science and religion. Same goes for smoking. Or adultery. Habit is the royal avenue for the soul. When you surrender habit there's no way left for the soul to go to heaven. Or hell.

He went into the bedroom. Jacquelyn turned over. He kissed her cheek. His eyes fluttered open. She really did have the most magnificent tits.

"Morning, love."

"Kiss me, really."

He bent over and kissed her.

"Touch me."

"For Jesus' sake, what's the matter? Didn't you have enough last night? Damn it."

He was smiling as his fingers explored her. She put the sheet away and watched him.

"Would you like the scourge of my tongue on you?" he asked.

He squeezed into bed beside her. Ah, Lord, she was like melting butter. He was drenched in the honey of her.

Merrill arrived late that afternoon. From the window of the upper bedroom Brian saw her uncoil out of Sean O'Connor's taxi. (Damn the man, he could have telephoned to warn him!) Brian quickly got into his trousers, hopping about first on one leg and then the other.

Jacquelyn asked sleepily, "What is it, darling?"

"Someone's come to see me. I'm going down."

"Who is it?"

"Merrill."

He pulled a velour sweater over his undershirt and went down the stairs two at a time, balancing against the walls with his hands as the staircase turned.

He slowed down abruptly as he entered the living room. Merrill was coming in the door.

She dropped the small valise she was carrying. What a rocklike thud on the bare floor. What was she carrying in it—her hope chest?

"Brian . . . darling!"

He took her properly in his arms. She wanted to be held. Except when women were in actual heat, it was his observation that they mostly wanted to be held, not kissed or embraced or stirred up. Snuggled.

"Oh, Brian, I came as soon as I heard."

"How did you hear?"

"Lester Mitchell told me. I kept calling the set to find out where you'd gone. There was never anyone around. I finally got Lester at his hotel. He told me the entire production has been suspended."

"It's true."

She drew back to look at him as though she could read the cause of the disaster in his face.

"How could a thing like that happen?"

"It's damned hard to persuade people they ought to work for nothing."

"You ran out of money?"

"Yup. Scraped the very bottom of the barrel. I was planning to go to New York today to see what I could do about it. I'd thought everything was set—with Lyle Wesley's company backing us. It *was* set; it just wasn't signed. Lyle backed out of the deal. I can't blame him. He was having his arm twisted."

"There's no reason for you to go to New York, darling. I can get the money to help you finish the production."

"I don't want you going to your father."

"He'll be glad to help. It's an investment. Besides, I feel responsible for you being in this predicament. Your doing this movie was partly my idea; I encouraged you. The least I can do is stand by you when there's a crisis."

Old Billy bicycled into the front yard, a perspiring, gaunt, and ancient figure. He parked the bicycle against the wooden fence and limped into the room with a greeting prepared for a woman he made out dimly in the room with Brian.

"Jacquelyn, I'm glad to see you're awake ..." The words were out before he saw who was really there. Old Billy blushed. A scarlet stain spread upward from his wattled neck. "A pox on a rash tongue. Is this the new one?"

Merrill moved her gaze slowly from Old Billy toward Brian.

"Is Jacquelyn here?"

"Yes. She arrived last night."

"Now? In this house?"

Brian's gaze traveled to the stairs and ascended them.

"How smashing." Merrill's tone had turned shivering cold.

"I didn't invite her. She just came." The tone did not sound as apologetic as he meant it to.

"Of course," Merrill said sweetly. "And black is white and night is day."

"You can believe it or not. I don't have room in my life right now, Merrill, for anyone to take offense against me."

Merrill's face looked very pale against her blond hair. "The last I heard, Jacquelyn was in Rio. Do you wish me to believe that she got up one morning and simply decided to take a plane here to spend the time of day?"

"I wish you'd alter that tone of voice. I don't appreciate it."

"I'm sorry. But when I discuss something I feel deeply about I can't do anything about my tone. You know how it is—free thought, free speech! I thought you favored everyone being completely free to say what they think. Doesn't that include women?"

She stopped. Jacquelyn was coming down the stairs. She had put on a long white wool robe with wide trumpet sleeves and black frog closings down the front. Her figure, Brian thought, would look provocative in a suit of armor.

"Good morning," Merrill said, in *that* tone. "I hope you slept well."

"Reasonably," Jacquelyn said.

Merrill leaned back against the fireplace and watched Jacquelyn as she found a pack of cigarettes in the cupboard.

"I didn't expect to see you here," Merrill said.

"I'm sure you didn't." Jacquelyn lit a cigarette, seeming to take pleasure in the frictional moment when the match burst into an orange spout of flame.

Brian cleared his throat. He had an odd impression that the tinge of his face was a shade toward purple.

"Jacquelyn heard about *Oedipus* going on the rocks and came here to ask if there was anything she could do."

"I don't imagine even you believe that," Merrill said. Still leaning against the fireplace, she turned her attention to Jacquelyn again. "What is your real reason? Did you hope to win Brian back?"

"I'm still his wife. Who," Jacquelyn asked, "are you?"

For a second, Brian thought Merrill's poise would desert her. There was a throbbing in a neck muscle and a rosy glint to her complexion that was foreboding. She sauntered across to Brian and took his hand in hers. She faced Jacquelyn, holding Brian's hand firmly.

"Brian and I are going to be married as soon as you set him free," she said.

In a detached way he admired her effort, but it was not effective. A good deal too much posturing.

Sure enough, Jacquelyn spotted it.

"Oh, dear," she said. "I do wish you'd stop making casual trips across the room or leaning on fireplaces or clasping hands. In a moment you may give him one of those tender little looks, and I'm afraid I'm going to laugh out loud."

Merrill clasped Brian's hand tighter.

"You just can't accept when you're beaten, can you, Jacquelyn? It should be perfectly apparent by now that Brian is finished with you. He doesn't want you anymore."

Jacquelyn wasn't finished. "I can't help disapproving of the performance in a professional way. It seems to me you're just repeating the gestures, the looks, the kind of snobbish little set speeches that you feel are effective and establish your identity as a member of the upper *clahss*.

Amateurs can't get away with it. That kind of performance should only be given by real actresses."

Merrill's demeanor changed; she threw up her arms as though in a choppy sea.

"Brian, please ask her to go. I have to talk to you alone."

Old Billy creaked to his feet—Brian had forgotten his father was still in the room. The old fellow had been enjoying the show; that was clear from his reluctance to leave.

"I'll be taking me bones down to the Olde Lion for a bit," he said. "If there's company for dinner, Brian, you should know that there's naught in the house but salmon."

Old Billy touched Brian's arm. "Did you ever see the headstone that lies hard by the Rock of Cashel in Tipperary?"

Brian looked a question at him.

Old Billy said, "This is engraved on it. 'Remember, Man, as you pass by—as you are now, so once was I.' Luck, lad."

When the door closed, no one in the room moved. Then Jacquelyn slowly ground out her cigarette.

"I'm not going to pretend I haven't been badly hurt by this," Merrill said. "I know it isn't your fault, Brian, but you might have used better judgment. You know what sort Jacquelyn is, and what she's after."

Jacquelyn made one of her monster faces with her wrists up and her hands hanging down like claws. Brian tried to keep a serious expression, but it wobbled.

"I don't see anything particularly funny about the situation," Merrill said. "What it comes to is this, Brian. You've got to tell Jacquelyn once and for all exactly how things stand. There can't be any further misunderstanding. I've never said anything to you like this before, Brian, but I can't have this sort of thing."

Merrill's eyes, unexpectedly brilliant, fastened on him.

"What sort of thing?"

"You're not going to pretend nothing happened in this house last night!"

Ah, there it was. When the last philosophy has been uttered, the final moral redoubt stormed, it comes down to who did you stick it into last night? No wonder I am paranoid, schizophrenic, and hostile. Anyone who is not is out of touch with the real world. His mind became an absolute blank in which there did not even exist the will for denial.

"I don't have to pretend anything."

"Do you admit it, then? Tell me the truth."

He shrugged. "Oh, we had a go at it."

Merrill's eyes widened and she seemed to crumple as though she were a toy balloon he had popped.

"Brian," she whimpered, "how could you?"

Damn it, she had asked him. Then he realized that what she objected to was his telling the truth, and she was right. It did mean something.

He started a gesture which she misunderstood.

"No, Brian ... don't apologize ... it's too late for anything like that. There's only one thing you can do now."

"What's that?"

She held back tears at the underlash. "Do you love me, Brian? Do you really love me?"

He considered cunning, and dismissed it. "No matter how fond I am of you, Merrill, I will never look on marriage as the act of entering a monastery." He was genuinely sorry if anything he said hurt her, but he had been suffering, more than he could bear, from excess of femininity. "That doesn't mean I'm incapable of feeling. It's just that I'm no better than I am."

She stared at him, struck dumb. "What you want is a harem—with your wife as the number one courtesan." She meant to be scathing, but there was an undertone of pleading as though she wanted him to deny it and attempt to reinstate himself. "I've put up with everything until now, Brian, because I love you. But you can't ask me to keep on unless you're willing to make some concessions too."

"What sort of concessions?" Brian inquired suspiciously.

"You might begin by telling Jacquelyn that she no longer has any place in your life. Make clear to her that you want a divorce."

"And then—what else?"

"I don't expect miracles. I don't want you to change your ways overnight. But I simply can't settle for a marriage in which my friends laugh at me, or feel sorry for me. I expect you to be faithful to me once we're married, Brian."

He was hardened to the defense of the devil by which

he was possessed. "I can promise to go to the mat with my evil nature. I can't promise I'll win."

"And Jacquelyn? Will you promise never to see her again?"

"Hold on now," Brian said. "I'm no prize pig at the auction. I make up my own mind about my own friends."

"How about last night? You admit that you slept with her."

"I didn't take anything from your greens, and I never will. I don't believe in keeping a woman unsatisfied. It makes her cross and nasty. Do you have anything to complain of?"

"That's entirely beside the point. And I think your way of putting it is contemptible. It's revolting. You're revolting."

"I do not prowoke."

"What's that?"

"Something Akim Tamiroff said in *For Whom the Bell Tolls*. He didn't prowoke. That's the reason he outlasted Gary Cooper in the movie. He didn't want to be the hero—just the man who lived longest."

Merrill's mouth went a little slack. "You're not making sense. I want an answer. Will you tell Jacquelyn you never want to see her again?"

Brian turned to give Jacquelyn a long clinical stare.

"That would be a terrible pity," he said. "She's about the prettiest woman I ever saw."

Merrill gave a small gasp of astonishment. "I won't forgive this, Brian. I'm warning you. No woman with any pride could possibly put up with it."

Jacquelyn said, "There are a lot of things easier to live with than pride."

Merrill moved away from the fireplace into the strong daylight. It made her features seem solidly constructed; one could see how each bone contributed to her good looks.

"I hope you understand what you're doing, Brian. You can't really mean to have it end like this."

"I'm not the one handing out ultimatums."

"When I walk out of this room so does your last chance. You're not only losing me. You're throwing over your entire career, your hope to amount to something."

Brian never reacted well to the feminine art of blackmail.

"By the holy wounds of Jesus," he said, "I do think

Jacquelyn was right. You're trying to act a part in a movie."

Merrill answered with a long sorrowful look. As she was leaving, she stopped near Jacquelyn. "This is what you've wanted all along. To win Brian back. Well, you can have him. Perhaps he can treat you like his favorite whore—but he can't treat me that way. I suppose, in the final analysis, that's the difference between us."

"Just one of the differences," Jacquelyn said pleasantly. "There are others."

As she walked to the front-yard fence, Merrill showed the stiff indignant curve of her back. She started down the road without a glance back at the house. Too bad she had not arranged for Sean O'Connor to pick her up, Brian thought. It was nearly three miles back to the village.

She dwindled down the road, into the haze, like a magician vanishing into the smoke of her own illusion.

"A good woman," Brian said. "Much too good for me, really."

Already the shock was giving way to relief, and he began to feel like one from whose finger a thorn had been plucked.

"Did you ever get along together?" Jacquelyn asked.

"I admire her, Jacquelyn. I guess I always will," Brian shook his head in a faintly exasperated way. "Do you think she'd have been happy—married to me?"

Jacquelyn said, "She'd have been miserable. She wouldn't know how to cope with you, and she wouldn't quit either. She'd be in there trying until you broke her heart."

"How about Jacquelyn Stuart—how does she feel about it?"

"You know the answer, Brian. It's why I'm here."

"Or else Meyer didn't cut the mustard with you—and you translated the whole struggle of the flesh to the high moral plane. All that business of who and what you are."

"Think what you like. I don't know all the answers myself."

"What we had last night isn't what most people call love. That kind of thing doesn't last, they say. It's only part of the mystery. It's Low Mass."

"It's seen me through a few years with you. For all I know it'll keep on. Or if it goes away, maybe it will leave something else in its place."

"Or maybe nothing."

"At the moment I don't know—and I don't much care."

"We suit each other. That's the truth of it. I'd rather bed you down than any other woman I can think of."

"Thank you. But that isn't all you want. Or you wouldn't have left me for Merrill."

"We had our temperamental differences. You can be a bitch to handle in your own right."

"I'm talking about you. Not me."

"Oh, who can say what a man wants? Except something he hasn't had yet. Something just over the hill. Something just beyond the reach of his fingertips. I've never known what I was after." He looked about the plain room, with its stone walls and the slanting thatched roof. "I'd like to be better than I am," he said, and was a little surprised that the words beat out of him with such conviction.

"A lot of the trouble was that you became thirty-eight and decided it was time you proved something to yourself."

"*To* myself?

"No—to the world."

She did not mention what they both knew. Drink was his defeat—his life was in sober truth, being liquidated. He had little time in which to do what he wanted. A few years, perhaps. If he could learn to be careful, perhaps a decade. No longer than that.

"I admit to being an inordinately ambitious man."

"You have a real talent, Brian. I don't have any—certainly none that can match yours. You were playing my game by appearing in my kind of picture. You weren't using your strength as an actor—you were lending it to me."

Worse. With the descent into commerce his skills had diminished in scale, had become smaller as the demands on him became smaller. He knew that he was still capable of fine moments but he could not be sure of sustaining a whole performance.

"It's true I am not content to be a matinee idol. That's why I jumped at this chance to be an actor again. But you see what's happened? I've come to shipwreck."

"Supposing you can't get money in New York, what will you do, Brian?"

"Take some job, I suppose. Try to save up enough to try again."

"And how about me?"

"You'll get your million for *Death of a Peacock*. It'll be a big hit."

"That isn't what I was asking."

"Oh, I suppose we can try again, if you're willing. But when you finish *Death of a Peacock*, I won't do another of those movies where I pant and slobber over you, and you show up for at least one sequence in the nude. It wasn't a bad life, Jacquelyn, and we did have good times. But I will never go back to that again."

"I don't want you to. If you do, the same problem will start again. You'll get that itch to really be an actor of consequence, to show you can fulfill all that early promise. And somewhere along the way there'll be some other Merrill Yeaton, with money enough to hold out hope to you that you can be what you want and you'll go away again."

"I've learned my lesson."

"You may go more reluctantly, but you'll go. And the next time will be forever. There'll be no way back."

Brian, puzzled, looked off at the fireplace where a pleasant-looking Jesus was impaled on a wooden cross on the mantlepiece.

"You mean there's no future for us?"

"Only one."

"What is it?"

"I believe in you, Brian. I think you should have your chance to prove yourself as an actor."

"Oh, another one will come along sooner or later."

"I mean now. I mean with *Oedipus Rex*."

"If you bend close and listen you can hear the start of the death rattle."

"All you need is money to bring it to life."

He got up from the chair where he had been sprawling and went to the window. The sun's last rays were striking the hills, turning them dark blue with lacings of purple. Other colors, cobalt and magenta and green, were fading away into the solid dark.

"You're not offering to buy me, are you? I can't have a woman paying my way. I'd feel like Dapper Dillettante with his scrubwoman wife at home."

"I wasn't offering to put up money, Brian. I couldn't, even if I wanted to. I don't have that much and what I do have is tied up in trust funds."

"What are you suggesting then?"

"To help you to raise the money."

"How?"

"Is it true Dame Sara Thomas has quit to accept a stage role?"

"What of it?"

"I don't think you'll have trouble raising the money for *Oedipus Rex* if I appear in it with you."

He felt the chill in his veins, so light that it seemed hardly a ripple across his blood. His breath caught short.

"You mean *you'd* play Jocasta?"

"I'm probably not equal to it as an actress. But you did say once that I can do heavily emotional things on instinct."

"You'd be marvelous. But Jocasta is a much older woman. Good glory to God, she's my *mother!*"

"She's also your wife, isn't she? That's what the play is all about, so she has to look young and attractive enough to *be* a wife."

"She'd still be twenty years older than you look on screen."

"I can look older. You've heard of makeup."

In a little rectangular square of window his face looked back at him, dark with incredulity.

He turned to her. "Do you mean to tell me you'd give up *Death of a Peacock* to take on a secondary role in my movie? As an older woman? It's a damned generous offer. But I can't let you do it."

"I want to, Brian," she said simply. "I really want to."

He received the full impact of her eyes that could speak to anyone who had the heart to hear.

"There's still light. We could go for a walk and talk about it more."

Even with dusk coming on, the high tide of green surged across the meadows. Heavy leaves hung green from the hardwoods and burst in hedgerows, and green lines were drawn on the rich dark soil. Green-golden grass ran in ripples before the wind across the lowland fields and through pasture lanes and to the edge of country roads.

They walked hand in hand along a dirt road.

"Do you think you could get out of your commitment to *Death of a Peacock?*" he asked.

They had been talking half an hour, and this was the first clear indication he had weakened.

"I'm sure I can. We've hardly begun shooting. Morey

Bloom can get me out of it. That's what agents are for—to pull off the difficult deals."

"He'll think you're crazy."

"Probably. But Gerda Andersen is a client too. And she's been dying to do it. That will heal his wounds."

"He won't get a million with Gerda."

"She'll be around longer. Gerda is twenty-eight. I'm thirty-two. He'll be collecting his ten percent from Gerda for more years."

"You're talking like an old lady."

She smiled up at him. "Getting ready to play Jocasta."

Outside, the wind was blowing rain, but in bed it was warm. Rain struck in pattering slashes against the glass. The thin white curtains trembled.

Beside her Brian snored. What had happened to her in the past half hour would keep her warm for hours yet. She was so highly charged that everything had a physical meaning—the slightly damp air, the crisp touch of the sheet against her body. It was good to lie here beside him now in the late night, the first hour of morning really, like a traveler at the end of a journey. She had been at the beginning of a different road, a long, empty stretch of gray, with no end in sight for the weary frightened heart. But the cold of that other road could not get through to her now.

In the evening, just after dinner at the hotel, she had spoken with Morey, who had been predictably astonished. He had argued with her, pleaded, logically explained the folly of her decision, and somewhere in the course of a forty-five minute overseas telephone call he had begun figuring the angles and realized he had little to lose with Gerda. Thereafter his protests became increasingly perfunctory. Their dinner had twice been disturbed by calls afterward: a return phone call from a financier in New York (where it was still afternoon) to say he had discussed Brian's offer of a participating interest in *Oedipus* costarring Brian and Jacquelyn and that while the issue had to go before the directors for a final decision he had already spoken to them and was sure there would be no trouble. The other phone call had been from Lester Mitchell, returning Brian's call to assure him that he was enthusiastic about working with Jacquelyn in the role of Jocasta. The production would start moving forward on schedule as soon as Lester and his assistants could round up some members of the cast and crew who had already left for other destinations. Lester also wondered if now that they had Jacquelyn co-starring they shouldn't try to increase the budget and furnish the picture with added production values. Brian thought that was a good idea.

And now here they were, in a bedroom at the hotel, where Brian flushed and exultant with the day's triumph, had rollicked with her like a conquering hero. Ahh, Mother Jocasta! he cried as he came in long shuddering spasms. She could never be maternal between the sheets, but she would play Brian's mother in the movies with streaks of gray and wrinkles and perhaps a little padding. She would not need too much padding if she simply ignored her diet. It would be relaxing to eat anything she liked for a time. This might be the beginning of a long process of deglamorization. Out of Jacquelyn Stuart, film star. She had often been happy before but never from the inside. Possibly now, if very carefully she lifted the edges of her skin, like a carpet, she would discover the grateful network of nerves, gossamer of shining muscles and quivering delicate exquisite sensual apparatus. There would be the secret her in communication with herself. I need Brian and I love him well, yet he is only my way of reaching myself. If Brian was summoned away, if the knock came on the door and took him, she would not abandon her faith. There would be some alternative for her, who would carry the same message beneath a changing countenance. How strange her thoughts would appear to those who withdrew from temptation, who dropped desire and lust as a pack too heavy to carry on their journey. But the pack was life, and to live at all, really live, we must carry that burden.

At last, quite naturally, without being aware, she drifted off into sleep. She dreamt of Dan. He came to a great ballroom where she was dancing with any man who asked her, slightly drunk, telling herself what a wonderful wonderful time she was having.

He said to her, "Okay, honey, we're leaving."

"I don't want to. I'm having such a good time."

"No, you're not, baby. You're *trying* to have a good time and it doesn't work that way. Don't be a hypocrite. You can't change what kind of human being you are."

"I want to. I want to have a good time without feeling guilty."

"You'll never make it trying too hard. Relax. You like being one man's woman. I'll show you what I mean."

As he was taking her into his arms, kissing her, she woke up. She must have cried out because Brian muttered a little and rolled over. She reached out to touch him, summoning him back to wakefulness and her. Slowly his eyes opened.

She smiled. He had got her call. Soon they would be making love again in the wild dark.